A missing daughter; a missing mother—*Ladies' Day* is beautifully written; a compelling, emotional journey of grief, hope and above all else love. I couldn't put it down.—**USA Today Bestselling Author Marlene Adelstein** on *Ladies' Day*

"...a heartfelt examination of what it means to be and to have a daughter."—**Library Journal** on *Ladies' Day*

"Libraries and readers looking for a tale which promises entertainment, then delivers a powerful punch of social inspection, will find *Between the Sky and the Sea* compellingly easy to recommend and hard to put down."—**Midwest Book Review** on *Between the Sky and the Sea*

"A fun read from cover to cover, "Ladies' Day" will hold a very special interest for fans of contemporary women's fiction and prove an enduringly popular pick for community library collections."—**Midwest Book Review** on *Ladies' Day*

"Notably unsentimental and more mature in its treatment of adolescent physical and emotional changes than many novels for this age group, this satisfying, engrossing read will appeal to fans of historical fiction."—**Booklist** on *Eleanor Hill*

"Themes of family loyalty, friendship, and self-sufficiency are artfully woven through this delightful coming of age tale, with appropriate sentiment and historical detail for the middle school and junior high audience."—***Voice of Youth Advocates*** on *Eleanor Hill*

"...a marvelous book."—**Author Ellyn Bache** on *Between the Sky and Sea*

"Heartfelt and tender, *Ladies' Day* is a story of the enduring bonds of family, assuring readers that love, even when tested, is never truly lost."—**Author Kim Wright** on *Ladies' Day*

the
Bristlecone
WRITERS'
Group

the *Bristlecone* WRITERS' *Group*

LISA WILLIAMS KLINE

HARPETH ROAD
PRESS

Nashville

HARPETH ROAD PRESS

Published by Harpeth Road Press (USA)
P.O. Box 158184
Nashville, TN 37215

Paperback: 978-1-963483-55-0
eBook: 978-1-963483-54-3
Library of Congress Control Number: 2026936726

The Bristlecone Writers' Group: A Story of Friendship, Loss, and the Power of Words

This is a work of fiction. Names, characters, places, and incidents are the product of the author's imagination or were used fictitiously, and any resemblance to actual persons, living or dead, business establishments, events, or locales is entirely coincidental.

Cover Design by Sarah Hansen
Cover Images © Shutterstock, Adobe, Depositphotos

Harpeth Road Press, April 2026

For people who write,
Or want to write,
Are afraid to write,
Or never had time for it when they were young.
And people with stories they've never told.

CHAPTER I

ABE

Whenever Abe Goodman reflected on what happened to Margaret after the writers' group that day, his thoughts fluctuated wildly, like a lie detector needle, between thinking he could be blamed and admitting no responsibility at all.

Traditionally, the first to arrive at the Friday afternoon writers' group read from their work-in-progress first, and on that day early in April, Abe was determined that it would be him. He was proud of his attempt to write from a woman's point of view, something he never would have tried as a younger man. As he crossed the unkempt Bristlecone Village courtyard, passing the ancient bristlecone pine with the plaque and the bench next to it, a dated red Mustang convertible squealed into the handicapped spot by the front door of the two-story brick administration hall. Abe quickened his steps as Margaret Tinker emerged, brandishing her cane as her pot-bellied husband hoisted her from the low seat.

The oldest writers' group member at eighty-two, frail and disheveled, Margaret wore a jacket with padded shoulders that might have been avant-garde during the 1980s. She never came prepared with anything written down. Each week, she used her time to tell unbelievable stories that were surely the product of a declining mind. It irked Abe that the others were too kind-hearted to kick her out.

Abe could not let her beat him to the conference room.

To attempt an end-run, Abe hurried through the side door of the admin building and took the stairs two at a time to the dated second-floor library and conference room, with its yellowed copies of *The Great Books* and *Encyclopedia Britannica* and its smells of leather and dust. But as his doctor warned he might, Abe became winded from the exertion and had to stop on the stair landing to take a few breaths. Adjusting to this new way of being was most annoying.

"You doing all right, Dr. Abe?" the young Black woman with the sweet face and long braids at the reception desk called up to him, half-rising from her chair.

"I'm fine." Abe waved and nodded, feeling embarrassed that the young woman had noticed him slowing down, and also slightly guilty that he could never remember her name and now was too far away to read her nametag. Was it something biblical, perhaps?

Before he reached the second floor, the elevator door dinged, then opened, and Margaret and Roy emerged.

Damn!

"Ah, you beat me. Hello, Margaret. Afternoon, Roy," he said, hoping he sounded more cordial than he felt.

Roy, with his ruddy, youthful face, left Margaret with Abe, refusing to meet his eye as he headed down the stairs, tossing "See you at five" over his shoulder as he went. Conveniently for him, Roy normally squeezed in nine holes of golf during writing group. Roy was always late to pick Margaret up, smelling like cigars and beer.

As Abe helped Margaret into her chair beside the scarred pine conference table, she gripped his arm like a vise.

"Thank you, young man," Margaret said with a toothy grin as he helped her get settled in one of the ancient pleather chairs. Margaret was partially deaf, and throughout their meetings wore a hearing aid that emitted intermittent high-pitched squeals loud enough to make a dog yelp.

"Sure, my pleasure." Young man, indeed. Abe was possibly seven years younger than Margaret.

One of the shortcomings of the writing group at Bristlecone was that anyone who lived at the Bristlecone retirement community was welcome to attend. In circumstances such as these where anyone, regardless of talent (or lack thereof), could be admitted to a group, sometimes one had to endure situations that weren't ideal. Of course, Abe didn't actually know if Margaret had writing talent, as she never brought anything she'd written.

Abe tried not to seem impatient. "Here's your briefcase." It weighed no more than a feather, as usual, proof that once again this week she hadn't written anything. Why did she even bother to carry it around?

"Oh, thank you. I don't want to let that out of my sight."

"Hello, everybody." Jennie Rossi arrived a minute or so after Abe, and he was relieved not to be alone with Margaret any longer. Jennie was a kind, attractive, and fit woman in her early seventies, a little younger than Abe, with olive skin that tanned easily, and white, corkscrew hair with a mind of its own.

Abe had seen her helping teach the wheelchair yoga

class that met on Tuesday mornings in the exercise center but really didn't know her outside of the writers' group. He did know she was working on a novel that she'd never had time to pursue during her days as a social worker.

Abe grudgingly admitted that Jennie's writing was quite good, though he often felt obliged to offer his expertise, since her manuscript was a historical novel about Enheduanna, a princess and priestess from ancient Iraq, and supposedly the world's first known author. The Middle East had been one of his specialties while teaching at the university. Sometimes he heard a hint of pompousness in his voice as he commented on Jennie's manuscript and tried, without great success, to rein it in. His students used to be enthralled, but these women seemed less dazzled by Abe's oratory. That was a part of retirement that had been hard for him to adjust to over the last two years.

Willoughby Philpott arrived last.

"Hi, folks, you'll be happy to know I didn't forget the egg timer" From her large purse Willoughby produced the small five-minute egg timer they used to time their readings. It was antiquated, a holdover from a writers' group Willoughby had been in years before, but they liked the symbolism of it. When she forgot the hourglass, they simply used the timers on their phones, but it wasn't the same. Willoughby had been the one to organize the Bristlecone Writers' Group a year ago, explaining that after she'd transferred her husband to the memory-care wing she needed something to look forward to.

Abe had always appreciated the fact that Willoughby wore her gray hair shoulder-length, longer than many women in their sixties and seventies wore it. She was tall—almost as tall as Abe—Southern, and athletic. Abe had noticed her agile play several times on the pickleball court, and he thought she looked young for seventy-one.

Willoughby, he thought, might be a family surname, as prominent Southern families sometimes followed that tradition with daughters to remind others from whence they came. Abe sensed, through her writing, that Willoughby was lonely. Her husband lived in the memory-care wing, and she lived on her own. She was the only one in their group who had published a novel, called *Between the Shelves*, about the secret inner life of a shy librarian, which was indeed what Willoughby had been before she retired. Although in Abe's view, Willoughby was now anything but shy. He saw her as the leader of the group, the glue that held it together. Had she been shy when she was younger, perhaps? Abe fully intended to read Willoughby's book out of courtesy but just couldn't seem to get around to it.

"So who was first?" Willoughby looked around as she settled herself and laid her pages on the table.

"I was." Margaret's voice quavered. "I didn't write anything down, but I'm going to talk about the story I'm going to write." Her hearing apparatus squealed with electrifying vigor, and they all winced and tried not to put their fingers in their ears.

Abe sighed. Of course she hadn't written anything down. For God's sake, this was a *writing* group.

Willoughby glanced reprovingly at Abe, which he didn't think was necessary. She put on her bright blue reading glasses, looked over the tops at Margaret with a kind and patient expression, then said exactly the same thing she always said. "Margaret, we'll let you use your time by talking about your story today. Next time, please bring something you have actually written." She turned the egg timer over. "Timer starting now. You have five minutes."

Margaret looked crestfallen, but only for a few seconds. "All right, then, I'll go quickly. The story I'd like to tell is about a family who kept moving their deceased patriarch to more prestigious cemeteries to burnish their family reputation and possibly erase failures, bankruptcies, and sins of the past."

Abe, trying to keep his expression neutral, made a brief note about the legality of moving people who had already been buried.

As usual, Margaret rambled on with her imaginary and slightly implausible story. She finished at last by saying that in her story, the patriarch did in fact regain previous status and the past was successfully erased, and those who remembered the fall of the family questioned their own memories. Margaret's hearing apparatus squealed again.

"It's a true story," Margaret concluded. "And that's only the beginning. Just so you know, everything's in here." She patted her empty briefcase.

Abe couldn't believe that after all of Margaret's nonsense, the other women nodded politely. Why didn't they just kick her out?

"Time's up," Willoughby said, as the last few grains of sand slipped to the bottom of the hourglass. "Comments?" Each group member took a few minutes to comment on Margaret's story, going in clockwise order around the scarred old table.

"That sounds like a thought-provoking and hard-hitting story about the ways that people try to cover the past," Jennie said in a kind tone that Abe never could have mustered. "I do hope you write it down."

Willoughby was also extremely kind, complimenting

Margaret on the unusual nature of the story and its metaphorical strength, and encouraging her to go back to her room and put the story on paper.

Abe couldn't help himself when his turn came. "I haven't actually done the research on this, but can people move their deceased relatives?"

"I believe they can," Jennie said.

"I have no comment," Margaret said, staring at the ceiling.

Willoughby gave Abe another reproving look. "I don't think it's that important, do you, Abe? It's a metaphor."

"Well, I think we should strive for accuracy." Margaret reminded Abe of the students in his classes who didn't do their work and tried to get away with it.

Margaret fixed her dark, heavily lidded eyes on Abe. "When you're old, people don't take you seriously and try to push you out." Her deep quavering tone hovered close to tears. "One day it will be you and you'll see what it's like."

The air rushed out of Abe's chest as if he'd been punched, and he felt so ashamed that goosebumps broke out over his scalp. Silence hung in the air for long seconds. Both of the other women seemed at a loss for words at this strangely prescient and hostile statement coming from Margaret.

"Let's go ahead and move on." Willoughby raised her eyebrows and cleared her throat. "Abe, you were next?"

Abe nodded, strangely self-conscious, and began to read his work. "Abby tried on a tight fuchsia sweater that accentuated her breasts, then took it off. He would make assumptions. She then put on an oversized gray sweater that swallowed her and made her look frumpy. She took that off, too. Her third option was a plain, high-necked, navy-blue top that her mother might have approved of but that did absolutely nothing for her. Oh, God, maybe she'd just go in her bra." It went on from there. Abe told himself that he didn't care what the other members, all women, might say about these pages written from the point of view of a widowed, middle-aged woman getting ready for her first online date.

Willoughby cleared her throat as soon as Abe finished reading. "As librarians we were discouraged from acquiring books written by outsiders. For example, a White person trying to write about the Black experience. Or a man trying to write about what it's like to be a woman."

Abe put down his pen. "But isn't it one of the great benefits and challenges of reading and writing books to understand what it might be like to be inside the head of a person who is different from you?"

"Though I did identify with the agony of trying to represent the entirety of oneself with one outfit, Willoughby is probably right that you might have a tough time publishing this," Jennie said. "If you indeed wanted to publish it."

"It could be risky, that's all," Willoughby said, in a kinder tone.

Abe leaned forward. "Well, now that I'm in my seventies, I figure, what the hell? I'll take a risk. I have always liked women. I respect women. I don't know why I can't try to write from the point of view of one. Barbara Kingsolver wrote *Demon Copperhead*, and that's a male written from a female point of view."

"I don't mean to be discouraging, Abe. Brilliant writers can do whatever they want," Willoughby said.

"You don't think I'm brilliant?" he joked, then rushed on when they didn't laugh. "But what did you think about what I actually wrote?"

"As I said, I could identify with it," Jennie said.

"I still wear many of the sweaters that I wore as a young woman," said Margaret.

"I do appreciate the value of you doing this. But a woman trying on multiple outfits before a date might be considered by some to be a bit cliché." Willoughby took off her bright blue glasses, smiled kindly, and turned over the hourglass.

Willoughby's comment, more critical than usual, Abe thought, struck a nerve. After Ellen died, Abe had tried on at least five shirts before his first online date a year later. He'd limited the scene he'd written to three changes because five had seemed like overkill. Abe traced the soft skin of his empty ring finger. He kept his wedding ring in the top drawer of his dresser, between some handkerchiefs.

When Jennie read her piece about Enheduanna, and when Willoughby read her piece about the reclusive, nearly agoraphobic author who refused to make public appearances, Abe was aware that out of sheer spite he made biting, scathingly critical comments. At the end of the meeting, he stood, gathering his pages. Maybe he just wouldn't return. He was tired of being the only male in the group anyway.

Still, trained by his mother, Abe courteously helped Margaret out of her chair, despite her belligerent comment earlier. Just ahead of Jennie and Willoughby, he escorted Margaret from the conference room and into the hallway. As usual, Roy was nowhere in sight.

"The golf course may have been crowded. Maybe we can meet him just outside the building," Abe suggested, leading Margaret toward the elevator. But the professor in him could not resist a dig. "And I feel confident that next week you will grace us with actual pages you've written. Am I right, Margaret?"

To Abe's surprise, Margaret glared at him, shook him off, and lurched toward the staircase. As she jerked her arm away, she lost her balance. The rest of them watched in horror as she fell down the stairs, tumbling loudly over and over like an unbalanced load of laundry. At the landing, her head smacked the floor with a spine-chilling thud, and her ear apparatus began screeching non-stop.

"Oh my Lord!" Jennie skimmed down the steps ahead of Abe and kneeled on the landing beside Margaret's prone form. "Margaret, are you okay? Can you get up?"

Abe raced down and started to help Jennie pull Margaret up. The incessant screeching of her hearing aid continued, adding to the general sense of panic, until Abe yanked it from her ear and unplugged it. The silence was glorious.

"Stop!" Willoughby said, running down after them. "I don't think you're supposed to move a person. She might have broken something."

"Oh, of course." Abe stood back and looked down from the landing to the lobby, where the young woman at the desk had seen everything. "Miss, could you—"

"I'm on it." She had already picked up the phone to call for help.

Margaret lay on her side. She seemed barely conscious, and one side of her grayish face sagged. Jennie remained on the floor beside her, holding her hand, telling her that help was coming soon. Meanwhile, the attendant—Abe now saw that her nametag said Destiny—raced up to the landing.

"I know CPR," she said, kneeling and tossing her long braids out of the way to begin chest compressions.

Within minutes, two of the Bristlecone Village medical staff arrived, checked Margaret's vitals, and lifted her onto a stretcher. The bump on her forehead was already the size of a Ping-Pong ball. Abe, Jennie, and Willoughby, who had taken Margaret's empty orange briefcase from Destiny, followed them down the sidewalk toward the nursing wing, between the leggy azaleas and half-hearted clumps of tulips trembling in a slight breeze.

"Wait, does anyone have Roy's cell?" Abe asked.

Willoughby and Jennie shook their heads.

"Maybe I should stay here in the lobby to tell him what's happened," Abe offered.

"Good idea, and we'll go with her," Willoughby agreed, and they both hurried off behind the stretcher.

Abe stood outside waiting, contemplating all that had taken place, regretting his impatience with Margaret, knowing the other two women were disgusted with him. He rejected his previous thoughts about leaving the writing group as being completely juvenile, the impulse of someone who was seventeen and not seventy-five. Roy's ancient red Mustang squealed into the lot.

Roy rolled down the passenger window, his eyes wide, a cigar in his hand.

"Margaret fell down the stairs. She's in the health-care wing."

Roy leaped out of the car and they jogged thirty yards across the courtyard to the rather outdated Bristlecone medical wing, with its brick and white trim façade. Abe headed inside, holding the door for Roy, who still had his cigar. "I don't think you can smoke in there."

He grunted and tossed the cigar into an already ailing flowerbed before heading inside. Abe went over and stomped on the still-burning tip before going inside himself.

"My wife Margaret was just brought in here." Roy clutched his golf cap in his hands and he sounded short of breath.

"Come with me, sir."

Abe joined Jennie and Willoughby on the dated flowered couches in the waiting area as the attendant led Roy to be with Margaret.

"Did they say anything about her condition?" Abe asked Jennie and Willoughby.

Jennie shook her head. "They just rushed her back and told us to wait out here since we're not family."

The three sat in silence for a few moments.

"I bet Roy is going to blame us," Abe finally said, sotto voce. He did feel guilty for not being able to grab Margaret's arm in time. Could it, in fact, have been his fault?

"You tried to help," Jennie said, which endeared her to Abe.

"We need to talk to her, and to Roy," Willoughby said. "I think it's time she stopped coming to the group. I'm not even sure she can write anymore."

Abe nodded. "I've been thinking that for months!"

Jennie's eyes welled. "Maybe you're right. But I just hate this. She deserves to be able to express herself somehow. Don't we all?"

The physician's assistant, with a solemn expression and tired eyes, came into the waiting area and addressed them. "I'm so sorry to tell you this, but your friend has had a seizure and died."

～

Abe, Willoughby, and Jennie stood in the waiting area, stunned. How could she be dead? They'd only just been subjected to yet another of her rambling stories. Abe swallowed, glancing at Jennie and Willoughby's shocked expressions. They thought Roy might come back through the lobby, but he didn't.

"Maybe he went out the back to wait for the funeral home attendant," Abe suggested.

"I feel terrible about how badly we treated Margaret," Jennie said.

"I, on the other hand, feel we had the patience of Job," Abe said.

"Yes, we were patient." Willoughby held up the empty orange cloth briefcase. "I still have this. How will we get this back to Roy?" As Willoughby held up the briefcase, the corner of a sheet of paper stuck out the top. "Look, she did have something in it after all." Willoughby squinted. "I don't feel right about pulling the whole thing out, but here at the top it says, 'Are You There God? It's Me, Margaret.'"

"That's certainly odd," Abe said.

"That's the title of a book," Willoughby said. "My daughter, Courtney, loved it so much I read it, and I loved it too. It's about a young girl coming of age. By Judy Blume."

"I loved that book too!" Jennie said. "Such honesty about something people never used to talk about. So refreshing. It was one of the first books that made girls feel normal about the changes their bodies went through."

"I've never heard of it," Abe admitted.

"I wonder why Margaret wrote that title down, though," Jennie said. "Does it mean anything?"

Abe shrugged. He recalled with slight embarrassment Margaret's warning to him about being old but reassured himself that her cognitive abilities were diminished. He wondered if they'd look for a new member for the Bristle-cone Writers' Group, but he knew it was boorish to mention it so soon. Frankly, he intended to recruit another man so he wouldn't feel quite so outnumbered. Then, as the sun slid lower and dusk began to fall, Willoughby headed off to visit her husband in memory care, and Jennie went back to her apartment for dinner.

Abe, striding almost silently through the pine-needle covered paths back to his own dark, 1960s cottage, reflected on the bristlecone pine at the end of the courtyard. It was neither graceful nor beautiful nor majestic but dwarf-like, gnarled, and stubby. Long life, that's what the bristlecone pine had going for it. *Was it worth it?* he wondered and considered his own life.

After childhood and an early career in New York City, Abe had in later years enjoyed the bucolic joys of teaching at the small university of Eden Forest in the North Carolina piedmont, his alma mater. Teaching at Eden Forest had carried a bit of prestige, which was why he had elected to stay in the immediate area and chosen Bristlecone Village for his retirement. It was not the most highly regarded of the various retirement options in Eden Forest, but Abe had received a meaningful discount by making his deposit in advance.

Bristlecone Village covered about twenty acres and featured several different types of residences, from the older two-bedroom brick cottages like Abe's, to smaller one- and two-bedroom apartments in the main building, and larger two- and three-bedroom condos in the new building. There was also an assisted living center and a memory-care unit. Bristlecone boasted two restaurants—one casual, featuring pub fare, and the other more formal, with white tablecloths, good cutlery, and fine china. The grounds, though not particularly well-maintained, featured wooded walking paths for active residents, courtyards with gardens, and four pickleball courts that needed their lines repainted.

He didn't feel like meeting his regular group for dinner and sent a text saying he couldn't make it. His son Jacob had called, but Abe wasn't in the mood to talk to him either. He poured himself a glass of red wine when he arrived home, which his cardiologist had recommended over any other types of spirits. He sat in the maroon leather chair that Ellen had chosen for him so carefully all those years ago and tried to read the new issue of *The Bristlecone Weekly*. Still in a daze over what had happened to Margaret, he read entire articles without processing the words. He kept seeing Margaret tumbling down those stairs.

Unbidden, the experience of his heart attack came back to him, with vivid memories of excruciating pain.

There but for the grace of God go I, he thought.

Then he was taken back to the last week of Ellen's life, when she lay in the big white bed in hospice, wearing her white turban, and had asked him to get her a newly published book on near-death experiences and life after death. He'd raced to the quaint Eden Forest bookstore on Main Street and got her the book, knowing she no longer had the stamina to read it, but being so grateful there was some small thing he could still do for her. He had spent swaths of her last week reading to her from it, lying in the bed next to her, though he now wished he'd simply held her since he didn't believe in life after death then, and certainly not after Ellen's passing.

He forced himself to return to the newspaper, skimming an article buried in the back explaining that the bristlecone pine could be the longest-lived species on earth, surviving in some cases up to five thousand years. Scientists had core-dated one somewhere in California at over forty-eight hundred years. The scientists had named it Methuselah, after the nine-hundred-year-old man in the Old Testament. Its location was being kept secret by the forest service to prevent vandalism. A shame, Abe thought, that even a tree needed to be put in the witness protection program in today's fractious times.

Bristlecone pines were native to California and the Southwest, he read. The article featured a photograph of the oldest bristlecone pine in the Village, in the back Bristlecone courtyard, with its gnarled, dwarf-like trunk and thick-growing blue-green needles. A bronze plaque near the foot of the tree stated the genus and species: "*Pinus Aristata.*"

The article went on to tell a "myth," or "fable" about that ancient pine. Apparently, back in the 1980s, a new Bristlecone administration had planned to cut down the tree to build new apartments, but a retired botanist from Eden Forest College, where Abe himself had taught, wanted to save the tree because it had been core-dated at over 450 years old, which meant it had been growing in the North Carolina piedmont back when the Catawba Indians made their homes there. The botanist found the presence of such an old bristlecone pine extremely mysterious, as bristlecone pines were not native to North Carolina. How could a non-native species have appeared here 450 years ago? Had a seed been carried from another location by a nomadic tribe, or by a horse or pig that had eaten a pinecone centuries ago? Or maybe it had been dropped by a migrating bird, such as a finch or crosshatch? No one knew, and perhaps no one ever would.

But the mystery of it was intriguing enough that when the bulldozers came to clear the land, a group of retirees sat peacefully around the tree, arms linked, refusing to move, until the administration backed down and located the apartments elsewhere. After that, the plaque and bench appeared.

Abe folded *The Bristlecone Weekly*, thinking he'd rest his eyes for a few moments. That story was certainly archetypal, but Abe didn't know whether he believed it or not. Tonight, after all that had happened with Margaret, he felt as old and gnarled and endangered and out of place as that lone North Carolina bristlecone pine.

CHAPTER 2
WILLOUGHBY

Willoughby and Jennie walked together down the paved path toward the newly constructed memory-care wing. They paused at the fork where Jennie would peel off to go back to her apartment but didn't part company yet; they couldn't stop talking about Margaret's death.

"Can you believe Margaret's dead?" Jennie's dark eyes went wide with disbelief, and she raked her hand through her wild, white, corkscrew hair.

"What a shock! I feel so damn bad that I lectured her about her writing. Or lack thereof." Willoughby, still shaking and a little nauseated from the whole experience with Margaret—that awful fall, then waiting for so long in the health center—adjusted her briefcase, pushing the small hourglass more deeply into a side pocket so she wouldn't lose it. She tucked Margaret's nearly weightless orange satchel more tightly under her arm.

Dusk had fallen and the entrance lights around the building flickered on. Though Willoughby couldn't see the stringy wisteria climbing the wall of the memory unit, she could smell its sweet aroma. She wasn't exactly dreading going inside to see Gary, but she didn't mind putting it off a few more minutes to chat with Jennie. Okay, well, maybe she was dreading it a little. She pretended she was handling the situation, but it was becoming more of a struggle.

"Don't feel bad, Willoughby. She really hadn't been seriously participating in the group for a while. You know Roy just brought her so he could escape to play golf." Jennie patted her arm gently. "I mean, he deserves to get away to play golf, of course, but he really should have hired someone to watch her rather than using us as sitters. It was a horrible accident but that's all it was—an accident. It wasn't anyone's fault."

"I know, I know, you're right. Thanks for the reassurance. Just, I keep hearing that thud when her head hit the floor." Willoughby shuddered.

"I know, me too." Jennie hesitated. "I wonder if there'll be a funeral."

"We'll have to find out. What the hell am I going to do with this briefcase? When will we see Roy again?"

"Do you want me to take it? I can get it to him," Jennie said. "I don't mind. You have to worry about Gary—let me take it."

Willoughby didn't want Jennie to think she needed help because of Gary, but agreed immediately, handing the garish, featherweight thing to her. "Oh, that would be great, thank you. I don't even think there's anything in it other than the sheet of paper with 'Are You There God? It's Me, Margaret' written on it."

"And I wonder what that's all about. Anyway, I won't look inside, obviously, but I'll get in touch with Roy."

"Thanks. If anyone should feel bad, it's Abe. Could you

believe the way he kept going on about moving dead people?"

Jennie said quietly, "Well, I don't know, I think we were a little hard on Abe today."

Willoughby considered this. "You mean about writing from a female point of view?"

Jennie nodded. "It was his first attempt, and we're supposed to be encouraging each other to take risks and try new things. I didn't think his scene with the woman changing tops was that bad. Sometimes I think we try to encourage other women, but not necessarily men."

"Oh, come on, Jennie, it was totally clichéd." Willoughby thought Jennie was too forgiving. She was always letting people off the hook. To tell the truth, though, if Willoughby was being completely honest with herself, Abe's pomposity got on her nerves.

"Well, you see scenes like that in movies all the time. Sometimes things are clichéd because they're true. I changed my outfit a few times before I met my son Elijah's new girlfriend, Amanda, for the first time. It's something we all do when we're nervous about making a good impression."

"Maybe you're right," Willoughby conceded, "but do you think it will ever get published?"

"Maybe publication isn't really Abe's goal."

Willoughby glanced away from Jennie's shadowed face. Willoughby had dreamed of being published her entire life, since her childhood as the competitive younger sister of two older brothers. She had written stories in second grade, on the paper with the dotted lines, and even illustrated them, giving her brothers plenty of ammunition for teasing. Yet, it seemed nothing that had ever happened to her was real until she had written about it. She hadn't craved lights and fame, not at all. Just a book to hold in her hand, with her name on the cover. A concrete symbol: *I was here.* She hadn't known if she could do it.

And then it had happened when she was fifty-five, years after subverting her writing dreams into a master's in library science. Maybe it had something to do with her new life with Gary, with the newfound outspokenness and confidence he'd inspired in her. She'd published her first book, *Behind the Shelves*, a novel about the secret dreams of a quiet librarian, with a New York publisher. The book had been more autobiographical than she'd ever admitted. Then came the laudatory, starred review from the reviewer well-known as the most difficult to impress. Willoughby could still remember word-for-word what it said:

Ms. Philpott captures the ephemeral desires of a quiet librarian in a highly authentic and poignant way that should remind us all that our society needs to hear more from quiet people.

That review had thrilled her publisher. Even her older brothers, who she saw once a year at their family reunion on Bald Head Island, seemed impressed. Then her book had won a state library award, which had thrilled Willoughby, while she also secretly wondered if her library friends had voted en masse in the state library book competition and thus skewed the results. Impostor syndrome set in.

Despite her self-doubt, her modest success had inspired Willoughby to write more books. But because her first book had ended up not selling well in spite of the good reviews and the award, Willoughby had lost her agent and her new work had not been accepted by any more New York publishers. Willoughby had lived in a state of frustration about her writing for years afterwards, thinking that if only she worked harder and improved, something else would happen, but it never did. She had come to half believe she deserved it.

Willoughby shook her head, realizing that Jennie was right. Willoughby was herself so focused on publication that maybe she'd misinterpreted the goals of other people when she organized the group. But Abe was so damn pompous! To be brutally honest though, maybe the main thing that annoyed her about Abe was that he still had his cognitive abilities, while Gary did not.

"You're the only one of us who is seriously focused on publication," Jennie said. "I think the rest of us are just expressing ourselves. Certainly that was true of Margaret." Jennie lowered her voice. "I sometimes wonder when Abe writes about women if he's writing about one of us. I mean, he doesn't wear a wedding ring. Do you think he thinks we think...?" Jennie giggled.

Willoughby couldn't help laughing too. Jennie had an infectious giggle. "Think he thinks we're interested in him?" Abe was not a bad-looking man—fit, slim, with intense, hawk-like blue eyes, a well-trimmed beard, and white hair that he kept cropped but which might have curled if allowed to grow.

Jennie nodded, still giggling. "We better stop. The next time he reads his stuff, we'll burst out laughing."

Willoughby hooted with laughter at the thought of that as she glanced at her sports watch. "Well, Gary will be wondering where I am." The truth was that Gary did live for her visits, and she was able to get him to take meds and showers when the nurses weren't able to, which did make her feel needed but also added pressure.

"How is Gary?" Jennie touched her arm.

"Same old, same old."

"I know it's hard."

"Yeah. Writing group helps keep my mind off it. I escape to the world of my super shy heroine."

"Sure. Hang in there, Willoughby."

They didn't usually hug each other good-bye but tonight they did, feeling closer after all that had happened that afternoon.

Willoughby punched in the code on the locked memory-care unit keypad, waited for the heavy door to open and close, then headed down the hall toward Gary's room, listening to the echo of her footsteps on the hard, tiled surface and saying hello to the tired staff members on duty. Gary had been here for a year, so she knew pretty much everyone. Mrs. Burns slumped outside her room in her wheelchair, and Willoughby gave her a smile as she passed.

Outside Gary's room, she stopped and took a deep breath. Last week Gary had called her by his first wife's name, Sally. But it had only been that once, and he had been doing pretty well since then. She had to be ready for whatever version of Gary she got. Sometimes he demanded that she take him home, and it was nearly impossible to convince him that this was his home now. She reconsidered constantly: Should she take him home and try again to care for him there? She straightened her shoulders and went in.

"Hi, honey!"

He was sitting in the leather armchair she'd moved from their apartment, the expensive blue one that had been "his" at home. She'd moved their bed here, too—the queen, with the high-end mattress—and in her own place slept on the bed they'd had in the guest room. Willoughby had put photos on every available surface—of Gary with her, of

Gary on-air at the television station, in a tux at a ceremony when he'd won an award for on-air reporting. His dynamic and charismatic personality shone from every photo.

When she reached him, she leaned in to kiss his forehead and smoothed her hand over his. Gary's previously robust and virile body was frail now; he'd lost about forty pounds. He needed a shave. She gently brushed crumbs off his shirt. "How did you get along this afternoon?"

"I'm perfect."

"Great, great."

"I thought you would never get here."

"I had a hold-up today. I'm sorry, honey."

"They wanted me to take a shower, but I told them not until you got here."

"They can give you a shower, Gary. I have given them my permission. They're here to help you." Having him in memory care was easier in some ways, but she was still his main caretaker. She seemed to be the only person who could convince him to take a shower.

"I only want you to give me a shower." He raised his eyebrows, gave her a meaningful look with those amazing brown eyes, reached his arm around her, and patted her on the ass. He was still so persuasive. She had initiated the idea of taking a shower together just to get him to take one, and joined him about twice a week, but now, obviously, it was getting out of hand.

"Gary, honey, not a good idea right now." Mrs. Burns across the hall peered at them from her wheelchair. "Tell me, did you eat dinner with the group tonight?" She tried the redirecting tactic that had been explained in some of the Alzheimer's self-help books she'd read. But Gary might not be able to remember if he had eaten with the group, so that was not a great move. She wasn't on her game tonight after what had happened to Margaret. This was like a delicate dance, and even after a year, Willoughby hadn't yet learned all the moves.

"Come on, baby, let's take a shower," Gary insisted, pulling her closer.

He'd had such a beautiful head of hair when they met—wavy, dark, and full. She used to lie in bed with her first husband, Steven, and fantasize about running her hands through Gary's hair, and that still gave her the shivers. They'd both been married when they met, during a fundraiser the library had in partnership with the public television station where Gary was an on-air reporter. On the first day of the event, Willoughby's supervisor had been hospitalized for an emergency appendectomy and Willoughby, shy Willoughby, had to take over the on-air responsibilities. She had been terrified, and Gary had noticed her hands shaking when she tried to pin on her mic.

"Let me help," he'd said kindly, leaning in close and taking the mic from her, pinning it to her shirt just above her breast. "And if you just imagine everyone else in the studio naked, you'll relax and you'll be fine."

Willoughby did try to imagine the cameramen and volunteers naked, and for whatever reason, it worked. She'd felt her shaking subside.

All it had taken was that moment of closeness. She felt immediately connected to him, and when Gary stood beside her in front of the camera, she gained confidence she never knew she had. Willoughby and Gary had been on-air together during that week and Willoughby wondered if the viewers could feel the chemistry between the two of them, sense that they practically wanted to rip each other's clothes off, like the characters on *Poldark*. Being on-air and meeting Gary had been like flying free, like a butterfly emerging from a chrysalis. Willoughby hadn't even realized until then that she had felt trapped. She turned into practically a different person.

The divorces had been painful and messy and riddled with guilt. Willoughby felt fortunate her daughter, Courtney, who had been in her early twenties at the time, had at length forgiven her. But her older son, Adam, and Gary's married children, had not. She had tried numerous times to re-establish a relationship with Adam, but he continually rebuffed her, never able to forgive her for leaving his father. It was one of the greatest sorrows of her life.

It had been almost fifteen years ago now, but it was only in the past year, once Gary couldn't communicate as well on his own, that his kids had been forced to communicate with her. Finally, they'd seen what she was doing for him and had thawed.

Gary's hair was silver now, but still the kind of hair you'd want to run your fingers through. The twelve-year difference in their ages hadn't seemed that important when they were in the throes of passion early in their relationship, but her seventy-one to his eighty-three was making an impact now.

In the early stages of his decline, Willoughby had kept him in the apartment with her for as long as she could. She made sure he still looked good. She helped him shave and wash his hair. She chose his clothes every day. He had fans, after all. She'd done all of it until she realized she was running on empty all the time and had not a minute to herself. She'd come down with shingles, out of sheer exhaustion probably, ignored it for far too long, and allowed herself to become so sick she'd ended up in the health-care unit. When she was there, she'd been forced to give permission for Gary to be moved to memory care. That was a year ago.

"Come on, baby, let's take a shower," he repeated, squeezing her ass.

Willoughby's phone pinged. Her daughter, Courtney.

> Dad's being kicked out of rehab next week. They can't release him until he has somewhere to go. Can you help us get him into Bristlecone? It would be easier for me, too, having one central place to visit you both.

Why was Steven in rehab? Willoughby's scalp prickled at the thought of Steven being in the same retirement center as her and Gary. He had never remarried and counted on Courtney a lot. Willoughby imagined the awkwardness of running into Steven, or Steven and Courtney, in the restaurant or in the lobby picking up mail. What an impossibly awkward triangle! She quickly typed that she would call Courtney as soon as she could. What were the chances she could get Steven into Bristlecone on short notice like that? And what were the chances she even wanted to? Yet, dammit, she would try, for Courtney.

Willoughby smiled at Gary, squeezed his hand, and then winked at Mrs. Burns as she shut the door of Gary's room. She silenced her phone. Gary was having a good day today. He remembered her. He was being affectionate. And after all, it was Friday night.

A few hours later, back in her own villa, Willoughby poured herself a beer and sat down at her cluttered kitchen counter. She would have chosen a more modest one-bedroom in the main building, but when they had moved in three years ago, when Gary turned eighty, he wanted one of the newer, larger villas with a den. So that's what they had done.

She stared out at the April blooms that filled the courtyard and tiny patio outside the picture window and called Courtney. Even though she and Courtney had reconciled five years ago when Courtney married Scott, their relationship was still fragile. Courtney lived in Charlotte, about forty-five minutes away, with Scott and their two-year-old son, Clay.

"So why is Steven in rehab?" Willoughby asked.

"He was diagnosed with pancreatic cancer and had to have a Whipple procedure."

"Oh my. That's serious." Willoughby hadn't had any idea. The last time she'd seen him was at Courtney's wedding, five years ago. Steven had never been very good about slowing down, nor was he any good with pain. She was sure he was a horrible patient.

"He's stayed in rehab as long as his insurance allows, and now, since there's no one at home to take care of him, the doctors are recommending assisted living. Bristlecone's the most affordable in the Eden Forest area—can you possibly see if he might be able to get in?"

"I think they have a waiting list of about a year, sweetie."

"But maybe if he came in as a family member or something...?"

"I have no idea if that would work." Willoughby supposed Steven was family, though she only knew what was going on with him through Courtney. He had remained deeply hurt about their split for many years, and he'd had some rocky times. Willoughby still felt guilty, and coupled with trying to please Courtney these days, no matter what she wanted, she reluctantly said, "I'll try to find out something tomorrow, though since it will be Saturday, I might not be able to get answers right away. Anyway, how are you feeling?"

Courtney was seven months pregnant with her second child and feeling much more tired than the first time around. Her nausea had lasted almost five months. Clay, Willoughby's only grandchild, was headstrong and precocious, and parenting him required a huge amount of energy.

"Just exhausted—obsessed with sleep."

"I can come watch Clay anytime you need a nap."

"I will take you up on that, Mom, thank you."

Clay was already in bed, or Courtney would have put him on. He called Willoughby "GiGi," which she had agreed to at Courtney's request. He called Gary by his name, which seemed a bit odd to Willoughby, but Courtney insisted it was appropriate since Gary wasn't Clay's grandfather. Willoughby supposed that was right, but it hurt her heart.

When she was young, Willoughby had hated her name. It had been her grandmother's surname, and her mother had been proud of it, but Willoughby thought it came off as pretentious. Plus, in college she'd learned that Willoughby was the name of a rake who dumped sweet Marianne in Jane Austen's *Sense and Sensibility*, and it rankled that people might assume she'd been named after such a heartbreaker. Yet in mid-life, having an affair and ruining her own and someone else's marriage, she sometimes wondered if that was kismet, and she was just living up to that character's name.

Leaving Steven had been the most out-of-character thing she'd ever done. And she deeply regretted the effect it had on her relationships with her children. But she would never trade the years she'd had with Gary.

After she said good-bye to Courtney, Willoughby sat down with her work-in-progress in the guest bedroom, which she'd turned into her office. It was the story of a reclusive writer who hires a younger, more attractive, and outgoing woman to pose as her during publicity appearances. Willoughby intended for the younger woman to eventually begin writing herself, and possibly try to take over the identity of the reclusive older writer, but she wasn't completely sure yet. Her previous books had developed organically, without a lot of planning, but she was trying to be more focused on plot this time. She'd begun the story as a contemporary one but then considered that it might be more believable as a historical piece, set during the 1920s, when authors did make public appearances but photography was not so widespread.

Working on the story was a joyous break from caretaking, and a few hours quickly flew by.

At the end of a chapter, Willoughby paused and stared at the screen. She'd been pulled out of her own story by wondering if she would have to do additional caretaking for Steven if he indeed moved into Bristlecone. She also wondered how Adam felt about Steven moving in—did he even know about Courtney's plan? Willoughby hadn't seen Adam since Courtney's wedding. He lived in New York City. Courtney and Steven had gone to his wedding to his partner, Diego, last year, but Willoughby had not been invited. After multiple fruitless efforts to reach out to Adam, and many years of painful therapy, Willoughby had accepted the fact that her actions had caused this rift, and it might not be possible to repair it.

But now, if Steven moved to Bristlecone, presumably Adam would come to visit and there would be a chance for Willoughby to reconcile with him. Seeing Margaret die so suddenly had opened her eyes to the fact that she might not have much more time to make amends with Adam.

CHAPTER 3
JENNIE

"I'm home!" Jennie shut the door of her two-bedroom garden-level Bristlecone apartment, dropping the key on the tiny antique hall table.

Her overweight Siamese cat, Sir Arthur, came running like a dog to greet her, weaving around her feet and meowing, his chocolate tail swaying as if to music. Only pets weighing less than twelve pounds were allowed to live in the Bristlecone retirement community, and Jennie joked with people about the fact that Sir Arthur was constantly on the verge of eviction. Sir Arthur was named after Sir Arthur Conan Doyle, who many people did not realize was an eye doctor—Michael's profession.

Jennie took a moment to process the silence, and caught herself waiting for Michael to say, "I'm in here" from the den. She put Margaret's briefcase on the hall table, scooped up Sir Arthur, and buried her face in his soft neck, blinking away the tears.

Sir Arthur responded with a loud, motor-like purr, closing his blue eyes in delight. His dish was probably empty. Sir Arthur's affection was rarely without an agenda.

A typical conversation with Michael unwound itself in her imagination.

Oh, my gosh, Michael, she might say. *Do you remember me telling you about Margaret, the oldest woman in our writing group?*

Michael would look up from a large print book he was reading. His meticulously kept two-day growth of beard would look sexy in the waning light.

The one who doesn't write anything down but tells those crazy stories? Michael's liquid brown eyes would spark with humor, and his lips would twitch.

Yes! She fell down the stairs and died!

Died? That's horrific.

I know—we all saw it happen, like in slow motion.

Jennie, Sir Arthur at her heels, looked into the den. She could almost feel herself clasping Michael's hand and bending to kiss him, as she always used to do. She could almost smell his aftershave. See him wearing high-end workout clothing and some expensive running shoes in an electric shade of red—the bright colors an attractive contrast to his dark, African American skin. He'd always dressed fastidiously, spending more on his clothes than Jennie ever had, and wasn't unaware of appreciative glances from women of all races.

Jennie, then, used to squeeze into the chair with him and would tell him everything.

The whole experience was surreal, Michael. I mean, at a place like Bristlecone, we lose people almost every month, but seeing it happen before your very eyes is shocking.

Seriously. How long had she been in your group?

Ever since we started last year. We'd discussed whether she might be getting dementia. Willoughby and Abe wanted to be

*strict with her and kick her out, since she wasn't writing
anything, but I couldn't have that on my conscience.*

Michael would have smiled at her. *Of course you couldn't.*

She missed him so much. She used to tell him everything. He thought she was too soft-hearted. But she
thought he was too.

Jennie ran her hand over her eyes, then headed into the
kitchen to feed Sir Arthur. A knock sounded on her door.
Uh-oh. She knew who it was—her new neighbor across the
hall. Bernice had started coming by to walk down to dinner
together. Yes, Jennie was an introvert and sometimes
wanted to eat alone. But also, there was an awkwardness
about Bernice that Jennie couldn't put her finger on. Reluctantly, Jennie opened the door.

"Hi, Bernice." She tried to think of an excuse for why
she wasn't going to dinner but was too tired to think of one.
And she was definitely too tired to cook. "Let me get my
phone."

"Sure." Bernice had moved in four months ago from the
Midwest to live closer to her son, almost a year after
Michael died. Bernice was in her seventies, an attractive
woman with coiffed silver hair, a curvy, full-breasted figure,
and beautifully applied makeup. She wore the creamiest
lipstick Jennie had ever seen. She had seemed to be lonely,
and Jennie had been trying to reach out to others to cure
her own grief, as she'd learned to do through her social
work, and she'd invited Bernice to walk to dinner together a
few times. Conversation had been awkward, but Jennie
couldn't figure out why, and she had stopped asking.
Strangely, Bernice kept knocking on her door at dinnertime,
wanting to eat together. Jennie, soft-hearted, as Michael
would have said, rarely said no.

"I don't believe I have ever seen a briefcase that exact

color of orange," Bernice commented. She had disconcerting, darting eyes and deep lines around her mouth that made her look judgmental, though Jennie told herself that didn't mean she *was* judgmental.

"Oh, it's not mine—it belongs to a woman in my writers' group who unfortunately died today. That reminds me, I need to call her husband so I can take it back to him."

She told Bernice what had happened to Margaret as they walked down to the dining room. Bernice seemed shocked but preoccupied. Once they were seated, the handsome young server, Jax, who all the women had been talking about, approached them and asked what they would have to drink.

"No spirits for us, young man," said Bernice. "We'll have water. What's the special?"

Jennie sighed. She was really wanting a glass of wine after all that had happened today, but she was too tired to protest.

After Jax described the trout special, they ordered, and he left, Bernice launched into an account of her day. "I've been volunteering at the Youth Activity Center and reading books to the children, and I've become horrified," she exclaimed. "Books about pooping! Books about butts! Books about having two mothers, or two fathers. A book with a naked boy on the cover. And, for the teens, books about suicide, and books about being gay. Books about slavery. Why give them ideas?"

"I think the center tries to offer books that might speak to many children and teens and their lives," said Jennie carefully, as she also volunteered there. She had, in fact, been pleased by the variety and openness of the books. She'd enjoyed sitting on the pillows in the open room and reading to the eager children. They snuggled next to her, and feeling their affectionate warmth made her heart bloom. It was just what she needed to help fill the hole in her heart after Michael died. She had taken pleasure in reading them any book they chose. "Besides, slavery happened. Why shouldn't young people learn about it?"

"I don't think children who had nothing to do with slavery should be made to feel guilty for it. I took a stack of the books that I disapproved of to the director and told her she needed to remove them from the collection," Bernice said.

"Oh, really?" Jennie crafted a carefully neutral response, though her heart beat faster. "And what did she say?"

"I was terribly annoyed; she said she wouldn't remove them."

"Well, they have an open policy about books, I know."

"How do you know?"

"I volunteer there. They hope the kids find their own stories in the books."

"Well, I won't go back. Not if they have those kinds of books there."

Jennie cast around for a nonconfrontational response. "There are lots of other places you could volunteer." Sometimes she wished she wasn't so conflict-averse.

"I suppose." Bernice had finished her chicken and stood. "Ready?"

Jennie stood with a sigh that she couldn't hold back. She was happy for this dinner to be over. After what had happened to Margaret, and thinking about how much she missed Michael on her arrival home, she hadn't been that hungry anyway.

∼

Back in her apartment, Jennie poured herself a glass of pinot grigio and took it into the office. She'd been looking at her budget before their writers' meeting, and the calculations were still spread on her desk. She shoved the papers back into the file folder, not wanting to think about them after such a draining day. Her financial adviser had told her that because Michael had to retire earlier than expected because of his eyesight, meaning he could no longer do surgery, their nest egg was not as large as it should be, especially with some of the prices at Bristlecone going up. Jennie wasn't sure what she was going to do. She could consider one of the smaller apartments, a one-bedroom, since she was alone now, but there was a waiting list. In the meantime, she was just going to have to watch her expenses very carefully.

Jennie glanced up, and the sight of Michael's medical diploma on the wall brought back memories of when they met in 1979, at an anti-apartheid protest in Chapel Hill. Jennie, after working for a few years after college, had gone back to school for a graduate degree in social work. She'd planned to go to the protest with her roommate, but Nancy ended up being hungover and canceled at the last minute. Jennie, upset by the atrocities she'd heard were taking place under apartheid, decided to go alone.

It had been a sunny, breezy Saturday morning in March, one of those where the bright blue sky makes you think it's warm but the day really requires a heavy coat. Franklin Street had been blocked off and teemed with students. Chanting and singing with the others, Jennie accidentally tripped over a curb and fell. Her glasses slipped off and landed on the street. A second later, someone crushed them. In the press of people, she had been able to scramble back to her feet but had not been able to retrieve her glasses. Jennie panicked. She had driven to the march from her apartment in Carrboro and parked her car a few blocks away. Severely nearsighted since birth, she couldn't drive home without her glasses.

She pulled herself out of the flow of people and onto the sidewalk, figuring she could use the phone in one of the shops to call Nancy to come get her, take her back to the apartment to get her spare glasses, and bring her back to her car.

At the same time, she realized she'd been nervous about protesting, since she'd never really done it before. She hadn't known what to expect, and been on edge, which was probably why she tripped.

Someone touched her shoulder. She turned to see concerned brown eyes looking into her own—eyes that could melt a girl. "Are these your glasses? Correction, *were* these your glasses?"

"Oh!" Jennie took the crushed glasses from his warm hand. One of the earpieces hung at an angle and a lens had popped out, while the other had spider webs of cracks lacing through it. "Thank you so much. I tried to grab them but kind of got swept away."

"Yeah, I was behind you and saw it happen, so I was able to snag them." The young man wore an impeccably ironed white shirt that contrasted beautifully with the dark tone of his skin. She realized now that she recognized him from her next-door neighbor's party a few weeks ago.

"You're so kind, thank you. Hey, I met you at Leonard's party, didn't I?"

"Oh, right, the one in Carrboro. Where Leonard was getting everyone high with nitrous."

"Yeah, Leonard likes to brag that's one of the benefits of being in med school." Jennie's neighbor Leonard was in medical school and had access to nitrous oxide, which everyone called laughing gas. He'd set up the tank in the bedroom, and everyone lined up to breathe in the gas, using the effects on their vocal cords to say something in a really low voice, like "The Force is strong in this one" from *Star Wars*, and then pass out on the bed for about thirty seconds. It had been a blast.

They both laughed in recollection. "That's right—you did a great imitation of Lauren Bacall."

Jennie had had just enough beer to be brave enough to try it and say, "Just put your lips together and blow" in a deep, sultry voice after she inhaled the nitrous and before she proceeded to pass out.

She blushed, searching his eyes and getting a little lost in the intensity of his gaze. Looking down, she saw blood running down her arm. "Oh!" She'd badly scraped her elbow in her fall. She searched in her pocket for a tissue, but the young man beat her to it, holding out a neatly folded handkerchief.

"Oh, I couldn't."

"Don't worry, my mother gives them to me by the dozen."

"Well, thank you." She noted the handkerchief was monogrammed and hesitated about getting blood on it. But the blood was now running quickly down her elbow, so she laid the handkerchief over the scrape. She felt a stinging on her knee and looked down and saw it was scraped and bleeding too.

"I'm in med school with Leonard," the young man said.

"These are pretty thick lenses—are you able to see without them? Do you have a spare pair?"

"Yes, at home."

"How are you going to get back to Carrboro?"

"I can call my roommate."

"I can give you a lift."

Jennie hesitated. She didn't like the idea of getting in a car with a virtual stranger, as appealing as he might be. "No, that's okay, I'll just call Nancy."

"Okay, as long as you have a way home." He seemed to be struggling with whether to repeat his offer or avoid pressuring her. Then he glanced out at the street, where the crowds were thinning, and gave her a small thumbs-up. "Hey, see you at the next nitrous party. Keep up the Lauren Bacall." And he was gone.

The long-haired guy behind the lunch counter at the nearby vegetarian restaurant let her use the phone to call Nancy, who groggily answered and said she'd meet Jennie at the corner of Franklin and Kenan in twenty minutes.

Jennie headed down Franklin toward Carrboro. The bleeding on her arm had stopped, but as she walked, her knee still trickled blood. She couldn't read any signs. She knew the way, of course, but still felt vulnerable. She wished she'd taken the young man's offer of a ride. Fuzzy shapes approached her and passed. She couldn't see faces to smile or say hello. Cars whizzed by in a blur.

Jennie arrived at the corner of Franklin and Kenan and waited. And waited. Nancy was notorious for falling back asleep. She could walk, but it was over two miles back to the apartment. She looked at her watch, waited fifteen minutes more. Nancy had definitely fallen back asleep. Jennie figured she'd go for it. She retied her shoes and headed off.

She'd been hoofing it for fifteen minutes and was feeling the sting of a blister on her heel when a car slowed beside her. She glanced over her shoulder to see a tiny, bright orange car that looked like it wouldn't be out of place in Europe.

"Sure you don't need a ride?" From the blurry face came the voice of the young man who had returned her glasses. "I'm heading over to Leonard's now."

"Sure, okay."

Jennie was thrilled; her heel was killing her. She stepped down from the curb to get into the car and nearly fell again but at the last minute caught herself on the side-view mirror. She straightened and took the door handle.

"Hop in."

"Easy for you to say."

He laughed, a loose and somewhat intoxicating chuckle. Sitting close to him inside the small car caused a pleasurable buzzing tension that Jennie felt a little embarrassed about. It made her insanely happy, though, to have made him laugh.

"This is a really small car."

"I know, it's more like two motorcycles strapped together. When I finally saved the money from my three jobs, I went to the dealership and asked for the cheapest car they had. This is it."

"And so easy to spot."

"Yeah, not the most popular car color, hence the affordable price."

Jennie's apartment was on the third floor and the young man insisted on helping her up the stairs. She let herself in, and at the end of the living room saw Nancy's closed bedroom door.

"I knew it! Still asleep!" She realized he could leave now

but she didn't want him to. "Want some coffee or something?"

"Sure."

"Let me get my spare glasses first so I can see the coffeepot."

He laughed again, making her feel ever so clever as she headed back to her bedroom. She found her glasses on her nightstand and put them on, then glimpsed herself in the mirror and cringed, seeing the out-of-style frames and thick lenses.

"These are my Mr. Peabody look-alike glasses," she said lightly as she returned to the living area, where the young man was reading the spines of the books in her bookcase.

He looked up and saw her. "You are indeed near-sighted."

"Yes, not legally blind, but close to it."

"You know, your book collection is pretty intense for a person who hangs out at nitrous parties. You have some heavy books here. *Things Fall Apart*." He pulled out her tattered, red-jacketed edition of the Chinua Achebe novel.

"Yeah. I guess there is kind of a ridiculous dichotomy to our lives as students."

"True. You're in school for social work?" He gestured to the textbooks on her bookcase.

"Yes. But my father wants me to go to law school." She turned away from the coffee-maker to make a pained face.

"Well, it's definitely frustrating to feel pressured to become someone we're not, but I hope you don't mind me pointing out that the upside of that is that it's nice to have a father who cares what you do."

Jennie kept filling the coffee carafe but caught her breath. With one sentence, this young man had been able to help her see her father from another point of view and also to tell her, perhaps, something about his own father. Her heart pounded as she fitted the filter into the basket, filled it with fresh coffee, and pressed the button to brew.

"I don't like confrontation," she finally settled on as her response. "So I don't think I would do well as a lawyer. Anyway, we're talking about our fathers and we don't even know each other's names. I'm Jennie."

"Michael. I'm sorry—I might be getting into personal stuff too early, considering we've only known each other for an hour." He came over and sat at the café table with the red Formica top in her small kitchen.

"I can try to get the blood out of your handkerchief and get it back to you," she said. She could have offered to give it to Leonard, but then she wouldn't see him again. And well, she admitted that was no longer an option she'd choose.

"Don't worry about it. Like I said, I have dozens."

"Please, I insist."

At that moment there came the ear-splitting sound of squealing brakes in front of her apartment building. Two seconds later, a thunderous crash.

They both froze. A few seconds of loaded, tense silence followed. Then sirens.

"Oh my God, I hope no one was hurt," Michael said. He stood.

Jennie had been thinking the same thing, but was surprised by Michael's humane reaction, since most guys she'd met in graduate school didn't have a lot of empathy to spare. She felt a sudden warmth toward him, a softening and blooming in her heart.

Nancy's bedroom door cracked open, and she poked her tousled blonde head out, her eyes swollen and bloodshot. "What the hell was that?"

All three of them ran out onto the balcony to look out

into the street, and then, while Jennie and Nancy continued to watch the accident, Michael left and rushed down three flights of stairs and into the street to help both drivers, fortunately uninjured, get out of their cars.

Nancy grabbed Jennie's elbow. "He's not only ripped, he's like a bleeding-heart hero. Just your type."

Goosebumps pricked their way over Jennie's scalp and neck. "I know," she said. She was a goner after that.

Thank God Nancy had slept in.

Sir Arthur broke into Jennie's reverie by jumping onto her lap and gently nibbling her ear, his loose, low-hanging stomach wobbling from side to side.

Jennie turned on the lamp and looked at the clock; it was close to seven thirty and the light had faded on this spring night.

She focused on a desktop photo of herself and Michael on the night they'd attended *Hamilton* in downtown Charlotte several years ago, both dressed up, looking their best, with gleaming hair and eyes. That had been a spectacular evening. She thought about the lyrics to one of the songs, about being so lucky to be alive at that moment. She'd gotten goosebumps and taken Michael's hand, gratitude sweeping over her.

Sir Arthur purred as she ran her fingers over his silky cream-and-chocolate fur.

He's a one-woman cat, she could hear Michael saying in her head. *I'm chopped liver.*

Darth Vader liked you better, she would remind him. Darth Vader was their first cat, black and sleek. Named, really, after that nitrous party where they had first met.

Darth Vader had lived twenty years. Their second cat, a sassy tortoiseshell named Bacall, had lived for fifteen. Now she'd had Sir Arthur for seven years, the first five of them while Michael was still alive. Over forty years of marriage, in cat lives.

One of the constants in their marriage had been lying in bed together, forehead to forehead, with a cat snuggled between their feet.

The familiarity of sitting with Sir Arthur, sipping wine, and reviewing the day began to calm her after the bizarre experience of Margaret's death and the tense dinner with Bernice. She drifted into another imaginary conversation with Michael.

You know, we only tolerated Margaret in our group. I think she annoyed Abe and Willoughby. I felt sorry for her. And, actually, I feel sorry for Bernice too.

Of course you do. But, really, Jennie, why?

Do you know that Bernice actually thinks young people who had nothing to do with slavery shouldn't be made to feel guilty about it by reading books?

Once, I ran ahead of my mom when we were going to the public library, and they wouldn't let me in—not until she showed up and told them I was her son. I couldn't go by myself until my early teens. Whites only. Only because my mom was White.

I know. Things like that should be known.

Then, don't back down on the books with Bernice. Is that all that's bothering you?

Well, Abe questioned whether I should be writing from the point of view of a Mesopotamian woman.

Why should that be a problem?

Because he believes I'm not a Mesopotamian woman.

Wouldn't you need to be four thousand years old?

Jennie almost laughed out loud. Honestly, people would think she was weird, imagining Michael making a joke and then laughing at it. Abe didn't know Jennie had Iraqi heritage from her mother, and she hadn't felt like sharing that. Not after 9/11 and the war in Iraq. People might feel prejudiced toward her.

Prejudiced? She could just imagine Michael raising his eyebrows in an ironic way.

I mean, even more prejudiced. Jennie certainly wouldn't argue with the fact that some people at Bristlecone used to give her and Michael, as a biracial couple, disapproving glances. Jennie was pretty sure they'd be even more disapproving if they knew that her mother came over from Iraq during the 1930s. She would most certainly be classed as "other." Keeping that secret to herself wasn't completely honest, but it made life easier.

Jennie went down the hall, to go back into the kitchen, preoccupied, and found that Sir Arthur had clawed his way into Margaret's orange briefcase and knocked a pen onto the floor, as well as a sheet of paper. Jennie wasn't a snoop, but there was no ignoring this. On the paper, Margaret's wobbly, spiky, arthritic handwriting started with the title *Are You There God? It's Me, Margaret,* as she had seen before, but now more book titles were revealed, including many Jennie knew, such as *Animal Farm, Their Eyes Were Watching God, The Catcher in the Rye, To Kill a Mockingbird, 1984, Lady Chatterley's Lover, The Bluest Eye, The Adventures of Huckleberry Finn,* and *The Color Purple.* Some of the titles she didn't know, such as *This Book Is Gay, Nineteen Minutes, The Hate U Give, Speak, Me and Earl and the Dying Girl,* and *The Absolutely True Diary of a Part-Time Indian.* And then there were a few classic children's books like *Charlotte's Web* and *Alice's Adventures in Wonderland.*

Jennie stared at Margaret's list. So many classics. Was this a list of books Margaret had read? Planned to read? Or did it mean something else entirely? Jennie was intrigued. She needed to get the briefcase back to Roy, of course, but it would probably be best not to bother him with such a small thing for a day or so.

CHAPTER 4
DESTINY

It was almost eight, and Destiny was about to get off work. The outside lights blinked on automatically and blanketed the daffodils in the Bristlecone courtyard with brilliance as residents strolled back to their cottages and apartments after dinner. That old lady, Miss Margaret, who fell down the stairs, was still on her mind. When the trainers said new hires had to practice CPR on those flesh-colored dummies—Why weren't they ever Black?—Destiny never figured she'd really have to do it. This was a desk job, right? At least she got it partially correct, but she couldn't help but wonder if they were able to bring Miss Margaret to.

Destiny kept replaying, over and over, what had happened that afternoon. She was thinking about going over to the medical wing to see what had happened to the old lady.

Those four old writers had been meeting upstairs in the conference room every Friday since Destiny had been working at the Bristlecone front desk, going on a year, which was, not bragging, probably the longest time anybody had ever stayed at this brain-numbing job. It was the perfect job for Destiny though, since it gave her time to work on her homework from community college and her poetry. Destiny had to admit, it was lucky that Mama knew her boss, Ms. Robinson, from her sorority, because that had given her a chance to apply.

As she recalled it, the old writers had finished their meeting, and down at the desk, Destiny could just see them at the top of those L-shaped stairs outside the conference room. There was Dr. Abe, probably in his seventies, a professor type with a short beard, wearing wrinkled khakis and a geeky short-sleeved shirt. The really old one, Miss Margaret, who dyed her hair red, had a screechy hearing aid and wore an ancient jacket probably from the nineties or even earlier. No lie, her jacket was literally older than Destiny herself.

Then there was Miss Willoughby, tall and buff with shoulder-length gray hair and freckles. Destiny had looked her up and discovered she had actually published a book, so she was, like, really a writer. And then there was Miss Jennie, who Destiny guessed might be Italian. Miss Jennie was short, with olive skin, lighter than Destiny's but darker than most of the pale folks at Bristlecone, and had wild-ass curly white hair and those deep brown eyes that stared into a person's soul. Miss Jennie always seemed like the friendliest one; she always stopped to say hello to Destiny.

They'd finished their meeting—and Destiny knew it had been kind of a hot mess. She knew because she'd figured out how to use the intercom at the front desk to eavesdrop on their meetings.

Why did Destiny bother snooping on those old people talking about writing, anyway? Reason being, she'd wanted to be a writer ever since she read *Their Eyes Were Watching*

God by Zora Neale Hurston in tenth grade, which was the most electrifying book she ever read. After that her English teacher, Mrs. Patterson, told her she should be a writer because she was "not afraid to tell the truth." Destiny joined the poetry slam club, Drop the Mic, at school that very day, channeling Amanda Gorman. She felt like that could be her superpower. Not that her parents cared.

"Something professional that earns you a good living and allows you to stand on your own two feet, Destiny," Mama always said. "Making up stories is not a real job."

Destiny had heard recently that *Their Eyes Were Watching God* wasn't allowed to be taught at her school anymore, which really pissed her off. That was crazy. That book had changed her life.

So anyway, there they all were at the top of the stairs, and next thing Destiny knew, Miss Margaret was tumbling down. Her head bumped with a sickening sound, like a dropped cantaloupe, and she just lay there on the landing like a rag doll. Miss Jennie, the short Italian one, was the first running down after her.

"Margaret, are you all right?"

Then Miss Willoughby came behind, yelling, "Stop! I don't think you're supposed to move a person."

Destiny was halfway to the stairs when Dr. Abe said, "Miss, could you—" Destiny had greeted him every Friday wearing her "Destiny Johnson" nametag right above her boob for a year, and he still called her "Miss." Really? And that was after he'd reminded her no less than three times that he was to be called "Dr." But, whatever.

"I'm on it," Destiny said, running back to grab the phone. They said they were on their way, and Destiny headed back up the stairs to try CPR—part of her training.

Miss Margaret's face was sagging on one side and all

gray looking. Destiny lifted her skinny wrist, took her pulse —nothing—and lay her own hands on Miss Margaret's bony white chest, carefully splayed, the way she'd been taught. She had barely done twenty chest compressions when the med techs showed up, one of whom was that cute, buff one named Marcus, with the expressive eyes and the dimple. Destiny had seen him around a couple times.

They put Miss Margaret on the stretcher, rushed her down the stairs and out.

Her orange briefcase was still lying there. Destiny picked it up, and it felt like there was barely anything in it. A sheet of paper poked out and Destiny glimpsed one line of her wobbly handwriting—the title of the book *Are You There God? It's Me, Margaret.*

What the hell?

"I can take her briefcase, Destiny." Miss Willoughby held out her hand.

"Sure, yeah." Destiny handed it to her. Miss Willoughby gave Destiny this look that made her wonder if she'd suspected all along Destiny had been using that intercom. But at least she knew Destiny's name.

So now an old guy had returned a library book—by James Patterson, was it humanly possible for one person to write so many books? —to the gathering room just behind her desk and couldn't remember how to write it down in the "honor system" ledger. Plus, his old, wrinkled, white hand shook so much it was hard for him to write, so Destiny helped him. But other than that, the desk had been dead as a doornail. Not that Destiny minded that whatsoever. More time for studying and writing.

For her community college poetry class, Destiny had been listening to Maya Angelou recite her poem, "Phenomenal Woman." Destiny loved the way the syllables rolled off her tongue when she wrote about the mysterious power of being a woman. She ran it back to listen again when the front door opened. That ripped med tech from this afternoon, Marcus, with his slightly disheveled Afro and cute dimples, still in his uniform, came in. You wouldn't think Destiny would notice a guy in the midst of somebody falling down the stairs and then giving them CPR, but you would be wrong.

"Hey." His eyes looked weary, with dark circles underneath, but there was a spark, and all of a sudden, Destiny knew it was for her.

She was still thinking about that Maya Angelou poem, about a woman's smile and inner mystery. So many spoken word poets wrote about men doing horrible stuff and Destiny knew for a fact that they did, but she liked that poem being different. There were good men in the world, her daddy being one. He went to work every single day and took pride in his work with HVAC systems. He changed filters and light bulbs, mowed the grass, sat next to Mama at church, listened to Mama complain about how tough it was to be a school principal, and fed their little pittie dog, Rosa, named after Rosa Parks. Mama called Daddy her sweet thang, which embarrassed Destiny and her brothers practically to death.

Destiny would like to find a good man like her mama had. She'd like it if Marcus turned out to be one. But she knew Mama thought "not yet." Twenty-one, in Mama's opinion, was still wet behind the ears

Marcus was a gym rat; she could tell right off. A few inches taller than she was, with muscles toned in all the right places. She had to say that she was not opposed to gym rats. He also had kind eyes. She took out her earbuds and put them in her bag.

"Just wanted to circle back to let you know. That old lady didn't make it."

"Oh no." Destiny thought about Miss Margaret's old, padded jacket, her wrinkled face, that almost empty brief-case. That was sad. And since Destiny had listened in on some of the writers' meetings, she knew Miss Margaret never brought a single thing she actually wrote. And what did that mean, Miss Margaret writing down the title of the book, *Are You There God? It's Me, Margaret?*

"Yeah." Marcus put his hand on the desk, kind of gently patting it, like he might like to pat Destiny on the arm, but that was maybe too much, since they'd hardly just met, so he patted the desk instead. "Good job trying, though. Sometimes, you know, it just doesn't work out. But I thought you'd want to know."

"Yeah, thanks. That's nice of you. I had the training, but I never tried it before."

"I saw you doing the chest compressions when we came in; you were doing great."

"Well, thanks." Could she have saved Miss Margaret? If she had gotten there sooner, placed her hands in a more perfect position, or done more compressions?

"Working in a place like this, you'd think we'd get used to people dying."

"But we don't." She finished his thought. Everyone joked about it—with tons of flippant, dark jokes about death—but how many times had she caught someone in the break room crying, or had other people caught her crying?

He noticed she had her bag over her shoulder. "You going home now?"

"Yeah."

"Where're you parked? I'll walk you."

"You don't need to do that."

Bristlecone had a serious rule about employees dating. One of the girls Destiny had gotten to know a little bit had been fired for going out with her supervisor. The supervisor had been fired too. Destiny had been there in the break room when Melody had to clean out her locker. Destiny and Marcus weren't in the same department, but at Bristlecone, it didn't seem to matter.

"I want to."

Well, it was just a walk to the parking lot, not a bona fide date. And she had to admit it would be nice after such a tough day. "Okay. I'm in the lot around back."

They walked together around the building and through the back courtyard with the old bristlecone pine tree with the plaque. The spring air that evening felt soft.

"That was a poem you were listening to?"

"Yeah. For a poetry class. Maya Angelou. She taught at a university not far from here. She was...amazing. I wish I could have taken a class with her. Do you know 'Still I Rise'?"

Marcus shook his head. "I don't know jack about poetry. You a poet?"

"Trying to be. Spoken word."

"That's cool. Speak one for me."

"Oh, we have to know each other a lot better for me to do that." Destiny laughed a little and cut her eyes at him in a way she knew was flirty.

"Oh, really?"

"Really." She stopped beside her black Toyota. "This is me."

"I like your name—Destiny. Sounds like your parents want you to do something with your life."

Destiny laughed again. "Well, you're right about Mama. She has no patience with slackers."

"Well, Destiny, I think I might want to get to know you better so I can hear some of your spoken word poetry."

"Is that so." She put her hand on her hip, like she wasn't impressed.

"Yeah, that's so. Can I get your number?"

"You know employees are not supposed to date, right?" She acted even less impressed, though her heart gave a little squeeze. "We could be fired." She unlocked her car door. "Remember that girl Melody and her supervisor who got fired a few months ago? I mean, I need this job to save for school."

"I hear you; I need it too—I help out my mom." Marcus hesitated, ran his hand through his hair. "Just as friends, then. I'd like to hear one of your poems."

"My writing is personal to me. I don't show it to just anyone. I mean, when people write—or when I write—I'm telling what's on my heart." Destiny lay her hand over her heart, just to show him she was serious. "And I don't necessarily want to put that out for just anyone. Especially anyone who might end up hurting me." Destiny realized she'd never really said that to anyone, but that was how she felt about her poetry.

"Has anyone done that? Hurt you, I mean?"

"No," Destiny lied.

Yes, there had been the guy in junior year who had ended up ghosting her, who then literally fell off the face of the earth. She'd cried herself to sleep for a week, with Mama rubbing her back and saying, "See what I told you? Keep your eye on the prize, baby." And Destiny had decided Mama was right and hadn't given anyone the time of day after that. But that was way too much to tell Marcus right now.

"Well, that's good, because I wouldn't want anyone to hurt you," Marcus said.

Destiny thought that sounded like a player's line and gave him a look that said so.

He backpedaled. "I tell you what, I'll give you my number, and you decide when you want to text me." He held out his hand for her phone.

Destiny looked at him for a long minute. The deep, soulful, and very kind eyes made even more so by the pleading look on his face. Those dimples. The messy Afro. She wished she could just neaten it up a little for him. The ripped gym rat torso. She couldn't argue; he was definitely her type. Still hearing Mama's voice about keeping her eyes on the prize, she pulled up the "add contacts" screen and held out her phone to him.

And here's what she was thinking: *I'll remember that the day I first talked to Marcus is the very day Miss Margaret died.*

CHAPTER 5
ABE

The Saturday morning after Margaret fell and died, after his coffee and his cholesterol-lowering oatmeal, Abe read the last pages of *The Bristlecone Weekly*, as he had fallen asleep while reading about *pinus aristata* last night. Two things caught his attention.

First, there was a reminder to residents that pets could not weigh over twelve pounds. Abe, frankly, hadn't even realized that pets were allowed here. He'd seen them occasionally but assumed they were visiting. Could Solomon possibly live with him? Margaret dying had made Abe realize how alone he was. He decided to call Nicole after his workout, while on his daily three-mile walk. Solomon was a very friendly dog. He might help Abe make friends.

Second, a photo on the "Welcome Newcomers to Bristlecone" page caused Abe to flush with recognition. The woman looked an awful lot like Allison Wilson, the girl he'd dated his junior year of college. It was not exaggerating to say Allison had been the lost love of Abe's life. The last name was different. Her married name, probably. He couldn't remember. He could, however, still picture seeing her for the first time, reading a book on a bench on the quad. He vividly recalled her wavy, honey-colored hair, her petite girlish figure, her full lips, always laughing, with a hint of a smile at even serious times. Such a foil for solemn Abe. He and Allison might have married, except for a confluence of circumstances.

Abe stared at her photo; she had silvery spiked hair—a definite change—and a come-hither mouth. Was that indeed Allison? His heart gave one aching throb. How could fifty years have gone by, yet his feelings for her hadn't changed in the least? Or maybe it wasn't her, after all.

The memory was as vivid as yesterday. On their first date, only weeks into their junior year, Abe invited Allison to go for a ride on his motorcycle, a royal blue Honda 350. He couldn't afford a car. He wasn't sure that the girl he'd met on the steps of the library would have an interest in motorcycles, but he was wrong. She accepted with enthusiasm.

"My senior year of high school I only dated guys with motorcycles," she'd told him. Her gold-flecked hazel eyes sparked with fun, and she pushed her unruly, waist-length, honey-colored hair behind her ear with a practiced motion. Her answer had been surprising since he'd seen her, night after night, sitting in a study carrel in the library not far from the one he always chose, reading Eudora Welty and Shakespeare and Carson McCullers and F. Scott Fitzgerald and taking copious notes. He'd thought she might be too studious.

He wasn't sure what to think about the statement about dating guys with motorcycles, but his mind went to:

1. *She has her choice of guys to date.*
2. *She is a risk-taker.*
3. *Maybe she isn't a virgin.*

The motorcycle date wouldn't cost anything, other than a few teaspoons of gas, which was good, but now that she'd said yes, he had to come up with a spare helmet. He borrowed one from a fraternity brother, but it ended up being far too big and it bobbled on her head when he carefully joined the clasp under her chin. He took her for a drive around the town, ever-conscious of her breasts nestled against his back and her thighs behind his on the 'cycle. Her roommate's parents were impatiently waiting to drive her home with them for semester break, so the ride was shorter than he'd planned.

He had been wrong about the virgin part. After dating for almost six months, he decided it was time for the "big night." He bought her an expensive dinner consisting of tiny portions and a bottle of Pouilly Fuissé. Once again, Allison surprised him, because he'd expected her to be shy and need coaxing, but once the first time was out of the way, she sometimes seemed more interested in sex than he was.

When he took Allison up to New York to meet his parents, Abe's father took him aside and asked, "What are you doing with this girl? Is she going to convert?"

"I don't know, Pa, we haven't discussed it."

"Haven't discussed it?" His father seemed incredulous.

And then, only a few weeks after that visit, Allison had nestled beside him on a bench on the quad one night after studying together and asked, "Could you see us married some day? With a family?"

But Abe's goal was a PhD in Middle Eastern history,

years in the future, and marriage wasn't even on his mind. He told her so.

Things with Allison unraveled after that. For reasons unknown to Abe, she became whiny and clingy, and Abe, annoyed, suddenly found her less interesting now that he no longer needed to pursue her. He began to date other girls. Since she lived in the dorm right across the quad from his, she knew about the other girls, even saw him with one. She retaliated by dating some of the wildest guys on campus. Abe once looked out his dorm window after two in the morning and saw Allison walking alone on the quad with her high heels in her hand, singing "Piece of my Heart," with the abandon of Janis Joplin.

He called her the next day. "I saw you staggering across the quad last night. You need to straighten up."

"I need to straighten up?" She laughed gaily.

"Seriously, we need to break up," he said. "Things aren't working anymore."

She hung up on him, and he wondered if she'd been drinking.

He didn't see her studying in the library in the evenings after that, and he learned that she had decided to take a semester abroad. He was careful about who he asked about her, but her old suite-mate finally told him that Allison had later transferred to Chapel Hill. Abe briefly wondered if it had anything to do with their breakup, but then decided she probably just changed her major. A year after that, he graduated.

Abe moved back to New York and went to graduate school. His first year, he was so lonely he finally got Allison's old suite-mate to reveal her phone number and called her over and over. She usually didn't answer, but once she finally picked up. He'd had a few drinks and offhandedly asked if she might consider converting. She said no.

Something about the fact that he was her first love made him sometimes think they were forever connected, even though, logically, that wasn't true. The next thing he knew, he heard from that same suite-mate that Allison had met someone else and married him. The following year, Abe met Ellen, who was Jewish, and made his parents incredibly happy.

Life with Ellen had been good. She'd had a great sense of humor, she'd been tremendously proud of Abe's scholarly accomplishments, and they'd had two boisterous sons, Jacob and Noah. Neither had been as obedient as Abe had been as a boy, but their lives had been chaotic in a wonderful way. Ellen had been a high school teacher, and since they both had summers off, they usually went to Cape Cod for a month, and they also tried taking the boys on wilderness trips out west. Later, when Abe received a job offer from his alma mater at Eden Forest, they'd moved from New York back to North Carolina. A few months after their younger son, Noah, married, Ellen's cervical cancer was discovered. She lived two debilitating years after that.

About a year after Ellen's death, Abe looked for Allison's new number on the alumni website. He imagined they might have an hour-long conversation, seamlessly bridging thirty-five years. He imagined the memory of that lost love between them infusing every word they spoke. It was a dream-like conversation that soothed Abe's aching heart, but he never gathered the courage to call her.

A few weeks later, he met Nicole, a tall CPA nearly twenty years his junior, with glossy strawberry blonde hair past her shoulders. She was a new partner in the financial firm he'd used for many years. She started out just being his accountant, but she flirted with him even on their first meeting in mid-March. Pretty soon, he was inventing reasons to drop records off at her office rather than just sending them electronically. Being with Nicole pulled him from the year-long depression he'd sunk into after Ellen's death. His sons didn't like it, but he proposed to her after knowing her for only seven months.

They had gotten married in Naples, Florida in October, with only a photographer present, which simplified things since his sons were making such a nasty fuss about everything. Nicole had been married once before but had no children. He sold the house he and Ellen had lived in, split the proceeds between the two boys, hoping to appease them, and moved into Nicole's gorgeous lakefront house.

After he retired from the university, they went on vacations, they played golf, they went out to trendy restaurants and plays. Abe was invited to be a guest lecturer in a few exclusive places, which impressed Nicole. Things were fantastic for about ten years.

Abe, surfacing from his memories, put his coffee cup in the sink, sighed, and put on his workout clothes. He headed for the Bristlecone workout room in the admin building as he did every day, rain or shine, stepping out into the spring warmth and crossing the grassy courtyard. The grass grew wildly this time of year, and the crew could not keep up. For today's workout, according to his usual routine, he'd focus on his legs and core, with dead lifts, lunges, planks, and crunches. He found a spot inside the workout room where he could watch the pickleball court while he worked out.

Nicole loved pickleball. She was a jock, really, better at

golf than Abe was, and was also great at tennis. Sometimes he saw Willoughby playing pickleball and thought of Nicole, as she was tall, too, and also played aggressively. He'd thought that Nicole might want to play here.

So when the reservation he'd made at Bristlecone when Ellen was still alive miraculously made it to the top of the waiting list, he had been eager to tell Nicole. He was eligible to move into one of the independent cottages, but if he didn't take advantage of it within eighteen months, he would have to go to the end of the waiting list again. Abe had had a few heart issues and liked the idea of being near the medical services at Bristlecone. Nicole didn't cook, and he had never learned, so he also thought it would be good to have a meal taken care of once a day. He assumed Nicole would too.

That morning, as he sat on the bed putting on his new walking shoes, he suggested moving to Bristlecone to Nicole, but she looked shocked.

"Are you kidding me? I'm not going to any retirement community! I'm barely sixty—the new fifty! I love this house. I love this neighborhood and my friends. I love the golf course." Nicole zipped up her golf skirt and quickly braided her long red hair. She looked far younger than her age. She hadn't gained any weight since they had married, and she'd had some work done on her face. A few times people who met them thought she was his daughter.

"Well, if I need taking care of, Nicole, will you take care of me?" he said with a joking tone to his voice. The difference between their ages hadn't really been an issue before.

Nicole shook her head. "That was never part of our deal.

I love you to pieces, but you are going to have to keep up, Abe." She jammed her golf cap on and pulled her long braid through the hole in the back. "I'll be back after dinner; it's ladies' day at the club and I'm eating with the girls."

Arguments with Nicole about Bristlecone had gone on for a full year. Around that time, Abe had a heart attack on the golf course, collapsing on the eighteenth hole. His golf partners, in a later attempt at dark humor, joked that he had a heart attack from shock after making a twenty-foot putt. His partner, Pete, told Abe that he lay there looking blue as Pete tried CPR, and the shadow of a cloud moved over his body in a most eerie way, before the rescue squad arrived.

The paramedics got Abe to the hospital in time, but he had to have a triple bypass. The recovery had been agonizing. He'd felt like his body had been sawed in half. And, truthfully, it practically had. He still had the big brown teddy bear they gave him after the surgery to hold to his chest when he coughed. He hadn't felt like an old man before. Now he did. Nicole had been prescient; she was not a good nurse.

The heart attack changed his life. He had gone on the Mediterranean diet, thrown himself into the physical therapy afterward, lost thirty pounds, became the star graduate, and even after all that continued working out religiously. Which was why he was there in the workout room every day, as well as walking three miles afterward.

He had called Bristlecone a month before his eighteen-month window was up and, in a fever, said he'd take the next available cottage. His sons, Jacob and Noah, were in full agreement, though Abe worried that it was because they still just didn't like Nicole. When he moved to Bristlecone, Nicole didn't help him, as they were barely speaking, and once there, he didn't tell anyone he was married. There were one or two acquaintances from college also residing at Bristlecone, but he doubted they even knew anything about him since Ellen's death. He removed his wedding ring and slid it into his handkerchief drawer.

It was unspoken but, since Nicole refused to move to Bristlecone, they were separated.

As soon as Abe finished his workout, he headed out on Bristlecone's walking trail, which connected with the Carolina Thread Trail through the small town of Eden Forest. His route circled past the bookstore, coffee shop, and library in the downtown area, and various suburban neighborhoods and playing fields, where he saw the occasional soccer or softball game, with kids piling on each other and parents yelling on the sidelines. Eden Forest was an enjoyably walkable town. Once he got into the woodsy and more private part of the trail, Abe called Nicole.

"How are you? Are they feeding you okay there?" She sounded like she was talking to a son she'd sent away to camp.

"The food's not bad. They hired a new chef."

"That's good. How's your heart?"

"Okay. A little sore sometimes. How's Solomon?"

Nicole had adopted the sweet and loyal eight-pound chihuahua against Abe's wishes, but he had become quite fond of Solomon. He hadn't dared to ask for Solomon when he first moved into Bristlecone and still considered it a long shot.

"He misses you."

"I miss him. Does he still play with that dead chipmunk toy?"

"He takes it to the door to meet you every day."

Abe sighed. A short pause, with obvious awkwardness, since neither of them mentioned missing the other. Then, as usual with Nicole, the conversation took a turn that Abe couldn't have foreseen. Before Abe could even bring up the idea of bringing Solomon to live with him, Nicole said, "It's been a year, Abe. According to North Carolina law, we can get a divorce now."

He was silent, a bit stunned. He couldn't think of anything to say. He didn't know if he wanted a divorce or not. He had never thought he'd be twice married, let alone widowed and divorced. The events of his life still baffled him at times. He tried not to think about Allison but didn't succeed. He had read novels about the folly of revisiting lost loves, such as *Long Island* by Colm Tóibín but somehow could not help himself. He was aware that part of what intrigued him about Allison was the unfinished nature of their relationship.

A group of bikers approached Abe on the path, and he waited for them to go by before answering.

"Abe. Don't you have an opinion?"

"Have you met somebody?" It was spring. Tax season. He pictured Nicole flirting with a younger version of himself as they discussed deductions over the satiny poplar of her conference table.

"I don't know."

"That's an odd answer. It would seem that you'd know if you'd met someone."

"Why don't you move back here?" Nicole said.

"Why don't you move *here*? There's room for two in the cottage. And the closets are big." Nicole had a lot of clothes.

"Abe, I love you, I do. You are my best friend. I absolutely love discussing almost everything with you. But we've talked about this ad nauseam. I can't picture myself there. I'm not even sixty yet. I can still run a 10K. I can still break fifty for nine holes. You and I agree on just about everything in life except where we want to live. I am not ready for Bristlecone. I mean, we've been over and over this."

He sighed. "It's just...the heart attack scared me, Nicole." He almost whispered, as if admitting this within earshot of some passing walker would be admitting weakness.

"There are a lot of things in life that are scary. I think we just have to step up."

"That's easy for you to say. You don't have any health problems, Nicole. I like the fact that there are nurses and doctors on staff here. So are we at an impasse?"

"I guess we are. Donna will send the papers over."

Donna had been their lawyer. Now Abe supposed she was Nicole's lawyer.

"Well, the kids should be delighted," he said, knowing he sounded petty but saying it anyway. He was coming up on a peewee soccer game and had a bit of trouble hearing over all the yelling.

"Well, maybe you can repair your relationships with Jacob and Noah and your grandson Levi without me in the picture." Jacob and his wife had chosen not to have children and Noah, who lived in San Diego, had nine-year-old Levi.

"Repair my relationships? What's wrong with my relationships with Jacob and Noah? And I don't really know how deep a relationship I could have with a nine-year-old boy who lives three thousand miles away." He realized he was yelling over the shouting of the game.

"If you don't know, Abe, there's no sense in me wasting my breath."

"Well, I don't know what you mean." Abe kicked a soccer ball back to a bunch of kids who had kicked it out of bounds. But then, abruptly, "Can I have Solomon?"

A moment of silence. "You want Solomon?" She sounded stunned.

"Yes, I didn't think Bristlecone allowed dogs, but they do."

A longer moment of silence. Then, her tone sounding almost amused, "Okay, sure, yes, you can."

Abe let his breath out, feeling previously unimagined joy just at the thought of walking Solomon around the grounds of Bristlecone, or of the comforting weight of Solomon sleeping on the bed on top of Abe's feet. He'd been so lonely. And he'd been prepared for an argument, but she'd agreed almost instantly, which threw him off-balance. But truly, everything about Nicole had always thrown him off-balance.

"I've got some things to take care of, but I'll text you with a few times you can come pick him up."

"That's great."

Abe returned to his cottage, started a load of laundry— which was something he had learned to do after Ellen died —and worked on his manuscript at a breakneck pace over the next day or two, while waiting for his divorce papers and "custody" of Solomon. What he was writing was far too autobiographical; even he knew that. It was incredible how this personal form of writing was so much more cathartic than the academic writing he'd done in the past.

The act of writing was, in fact, almost helping him make sense of his past and the losses he'd experienced.

He invented a name for Allison, gave her long dark hair instead of long blonde hair, and made her tall instead of short. He gave a thorough description of their relationship, in some parts from Allison's point of view, and gained insight into her clinginess. He came to understand that many Southern women of his generation believed that once they'd had sex with a man, they should marry him.

He went on for pages about the loss of Ellen.

Later in the manuscript, after he met Nicole, he made himself better-looking and more successful than he really was, which gave him a faint burst of satisfaction. If you couldn't make yourself a nine instead of a five when you were writing, why do it, right? Of course, his character was chairman of the department.

Interestingly, writing from Nicole's point of view did give him a new perspective on their age difference. What if he were twenty years younger than she was? Would he not be impatient? Would he not feel stifled? What if he, like Nicole, was interested in pickleball, but he had an older spouse, like Abe, who had to be careful about physical activity due to a heart attack and a newly discovered clotting disorder? Writing about himself as Nicole might see him, on the other hand, gave him a somewhat uncomfortable feeling. When he read it back, it sounded whiny. A little like he thought Allison had been, over fifty years ago.

Fifty years was a very long time. If he'd married Allison, and they'd indeed started a family as she'd wanted, their children would be almost fifty. Only, actually, ten years younger than Nicole. Unbelievable.

He plowed on with his rusty prose. Willoughby and Jennie knew practically nothing about Abe's life. They would never know that most of it was true. He thought about possibly seeing Allison again, at Bristlecone, if it was actually her. It wasn't that big a place—only about three hundred residents. He was bound to run into her somewhere. How might she have changed after all these years?

CHAPTER 6
WILLOUGHBY

On the forty-five-minute drive to her daughter Courtney's house, the day after Margaret's death, Willoughby sunk her mind deeply into the thriller she was working on. She admitted that escaping into the world of her writing was a way of coping with the situation with Gary. Truly, it did help.

The concept, she thought, about a reclusive writer and the younger woman she decides to hire to make appearances for her, had a lot of potential. She tried to imagine herself as Dorothy, her main character: private, lonely, weakened by ailments, interviewing the much younger, vibrant, extroverted, and mysterious woman named Astrid. She pictured Astrid with flaming red hair, of course. But maybe Dorothy's hair had once been red also.

"Do you have any problems with having your photo taken, first of all?" Dorothy might ask, meeting Astrid in a coffee shop or café somewhere in the South, in the early 1920s.

"No," Astrid said, raising her chin in a sensual, almost arrogant way. "I have had my portrait made several times and received compliments on it."

"I am sure. Would you have any problem with having your photo displayed as though it were me?"

"Not at all."

As a librarian, Willoughby had always been fascinated with female authors. She'd done some research and knew that, for hundreds of years, women had hidden their authorship of novels. Before the turn of the twentieth century, it wasn't even considered acceptable for women to write much of anything, let alone novels. Female authors had disguised themselves in many ways. They wrote, like Jane Austen, as "a Lady." Or as "Anon." Or they used men's names, like George Sand and George Eliot, or only their initials when they wrote, even as recently as J. K. Rowling.

The era in which Willoughby set her story was all-important. It had to be after authors began making personal appearances in connection with their books and before photography became commonplace. It also needed to be before the proliferation of personal information via broadcasting and the internet. The sweet spot for her story was possibly the 1920s. She'd always loved that time period because it was a time of freedom of thought, behavior, and dress for women, after the confining restrictions of the Victorian age. She'd written her thesis, years ago, on Virginia Woolf and the Bloomsbury group, so she was familiar with the time period. In the café scene, her characters could be wearing slim twenties-style sheaths with tiny hats cocked at an angle.

Just as Willoughby reached Courtney's house, lost in her story, her cell phone rang. It was Jennie.

"Hi, Willoughby, have you got a minute?"

"Sure." Jennie never called her except with writers' group news, so this was a little out of the ordinary.

"I promise you that I am not a snoop—I have called Roy

and left a message about returning this briefcase—but he hasn't called me back."

"Oh, Jennie, of course you aren't! That would never cross my mind." Willoughby turned off the engine. "That briefcase is the last thing on his mind."

"Sure. But my cat crawled into it and pulled out that sheet of paper we all saw, but it is kind of strange. It has a bunch more book titles on it, a lot of which I recognize and have read, but some I've never heard of."

"I am amazed there was anything at all in Margaret's briefcase. I always thought it was completely empty."

"Me too. But it's a kind of weird, eclectic list of books."

"What are they?"

"Let's see...*Are You There God? It's Me, Margaret*, *1984*, *To Kill a Mockingbird*, *The Catcher in the Rye*, *The Bluest Eye*, and *The Adventures of Huckleberry Finn*, those I've read. A lot of others I don't know, like, *The Absolutely True Diary of a Part-Time Indian*, *Speak*, *The Hate U Give*, *This Book Is Gay*, *Gender Queer: A Memoir*, *Nineteen Minutes*, and *Me and Earl and the Dying Girl*."

"Hmm, some are children's books, some are for adults. Some are classics, some more recently published. I'm not familiar with all of them. I wonder what the relationship between them is." Willoughby looked quickly in the mirror on the back of the visor and ran a brush through her hair and slid lipstick across her lips. She always wanted to look put-together when she saw Courtney.

"Yeah, I wonder too. It seems important somehow. I feel like we need to figure out what they mean," Jennie said. "I mean, obviously, we barely knew Margaret, but I know she didn't have children or grandchildren, so these children's books wouldn't be gifts for grandchildren."

"You learn a lot about a person from what they read and

write," Willoughby said, looking at her watch. Courtney might wonder why she was sitting in the car. She couldn't wait to see her and, of course, Clay. She loved Scott too—he was such a perfect husband to Courtney. "Maybe we can talk about this at our meeting on Friday."

Jennie seemed to sense Willoughby needed to go. "Sure, we can talk about it then. I'll bring the briefcase with Margaret's list. I don't know, I just wonder if the list means anything. Remember at our meeting when she patted it and said, 'Everything's in here'?"

"Oh, I do remember that, now you mention it."

"Let's think on it until Friday. I can return it to Roy after that."

"Sounds good."

Willoughby climbed out of the Lexus and up the rather steep stairs to Courtney's front door. When she was married to Steven, their careers, hers as a librarian and his in corporate IT, would have never afforded them a Lexus—it had been a less expensive Honda Civic—but life with Gary the news anchor had been different. Gary had felt it was important, as the face people saw on TV every night, to drive a nice car.

It was probably true, but she had been swept away not by Gary's expensive clothes, big personality, or celebrity, but by how kind he'd been. He'd focused on her alone. He'd made her feel like the only person in the room. She'd truly been in a state of disbelief that such a magnetic man had fallen in love with her, Willoughby, the quiet librarian.

Courtney and her husband, Scott, kept a beautiful yard, with dogwoods and cherry trees and climbing roses on a trellis in the front garden. Hot pink peonies that Courtney was quite proud of were just beginning to bloom by the mailbox. She'd had the door painted a vivid indigo and hung a handmade wreath on it. It was a Saturday afternoon, and Scott was outside mowing the lawn. He waved at Willoughby over the roar. Willoughby tried to see them at least once a week, usually to help them out with Clay on the weekend.

As Willoughby rang the bell, Courtney's black lab, Keanu, raced to the door, barking. When Courtney opened it, the dog jumped all over Willoughby, which nearly knocked her off her feet. Willoughby had never been much of a dog person.

"Keanu, no! Hey, Mom." Courtney grabbed Keanu's collar and pulled him out of the way. She was built like Willoughby, tall and fit, with curly blonde hair like Steven's that she wore chin length. Her waist had "popped" more quickly with this pregnancy than with the first one, and now she was seven months along.

"Oh, you look fantastic!" Willoughby hugged her daughter tightly. The "pregnancy glow" had not hit Courtney this time. "Oh my gosh, your bump has grown even since last week. How're you feeling, honey?"

"Tired. I am *obsessed* with sleep."

"Why don't you take a nap? I can watch Clay, clean or do laundry for you, run errands, whatever you need. We can talk about what I found out for your dad after."

Willoughby, totally aware that she was forever trying to overcompensate with Courtney after leaving her father, couldn't seem to make herself stop. She was still processing what she'd found out about Steven getting into Bristlecone and how she wanted to present it to Courtney; taking care of Clay would buy her some time.

"That would be great. Thanks, Mom."

Willoughby followed Courtney inside, and Clay came

running into the hallway in no pants, just a saggy diaper. "GiGi!"

"Hey, buddy!" Willoughby knelt to hug him, as she was afraid her back couldn't handle picking him up. His damp, light brown curls tickled her face, and his skin smelled so sweet, but he definitely needed a clean diaper.

"Sorry, I was just about to change him."

"I'll do it." She took Clay's hand. "C'mon, buddy, let's get changed. Where are your pants?"

"No pants."

"He's been rebelling against pants. Don't ask me why." Courtney pushed her bangs off her forehead with an exhausted sigh. "I just...can't fight it."

Willoughby laughed and stroked Courtney's arm. "I get it, honey, I get it!"

Courtney took Willoughby's suggestion and went to the bedroom to lie down, poking her head out before collapsing onto the bed, saying, "Do not, I repeat, do not let him go to sleep before two o'clock under any circumstances."

Willoughby changed Clay and was headed out the front door when Keanu joined them, wagging his thick black tail vigorously at the prospect of a walk.

"I'll take Keanu too," Willoughby called out to Courtney.

She wasn't your average seventy-some-year-old; she could surely handle a dog and a toddler. Wasn't that why she kept up the pickleball and Pilates, after all? Not to be too competitive, but she was among the most fit at Bristlecone. She wouldn't even be living there if it weren't for Gary. She grabbed Keanu's leash and Clay's hand and started out around the neighborhood, sans pants, which was the path of least resistance, and really, what did it matter? Her younger self would have insisted, but she had softened in her old age.

"Hey, buddy, we're going on a nature walk. Let's look for birds, butterflies, and bugs." Willoughby enjoyed the alliteration. And knew Clay was a huge fan of anything to do with nature, dinosaurs, or bugs.

"Bugs!" Clay shouted.

Clay's little legs had sweet, chunky rolls, almost like a pastry, and his light brown curls hung in his eyes—Willoughby knew Courtney did not have the heart to cut his hair yet. Sometimes Willoughby thought she could just hug him to pieces—her love for him was not tempered by the responsibility and aspirational competitiveness that had colored her own parenting. She didn't care whether Clay was the most advanced two-year-old; she now understood that the simple fact he existed was a miracle. She wished, in fact, that she'd had such existential wisdom back then. Courtney's parenting was much less strict than Willoughby's had been—and Willoughby was proud to say that most of the time she managed to keep her mouth zipped.

She took Clay to a small neighborhood playground. Keanu watered a nearby tree, then lay in the shade, panting, while Willoughby pushed Clay on the swing, singing "Up in the Air, Junior Birdman," a song she used to sing forty years ago with her sorority sisters.

She had no idea why that song came to her mind, but Clay seemed to like it. Later, sitting at the picnic table under the nearby pergola, she showed him how to form the Junior Birdman goggles with her thumbs and forefingers upside down on her face, and he collapsed in giggles.

He tried it. "Can't do it, GiGi."

"That's okay, it's not that easy for me either." She had

increasingly stiff joints, despite her pickleball and Pilates classes. Speaking of which, she realized that a need to pee had come over her quite suddenly, which also was disconcerting. Willoughby didn't think of herself as old or out of control.

She looked at her watch. One-thirty. "Time to go home, buddy."

She grabbed Keanu's leash. On the way home, they saw a small gray rabbit, frozen beside a clump of well-chewed red impatiens.

"Look, Clay. A bunny rabbit. See the way he sits so still?"

"Bunny wabbit." Clay waddled up the neighbor's driveway toward the rabbit, pointing.

The rabbit, either exceedingly brave or too scared to move, waited until the last minute to scamper away. Keanu's ears pricked up and though Willoughby wrapped the leash around her wrist one more time, it was too late—Keanu lunged toward the rabbit, yanking her to the ground.

Willoughby had the wind knocked out of her but scrambled to her feet, running up the driveway to catch Clay's hand. Keanu had raced around the back of the house after the rabbit but now trotted back, unsuccessful, but then proceeded to squat and deposit a large poop on the neighbor's pristine yard.

"Keanu!" Willoughby picked Clay up, jogged across the lawn, and grabbed Keanu's leash. Putting Clay down, she struggled to pull out and open a poop bag—how could they possibly make it so difficult?—and bent to scoop up the incredibly large poop with one hand while trying to hold Clay's hand with the other. The homeowners were probably peering judgmentally out their front windows.

How did Courtney manage all this? Willoughby was so relieved she was only visiting. No wonder Courtney was so exhausted.

Finally, she managed to head in the direction of Courtney's house, covered in sweat, with Clay's hand in one hand, and Keanu's leash and the steaming bag of poop in the other, when Clay reached up with his chubby arms.

"Carry me."

Why in the hell didn't I bring the stroller? She'd completely forgotten something she'd never have forgotten as a mom.

"I can't, buddy, you're too heavy." She'd thought nothing of carrying around a thirty-pound toddler back in the day. There was no way that was happening now, especially with Keanu and the giant poop. Besides, if Clay kneed her in the stomach, she'd wet her pants.

"Carry me!" He dug his fists into his eyes, a sign that she recognized as him being overtired, reached up to her again, and began to whine.

"It's okay, let's just sit here and rest for a few minutes." She sat on the curb and patted the spot next to her. Sitting down relieved the urge to pee. Keanu lay down in the street, panting, with a heavenly smile on his face that made Willoughby wonder if he had some way of getting high. And he certainly felt the freedom to pee whenever he wanted to, as long as he was outside.

She could call Courtney or Scott to come bring the stroller but hated to bother them—they both had so much on their plates. She was supposed to be helping them and then she would only be causing more trouble. She and Clay were only about a half a block away from home. Surely they could make it.

"Carry me!" Clay was starting to melt down. She'd

pushed too close to naptime. Squatting to make sure she used her legs instead of her back, she gripped him under his armpits and, wobbling, lifted him to her waist. She'd walked past several houses when she realized—she'd forgotten the poop!

She looked back at the black plastic bag, lying in the street. She couldn't. She just couldn't.

"Wrap your legs around me, buddy, that's right." Willoughby headed down the street, with Clay burrowing his face into her shoulder, stopping every fifteen steps or so to bump him higher on her hip and try to squeeze in a Kegel or two. She was practically staggering by the time she reached Courtney's house. Worse, Clay was fast asleep, drooling on her shoulder. She knew immediately there was no way in hell she could get him and the dog up the steep front steps.

Courtney was probably still asleep, and mower sounds now came from the back yard, which meant Scott couldn't see or hear to help either. Damn her seventy-year-old bladder.

She sat on the bottom step holding Clay as he slept, stroking his head. Keanu, thoughtful as always, began to sniff and then lick her legs.

Scott came around the house, pushing the now-quiet lawn mower. "Willoughby, did you carry him? Why didn't you take the stroller?"

"I forgot it."

"Let me take him." Scott parked the mower, then bent and picked Clay up with ease, gently, without waking him. He grabbed Keanu's leash too. "Come on, boy, up the steps. I'll take him up to his crib. Do you need help on the steps?"

"No, no, I'm fine. I'll be up in just a minute. But I left an enormous bag of poop back there in the street." People never used to ask her if she needed help. Now they did all the time.

"I'll get it, don't worry."

"Thank you, Scott." Willoughby raced up behind Scott and ducked into the powder room just off the front hall. *Whew! Barely made it.* She discovered a bloody scrape on her knee that she hadn't even noticed before and cleaned it the best she could.

Scott was upstairs with Clay by the time Willoughby came out of the powder room. Keanu was sprawled on the kitchen floor, his forelegs framing his water dish, slurping loudly, and Courtney was still sleeping in their downstairs master suite.

By the time Courtney woke up, Willoughby had unloaded the dishwasher and folded a load of laundry.

"Mom?" Courtney ran her hands over her face, still waking up. "Thanks for doing all that. I feel a lot better."

They sat on the kitchen stools and dipped some carrots and celery Courtney had cut up into blue cheese dressing. Clay was still napping, and Scott was making a quick trip to the hardware store for a new string for his Weed eater.

Keanu had developed a new level of affection for Willoughby and repeatedly licked the scrape on her leg, as if to atone for pulling her down.

"So glad you got some rest." Willoughby was careful not to ask too much—Courtney sometimes thought she was overly protective. Willoughby had once suggested that Courtney forgo a business trip early in her pregnancy and Courtney had exploded at her and gone anyway. Fortunately, all had been well. Now Willoughby was more careful and picked her battles.

"So, Mom. What's the story on Dad? Can you get him into Bristlecone?"

Willoughby drank in her daughter's hopeful face, and it meant everything. "I finally decided to say he was a member of my family—which was a teeny tiny lie—and they offered for him to move into the first room that opens up in health care, which they anticipate will be in the next few days. One guy's close to death and another woman has improved and will be moving back into assisted living. So two possibilities." Willoughby didn't mention to Courtney the mental and emotional gymnastics she'd gone through before taking the step of saying Steven was family. She didn't want Courtney to be burdened with that.

"Oh, that's great!" Courtney threw her arms around Willoughby, and Willoughby felt herself melt with joy. Keanu, always wanting to be in on any physical affection, tried to wedge himself in between them, his tail thumping. "Thanks, Mom. Face it: You owed him this."

"Did I?" Willoughby pulled away, feeling a flicker of anger. Steven hadn't been perfect in their marriage, so it was difficult for her to always feel like she was taking the blame. Keanu licked her leg again. Willoughby exploded. "Keanu, stop it! Leave me alone!"

"Keanu, no." Courtney pulled Keanu away. "Mom, you don't have to yell at him. He's just a dog."

Willoughby drew a deep breath. "I'm sorry, I lost my patience. This stuff with your dad is just stressing me out."

"Mom, I mean, I know being married to Dad had to have been a challenge. I get it. But this is the least you can do, now that Dad's old and sick."

Willoughby bit her tongue, not wanting to get into it. She felt like she could never atone for leaving Steven. Had Steven's multiple job losses seriously gone that unnoticed by the kids? At least Courtney conceded that he wasn't easy to live with, but the kids didn't seem to pick up that she hadn't been happy. If she had been, she wouldn't have found something she needed in Gary. She drew a deep breath and stood up. "You and Scott will move him, right?" She took Clay's laundry she'd folded and tiptoed upstairs to his room and lay it outside his closed door.

"Yes, if you can keep Clay for the day, Scott and I will do it," Courtney called up the stairs after her.

"And you'll need to take care of him," Willoughby said when she came back downstairs. "I can't." She took the laundry she'd folded for Courtney and Scott and lay it on top of the small bookcase in the hallway right outside their room. "I have Gary to take care of."

"Yes, Mom, we'll take care of him." Courtney wasn't facing Willoughby but she could picture her daughter jutting her jaw the way she did when she was annoyed.

It made no sense to even tell Gary about Steven, of course. He wouldn't remember him. But she still felt...odd? Guilty? There were a few seconds of silence.

When Willoughby came back into the kitchen, after a short hesitation, Courtney reached out to hug her. "Thanks, Mom, I appreciate it so much. How's Gary doing, anyway?"

Willoughby almost said, "I thought you'd never ask," but she bit her tongue again. "Good days and bad days. At least he still knows me every time." She smiled and shrugged. Just a little lie.

"Well, that's good."

Willoughby picked up her purse to leave but couldn't resist her desire to know about Adam. "Any news from your brother?"

Courtney blinked and looked away. "He's fine. I talked to him a few days ago." She hesitated, as if considering whether to share more information. "He's probably coming down in a few weeks to see Dad."

Willoughby couldn't hold back. "Oh, great, maybe I'll see if he'll have coffee with me. Do you think he would?"

Courtney pursed her lips. "I think you should accept that he doesn't want to see you, Mom."

Defeat oozed through Willoughby like a heavy sludge, weighing her down. "I can't give up, Courtney. I just can't."

"Maybe you should talk to someone about it."

"I'd like to talk to Adam about it."

"I mean a therapist."

Willoughby sighed and picked up her purse to leave, then paused. "You and Scott want to go out? It's Saturday night. I'll stay with Clay?"

"No, we're going over to some friends tonight and taking him. They have a little boy about his age."

"Okay, well, sounds fun. Tell Scott thanks for helping me with Clay on the steps."

"I will. And thanks for all the help this afternoon, Mom. It means a lot."

Courtney and Willoughby hugged again, and Willoughby headed down the driveway to her car. Backing out, she waved as Courtney waved from the doorway, then looked in the rear-view mirror and saw the enormous bag of poop still lying in the street. Someone had partially run over it. She sighed, got out of the car, jogged down the road, peeled the poop bag from the asphalt, and put it in Courtney and Scott's trash can.

As she drove back to Bristlecone, she managed to put her anguish over Adam out of her head and instead forced her thoughts to return to Steven. Her mind churned with scenarios. Steven needing someone to visit him while Courtney and Scott went on vacation. Steven needing someone to coax him to eat, to help him to the bathroom, to walk the halls with him while Courtney worked, took care of Clay, and, of course, gave birth.

Did Willoughby owe Steven? She didn't think so.

Would she do it for Courtney? Absolutely.

CHAPTER 7
JENNIE

Jennie hesitated, her cursor hovering over the "Send" button. Her hand shook. She let go of the mouse and squeezed her hands together. Then she scrolled back to the top of the entry form to reread her query letter to a small publisher. Sir Arthur sat on her lap, kneading his paws on her thighs. Then he stood and stuck his wet nose in her ear, purring as loudly as a helicopter.

"It is not even close to dinnertime yet, Sir Arthur. Give me a little while longer."

It was Monday, a few days since the writers' group meeting when Margaret had died, and Jennie was finishing up the edits to her manuscript that the group had suggested. Still not satisfied, she'd gone back to reread and edit her manuscript again. The same manuscript that she'd changed from first person to third, reordered, put back in the original order, added descriptions to, scrubbed adverbs from, and generally agonized over for months.

Now, in her cover letter to the publisher she was querying, she'd decided to do something she had never done: She revealed her mother's Iraqi background. Maybe it would give her a leg up in writing about Enheduanna, add a note of authority to her writing.

Ninety minutes later, as the light drained from the extra bedroom she used as an office and indigo shadows fell, her cursor hovered over "Send" once again. She got up, paced the room, came back.

Do it! Just do it! Michael's voice sounded in her head.

Michael would want her to do this. He wouldn't want her to back out because of fear. Finally she sat down, hesitating, her hand poised over the mouse, when Sir Arthur leaped onto her desk with a thud and stepped right on her fingers. Click. Whoosh.

Sent.

"Sir Arthur!"

He turned his blue eyes on her with an innocent look and meowed, as if he had no idea what she was talking about. He waved his chocolate tail cheekily, right in her eyes.

"All right, all right." She went to the kitchen, with Sir Arthur trotting along behind, and scooped food into his bowl. He dug in eagerly, his tail waving with satisfaction.

Would she have sent her manuscript without Sir Arthur? Most likely not. Sometimes—and this seemed crazy—she thought Michael's spirit was embodied in Sir Arthur. Of course, a human's spirit couldn't come back and inhabit a cat. That was ridiculous. Still, she let herself imagine it once in a while. She missed Michael's affection and was comforted when Sir Arthur kneaded his paws on her lap or purred in her ear.

Jennie's hands were still shaking in reaction to the unplanned "send", and she slid them under her armpits, then checked her phone for the time. It was close to seven and the dining hall closed at seven thirty. Maybe she'd go down there instead of eating limp salad alone again.

She stretched her back and blinked. In spite of getting up from her desk, Jennie's mind was still deep in the ancient world of Enheduanna—of priestesses, poets, princesses, the moon goddess, and of the laborious practice of writing cuneiform, one of the first writing systems of the world, with a stylus on wet clay. Enheduanna, the poet, had died four thousand years ago, yet lived on in the long and eloquent poems she had written in just that fashion, stylus on clay. For five hundred years, her poems had been used to teach Babylonian scribal school students.

During her research, Jennie had learned that, in one of her poems, Enheduanna had used the metaphor of child-birth for the process of writing. And last week, Jennie had discovered that Enheduanna might have been lesbian. It was all fascinating, but what Jennie loved so much about Enheduanna was the fact that she was the first to claim authorhood—to individualize herself and declare self-worth through her writings. Little was known about her, other than what could be gleaned in the lines of Enheduanna's poems, but there she revealed that she had at one point been thrown out of the temple. She managed to work her way back to power, and it was this story that Jennie told in her novel.

But what about Willoughby's warnings about writing about groups with which you couldn't claim identity? Jennie had used her imagination, her life experience, and had feverishly researched, but still. She had been mortified when Abe told her she should leave Iraqi stories to the scholars. Now to be writing about lesbians from centuries ago? Was she crazy to try? In her entire life, she'd had only two close lesbian friends and gone to one drag show, during a bachelorette party in her thirties. She'd known one trans person—a tomboy named Carla who had played with Elijah and the other neighborhood boys, and who became Carl in their mid-twenties. No one had been in the least surprised, and Jennie had been glad that Carl had finally found themself and had the resources to do so.

Had she started this project thinking she wanted to write about a character who was possibly lesbian? No. It was indeed amazing where the simple act of trying to tell a story might lead. And how illuminating that could be.

Jennie forced herself to return to the present, ran her hands over her face, yanked a brush through her ill-behaved white corkscrew hair, and dabbed on a bit of lipstick. That was one thing that had begun to get on her nerves about Bristlecone—when you went to the dining hall, you had to be presentable, and sometimes Jennie didn't feel like making the effort. Furthermore, occasionally you had to sit with other people, and often Jennie didn't feel like doing that either. These were among the times when she desperately missed Michael.

She headed down the hall, remembering the way they used to hold hands, so Jennie could help steer Michael around obstacles, if necessary. Michael's mother had been White and Jennie figured that growing up with her, it just being the two of them, had been one of the reasons he was attracted to White girls. He had not known his Black father until he was thirty-two, when the newspaper did a write-up on a new cataract procedure Michael had devised. Then suddenly his father appeared out of nowhere, wanting to establish a relationship. Michael had brushed him off.

Jennie, after seeing so many divided families as a social worker, had thought Michael should make peace and begged him more than once to give his dad a chance, but he refused. His father had died fifteen years ago, without reconciliation between them, which Jennie thought was a tragedy.

The estrangement certainly explained why Michael had gone to such lengths to maintain a good relationship with Elijah; he wanted to be the father he had never had. Elijah and Amanda were actually coming over for dinner next week, Jennie suddenly remembered. She needed to get her head out of the manuscript and clean her apartment and think about what she was going to fix. So it was actually a blessing that Sir Arthur had sent it.

It was late—she'd lied to Bernice about eating in tonight—and the dining hall was nearly empty, which offered just the peace and quiet Jennie preferred. Just as she sat down, however, Hannah, the dining hall hostess, came up to her leading an attractive, petite woman about Jennie's age. She wore dressy jeans and a pastel tie-dye T-shirt, her silver hair attractively spiked to show off the shape of her slim neck and head, as if she were Nefertiti.

"Hi, Jennie," said Hannah. "This is Alli Stone and she's new at Bristlecone—just moved in a few days ago. I told her I was sure you wouldn't mind if she joins you for dinner tonight?"

"Of course, please do," Jennie said, summoning a smile. "Welcome to Bristlecone."

"Thanks so much." Alli sat and put her napkin into her lap, giving Jennie a shy and pretty smile. "I've been unpacking all day. I'm exhausted."

"Time to relax. Are you from around here?"

"I went to college here, but then moved to DC, where I married and raised my family," she said chattily. "I worked in advertising, and my husband was with the NIH—sorry, the National Institutes of Health."

"What made you come back to Eden Forest?"

"Well, my husband passed away about a year and a half ago, but my daughter moved here to teach at the university last semester—she has a fondness for Eden Forest, knowing that I went here, and persuaded me to move here too. I'd always loved the town,"

"Yes, it has so many cultural advantages for a relatively small town, with the new art museum on campus, the independent bookshops, and the community theater. Does it make you feel like a college student again?"

"It does feel a little weird, like déjà vu, to be living in the same town where I went to college. But the town's changed a lot—grown so much."

"Oh, yes, my husband and I lived here for the past twenty years, and it has grown quite a bit even since we moved here," Jennie agreed. "I'm so sorry about your husband," she added, her trademark compassion blossoming. "I lost my husband about the same time."

"Oh, you did? I am so sorry. I honestly think it's one of the toughest things in the world."

"Yes, no question." She wanted to pat Alli's arm, show sympathy, even though she'd just met her, but hesitated.

"Plus, it was quite sudden," Alli added. "A stroke in the middle of the night. I woke up that morning and he was dead beside me." Her lip quivered.

"I'd say that was a shock." Jennie now did reach out and gently patted the back of Alli's hand. She felt an instant closeness with Alli, despite knowing her for only a few minutes.

"It was, yes. What about your husband?"

"Pneumonia. We had been so careful at first, with COVID, but he caught it somewhere—I'm kind of a homebody, but Michael loved to travel and he had planned a trip to Italy. That could have been it. Then it developed into pneumonia, and even though he was hospitalized for several weeks, and received all the new treatments, he just didn't make it."

"Oh, that's a shock too. Awful! Coping has been diffi-cult, hasn't it?"

"Yes, very much so." Jennie fought back tears.

At that moment, their server, Beverly, who Jennie knew well, came by. "Hey, y'all. What are y'all feeling like tonight?"

Both of them decided on the pasta special.

"Anything to drink? Wine? Beer?"

"I've been unpacking boxes, so I've earned a glass of wine!" Alli said gaily.

They agreed to split a bottle. Jennie realized she was beginning to enjoy herself. She had so much in common with Alli that she began to open up even more.

Alli gestured toward Jennie with her small, manicured hands. "Tell me about Bristlecone."

Over their pinot grigio, Jennie told Alli about the Bristlecone amenities, such as the pool, the workout room, and the library. "There's also a gathering room, where they hold various events, like memorial services, and concerts—someone told me an Elvis impersonator is going to be here soon."

"Elvis!" Alli laughed. "I love it."

Jennie warned Alli about the organizer of the pickleball schedule—a draconian guy who had been a coach at the college—and described the lecture series, the book club, and the music series.

"Are there any writing groups here?" Alli asked, bright-ening. "I've been writing poetry for many years. But lately I've become interested in fiction and memoir. I had a wonderful writers' group in DC—I loved a place called The Writer's Center in Bethesda—our group formed after we took a class together. That was one of the hardest parts about leaving. After so many years, we had come to know each other so deeply and truly loved each other."

"Oh, what a coincidence—I'm in a writers' group," Jennie said. What would Willoughby and Abe think about her bringing someone new, without even checking with them? Yet, they were now down to three, and it would be downright rude not to extend an invitation. "We're all writing fiction at the moment. In fact, we just—lost a member." Jennie didn't want to mention Margaret's death so soon after talking about losing husbands. "We meet every week—on Friday. Of course, you're welcome to come."

Alli's tired face opened in a delighted smile. She had lovely hazel eyes. "Do you mean it? I would love to! Thank you, Jennie, I can't tell you how grateful I am."

Jennie smiled, feeling good to have found a way for Alli to connect right away. Willoughby would probably be fine with Alli coming, though she did somewhat think of herself as the group's organizer. But what about Abe? Jennie backpedaled a bit. "You can visit, and we can all see if it's a good fit."

"Sure, that sounds very fair. What time and where?" Alli's face glowed. She pulled out her phone to add it to her calendar. Clearly this meant a great deal to her. She was really a lovely person.

"Friday afternoon at two, in the conference room above the main lobby," Jennie said. "We usually bring about five pages to read."

When Jennie got back to her apartment, she immediately went into her office to send an email to the group.

. . .

```
Dear Fellow Bristlecone Writers,
     You're not going to believe it, but my
cat sent my manuscript to a publisher today
by literally stepping on my fingers when I
had my hand on the mouse! He also found a
sheet of paper in Margaret's briefcase that
is kind of interesting that I'd like to
share at our meeting. FYI, tonight at
dinner I invited a woman who is new at
Bristlecone to visit our writers' group,
just to see if it's a good "fit." She had
been in one herself for many years when she
was in DC.


See you Friday.
     Jennie
```

She felt she'd covered all her bases and went out to the living room to read and listen to some Wynton Marsalis, which reminded her of Michael, before bed. Dinner with Alli really had been enjoyable. For one of the first times since Michael died, Jennie had actually forgotten her aching loss for a few minutes and felt happy.

She opened her tablet and began to look for just the right recipes to fix when Elijah brought his girlfriend, Amanda, for dinner. Elijah had mentioned that Amanda was vegetarian. Or was it vegan? She had been impressed with her when they'd met and hoped it would work out.

Sir Arthur jumped into her lap and began to knead his

paws on her thighs and nudge against her, trying to push his head under her hand to get her to pet him. She gave in and scratched his ears.

"Is that a good spot, Sir Arthur?"

He seemed very satisfied with himself, which reminded Jennie of the way he'd discovered the list of books in Margaret's briefcase. She got up and put Margaret's briefcase by the front door so she wouldn't forget it when she went to writers' group later in the week.

CHAPTER 8
DESTINY

Destiny was sitting at the front desk on Friday afternoon reading one of her faves, *The Hate U Give* by Angie Thomas. Her boss, Ms. Robinson, didn't like her to read while on duty, as Destiny guessed it made it look like she wasn't focusing on the extremely mentally taxing duties of this job. Consequently, she held the book under the counter so people coming in couldn't see it. Her boss didn't frown upon writing quite as much as reading, as Destiny supposed it did make you look as though you were concentrating on something important. That was one of the things Destiny liked about this job—the ability to get her schoolwork and poetry done while at work.

It was seven days since Destiny had met Marcus and he'd given her his number. Not that she was counting, haha. Truth: She'd thought every day about texting him, but she hadn't. She wasn't sure why; maybe she thought it would be good to play hard to get. She'd kind of been waiting for him to wander by, to see if he was still interested. Plus, thinking of the perfect intriguing-yet-casual text wasn't all that easy.

"Sup?" was definitely out. Overdone, plus she'd already told him she was a writer. She could do better than that. He'd be expecting it.

"Had any emergencies lately?" That was lame. Plus, at Bristlecone, there were emergencies every day. Well, until people died, and then there was no rush whatsoever.

What about a line from a movie or book, like one she'd practically memorized in *The Hate U Give* about Starr's friend accusing her of thinking she was "all that"? But maybe then Marcus would think Destiny thought she was all that. Which she didn't.

Destiny even thought about texting a line from a poem. In her English class they were reading Langston Hughes and Destiny had fallen in love with his poems. She loved the poem "I, Too," which described the Negro having a seat at the table, not having to eat in the kitchen. And also "The Negro Speaks of Rivers" and the way it described rivers all over the world as running with the blood of mistreated people from thousands of years of human history. Her teacher, Ms. Guthrie, said they could get extra credit for memorizing one of Langston Hughes's poems, and Destiny was deciding between those two. But probably Marcus would think texting a Langston Hughes line was pretentious.

Destiny, of course, didn't for a minute wish for anyone else to fall down the stairs so that Marcus would rush over and then be there with his ripped torso and kind eyes, even though she did replay the experience in her mind a few times a day.

Just then, one of the ladies in the writers' group, the wiry-haired one, Miss Jennie, came over on her way to the stairs. She'd always been the friendliest and always called

Destiny by name. She carried that messed-up orange brief-case that Miss Margaret had when she fell.

"Hey, Destiny, I wasn't sure if you knew. Margaret passed away after her fall last week."

Destiny nodded. "I did hear that, and I'm really sorry." She didn't mention that Marcus had told her.

"The rest of us didn't actually know her all that well, but thank you, it is sad. I'm sure she had more life she wanted to live. Thank you for trying to do CPR. It was so lucky that you knew how."

"Oh, no worries. I just wish it had worked."

Jennie nodded and pointed at Destiny's book, *The Hate U Give.* "I've heard of that book. Do you like it?"

"Oh my God, Miss Jennie, Angie Thomas is my idol. I would give my right arm to write like her, I mean, if I could have one tenth of the talent she's got in her pinky finger, I would be happier than a pig in shi—I mean mud."

Jennie laughed, then said, "I didn't know you wanted to be a writer."

"It's my dream. But my parents are not down with it. They want me to do nursing to make money as soon as I finish my associate's degree this spring. Which is why I'm here at this high-intensity job, waiting to see if I get into nursing school."

"When will you hear?"

"They say it's rolling, but by the end of May, I'm hoping."

"So in just a few weeks. And you may be leaving us?"

"In September, right, if I get in. I'm kind of nervous. My chemistry grade was borderline, though, and they don't let you retake it."

"Fingers crossed." Jennie smiled, crossing her fingers.

"I don't know what I want. I'm not even sure I want to go. It's mostly my mama's idea."

"Oh, really?"

"Yeah, I mean, I have these dreams of doing performance poetry, reciting amazing poems like Amanda Gorman, with people hanging onto my every word, if you know what I mean." Maybe Marcus hanging onto her every word.

"Not changing bedpans," Jennie said, with a laugh, nodding her understanding.

"Exactly, Miss Jennie."

"I know your mother means well. She wants you to have a profession that offers an opportunity to have a job wherever you might go, and nursing is definitely like that."

"Yeah, I know. She has my best interests at heart. But I'm twenty-one now. Old enough to vote and live on my own. She doesn't need to be pressuring me."

"There are a lot of aspects of nursing that are more rewarding than changing bedpans, I bet." Jennie nodded again, starting to say something, but then maybe changing her mind. "What's the main thing you like about that Angie Thomas book?"

Destiny didn't hesitate. "It shows you both big and little ways to be brave."

In the book, Starr didn't fit in at her private school with mostly White kids. Destiny realized that at her community college, she hadn't made many friends either. In high school, she'd been on the Dancing Divas, which was the half-time dance troupe, and Drop the Mic, the spoken word club, and those had been her main friend groups. Her community college didn't have a dance troupe, and she missed that. The community college spoken word group was really good, but she ended up working too much to participate very often.

Jennie smiled with understanding. "Being brave is really hard. "

"Yeah, I mean, Angie Thomas was even brave to write it. I mean, it's been banned a bunch of times. Sort of like *Are You There God? It's Me, Margaret.* Even though that one's pretty tame, if you ask me."

Jennie seemed to do a little double take. "Banned?"

"Yeah."

"It's so interesting that you'd mention that book." Jennie reached into the orange briefcase, hesitated a little, and then, with more confidence, pulled out a sheet of paper. On it was a list of book titles scribbled in some seriously wobbly handwriting, and she showed it to Destiny. "Margaret had the names of a lot of books on this sheet of paper, and the reason I'm so curious about your book is because *The Hate U Give* is one of the books on her list."

"Oh my God, *Their Eyes Were Watching God* is one of my all-time favorites too. *Alice in Wonderland* and *Charlotte's Web* are on this list? Excuse me, that is just ridiculous."

"Well, what do you think this list is? Banned books?"

"That would be my guess, Miss Jennie. But why *Alice in Wonderland* and *Charlotte's Web* would be banned is a mystery to me." Destiny whipped out her phone to look them up and found the answer. "*Charlotte's Web* was because of an objection to talking animals, and *Alice in Wonderland* might have been about references to drugs. People who don't think animals can talk better pay more attention to the whales and the birds." Inspired, Destiny switched to her camera app. "Miss Jennie, do you mind if I take a picture of that list? If somebody's going to ban a book, I want to read it so I can find out what it is they don't want me to know." Destiny winked, gave her a sneaky grin, took a quick photo of the list, then lay down her phone. "Why do you think Miss Margaret had a note listing banned books?"

Jennie stared at Destiny. "That's exactly what I'm trying to figure out." She put the sheet of paper away. "I'm going to bring it up at our meeting. Anyway, Destiny, I'm thrilled to learn that you love writing, and if you ever want to join us, or meet with us about something you've written, the door is always open."

Destiny managed to not even look at the intercom button. Probably best that Jennie didn't know that Destiny had already been meeting with them as a "silent partner" for a good while. "Oh, thank you, Miss Jennie. The powers that be here at Bristlecone probably wouldn't like that though."

"Well, if you ever get Friday afternoon off—"

"Thank you, Miss Jennie. Y'all have a good meeting."

It was nice of Jennie to invite her. It was. Destiny's mind whirled. Yes, she loved listening to their talk about writing, and she was learning about metaphors, character development, dialogue, scene-setting, and other stuff that she knew she'd never learn in nursing school.

But they were so old. And White. And probably Ms. Robinson, her boss, wouldn't like it.

After Jennie left, Destiny looked down again at the text she'd started to Marcus and had an idea. When they'd walked to the parking lot that first day they'd met, he'd wanted her to recite one of her poems. Quickly, she erased the old text, and typed instead:

Hey, I have to memorize a Langston Hughes poem for my English class, and I need somebody to practice it with. Will you be my guinea pig?

Then, before she could change her mind, she tapped "Send."

CHAPTER 9
ABE

When Abe approached the conference room that Friday, carrying the revelatory pages about the breakup with Allison that he'd written and changed and gnashed his teeth over, everything seemed to ratchet into slow motion.

Because he saw her. The coy tilt of the head, the innocent hazel eyes, the diminutive body. The Allison he'd fallen in love with junior year. The Allison he'd broken up with senior year. The Allison he hadn't seen in approximately fifty years. The Allison about whom he'd written the pages he planned to read.

She had hardly changed at all, except her wild blonde hair was now silvery and cut in stylish spikes, which looked very elegant with her slim neck. He would have recognized her anywhere. Just looking at her, he felt nineteen again. And he also felt like a foolish old man because his heart began to race, and he feared he would cry. That seemed to happen more often, now that he was older. Things seemed to get to him on an emotional level more than when he was young.

Through the glass door he saw Willoughby standing at the head of the table, pulling her egg timer from her purse and turning it upside down to reset it. Next to her sat Jennie, talking with Allison.

He stopped outside the glass door, tried to open it, became flustered, dropped his pages, and watched them float to the floor like feathers. Also spilling to the floor was a packet he'd just picked up in the mailroom that he was fairly sure were the divorce papers from Nicole. He couldn't imagine how they had been ready for his signature so quickly, unless Nicole had already had them drafted before she talked to him a week ago, which was nothing if not completely humiliating. Everything unraveling with Nicole had been so demoralizing. He hadn't even wanted to tell anyone at Bristlecone about her.

Willoughby came outside the conference room to help him pick up the pages.

"No, no, I'll get them!" He was aware his voice sounded tense and angry. No one in the room could read those pages. He could never read them now. He would say something had come up and he couldn't stay. He'd pretend to check his phone so he could cancel at the last minute.

"Okay," Willoughby said, with a puzzled look and hands-off gesture. "I'll just go back inside then."

One by one, Abe picked up the pages and made a show of pretending to check his phone. He even turned his back, holding the phone to his ear, and walked a short distance toward the staircase where Margaret had fallen so violently last week. The staircase suddenly seemed like bad luck, though, so he stayed a few yards away, his back still to the conference room.

His mind raced. If he left, Allison would surely suspect that it had to do with her. That would not be good. Did he have something saved on his phone, an essay, a blog post, that he could substitute for these pages about the breakup with Allison? Something clever, humorous, scholarly? Something that would impress her? This was an unmitigated disaster.

Sweat beaded at his hairline. What was left of it. He thought he might actually vomit. He had wanted to re-establish contact with Allison at Bristlecone, had in fact eagerly anticipated it, possibly as a chance encounter in the courtyard or the dining room. But not in his writers' group, for God's sake.

He had a vague memory of receiving an email from Jennie about inviting someone new, but he didn't recall if she had included the person's name, and in his state of frenzied denial of the divorce from Nicole, he had barely skimmed it. In his defense, Jennie often wrote emails about topics that didn't interest him, such as ways to build writing confidence, which Abe had to admit wasn't a problem for him.

Scrolling through his phone, he found a far from intellectual but engaging blogpost he'd written about Solomon, the beloved chihuahua that Nicole would bring to him as soon as their agreements were signed. He could read that. It was truly regrettable that it wasn't in the least erudite, but he felt such relief to find something to substitute for the breakup pages that he nearly fell down Margaret's steps himself.

Heaving a deep sigh, he headed into the conference room, greeting Jennie and Willoughby.

"Alli Stone, Abe Goodman," Jennie said, introducing them. "I mentioned Alli to the group in the email I sent. She's new at Bristlecone and was in a writing group back in DC, where she's from."

"Allison, we knew each other in college," Abe said, summoning what he hoped was a casual smile and reaching out to shake her hand, immediately wondering whether he should have revealed that they knew each other.

Allison, who had not been surprised to see Abe, as she had presumably read Jennie's email, half-rose and gave him a smile and a brief handclasp. "It's Alli now."

Her hand was so small; he remembered that. Almost like a child's. And her gold-specked hazel eyes still seemed to be so full of life. Affection for her swelled, which he immediately tried to quash.

"Alli," he repeated, clearing his throat slightly, as he took his seat across from her, beside Jennie. He would hate to have his blood pressure checked right now. It would no doubt be off the charts. "You changed your name?"

"I did. I never liked my name," Allison said.

"You didn't?" He'd always loved it.

"No."

He certainly had never known that. "Okay, I will try to make the adjustment. Forgive me if I slip." This was like meeting an entirely new person, not the soft and empathetic young woman he'd known at all.

"My husband made the adjustment, before he died, so I'm sure that if he could do it, other people can." Allison—Alli—smiled at him, but were her eyes hostile? Was there a sternness to her tone that she'd never had before?

He should have gone with the phone ruse. This was agonizing.

"Well, what a coincidence that you all knew each other, Abe and Alli. Small world," Willoughby said, seemingly unaware of any undercurrents. "Let's get started, then, I think everyone's here." She put on her bright blue reading glasses, as usual, and placed the egg timer in front of her on the pine table, with a polite, nervous cough. "I know it's a little awkward for all of us today, after what happened to Margaret last week, so I apologize for that, Alli. I arrived first, so I guess I'll start us off." She flipped the timer.

Abe, for once, was glad to be reading last and knew he wasn't his usual incisive self during the meeting. He struggled to focus as Willoughby read her pages about the reclusive writer meeting with the young woman who she planned to hire to be a body double for her appearances. He couldn't concentrate and thus could think of almost nothing to say by way of critique, which certainly was totally unlike him.

Had Willoughby changed the timeframe of her story from the present day to the 1920s? Or had it been that way before? Obviously, if he commented and it hadn't changed, it would appear he hadn't been paying attention, so he remained silent. He struggled not to look at Allison, not to stare at her: the small, neat hands, the hair which now was silver but seemed so similar to when it was blonde years ago, her small nose with the smattering of freckles, the hazel eyes which still looked so naïve.

Abe's concentration was equally poor when Jennie read her pages about Enheduanna. He had previously thought Enheduanna was heterosexual but now she appeared to be lesbian, but again, he didn't want to bring it up for fear of Jennie thinking he hadn't been paying attention in the first place. Should Jennie actually be lesbian in order to write about Enheduanna, then, like she ought to be part of a particular culture if she's writing about it? Abe no longer knew the answer to that, though he'd felt supremely confident about it at the last meeting. Willoughby praised

Jennie's changes and Abe chose the easy road and simply agreed with her.

Allison's pages were a portion of an essay about widowhood. The essay was so well-written and poignant and fresh that Abe found himself tearing up, as did everyone in the room. Allison wrote about emotions of devastation that Abe had experienced when Ellen died and had unsuccessfully tried to overcome in the years afterward. Abe had to admit: Allison was a fine writer. Listening to her words about her deep and complex love for her husband made Abe realize that she'd probably carry a torch for him the rest of her life, wear a wedding ring forever. He told himself he was happy that she'd found happiness with someone else, but could not help also feeling disappointed, and realized how much he had been counting on re-establishing their connection. He tried to tell himself that the tears in his eyes weren't completely self-pity.

When his turn came, people were still sniffling from Allison's reading. "I'm going to offer something more light-hearted than Allison's pages," he started out, his heart thudding, then scrolled through his phone to find the essay about Solomon.

"Alli," she corrected him.

"Yes, sorry, Alli." Abe felt the heat of a blush, and a generalized sense of being off-balance.

"That sounds nice—it will lighten the mood," said Jennie.

Abe began reading a blogpost from his phone that he'd written but never posted because he'd thought it was too precious. "Our eight-pound chihuahua, Solomon, is a social little dog who feels it to be his solemn duty to greet everyone we pass when we're out for a walk," he read. "He is the official greeter, like at Walmart. Every living being is his friend—every person, other dogs, even cats. Like his namesake, the biblical Solomon, he is a deeply wise little dog. It is a delight to be around such a happy creature. He brings joy to every life he touches. When my wife and I adopted him last year, the people at the adoption agency told us that he really knew how to work a room. And they were right."

Though people chuckled a bit, Abe was ashamed by the lack of literary content in the post; Allison certainly would not be as impressed with his writing as he had been with hers, which was an uncomfortable reversal from their relationship in college.

The reactions around the table were, amazingly, much better than usual, however, and Abe made a note to try more light-hearted pieces.

"Such a fun piece," Willoughby said. "So different for you, Abe. And you've never written about your wife before."

"We thought you were a widower," Jennie added, looking at his empty ring finger.

Now Abe felt himself blush. He'd forgotten that he hadn't even revealed to this group that he and Nicole were married. No way to keep it a secret any longer, after what he'd just read. "My wife Ellen died about twelve years ago, of cervical cancer. Nicole and I have been married for about ten years." Here he held up the packet he'd picked up from the mail room. "But these are our divorce papers."

"Oh, I'm so sorry," Jennie said, putting her hand over her mouth. The others echoed her sympathy.

"The only good thing about it is that I will get custody of Solomon. I hope he'll like Bristlecone." Being truthful about Nicole had suddenly made him feel closer to the others in the group, which was kind of surprising, and a bit of a revelation.

"I read that the community players are going to do *Legally Blonde: The Musical* and they're looking for a chihuahua to play Bruiser Woods," Willoughby said, which Abe suspected was an attempt to pivot to a lighter topic. "They advertised auditions in the local paper. Maybe you and Solomon might like to do something like that."

"Oh, I don't know," Abe said, shrugging, still recovering from all the emotions of this roller-coaster meeting. He liked serious theater. Musicals had never been his cup of tea, though Ellen and Nicole had both loved them. "Sounds like a lot of trouble." What would a dog do at an audition?

"Before we break up today," Jennie said, placing Margaret's old briefcase on the table in front of her, "I wanted to talk about something my cat found in Margaret's briefcase. I mean, it might be nothing, but there was a list of books in it. I had a talk with Destiny at the desk today about them, and she pointed out that these books might have been banned, and I can't help but wonder why—"

The glass conference door swung open. Roy, Margaret's husband, now a widower for a week, stood in the doorway.

The group's concentration had been deep, so everyone in the room gasped with surprise. The man looked like a ghost. Could a person actually lose twenty pounds in one week? His previously round and flushed face now looked like a shriveled prune. His golf pants, which had cinched his pumpkin-shaped stomach, now hung loosely and, in fact, looked in real danger of falling down. He gripped a printout in his hand. "Sorry to interrupt y'all," he said.

"N-no worries," Jennie said, briefly touching the briefcase.

"I-I had something to ask. I remembered y'all always met around now."

Everyone looked at him expectantly.

"Would you like to sit down?" Willoughby said after a beat, pointing at an empty chair beside Abe. "I tried to call you, by the way, and I left a message."

"No, I'll stand. I haven't been answering the phone. This'll just take a minute or two."

The man truly looked awful. Had Abe himself looked this bereft after Ellen's death? Abe ventured a glance at Allison, wondering what she must be thinking about this writers' group that seemed to be going completely off the rails.

"We're so sorry about Margaret," Jennie said. "I tried to call you, too, Roy, to see if you needed anything, and I also left a message. I have Margaret's briefcase right here that I need to return to you." She stood and handed him the briefcase, which he took without seeming to realize what it was. "I'd been looking for a memorial service to be announced but hadn't seen anything. How're you getting along, Roy?"

"Well, that's kinda what I came about. I mean, I feel like she was close to y'all. People get close in a writers' group, am I right?"

"Of course," Abe offered. "We reveal personal things about ourselves when we write." This was a bit of a stretch, truth be told, since he barely felt as though he knew Margaret, and he had spent most of the time annoyed by her. He straightened the pages about his breakup with Allison that he'd put face down on the table instead of face up.

"Well, I mean...I do want to have a memorial for Margaret. I mean, we were married for forty years. But..." And here Roy scratched the edge of one eye, which Abe now noticed was swollen and red. "By any chance, did y'all know what she wanted?"

"Wanted?" Jennie's voice was kind. "You mean—"

"Her service. What she wanted. What songs she wanted to be sung. Who she wanted to give her eulogy."

"You mean she didn't—"

"It was all so sudden, you know. I know it sounds crazy, but we'd never talked about it. I thought maybe, since you all were her best friends, that she'd talked about it with you."

Abe had a strange sensation he was sinking through his chair. He never would have considered Margaret a close friend, much less a best friend. They were acquaintances. How strange that people could understand the idea of friendship so differently. How lonely Margaret must have been to have thought they were close.

Roy hitched his loose pants a bit higher and began to scan the document he'd brought, which was, presumably, a list he'd made for Margaret's memorial service.

"One thing we did talk about, though," Roy said. "She did tell me that if she died first, that there was a very nice single lady in her writers' group that I should get to know. Jennie?"

The rest of them looked at Jennie, whose mouth dropped open. She flushed as red as a pepper.

"She told me one night, flat out, that I wouldn't be any good on my own and she thought Jennie was a good-hearted person and I'd do well to get to know her." Roy smiled congenially. "Are you Jennie?" He pointed at Allison.

Abe was gobsmacked by how forthright Roy was being.

"No, I'm Alli." Alli could hardly speak.

"Are you single?"

"Yes, well, widowed, but—" Alli looked wildly around the room.

Willoughby came to Alli's rescue, clearing her throat. "Roy, maybe we can get back to the issue of Margaret's service. There's a chaplain here at Bristlecone who can help you. In fact, I'm surprised she hasn't reached out to you."

"Oh, yeah, she's left a few messages. She even came by once, but I didn't open the door to anyone. Or pick up the phone. Today's the first day I've been out of the house." Roy suddenly began to cry. Tears rolled down the creases in his sunken cheeks. "Any of y'all lose your husband or wife?"

"Yes," Abe said.

"I have," Allison said, her eyes welling. "It's very hard."

"Me, too," Jennie said. "We know what you're going through, Roy."

"Roy, would it be helpful if some of us went with you to meet with the chaplain?" Willoughby asked. "I'm sure she could do Margaret's service, and some of us in the group could also say a few words about her. I'll go by her office with you right now." She looked at her watch. "It's almost five, so we should hurry to catch Deborah before she goes home for the weekend. Our meeting was about over, anyway." Willoughby stood up.

"I'll go with you," Jennie said, rising too.

"Jennie, you don't have to." Willoughby gave her a warning look, glancing at Roy.

Abe realized, belatedly, that Willoughby was trying to protect Jennie should Roy try any moves on her. And then Abe thought that he should possibly volunteer to go, even though he'd rather defend his PhD dissertation again than do so.

"No, I'll go with you," Jennie said. "It's the least we can do, Roy."

"Okay, let's go, we need to hurry," Willoughby said.

Roy obediently wiped his eyes and picked up his printout. He held the briefcase close to his chest, like he'd hold an infant.

And the three of them left Abe and Allison—Alli—alone together in the conference room. It wasn't exactly what Abe had envisaged, and he felt uncharacteristically nervous and dropped the packet with his divorce papers, which slid under the table to Allison's side.

Allison bent to help him pick them up, and there was a brief moment of confusion as she handed them back. She then collected her pages from the center of the table and put them, with her pen, inside a notepad made of soft blue leather. She completely skipped the small talk. "So how long have you been at Bristlecone?"

"A year." Abe picked up the remaining pages from the table and carefully folded them in half.

"You remarried after your wife died."

"Yes. A few years after. I was very lonely. And Nicole was very charming. She was my accountant before she was my wife. How long ago were you widowed?"

"A year and a half. When I woke up one morning, he was dead beside me."

"That must have been awful."

"Yes, it was. But it was surely awful to have your wife ill for several years as well."

"It was, yes."

They headed out of the conference room. Abe was exquisitely conscious of her body so close to his as he held the door open for her and she walked out, and he remembered the day she rode behind him on the motorcycle. Abe turned off the conference room lights, thinking that life was certainly curious—that something that had happened fifty years ago should come back to him so vividly, amidst all the many days of his life that had been lost in the mists of time forever.

They stood awkwardly in the hallway next to the stairs.

"I suppose I better go sign my divorce papers."

"You should take your dog to try out for that play," Allison said. "This is a tough time for you, and something fun like that would be a good distraction."

"Oh, I don't know. It seems silly." How did Allison know that Abe needed a distraction? Did she indeed still know him so well, after all these years?

"What have you got to lose?"

Abe looked at her face and it did, incredibly, still seem as innocent and hopeful as that day he met her on the quad. "Well, maybe I will. I will keep you posted." They parted and Abe was enveloped in a glow of pleasure all the way across the park until he arrived at his cottage, unfolded his pages, and saw that he had accidentally picked up Allison's pages.

Which meant that Allison had his.

CHAPTER 10
WILLOUGHBY

"Thank you for staying late to talk with us, Deborah," Willoughby said, as she, Jennie, and Roy filed out of her office after their meeting. What a relief they'd caught Deborah in time.

"Not a problem," Deborah called. "I didn't think we could pull it together for day after tomorrow, but we did it."

"Thank you kindly for your help with Margaret's service, both of you," Roy said, wiping his eyes. "I can never repay you."

"No need," Jennie said.

"Absolutely," Willoughby agreed, though she was still amazed by some of Roy's answers to Deborah's questions about Margaret's favorite music and readings. Was the theme from *The Good, the Bad and the Ugly* really Margaret's favorite song? Once again, she was reminded how little they knew her and what a mystery people could be.

In the parking lot, they said good-bye to Roy as he laid Margaret's briefcase gently in the passenger seat of his red Mustang, then climbed in and drove away, much more slowly than in the past.

"Poor guy," Jennie said. "But can you believe that he said Margaret's favorite literary reading was Crash Davis's soliloquy about believing in long and slow kisses from *Bull Durham*? I mean, did she even like baseball?"

"I know, right? And a reading about a constitutional amendment outlawing designated hitters and Astroturf. Is Deborah really going to read that at Margaret's service? And can you believe that he asked you and Alli if you were single? It's only been seven days since she died!"

Jennie laughed, but her usual compassion came through. "The poor man is probably still in a state of shock. People do funny things."

"You are too kind, Jennie."

"I do wish we'd figured out the meaning of that list of banned books in Margaret's briefcase. Now we don't even have the list anymore."

Willoughby shrugged, looking at her watch. Talking through the arrangements for Margaret's service had taken longer than she'd anticipated, and she was going to be late for her visit with Gary. She was also disappointed by her own lack of boundaries; she'd let them talk her into speaking at Margaret's service, since she was the unofficial "leader" of the writers' group. What the hell was she going to say? Back when Gary was functioning, he would have said, *"You're doing it again, saying yes just to please people."* He always had her back. Now she said, "Jennie, we definitely need to discuss that list of banned books at our next meeting, but I need to check on Gary before dinner."

"Oh, wait, Destiny took a photo of the list—so I can get it from her."

"Great. Also, my ex-husband just moved in here yesterday and I need to check on him too."

Jennie laughed. "Checking on two husbands. I'm sorry,

Willoughby, I don't mean to laugh—what happens in writers' group stays in writers' group. I hope this isn't all too much for you."

Willoughby nodded and smiled grimly. "I promised my daughter. She's worried about her dad. Talk to you next week."

She and Jennie parted ways and Willoughby hurried over to memory care.

Just outside Gary's door, Willoughby heard a crash and heard Gary yell, "I'm not eating this crap!" Willoughby cringed and felt her heart begin to race. A certified nursing assistant in her early twenties, with happy dog faces on her scrubs and a look of terror on her face, raced out of the room, nearly knocking Willoughby down.

Willoughby stood frozen, not even wanting to go in. But after a deep breath, she straightened her shoulders and marched forward. She had to. There was no one else to do it. The helpers did their best, but sometimes she was the only one who could get through to him.

Inside his room, she saw the red hibiscus she'd brought him the week before smashed on the floor in a pile of potting soil, and a plate of food overturned on the bedspread.

"Gary, what are you doing?"

"The food here is lousy!" Gary, in bed, kicked savagely at the plate and it crashed to the floor. Thankfully the plastic just bounced, but peas, chicken, and gravy flew everywhere. "Take me home! I want to go home!"

"Gary, stop this."

"I don't like it here. Take me home!" Gary's hair was standing on end, and his face was nearly purple with fury.

Willoughby knew what he meant; she wouldn't like it here either. She punished herself every day for putting him there, but there seemed no other answer. She could no longer look after him herself. Unsure exactly what might work to calm him, she touched his arm. "Gary, honey, let me give you a hug—"

"Don't touch me, Sally! Stay away from me!" He shoved her arm away.

Willoughby felt tears sting. To be called by Gary's first wife's name. And to be shoved. Her brain told her he didn't mean it but, oh, how it hurt her heart. All the guidelines warned about correcting a person with dementia, but against their advice she corrected him. "Honey, it's Willoughby, me, Willoughby."

Gary stopped and stared at her, uncomprehending, for a long moment, his eyes glassy.

"It's me, Willoughby," she said gently. She cautiously reached out and tenderly stroked the back of his hand.

Gary visibly relaxed, then tears came to his eyes. He put her hand to his lips and kissed it several times. "I've been waiting for you forever. Can we take a shower now?"

It had been a long afternoon and Willoughby had hoped she could get out of the shower with Gary tonight. The whole staff must be laughing their heads off about their ritual. But tonight, under the circumstances, she felt she had better go along with the program, since it seemed to be one of the only things that calmed him.

Willoughby crossed the room and closed the door, after smiling and waving at Mrs. Burns, who was glaring fiercely from her wheelchair, and started the shower.

Forty-five minutes later, Willoughby slid her T-shirt over her head and slipped her sandals back on while Gary slept. She fluffed at her wet hair, trying to air dry it with her fingers since Gary wasn't allowed a hair dryer. Her makeup had come off in the shower, but she did have a tube of lipstick in her purse that she used both as lipstick and blush.

She cleaned up and replanted the broken hibiscus plant, packing the soil back into the plastic container the best she could. She helped Josie, the aide, mop up the food from Gary's dinner and arrange the dinnerware back on his tray.

"Josie, maybe I'll have a talk with Gary's doctor on Monday about his meds. Maybe he needs more of something. Or less of something."

"That's a good idea," Josie said, nodding. "He's been having a lot of bad days."

After the writers' group, the meeting with the chaplain, and the harrowing visit with Gary, Willoughby was exhausted. Truly worn out. Maybe she could skip the visit with Steven and just go sometime tomorrow. Courtney would understand, wouldn't she? She sighed. No, Courtney was counting on her.

She grabbed the mistreated hibiscus, which she could regift to Steven, since its life seemed threatened in Gary's room, and headed across the courtyard to rehab, where they'd found a temporary spot for Steven until a unit opened for him. Now that the sun had set, the air felt cooler and a breeze teased her wet hair, drying it a little.

She wove her way through the maze of hallways in the rehab wing until she finally found the door with "Umstead" on it, the name that had been hers for twenty years. Jimmy Buffett's tune "Come Monday" wafted from inside. Cautiously, she knocked on the door. She hadn't seen

Steven in about five years, since Courtney's wedding. It could definitely be weird.

"Steven?" She poked her head inside the dim room. And immediately smelled pot.

It was unmistakable.

"Willoughby!"

Steven, thirty pounds thinner than she remembered, practically bald, his handsome brown eyes, his best feature, slightly bloodshot, was sitting in the easy chair beside his bed, in a pair of pajama pants with cartoon sloths on them and a "Life is Good" T-shirt. He was indeed smoking a joint, held casually between arthritic fingers.

It brought back, in a flood, memories of Steven, who was really just a big kid, never wanting to grow up, always wanting to keep having fun. Not just one drink but five. Not just one Grateful Dead concert but wanting to follow them around the country for the foreseeable future. Not just one week in Turks and Caicos Islands but actually considering moving there; Willoughby having to convince him that it was necessary to go home from their vacation to their jobs, hers at the library and his in a corporate IT department that bored him to death. Then there was his idea of traveling around the world while home-schooling the kids. She'd always felt she had three kids, not just two.

"Steven, are you getting high?"

He grinned. He'd always had the most devilish grin. "Medicinal. Totally legal."

Willoughby put one hand on her hip, dubious. "Really?"

"Really. Call my doctor." Steven widened his grin. "Want a hit?" He held the joint out to her.

"No, are you kidding?" Steven had not changed a bit. Not one bit.

He shrugged. "You were never any fun." He winked at

her. "Like Marian. Madam Librarian." He began to sing the song from *The Music Man,* as he always used to do, about needing to catch her ear and how he madly, madly needed her. "Or should I say, Willoughby? Marian and Willoughby have the same number of syllables, so it fits perfectly into the song."

"Well, it doesn't rhyme." Willoughby crossed her arms over her chest, but she was biting her lips to keep from laughing.

Steven sang on about his cause being lost, that he could not ever win.

"Steven."

He sang on about the sin of talking out loud with librarians. "Such as Willlllloughby."

Willoughby put her hand over her eyes and forehead, with rushing feelings she couldn't name or catalog.

"Have a hit," Steven said, holding the joint out to her. "It'll do you good."

Willoughby never used to get high with Steven. After one or two experiences in college, where she'd become cripplingly paranoid, Willoughby hadn't smoked, anything, really, for fifty years. Somebody had to be straight. Suffice it to say, she had absolutely no tolerance.

But goodness, this *had* been quite a day.

For reasons she didn't understand, Willoughby impulsively took the joint and, as Steven had once instructed her, inhaled deeply. The sharp, cloying smoke burned all the way down her throat, and she immediately choked and began to cough. Thick, musky smoke billowed out of her lungs.

"Oh my God, you did it!" Steven said, chuckling. "Was it my singing?"

"I brought you a hibiscus," Willoughby said, still

coughing a little, giving him the brilliant red bloom. "Gary threw it at the nurse so I thought it might be safer here."

"There were lots of those in Turks and Caicos," he said.

"Yeah. The iguanas used to eat the blossoms, remember?"

"I do. Remember sitting on the dock, feeding the blossoms to them?"

Willoughby then realized she should ask Steven how he was doing, since he'd had the very involved and dangerous nine-hour Whipple surgery for pancreatic cancer, and clearly had other serious health problems. That was the reason she was here, but the thought sort of floated out of her head.

"You wanted to stay there and live on that boat," she said.

"Can you blame me? It was gorgeous, all the woodwork, the beautifully maintained decks. All the cute and tiny stuff in the galley. The sun sparkling on the water."

"We didn't know how to sail."

"Details!"

Willoughby saw in a flash of amazing illumination that she had always limited Steven with her practicality and judgment. At that moment, she developed a sudden appreciation for his incredible, possibly brilliant, insights and regretted the way she had held him back all those years ago, smothering what she'd seen as excesses.

A thought sneaked into her head: This was the pot speaking.

His liquid brown eyes were incredibly expressive at this moment, as they had been when they first met at a keg party their freshman year of college. Her stomach flipped.

"Remember when you wanted to take the kids out of school and travel around the world? I kinda wish we'd done that," she said. Now, in hindsight, Willoughby felt she might have been excessively judgmental. Maybe she had in some way short-changed their children.

"*Now* you tell me." His eyes gleamed with amusement.

They meandered through a few other memories and then somehow Willoughby found herself whirling around Steven's room, singing "Landslide" with great expression, singing about being afraid of changing, building a life around someone else, and getting old.

"Remember when we went to see them in Charlotte and they played this?"

"And 'Don't Stop,' 'Gold Dust Woman,' and 'Rhiannon.'" She waved her arms as though she wore those flyaway sleeves and a long flowing gown like Stevie Nicks and landed on the bed.

"What year was that?"

"2004? 2005?" She lay there floating for a few moments, and then "Margaritaville" came on and Steven, looking directly at Willoughby, belted out the lyrics about knowing everything was his own damn fault.

"I was so bummed when Jimmy Buffett died," he said. "I loved that guy. I liked that song 'My Gummie Just Kicked In' on his last album.

"I know." Willoughby had immediately thought about Steven when she heard it. "Remember that concert of his that we went to in Key West?"

"At Crazy Ophelia's." Steven nodded, remembering. "Like another life."

"Do you really think that? That everything was your fault? I thought it was mine."

"Nope. It was both of us."

A knock on the door. "Evening meds." Steven's nurse

pushed the door open. She was in her forties, looking tired at this time of the night.

"Come on in," Steven said. "This is my wife."

"Ex-wife."

Willoughby thought she should get up from the bed where she was sitting to ask the nurse about the meds but realized she could hardly move. In fact, she was afraid she'd fall on the floor. She had been staring at the hibiscus blossom, wondering how a single flower blossom could be such an incredible symbol of unbridled beauty, of excess, of the amazing and breathtaking and almost garish variety of nature. How mind-blowing! A symbol of blood, truly blood red. And were she and Steven not blood, really, after the years they had spent together raising a family? What deep synchronicity had occurred, just in her bringing that hibiscus.

It was definite: The pot was infusing her entire being with ridiculous, ultra-sensitive woo-woo thoughts.

"Ex-wife," Steven repeated, taking her hand.

She thought about removing her hand from Steven's but realized she wasn't capable of doing so and, entranced, examined their fingers entwined together. She had forgotten what very nice fingers he had, even with the arthritis. A hair follicle on one of his fingers looked like it could be a portal to another universe.

She watched wordlessly as the nurse put the cup with Steven's meds on the tray and waited for him to take them and drink the cup of water. Willoughby suddenly became obsessed with the nurse's hands too. How worn they were, yet how careful their movements. She could not take her eyes off the nurse's hands. A nurse's caring hands could be a symbol of all that was missing in this world, all that the world desperately needed.

Then the nurse drifted out of the room.

Willoughby lay back on Steven's pillow. She literally could not get up, although it was possible that she might float up to the ceiling. Steven got up and fluffed the pillow for her, then climbed into bed beside her, stroking her still damp hair with his warm hand.

"Trouble," he sang in a whisper. She remembered so clearly watching old *Music Man* videos and the kids dancing around the house singing the songs. And what a sweet rake Professor Harold Hill was.

Willoughby felt Steven's breath against her cheek. She had never realized how much she had missed him, all these years. He was fun and oh, God, Willoughby needed fun.

He sang on about trouble, knickerbockers, rhyming, and pool.

The words of the song came back to her, and she whisper-sang, in answer to Steven, about remembering some ship, the pilgrim's rock, and the Golden Rule.

Willoughby drifted off, snuggling closer to him, her head tucked between his chin and shoulder in just the same old way they used to sleep.

Willoughby awoke, startled, in the deep center of the night. Where was she?

A narrow bed. A shirtless nearly bald man beside her with an angry scar on his abdomen. She sat up. She was incredibly thirsty and chugged down a container of water sitting on the bedside tray. She ran her hand over her face. Then over her T-shirt and capris. She was still clothed, right?

Steven. Omigod, she had fallen asleep in Steven's room! She had gotten high with him!

CHAPTER 11
JENNIE

Margaret's service, surprisingly lovely, was held the following Sunday afternoon in the octagonal gathering hall at Bristlecone. Light streamed through the circle of tall, elegant windows, shining on the few dozen chairs lined up in two graceful rows around Margaret's simple casket, which Roy had adorned with a single yellow rose.

Jennie saw Willoughby and crossed to sit next to her.

"Do you know if Abe is coming?" Willoughby asked her, after they hugged quickly.

Jennie shook her head. "I guess not. Plus, Alli never met Margaret, so I wouldn't expect her either."

Roy sat in the front row, a few seats down from a tall, patrician woman who looked like a younger, taller version of Margaret. Jennie wondered if that could be her sister. She knew Roy and Margaret had no children. He leaned forward with his elbows on his knees, in an ill-fitting black jacket over a lime green golf shirt, almost as though he was praying the entire time; his face was swollen and red.

Deborah, the chaplain, spoke eloquently about Margaret's long and eventful life and her love of travel. She introduced the woman on the row with Roy as Margaret's sister, Eunice. Willoughby's remarks were also well-crafted.

"I will remember Margaret as a writer and, really, a dreamer," Willoughby said, standing beside the casket. Jennie was so impressed that Willoughby used no notes at all. "Margaret was determined to keep coming to the group in spite of her health issues, and Roy faithfully dropped her off and picked her up for writers' group each week. She had a continuing quest to tell stories, even though she was no longer able to write them down. One of my favorite stories of hers was about a rather social-climbing family who kept moving their relatives to more prestigious cemeteries. Margaret showed such humor and wisdom with that story: Once we have passed on, truly, what is the meaning of social status? In fact, what is the meaning of social status at all? And how, indeed, will people remember us?" When Willoughby finished speaking, an acoustic guitarist played and sang "Brandy" by Looking Glass, with lyrics about the singer's lover and lady being the sea, which apparently was the hit song the summer Margaret and Roy met. Better than the theme to *The Good, the Bad and the Ugly*, at least.

Jennie never expected to cry, but she did. Margaret's life seemed especially lonely to her. "Should we introduce ourselves to Margaret's sister?" she asked Willoughby as they stood.

"Good idea." Willoughby stepped toward the tall, thin woman, who looked several years younger than Margaret's eighty-two years. "Hello, Eunice, I'm Willoughby Philpott and this is Jennie Rossi. We were in Margaret's writers' group and just wanted to express our condolences. We know that writing meant a lot to Margaret."

Eunice's smile didn't reach her eyes. "Aren't you sweet. Was she still doing that? I hope you didn't think that any stories she brought to the group were true. Like that story you told about moving the caskets to different cemeteries—I hope you didn't actually believe that. It was so far-fetched."

"Well...she told that story in our group, more than once, actually," Willoughby said, clearly a little taken aback. "It could have been a metaphor, of course."

"Believe me." Eunice leaned toward them, widening her eyes, with a light laugh. "Margaret was a very...fanciful person. There was no truth whatsoever in what she wrote." Eunice turned and left the room.

Willoughby looked at Jennie with a shocked expression on her face. "Wow, I have to say, that was pretty rude!"

"Agreed!" Jennie's face heated up with embarrassment. "No wonder Margaret never talked about her sister. I guess they weren't that close."

The two of them stopped to console Roy for a moment on their way out, who thanked them profusely for their help.

"It was a nice service," Jennie assured him.

A few days later, while having lunch with Alli on the patio outside the Bristlecone dining hall, Jennie received a call from a number she didn't know. She tried not to eat outside of Bristlecone, as the meals were already paid for, and Alli didn't seem to mind staying in the community.

"Go ahead and take it," Alli said. "I don't mind." She waved her hand and sat back, scrolling through her own phone.

"I don't know who it is. I'll just let it go to voicemail and check it later." Jennie and Alli had grown close quickly, to

Jennie's delight. They had been having an animated conversation about their children and speculating about the various local venue choices around Eden Forest for Alli's granddaughter's wedding reception.

"It might be a doctor's office calling you; I really don't mind," Alli insisted.

Jennie took the call. "Hello?"

"Hi Jennie, it's Roy, Margaret's husband. I wanted to thank you for all you did to help me with Margaret's service. I was just in a state of, I don't know what—as freaked as a long-tailed cat in a roomful of rocking chairs, I guess—and you helped." Jennie looked at Alli and rolled her eyes, mouthing, *Sorry*. She knew Alli could hear everything Roy was saying, even though he wasn't on speaker. His voice was that loud.

"Margaret was very fond of you. And I was wondering if you might want to join me for lunch at my golf club next week." He was breathing so heavily, he seemed almost to be panting.

Jennie thought fast. "Perhaps Willoughby and I—and possibly Abe, who is also in the writers' group—could join you there."

"That's okay, I don't want to bother the others. Maybe another time. I just felt like I should call you, since Margaret told me it would be good for us to get in touch. She said I wouldn't be good by myself, and she was right. I can't sleep. I have nobody to talk to."

Jennie took a few quick breaths, trying to figure out what to say. "Roy, I am very complimented by Margaret's esteem. But I'm still grieving my husband. I hope you understand."

She felt bad for him, as she knew what he was going

through was so awful that maybe he was losing perspective.

Roy made flustered apologies. "I just don't think I'm going to be any good at being alone," he said, and hung up.

"Everything okay?" Alli asked.

Jennie drew a breath, laughing with some embarrassment. "It was Roy, who you met at writers' group. Following up on Margaret's advice to contact me if she died before he did."

"That's so interesting." Alli sipped her coffee, her small, manicured fingers cupping the mug. "Fixing him up with you, basically from beyond the grave."

Jennie laughed. "That's one way of looking at it. I mean, I guess I could take it as a compliment that Margaret liked me."

"In a way it's controlling. But in another way, it's the most unselfish kind of love—trying to find a person who might make your spouse happy after you're gone. Did you ever do that? Think about a woman who might be a good wife for your husband, should you die first?"

How close she and Alli had become in just barely two weeks to be discussing things like this. The older she got, the more Jennie regarded friendship as an incredible gift.

"No, I always had complete confidence he would find someone himself," Jennie said. "Women found him very attractive. Once I went to the restroom during the intermission of a play, and when I came out a woman was trying to pick Michael up." She laughed. "How about you?"

"Oh, believe me, my husband did his own choosing before he died." A look of pain crossed Alli's face briefly; she waved her hand, dismissing the thought.

"That whole situation with Margaret," Jennie said, taking a cue to change the subject. "Kind of strange. Did I tell you about meeting Margaret's sister at her memorial service?"

"No."

Jennie shared Eunice's comment about Margaret's writing being untrue. "I mean, she was a very elegant-looking woman, much more so than Margaret, but she bordered on rudeness when she met us. She did not want us to take Margaret's writing seriously."

"That is really too bad, isn't it? Obviously, Roy didn't take her writing seriously either. She must have felt invisible."

"That does make me sad. I mean, we all have a story and deserve to be heard."

Then Alli's phone rang. She looked at it, puzzled. "I don't know this number either."

"Well, again, it could be a doctor's office..."

Alli shrugged. "Hello?"

Jennie heard almost every word. It was Roy again, explaining that he'd gotten Alli's number from the Bristlecone phone list and wondering if she might like to go to lunch with him at his golf club.

Alli looked at Jennie with wide eyes, pointing to the phone.

Jennie raised her hands to shoulder level, palms up, in the universal "I don't know" gesture. She mouthed, *Do you want to go?*

Alli vigorously shook her head. "I'm sorry, Roy, you're kind to call, but I'm not dating right now. Thank you for calling." Alli disconnected.

Jennie and Alli looked at each other for a second or two, then both burst out in unrestrained laughter so raucous that people from the next table looked their way with half-smiles and questioning expressions. Every time Jennie looked at Alli, she was provoked to laughter again. Tears ran down their cheeks.

Jennie hadn't laughed so hard in a long time. It had been so nice to meet Alli, really. And she had to admit that she admired how effortlessly Alli had responded to Roy.

"So I wonder what he's looking for," Alli said, gasping. "A nurse or a purse?"

Jennie could not remember laughing so hard since before Michael died.

"Yet," she said to Alli, once they were quiet, "I know how he feels."

Alli sighed. "Me too."

That night, Jennie opened the door to Elijah and Amanda, their young faces shining, Elijah cradling yellow tulips like a baby. She took the flowers with a sigh of joy, hugging him, and then hugged Amanda, with a sideways grin at Elijah. "Wow, you're having a good influence on Elijah."

"Hey, I can come up with flowers on my own." Elijah's tone was only mock hurt; he was clearly too happy to get annoyed. He was dressed more nicely than usual, wearing a cream-colored polo and golf shorts with a perfect crease. Elijah was lighter-skinned than Michael had been, with some of Jennie's sharp features, but he looked so much like Michael that a lump formed in Jennie's throat. How she wished Michael could be here.

I am here, came Michael's voice in her head. *Don't worry.*

"You both look so nice! What's the occasion?"

Amanda hugged her quickly, looking stunning, as always, with her braids pulled back in a ponytail and a short, yellow spring dress that showed off her long, graceful legs. Amanda was a beautiful and confident Black girl Elijah had met while running in a marathon a year ago. Jennie had met her several times and felt that Elijah seemed to have special feelings for her, deeper than any of his previous relationships. Might she be the one?

Jennie patted Amanda's arm with affection. She was clearly a young woman to be reckoned with. Jennie felt a little underdressed in her white capris and black top. Not to mention that Amanda was so much taller, nearly the same height as Elijah.

"Guess what?" Elijah obviously couldn't contain himself. "We've got a surprise!"

"What?"

Amanda held up her hand. A sparkling marquise-cut diamond shone from her finger.

"Oh my gosh!" Jennie's hand flew to her mouth. "Gorgeous! A ring!"

"Do you love it?" Elijah said with a huge grin. "I proposed on a five-mile run. Of course, I had to catch up with her first."

"You bet you did," Amanda said with a teasing laugh. Her nails were elegantly done in ivory and yellow that matched her dress and contrasted beautifully with the diamond and her dark skin.

"I am so thrilled for both of you." Jennie hugged them again, more tightly this time. "I am so very happy you two have found each other!" She lay the tulips on the counter, smiling to herself, thrilled to see Elijah so excited and proud. She took a vase from the cabinet and put the tulips in water, then turned back to them. "Oh, I'm so thrilled. Wish Dad could be here, you know. He'd be so happy for you two."

"Yeah." Elijah kissed Jennie on the cheek. "Me too, Mom."

Elijah would have to meet high standards with Amanda, Jennie thought, which was not a bad thing at all.

Jennie put Elijah to work setting the table while she tossed the dressing into the salad. Amanda wandered around her understated living area, looking at the family photos Jennie had displayed. She seemed particularly interested in photos of Michael. Even though Jennie had met them for dinner a few times, and even followed them one freezing cold Sunday morning when they ran a half-marathon together, Amanda had never been to her apartment.

"Elijah, you look so much like your dad," she said, picking up a photo of the family posing outside The Gantt Center in downtown Charlotte.

"Everybody says that." Elijah expertly folded the cloth napkins the way he'd learned when he was a server during college. The way he moved reminded Jennie of Michael. His voice. The way he smiled.

"I made the salad without meat, Amanda, but have chicken to add to it if you want it, Elijah," Jennie said as she placed the bowl on the table. She was still tickled by Elijah's childlike inability to keep the secret, blurting it out the moment they came in the door, just like when he was a little boy.

"Oh, I'm vegetarian now too, Mom," Elijah said. "No chicken for me."

"You both run and work out so much, I'm a little worried about your protein," popped out of Jennie's mouth before she could stop it.

Oops, Michael said. *Couldn't stop yourself, now, could you?*

"Oh, we get plenty," Amanda said quickly, with a slight

edge to her voice. "We eat yogurt, lentils and quinoa almost every week."

He must really be in love. Jennie could almost hear Michael's belly laugh. Elijah had eaten almost nothing but chicken nuggets for practically his entire childhood.

"So glad to hear it," Jennie said a little lamely. And firmly clamped her mouth shut.

The kids seemed to like the Caesar salad, though, and conversation ranged from their jobs to their workout schedules. Finally, they arrived at the topic of the wedding.

"Where do you think you'll get married?" Jennie asked. "Have you thought about it? Do your parents have preferences, Amanda?" Jennie assumed, as the mother of the groom, that she wasn't the first to know about the engagement.

"Yeah, we're thinking along the lines of—" Amanda looked over at Elijah. "Do you want to tell her?"

Jennie stiffened.

Don't overreact, came Michael's voice in her head. *You're just remembering the fact that most of your family didn't come to ours. This is a different situation.*

"Tanzania," Elijah said.

Jennie blinked. "Tanzania?"

A silence ensued.

"As in Africa, Mom. We want to get married on safari."

Jennie looked from one of them to the other, knowing that her mouth was hanging open. "You want to get married in Africa?"

"Yes."

Suddenly she needed to talk to her new friend Alli about this. She seemed so much more in touch.

"But—"

Don't say "but." Michael's voice in her head.

Jennie remembered introducing Michael to her parents. Her father had been borderline rude, and the two of them had left somewhat abruptly. Afterward her mother had run out to the car and said that they needed time, to please give them a chance to adjust to her new relationship. But Jennie had cried nearly the whole way home. She was determined she would not inflict that on Elijah.

So she shut her mouth and waited.

"We want a destination wedding, Mom," Elijah said. "We've researched it already and there's a place called the Serengeti Safari Lodge where we can have the ceremony before we go on safari."

Michael couldn't keep Jennie quiet now. Tears were in her eyes. "But I'd like to come to your wedding. It means the world to me to be there. I can't go to Africa."

"Why not, Mom?"

Jennie felt heat on her face as she flushed, not wanting to mention money or her fear of flying to her son. "Are your parents going to Africa, Amanda?"

Amanda nodded. "They've always wanted to go. They're going to combine it with a genealogical trip."

"What about your aunts and uncles, Elijah? Your cousins? What about your college friends? People who have meant a lot to you over your life. Are they all going to be able to go to Africa?"

Jennie... Jennie admitted that part of why she was upset was that the worst absence of all would be Michael, and that couldn't be solved even if the wedding were in this room.

"We were thinking a very small group. Just parents and siblings and one or two close friends. Maybe we could have a party for everyone a few months later."

Jennie glanced from one face to the other, shining with

happiness only an hour ago and now both set and defensive. She felt terrible about her reaction. Alli had explained to her that destination weddings were a trend with young couples. Truth: Elijah and Amanda weren't in their teens; they'd both been working for a decade at good jobs and could pay for it.

It's what they want, Jennie. Don't equate it to ours.

"I'm so sorry, I was just surprised. It sounds very romantic and exciting. But I'm afraid I can't afford it." Her heart beat rapidly and the heat of shame flooded her face.

"Mom, of course we'll pay for you."

"I would never take money from you, Elijah." She knew her voice sounded angry in spite of trying not to. In the resulting silence, as the kids possibly waited for her to offer a deeper explanation, or change her mind, Jennie somewhat savagely speared a cherry tomato, and it squirted directly into her eye. "Oh, shi—fiddle!"

She tried to wipe it with her napkin before the acid began to sting, but it was too late. The fire immediately spread all over her eye. "Excuse me." She raced to the sink and liberally splashed her eye with cool water. Finally, the burning ceased. She wiped her face—now makeup free—and sat down, drawing a deep breath, though by now she'd lost her appetite and tears still flowed down one cheek.

"Are you okay, Mom?"

"I'm fine." She picked up her salad bowl and took it to the sink, realizing belatedly that both Elijah and Amanda were still eating.

Jennie worked hard to smooth things over, but she could see that Amanda was feeling uncomfortable and wanting Elijah to leave. The kids left a short while later, but everything still felt awkward.

She felt so bad for not being able to control herself—her

fears, her traditional hopes, her sorrow about Michael not being there.

She wanted everything to be perfect. She was determined to welcome Amanda into the family with open arms, unlike the way her parents had greeted Michael. She thought about their sad but beautiful little wedding in their mutual friend Leonard's parents' backyard, a three-acre piece of land with a rambling, white clapboard house on the outskirts of Chapel Hill.

Leonard, the host of the nitrous party where they'd met, had taken pity on them and so had his hippie parents. She thought about the old Unitarian minister with the beard and ponytail, the only one they could find to marry them, the massive oak tree they stood under, the few friends who attended, and Michael's family, who made the effort and brought food and truly seemed happy for them. His mother seemed ready to adopt Jennie on the spot, especially when she began to cry when no one from her family came.

At the last minute, Jennie's mother and sister, Sofia, ran through the shrubs and trees to stand, chests heaving, in the back, but her father and brother did not come. After the ceremony, her mother had pressed several hundred-dollar bills in her hand and made an excuse that it was all she could give her, and she couldn't stay for the reception. Jennie had been so very grateful to Leonard's kind parents that she'd sent them Christmas cards every year and, of course, wrote them a note when Michael died.

Stop thinking about our wedding, came Michael's voice in her head. *Elijah and Amanda's situation is different.*

How can I stop? she nearly said out loud. *Of course, I'm thinking about it, Michael. I wish you could meet her, Michael. I know you'd like her. I feel terrible about the way I acted. I want to get them an engagement gift to make up for this, to show my support.*

Jennie began searching on her tablet and then stopped to look at a high-end coffee grinder. Elijah and Amanda were deeply into gourmet coffee. And she was almost sure she faintly heard Michael's voice.

That reminds me of when you made me coffee that first day we met. Good idea.

She called Elijah. He didn't pick up, so she left a voicemail, which she knew he often didn't listen to. "Hi, honey, I'm sorry that I said I couldn't come to your wedding. My reaction was maybe based on fear. I could not be more thrilled for you and Amanda—you are so lucky to have found each other, and I will do everything in my power to be there with you. Please forgive me. Love you."

She didn't know how she was going to make it happen, but she certainly was going to try.

CHAPTER 12
DESTINY

Tuesday night after she got off work, Destiny made a snap decision to wander through the health-care unit and pretend to run into Marcus. She'd been thinking about him constantly since they'd talked the previous Friday, but he hadn't answered her text about reciting the poem and she would not let herself text him again. She had her pride.

A couple of fluffy white flower arrangements were left over from a man's funeral service that had been held yesterday in the meeting room behind her desk. Destiny grabbed them and decided to pretend that she'd been assigned to rehome them. Her boss had on a few previous occasions asked her to do something like that, so it wasn't completely out of left field.

The sun had slipped down the sky to the tops of the trees as she headed to the health-care building. A thin yellow layer of pollen lay on the cars parked along the road and on the outdoor tables and chairs on the health-care café patio. The dogwoods were in bloom, which her mama had always loved.

She'd told Destiny that the dogwood flower represented Jesus's cross, with the brown marks on the edges of the petals representing where the nails had been in his hands. Destiny could never look at them now without thinking about that. Mama would most definitely not much care for Destiny "chasing" Marcus like this, but she was going to do it anyway.

Her code worked on the health-care door, and she shifted both flower vases to one arm while she let herself in. Heading down the long hall, with the impossibly shiny linoleum and supposedly inspiring framed sayings on the walls, she could see three or four med techs at the end in their green scrubs, hanging around the nurses' station, joking around and laughing.

As Destiny strode closer, she saw that one of the techs was Marcus, leaning back against the counter, while Sheba, a tech who wore her scrubs two sizes too small, probably to show off her boobs and her ass, was holding a stethoscope to Marcus's chest, making a big show of listening to his heart. Her hand was on his arm in what Destiny could only call a possessive way, and her head was angled with a disturbing familiarity toward his chest as she rolled her eyes, listening and laughing.

"Whoa, Marcus, your heart is speeding up!" Everyone laughed.

Destiny, heat rising to her cheeks, ducked into the first room she saw, ten yards before she had to pass the nurses' station, and plunked one of the flower vases on an old lady's dresser. "Enjoy these flowers, ma'am!" she said with fake cheerfulness. She didn't even give the poor lady dozing in her wheelchair a chance to say "thank you" before she turned around and scooted into a room on the other side of the hall and plunked the other vase on the dresser of another old lady, this one watching Little Joe ride across the screen on *Bonanza*.

"Flowers for you, ma'am." She gave another fake smile and started out of the room, just at the last minute realizing she'd left the card with "So sorry for your loss" sticking out of the white blooms. She crossed the room in two steps and ripped the card out of the flowers as the woman watching Little Joe cried, "Gracious, who in the world would send me flowers? Everyone I know has died!"

"Not everyone!" Destiny made an abrupt turn just outside the lady's door so she wouldn't see Marcus and went back down the hall toward the front door. Hopefully he hadn't seen her. Hopefully no one had. She had seen enough.

Once outside the building, she headed toward the courtyard with that ancient bristlecone pine and the parking lot behind it. She tossed her box braids behind her shoulder, angry at herself beyond words. What a hot mess. How totally humiliating. She could hear her mama's voice in her head, *Destiny, never chase a man. Let them chase you. Remember, you have your self-respect.* She sat on the bench beside the tree. She refused to cry.

Obviously, Marcus hadn't wasted two seconds thinking about her.

Didn't Mama get tired of being right? *Destiny* got tired of Mama being right, that was for sure. It brought back those awful memories of the guy who ghosted her, and Mama sitting beside her on the bed, rubbing her back while she bawled.

She sighed and stood up, searching for her car keys, scrubbing her hand over her face.

"Destiny!"

She turned and looked down the path. Marcus, running, then stopping, out of breath.

"Hey, I know you saw me. Why didn't you come and say hi?"

Destiny felt heat creep up her cheeks. How embarrassing that he'd seen her. "You looked pretty busy."

"Oh, Sheba and I were just kidding around, there is nothing going on with us. You never texted me, Destiny! What am I supposed to think?" Marcus threw his hands up in frustration.

"I did text you, Marcus! I asked you if I could practice reciting my Langston Hughes poem with you."

Marcus looked shocked, reaching for his phone. "You did?"

"I did."

Marcus rolled his eyes and looked at the sky. "I thought that was my little brother. I was going to see him the next day, so I figured I'd just ask him."

"Little brother?"

"I volunteer as a Big Brother, spending time with younger kids. Playing sports, helping with homework, stuff like that. I get together with him about once a week."

Destiny cocked her head, not sure she believed him. "That's nice of you. How come you don't know his number?"

"Well, he has the same area code as you. I'm bad about adding contacts. So I didn't open it. I assumed it was him and I called him." Marcus ducked his head.

"And what did he say?" Destiny was impressed that Marcus was helping a younger kid. If he really was.

"He said it wasn't him."

"And?"

Marcus shrugged. "Well, you didn't say, 'Hi, it's Destiny,' did you?"

"You deleted it, didn't you?"

Marcus started laughing. "I deleted it! I'd been checking a couple times a day to see if you'd texted and yes, I didn't realize it was you and I deleted it. I'm sorry. So can I have a do-over?"

"Do-over?"

"Yeah. And the thing with Sheba, there's nothing going on with us, we're just friends."

"It didn't look like there was nothing going on to me."

"Well, maybe she has a little crush on me, but to me she's just a friend. So come on, do-over?"

She gave him what she knew was a mistrustful look.

But then she took out her phone, pressed the red dot, and three feet away his phone rang.

"Hello?" He looked at her and grinned.

"Hello, Marcus?" She gazed at him. Those dimples.

"Speaking." His liquid eyes met hers.

"This is Destiny. Is this a bad time?" She smiled and raised her eyebrows.

"Hey, Destiny. No, this is a perfect time." He smiled too.

Destiny and Marcus agreed they'd hang out the next night, Wednesday, after they both got off their shifts, and Destiny even brought a short red dress to change into so it would feel like a real date. She hid it in the back of one of the cubbies in the break room. They were going to meet somewhere off the Bristlecone premises, so no one would see them leaving together.

She was at the desk, sorting the residents' mail and

sliding it into their cubbies, when her boss, Ms. Robinson, came up, looking kind of intense. Her usual neat bob looked like she'd run stressed fingers through her hair one too many times.

"Hey, Destiny, I'm going to need you to stay late tonight because of the Elvis impersonator."

"Elvis impersonator?" Destiny's mood plunged to the pit of her stomach. Not only was her date with Marcus in jeopardy, but Elvis was hardly in her top ten.

"We're moving it from the lobby to the large gathering room just behind you here. I need you to help us get chairs set up—they're stacked in the closets behind the stage—and I've asked some of the med techs to lend extra hands. And then leading up to the Elvis show I need you to help the residents get into their seats."

"Actually, Ms. Robinson, I sort of have—"

Ms. Robinson closed her eyes and held up her palm. "We are in emergency mode, Destiny. I thought maybe thirty of these old ladies would have a mild interest in Elvis. We are looking at a stampede of nearly all three hundred Bristlecone residents. Even the men. We need all hands on deck."

Destiny stood up. Ms. Robinson was her mama's soror. She had no choice. "How many chairs?"

Ms. Robinson threw her hands up in exasperation. "All of them."

Destiny set the little "Be Right Back" sign on top of the counter and followed Ms. Robinson to the closet behind the stage where the chairs were stacked. Ms. Robinson instructed her on how to arrange them in the gathering room, assured her help was coming, and raced away.

The minute Ms. Robinson was out of sight, Destiny texted Marcus.

Problem: I have to work late.

Surprisingly, Marcus texted back:

Me too.

Destiny sighed with disappointment. When could they find another night? That hot red dress was folded in the cubby in the breakroom, getting all wrinkled, and it didn't look like it was going to get worn tonight.

The chairs were stacked on rolling carts, which were easy to push, and Destiny got into the rhythm of lifting them from the stack and arranging them in the curving lines that Ms. Robinson had described. There were a lot of them, though, and she sure hoped someone would show up to help soon.

And, to her surprised relief, someone did.

Marcus.

And three of his med tech friends, including Sheba.

"Hey, Destiny, Ms. Robinson sent us over to help set up chairs. "

"Sure hope there are no 'code blues' while you're gone," Destiny said with a nervous laugh, not able to keep herself from checking out Marcus and Sheba's body language.

"Oh, we're only supposed to be here for thirty minutes, and there are two techs still in health care," Sheba said.

"I guess Elvis must be a medical emergency," Marcus said, and Destiny couldn't help laughing.

They lugged the chairs quickly now, and as the last few clattered onto the floor, the residents began filing in: with walkers, arm in arm with each other, in wheelchairs, or with canes, chatting and singing.

One ancient lady with a walker warbled the refrain to

"Don't Be Cruel." "But I can't remember any more of the words."

"'To a girl that's true,'" sang another lady beside her, bent over and with flyaway silver hair.

"No, no," said a third, with a cane. "That's not the right words. I think it's 'a heart so true.'" She looked at Destiny with a determined look on her wrinkled face and grasped her arm. "We have bad vision; we need the front row. So we can see him real good."

"Absolutely," Destiny said, smiling to herself, and helped them all the way down the aisle to the front row chairs, holding their thin white hands in strong grips so they wouldn't fall.

"I hope he plays 'Hound Dog,'" one exclaimed. "And swivels his hips."

"That hip swiveling was supposed to be illegal in several states," said the lady with the cane.

Things got flat-out crazy at that point, with excited old people pouring in, singing and talking, filling the seats. Destiny helped one person after another. She saw Jennie and Alli from the writers' group come in together and said a quick hello. Roy, who she recognized as Margaret's husband, came in and tried to sit next to Jennie, but someone got to the seat before he did.

"I'm worried about my memory," said one tiny old lady as she shuffled in. Destiny recognized her as the woman who'd been watching *Bonanza* yesterday. "Didn't Elvis die?"

"Yes," Destiny assured her. "This is an impersonator. Not the real Elvis." These old White people were as excited as Destiny had ever seen them, and she tried to imagine her own excitement if the impersonator was going to be doing Queen Bey, Alicia Keys, or Rihanna.

Out of the corner of her eye, she saw Marcus helping

the old ladies, too, with his gracious politeness—how they clung to his strong arm, and how he sweet-talked them.

Then Destiny and Marcus were standing by the door, scanning the crowd to make sure everyone seemed all right. The lights flickered, the residents gasped with excitement, and Elvis, carrying a boombox, sashayed in, twirling a scarf above his head like a lariat, in his signature move. He wore his jet-black hair slicked back, his trademark sequined white jumpsuit, the wide belt with the gold buckle, and he had probably thirty filmy multicolored scarves hanging around his neck.

"Wasn't Elvis taller than that?" Marcus whispered.

It was true. The Elvis impersonator was extremely short.

"I wonder how a person would decide they wanted to be an Elvis impersonator," Destiny mused to Marcus.

"Bruno Mars started doing it as a little kid," Marcus said. "That's how he got his start."

"No way." Destiny glanced at him.

"Yeah, I can show you a video of him singing 'Heartbreak Hotel' as a four-year-old."

"Evening, ladies and gentlemen," drawled the Elvis impersonator as he set the boombox on a folding chair on the stage. "Hope you enjoy our show tonight." He leaned down and, with a flourish, pressed "Play."

The opening guitar riff to "Hound Dog" blared through the room and Elvis swiveled his hips just like the real guy, belting out the lyrics.

The Bristlecone residents applauded eagerly, laughter and appreciation rippling through the crowd.

"FYI, Elvis loved playing music with Black musicians," Marcus leaned close and told her. "He made a bunch of songs famous that were originally performed by Black artists, like 'Hound Dog.'"

"How do you know all that?" Destiny crossed her arms over her chest.

"I'm into music trivia," Marcus said, with a grin. "Try me."

"I will."

The residents danced in their seats as Elvis leaped down from the stage, pulled a colorful scarf from his neck, and, with a dramatic kiss on the cheek, placed it around the neck of the lady who'd told Destiny she had to be in the front row. Well, that lady sure looked happy now.

Elvis then moved on to "All Shook Up," "Heartbreak Hotel," "Blue Suede Shoes," and "Don't Be Cruel." After each song, he jumped down during the applause and gifted a different old lady with one of his scarves. They all seemed tickled to death.

And, after almost every song, Marcus leaned over to Destiny and said in her ear, "Also originally recorded by a Black artist."

Elvis was giving the performance his all, with sweat pouring down his red face, and the audience members were whooping and hollering and swaying in their chairs.

"I was worried one of these old ladies was going to swoon," Marcus said. "But now my money's on Elvis. He's not looking so good. I think I'll turn up the air-conditioning." He left Destiny's side for a moment and then was back, and Destiny felt cooler air pumping into the room. Marcus really was a thoughtful person.

Elvis ended the concert with some slower songs and fortunately seemed to be sweating less. He crooned "Love Me Tender" and asked the audience to sing along, which they did with enthusiasm. The concert ended with "Can't Help Falling in Love." Every single person in the room sang at the top of their lungs on that one, and a few of the residents started to cry.

"Good night. And thankyouverymuch," said Elvis with his deep Tennessee accent, bowing low. "Thankyouverymuch."

The crowd roared.

Elvis was still making the rounds of the audience, giving the ladies scarves and kisses on their cheeks, when Ms. Robinson told Destiny and Marcus to help the residents get up and start putting the chairs back in the closet.

Destiny took the hand of the tiny lady she'd seen earlier and helped her out of her chair.

"Lord, when he kissed my cheek, he took my breath away," the lady exclaimed, fingering the silky blue scarf Elvis had given her. "But I'm confused. Didn't Elvis die?"

"Yes, ma'am, you are completely correct, that was an impersonator," Destiny reassured her again, patting her bony arm.

Within fifteen or twenty minutes the room had cleared, and Destiny and Marcus started stacking the chairs and wheeling the carts toward the closet behind the stage. Conveniently, Sheba and the other med techs had disappeared, and Marcus was the only one still helping.

"Thanks for staying to help," she told him as they lined the carts along the wall.

"I didn't think our first date would be to an Elvis concert," Marcus said. "Sorry about that."

"It was more fun than I expected. Guess I'll have to wear my red dress another time," Destiny said, in a flirty tone.

"I will hold you to that." Marcus peeked outside the closet, slid the door practically closed, put his arms around her, gave her a soft, brief kiss, and whispered in her ear, "Elvis has left the building."

CHAPTER 13
ABE

It was beyond absurd that Abe was standing on the front step of Nicole's sprawling stone-and-glass lakefront home on a halcyon Thursday morning in May, almost a month after Margaret died, holding his signed divorce papers, waiting for her to answer the door when it had also been his home for ten years, and he actually still knew the code. Unless she'd changed it. Which, frankly, she probably had. But he didn't live there anymore, which felt somewhat surreal, so he supposed he should ring the bell and wait.

After tax season, Nicole's firm allowed the CPAs to work from home some days.

Behind the door, little paws pattered, Solomon's high bark sounded, and he scratched the door in eager anticipation. Nicole would hate that scratching, Abe thought with satisfaction. Abe couldn't wait to see him. Things had been so up in the air with Nicole that he hadn't even seen Solomon more than a few times over the past year. For so many weeks he had been consumed with his health, and then the move, and all the drama with Nicole—yet he had missed Solomon every day. Nicole's steps sounded in the foyer—she had amazingly loud footsteps, so decisive and confident, even in bare feet—and the door swung open.

Solomon leaped out of the door and threw his entire tiny, buff-colored chihuahua self at Abe, wriggling, squealing, and jumping. Abe dropped the envelope with the divorce papers on the porch as he bent to pick him up. Solomon ecstatically licked his face, his hands, and then adorably buried his nose in Abe's armpit. His sweet, toasty doggy smell wafted up.

"Hey, Sol. Hey, buddy. I missed you too."

"Guess he doesn't remember you," Nicole said with the dry wit that Abe had always found so enjoyable, holding the door open and stepping back so Abe could come in. She looked wonderful, of course—barefoot, wearing a flared, multicolored golf skirt that showed her long, muscled legs, and a blue-green top that matched her eyes. The top presently showed some sweat spots that were, in fact, attractive to Abe, and her hair hung down her back in a long, thick strawberry-blonde braid.

"He's lost a little weight, hasn't he?" Abe put Solomon down, where he danced in circles and jumped up half a dozen more times as Abe picked up the divorce papers.

"Pining for you, I'm sure. Here's his bed, and I've got a bag with all his toys and food in the kitchen."

Abe followed Nicole through the white-tiled front hall with the enormous abstract painting in splashes of indigo, yellow, red, and pink, into the fully equipped, all-white kitchen with its enormous quartz island where almost no cooking had ever been done. "You played golf today?"

Solomon followed along, still turning in ecstatic circles, jumping on Abe, and letting out high-pitched squeals of joy.

"Yes. Sucked." She tossed her braid over her shoulder

with a shrug, handing Abe the bag with Solomon's toys. "But tomorrow is another day."

Abe put the envelope with the divorce papers on the gleaming quartz counter. He couldn't help but think of wise King Solomon from the Bible, who had arbitrated a custody dispute between two women over a baby by suggesting that the baby be cut in half, with half for each woman. The real mother showed her love for the baby by crying out to give the baby to the other woman rather than hurt it, and Solomon awarded the baby to her. What a savage and disturbing story. Abe had taught it in one of his classes on Middle Eastern culture. He frequently found himself thinking back on the ancient stories he'd taught.

Now here he was, in a sense playing out that biblical story with Nicole, sharing custody of an eight-pound dog.

"He's been hiding food again, so you might be finding little pieces in the seats of chairs and under pillows."

"Okay."

"And if you don't take him out about every three hours, he'll sneak in a bedroom and pee on the bed skirt."

"Still?"

"He's getting a little better. Not much."

Abe had a theory that Nicole didn't take the time to walk Solomon enough, but he kept his mouth shut rather than argue or blame her. When they had first gotten Sol, Abe's research had told him that chihuahuas could be exceedingly difficult to house-train, and that had been the case. Maybe that was why Nicole was suddenly willing to part with him. Or maybe there were other changes in her life. Abe couldn't help but wonder. A paramour who didn't like dogs, perhaps?

He pointed at the envelope. "Signed, also sealed, and now delivered."

"Sounds like the Stevie Wonder song."

They were both silent for a few seconds, since the next words in that song were not remotely appropriate today.

"Okay, thanks," Nicole finally said, leaning against the counter, seeming not to want to look at the envelope.

"So how are things? Everything going okay?" Abe picked up the bag of kibble and toys, trying to ignore his heart beating more rapidly than usual. This seemed so final.

"Of course." Nicole shrugged and smiled, a little sadly, meeting Abe's eyes only for a brief second, as they headed back through the foyer and stood by the front door.

"Well, that's good." Abe tried to think of something else to say, but she hadn't given him much to work with. "Since tax season is over you have more free time, I guess."

"Yes, except for the business returns. As for Solomon, I can of course keep him for you if you ever need me to, if I'm in town." Nicole definitely was not tipping her hand about anything personal or to do with her social life. Just business. He wished she would joke around, and tease him, the way she normally did.

"Oh, thanks, I can't think of anywhere I'm going anytime soon but you never know."

Maybe he would book a trip to Croatia just to make Nicole jealous. But was jealousy from Nicole completely a thing of the past? Evenings at conferences after young, fawning female students asked him questions that they'd clearly spent hours formulating popped into his mind; Nicole had done snarky imitations of them, which he'd enjoyed, especially when he realized she was jealous. But it had been years since that had happened. He felt as though he'd lost his edge.

"Sure, right. How are the boys?"

"Fine, they're fine." That was a surprise question.

It was thoughtful of Nicole to ask about Abe's sons, especially since neither of them had made much effort with her. Abe had found her crying once, standing just inside her closet door in her underwear, her nose all red and running. At first, she wouldn't tell him why she was crying, but she finally burst out with, "Your sons hate me!" After that one breakdown, though, Nicole had been stoic and pretended she wasn't hurt by it, that she didn't care at all, and sent gifts for years that were never acknowledged. She was pretty brave. Abe admired her strength and loyalty.

Nicole opened the front door, and there seemed to be little left to say. Solomon had spotted his dog bed by the door and was lying in it, but his anxious brown eyes shifted between the two of them, showing his confusion about what might happen next.

Nicole picked Sol up while Abe carried everything else. He put Sol's crate in the backseat and Nicole gently placed him into it.

"Be a good boy, Solomon. I'll miss you." The edges of Nicole's nostrils turned red as she hugged and kissed Sol, and Abe knew she was starting to cry again, just like the time she'd been hurt by his boys. He wondered again why she was letting him have Sol, since she hadn't even considered it when he first moved. What had changed?

Sol licked the tears on Nicole's cheeks, and Abe told himself it was because of the salt, not because he was going to miss her.

As Abe backed out of the driveway, Sol whined and watched Nicole recede as they drove away. He then curled in a tight little ball for the rest of the journey to Bristlecone.

When Abe and Nicole lived together, Sol had slept on the bed between their feet. Tonight, Sol wasn't able to get onto the bed on his own—too high up so Abe lifted him..

Sol found his way to the foot of the bed as usual, but then, with a hard-to-read glance at Abe, jumped down and trotted down the hall. He spent his first night with Abe curled on the front hall rug, facing the door.

Abe told himself that Sol was just a dog. He couldn't formulate sentences. Abe doubted that he had feelings.

The next morning, after his workout, Abe meandered with Solomon across the small, somewhat ragged park between his cottage and the main building at Bristlecone. Training Sol to walk on a leash had been a fool's errand. Solomon got his legs tangled, dug in and refused to walk anywhere, and stopped to sniff every leaf and flower and to water every tree, to the point where Abe wondered whether dogs could get prostate problems. Solomon also seemed obsessively interested in watching people and other dogs. He would stop and stare, which Abe had been taught was rude when he was growing up, but it was hard to teach that to a dog.

But just having his company stirred Abe to shake his lethargy and self-pity. Abe found himself straightening up and walking with more spring in his step.

Though it was only early May, hints of future summer heat threaded through the air. The peonies and gardenias at Bristlecone flashed their showy blooms, and the gardenias' scent reminded Abe of Ellen, as she had always commented on it. Solomon had already developed a fondness for anointing the ground at the foot of the ancient bristlecone pine, with its plaque in its own private courtyard, and Abe headed in that direction. Beside the tree, a young man in a cap and gown posed awkwardly for photos, with grandparents so proud that they literally clung to him and pinched his cheeks with affection.

Abe remembered his own college graduation. Before the ceremony, he and his father and mother and younger sister, Marcy, posed for photos on the quad in front of his dorm. It was unbearably hot in the caps and gowns.

And then Abe thought he saw Allison with her family —her parents, her sister, and her sister's children—posing for photos on the other side of the quad. But Allison had transferred, Abe was sure that was what her suite-mate had told him. But there she was. Allison wore a white dress, and her flyaway blonde hair floated in the breeze like gold threads. Her father helped her put on her graduation robe, which was too long and dragged on the ground.

"Isn't that the girl you brought home that time?" his sister Marcy asked.

"No," Abe said shortly. "She transferred."

"The girl you brought home?" his father asked.

"It's time to go to the stadium," Abe's mother said, brightly, cutting it all short.

If Abe had known that was the last time he'd see her for fifty years, he would have gone over and said something. For years, he'd remembered her with longing.

So when Abe saw Allison walking across the courtyard that whole memory unspooled and he felt twenty-one again. She was wearing workout clothes—vivid yoga shorts and a loose top—and her silvery spiked hair glistened in the sun. She still seemed so youthful.

She was on the phone and, as she approached, Abe caught her words. "It's nothing to worry about, sweetie, I promise you. I'll go to the website and take a look."

Allison looked up then and saw Abe. His immediate worry was that she had read the pages he'd written for the last writers' group meeting and known they were about their breakup. He'd thought about contacting her and apologizing and offering to return her pages but the whole thing had been so incredibly embarrassing he'd decided to do nothing. He thought maybe he'd hear from her—probably outrage—but at least he'd hear something. But no, silence. So maybe, with any luck, she hadn't read them, had just thrown them in the trash.

Now he wasn't sure he should even say hello, but he did. "Hello, Allison."

She smiled at him and pointed at her phone. Was her smile friendly? Guarded? Abe wondered if that might reveal whether she'd read the pages.

It would be awkward to greet her if she didn't, so he tried to keep walking, but Solomon completely foiled that plan. Solomon saw her, whirled in a circle of delight, and jumped up on her.

"Honey, let me call you back," Allison said into the phone, and then she bent to pet Solomon. "Oh my goodness, what a cutie! Hello little man." Solomon licked her hand. She looked up at Abe. "Is this Solomon?"

Abe nodded. "Yes. He loves you." Had he just said that? Abe wanted to kick himself. His entire body flooded with adrenaline. "I mean, he loves everyone."

Allison knelt and let Solomon jump all over her, lick her hands and face, and rub his nose all over her shoes. Afterward, Solomon seemed spent and lay on the sidewalk, looking up at her with adoration, his brown eyes gleaming, the end of his pink tongue hanging out.

Allison laughed, running her fingers over his silky ears. "Was it good for you?"

Abe felt caught in a time warp. He so clearly remembered the first time he and Allison had made love, how innocent and frightened she had been, how gentle he had tried to be. He laughed at her joke but could barely process the moment. Fifty years, he reminded himself.

Allison played with Solomon's ears. "Solomon, you should try out for *Legally Blonde*—you look exactly like Bruiser Woods! And you're so friendly, I bet you'd love to do it. And when you try out, you should tell them you're a Gemini vegetarian, just to show you have inside intel about the movie." Allison gave Solomon's ears a last scratch and stood as he continued to regard her adoringly. "What a personality."

"Yes, he charms everyone." Wasn't *Legally Blonde* a silly send-up of academia? What was a Gemini vegetarian? Abe couldn't be involved with anything like that. But he'd better determine if she'd read his pages. "Listen, Allison—"

"Alli."

"Oh, sorry, Alli." He shook his head, showing her that he wasn't being rude, but just trying to toss the old name out of his brain once and for all. "Listen, about that last crazy writers' meeting—Margaret's husband showing up and the orange briefcase and all the chaos—" He hoped maybe he could discern, without having to ask, whether she'd just chucked the pages or actually read them. And maybe get her to reveal what she thought.

She crossed her arms over her chest and regarded him with a directness that left him nonplussed. She'd had very little self-confidence in college, could hardly meet people's eyes. Her shy glancing away had been attractive and mysterious to him. Had that been an act? If not, she'd changed more than just her name.

Solomon lay down in the grass below the bristlecone pine, his nose between his little paws, his eyes angling between the two of them as if he knew they weren't going anywhere for a while.

"I assume that was our breakup you were writing about."

"No." Abe cleared his throat, feeling his face heat up. "No. Listen—"

"Listen? What is it you want me to listen to?"

"Give me a chance to tell you, it's just a figure of speech."

"All right." She took a breath, glanced at Solomon, and back at Abe.

"I've been writing some fiction for the writers' group, but some of it is more autobiographical than maybe I've admitted. Our experience and relationship have stayed vivid in my mind. I think about it a lot."

"Really?" She cocked her head, as if challenging him, as if she were about to say, *More than I think about it?*

The grandparents and their graduate grandson now crossed the courtyard on the path, approaching Abe and Alli. Abe had started to respond to Alli but waited in awkward silence for them to pass before continuing. Finally, when they were out of earshot, he spoke.

"I know now that I didn't really consider your feelings at the time. I was thinking only about how I couldn't be derailed from getting my PhD." He sighed. "And that was wrong."

"Yes." She nodded. "It was an awful time for me. We

were taught in those years that if we slept with someone, we should marry them."

"I realize that now. But at the time—"

"Abe, I look back now and see that because I was so helplessly in love with you, I allowed you to dictate the relationship. Also, quite a few of the other girls I knew were getting married. I thought I should marry you."

"Well, I realize that I never asked you what you thought. I just made the decision I thought was best since I had so many more years of school left ahead of me. And you did too."

She nodded. "True. And I admit, I did not stand up for myself. I didn't even give myself a chance to have my own thoughts, the way I've since learned to do. But I was young. Naïve. Raised Southern."

"We both were."

"You weren't raised Southern."

"Oh, no." He quickly added, "But that doesn't absolve me of being a jerk. I'm sorry for what I did. Obviously, since I've been writing about it, it's been on my mind, even after fifty years."

Her hazel eyes widened, even watered a bit. "Well, thank you. I guess I wasn't expecting an apology." She uncrossed her arms, rubbed her forehead as if the conversation hurt her.

"I think about our relationship a lot," he said.

"You do?" Alli seemed almost shocked.

"Yes." Abe's heart contracted, then relief surged through him. She had accepted his apology. "If we'd gotten married and started a family, our children would be fifty now. I actually tried to call you about a year after Ellen died." Maybe, somehow, they could continue this conversation over coffee. "Would you—" he began.

She sighed and glanced at her watch. "I have to call my daughter back." Then she seemed to reconsider, and looked up at him. "To be honest, those pages you'd written brought back so many feelings that I thought I'd deeply buried. I felt ignored and disrespected all over again."

Abe hadn't thought about that. "What do you mean? Ignored? I'm confused. Because I told the story?"

"Yes, revealing our relationship and breakup to strangers without getting my permission."

"But do I need your permission to tell a story that also happened to me?"

Alli's jaw tightened. "Absolutely, before you would publish it."

"I haven't even tried to publish it. I just brought it to the writers' group." Suddenly this was going even worse than Abe had feared. "If we hadn't mistakenly exchanged pages, you'd never even know I'd written it, because I purposely didn't read it when I saw you there."

"But you would have read it to strangers if I wasn't?"

"Well, yes. They didn't know who the girl was."

"Is it your plan to publish it?"

Abe shrugged. "I haven't published anything other than academic articles. My creative work has not gained much well, any notice. It was my thought, though, to send out some of my pieces, yes."

Alli raised her chin. "Well, in case you're at all hazy on this, I'd prefer you not send out the piece about me." She bent and said good-bye to Solomon. "Now, if you'll excuse me, I need to call my daughter back. See you this afternoon at writers' group."

She continued across the courtyard with a determined stride, pulling her phone from a side pocket in her yoga shorts.

Abe and Solomon watched her go.

Abe sighed. "We screwed up, didn't we, boy?" Solomon gave him a look that implied that he did not feel at all responsible for screwing up; in fact, he had done a stellar job of playing Abe's wingman and more than done his part to charm Alli. If anyone had screwed up, it was Abe. "Come on, boy, let's go home."

Solomon actually seemed to have picked up some of Allison's disdain for Abe; he was even worse about following Abe's commands than usual. He took his time about watering the ground below the bristlecone and then meandered home. Only minutes after they returned, Solomon went into Abe's bedroom, lifted his leg, and peed again on the bed skirt. So much for dogs providing unconditional love and companionship.

Abe nearly threw his back out trying to slide the bed skirt from between the mattress and boxspring, then sprayed it with something Nicole had sent along with Solomon's bed and toys and threw it in the washer. He'd forgotten about this particular aspect of living with Solomon. Then he turned on the tennis tournament he'd recorded earlier. The thwack of the tennis volleys reminded him of his contentious conversation with Alli. He didn't feel like writing. He didn't feel like going to writers' group in the least. He didn't feel like doing anything. He'd lost two women in one week. That seemed more like something that might have happened to him in college, not at age seventy-five.

Though, the truth was, he had probably lost them both many years ago.

CHAPTER 14
WILLOUGHBY

Willoughby unlocked the door to the conference room a little before two that Friday afternoon and put her battered leather briefcase in her usual seat, two down from the head of the scarred pine table. So far, from the email responses, everyone was coming, including Alli, despite that embarrassing scene with Roy at the last meeting. No one would have been the least surprised if Alli had decided never to darken the door of this conference room again. But apparently she was a brave individual, not easily cowed by the inappropriate behavior of men. She must really love writing. Willoughby could relate. If Willoughby couldn't write, she would have no way of processing her life.

Willoughby put the egg timer in the center of the table and watched the sand sprinkle through the tiny opening, almost grain by grain. Occasionally, time did seem to pass that way, excruciatingly slowly, but lately it seemed to be crashing through like a tsunami or a flood, in enormous, enveloping waves. She couldn't stop thinking about what had happened that night last week with Steven. Goodness, she should have checked on him again, but how could she? She was so embarrassed she'd fallen asleep in his bed!

What had she been thinking? She'd been heartbroken about Gary throwing the food and calling her by his first wife's name, yes. But to end up in Steven's bed? While Steven sang "Marian the Librarian"? Heat rose to her cheeks, just remembering. And what had he told their daughter? Courtney hadn't mentioned it. Maybe Steven would keep it their secret. Maybe he was honorable enough to do so, which increased Willoughby's worry over whether she'd made a mistake in leaving him all those years ago.

But taking care of Gary had been so hard lately. It was no wonder she was easily drawn into Steven's fun-loving attitude. She'd really missed that.

She'd also heard from Courtney that Adam was coming down from New York to see his father this weekend. What if Steven told Adam about what had happened when Willoughby visited? Adam would hate her even more. Should she show up in Steven's room unannounced and surprise Adam while he was there? She would do anything to reconcile with her son.

"Good afternoon." Abe entered the conference room, wearing his customary professor-style khakis, clutching his pages to his chest.

"Hey, Abe!"

Abe looked better-groomed than usual. His beard was carefully trimmed, his hair neatly combed, his white shirt was clean and starched. And there was a bright look of the hunter in his eye that she hadn't seen before. Willoughby remembered what Jennie had said about the group being hard on Abe and wanted to try to do better.

And in the next few seconds, as Alli entered the room,

Willoughby knew exactly the meaning of the sudden gleam leaping to his eyes, the flow of energy that animated him. Something was going on between Abe and Alli.

"Hi, Willoughby. Hello, Abe." Alli flashed a lovely smile and, after a bit of hesitation, chose the seat next to Willoughby, not Abe. Well, hmm, maybe something was going on in Abe's head but not Alli's.

"Hey there." Willoughby hoped to pick up more clues as the meeting progressed.

A moment later, Jennie came in, and Destiny from the front desk was with her. Jennie and Alli brightened when they saw each other. Jennie sat at the head of the table next to Alli and patted the seat next to her, indicating that Destiny should sit.

Willoughby suspected, as recent widows, that Jennie and Alli had developed a friendship outside of the writers' group. She felt a twinge of envy at their closeness, but it made sense that they had more in common with each other than with Willoughby, who now had not one but two husbands at Bristlecone. They certainly would not have any understanding of her feeling of envy.

"Before we read," Jennie said, "I've invited Destiny to join us for a few minutes to talk about Margaret's briefcase."

Everyone said hi to Destiny.

"Oh yes, I'm sorry." Willoughby felt terrible that she'd forgotten about Jennie's call and their agreement to discuss the list in the briefcase. She must be subconsciously avoiding the topic because of her own guilt from the past for allowing that book to be banned. "You called me about that, Jennie, and then we weren't able to talk about it last week because of Roy showing up. Go ahead."

"I had to give it back to Roy, of course, but the briefcase

was empty except for a list of books. Destiny, do you mind telling the group your thoughts about the list?"

"Sure," Destiny said. "One of my teachers at community college has talked a lot about banned books, and I looked these up, and believe it or not, the books on Margaret's list have all been banned, even these children's books like *Charlotte's Web*. So do you think that's what this list might be?"

Everyone looked at Willoughby, as she'd been the librarian.

"Of course!" Willoughby was chagrined that she hadn't noticed it herself. "Well, of course that's what they are." She slapped her forehead. She truly was all over the place these days. Her guilt about *Speak* was really doing a number on her. Even after so many years.

"I just wondered if anyone knows why Margaret might keep a list of banned books—there was literally nothing in her briefcase except that handwritten list—and if we should do anything about it?" Jennie said. "And remember when she said, in that last meeting, 'Everything's in here'?"

"I did hear her say that," Abe said.

"Maybe we should ask Roy if he knows anything about why she might have kept that list," Jennie suggested.

"I took a photo of it, because I wanted to make sure I read them," added Destiny. "I can send it to all of you, if you want." She stood up. "But I better get back to the front desk."

"Thank you for your help, Destiny," Jennie said, and the others joined in.

"No problem." Destiny gave a little wave as she left.

Willoughby turned to Jennie. "That's a good idea. Anybody want to volunteer to talk to Roy? Abe, what about you? You and Roy are fellow males—maybe you'd have better luck than the rest of us." Willoughby knew Abe wouldn't want to do it the minute she suggested it.

"Me? I just this moment found out about the situation."

"I'll volunteer to talk to Roy," Jennie said. "Would someone else do it with me, though? I don't want him hitting on me again."

"I will," Alli said, with a chuckle. "We can figure out some way to approach him."

"Well," Abe suddenly said, "I'm happy to join, in case the two of you need a male presence."

Willoughby almost laughed at Abe's sudden change of heart, but nodded, ignoring the wave of envy sweeping over her about the obvious growing closeness between the other group members. "All right, anything else? Should we get started?" Everyone nodded. "Great. I'll start, since I was here first for a change." She pulled out her pages and turned over the egg timer, clearing her throat. She'd written from the point of view of the extroverted and ambitious young woman, Astrid, who had just met with the older, painfully introverted author. Her antagonist, as it were.

As she read, she wondered if she might have channeled her thoughts about Astrid being an antagonist too heavily into the writing. Did she seem well-rounded enough, or did she seem too unrelievedly evil? Willoughby's dialogue sounded stilted, she realized as she read aloud. She broke out in a sweat, her anxiety about sharing her work rising, and stumbled on a few words. She had an uncontrollable desire to edit as she read and left out entire sentences. Her mind had been all over the place after the evening in Steven's room and she was finding it hard to concentrate on anything. She almost didn't want Abe to hear this; it was so obvious what his criticisms would be.

Jennie would be kind and encouraging, at least. Alli hadn't been in the group long enough for Willoughby to predict her reaction.

"This is a first draft," Willoughby said as she concluded. "I realized as I read that my own preconceived notions about who I know Astrid to be and what I know she is going to do are influencing the way I write about her." Preempting criticism wasn't something Willoughby ever did. It defeated the purpose of the critiques. She was completely off her game this week, maybe because of that night with Steven, and also because of how difficult things were getting with Gary.

"No apologies." Alli wagged her finger at Willoughby, then smiled and gave a small dismissive wave of her hand. "Sorry, that was my old group's saying. We didn't allow people to apologize for their work."

"We don't either!" Willoughby said. Alli's comment actually made her feel even worse. "I apologize for apologizing." She laughed at the absurdity of it.

"Except today," Abe said, chuckling, with a very brief glance and smile in Alli's direction.

"I know, I have no explanation, I walk back all apologies." Willoughby suddenly felt breathless and lightheaded, with a powerful urge to run from the room. She stood up, her heart pounding, pushing her papers together. "I have to go." She started to say, *I'm sorry*, but that would be laughable, so she bit her tongue, grabbed her briefcase, and slammed her chair tight against the table, then raced toward the door, breaking out in a cold sweat, hearing Jennie's sweet voice float from behind, saying:

"I thought it was a good scene, Willoughby, please don't leave."

But Willoughby did not stop. Something was happening to her that she couldn't control. Was it a panic attack? She was halfway down the stairs Margaret had fallen down when she realized she'd forgotten the egg timer. Oh, well, someone else would remember it. She was far too embarrassed to go back.

Willoughby raced past Destiny at the front desk, who gave her a wave as she slid the residents' mail into their cubbies, and ran outside into the fresh air. She leaned against the front column of the building, closed her eyes, and tried taking deep breaths. After a few minutes, her breathlessness and trembling abated. She sat in a rocking chair on the slate front porch for a few calming moments. She rocked slowly, laying her trembling hands flat on the wide armrests.

How embarrassing to race out of group like that. It had been so odd; she'd become totally unable to control the trembling, the breathlessness, and the overwhelming desire to flee. Honestly, though, they probably only talked about it for a few minutes and then went on with their readings. Younger people might have gossiped, but she'd observed that when people grew older, they often became kinder, having experienced more times of difficulty them-selves. Plus, maybe they'd just forget, unlike young people. Probably next week no one would even mention it. No need to apologize, she thought wryly. That word "apologize" again.

Now, though, she didn't know what to do with herself. It was too early to visit Gary; he was used to late afternoon. She suddenly recognized in herself a reluctance to go anyway. A sense of dread.

Rebecca, one of the CNAs, had said to her just the other

day, "Mrs. Philpott, don't feel like you have to come every single day and stay all afternoon. Give yourself a break. He doesn't remember. Go do something fun. He'll be all right."

She drew a deep breath and stood up, listlessly gazing across the expanse of bright green grass. He was literally slipping away from her. Willoughby could not believe it, especially when she thought about how close she and Gary had been. But she was thinking about cutting her visits to three times a week. Maybe.

Would she feel guilty? Would people think she wasn't a devoted wife? Would she *herself* think she wasn't a devoted wife? With how vibrant and energetic Gary had been, it was almost unbelievable, and certainly impossible to predict, that he would have such a precipitous decline. And his behavior was so mercurial. Sometimes he was affectionate, but other times so nasty. She'd talked to his doctor and possibly the change in meds might help.

Gary would get enough showers. Somehow, they would convince him. Even if he didn't, it wasn't the end of the world, right?

It would be nice to be able to get away and go some-where like Italy; some of her friends in the building had invited her to join their trip. Or Australia, before she got too old to make the flight. She'd said "no" to everything because of caring for Gary. She hadn't even wanted to consider anything else. But that sense of being trapped during writers' group... Maybe she did need a break.

Before she knew it, she was heading down the long hall in the rehab center toward Steven's room and knocking on his door.

"Come in!" His voice sounded clear and strong, welcoming, and when she entered the room, there was no pot smell.

"Not getting high today?" she asked with a laugh.

Steven, neatly dressed, sitting in his easy chair, freshly shaved, his hair washed and combed, acted startled. "Oh, it's you," he said. "I'm expecting Adam any minute."

Willoughby's heart pounded, her hand still on the doorknob. "Oh, really?"

He gave her a sideways look, a crooked smile. "Don't tell me you had no idea."

"I knew he was coming this weekend, but not exactly...I guess I thought he'd be here Saturday?" she trailed off, half-closing the door and moving farther inside the room. "You know me too well."

"I do know you pretty well. And I like you anyway." He gestured at the drawer where he kept his pot. "Want to get high after he leaves? That might be much more enjoyable. More to dish about."

"No, I don't want to get high at all." She rolled her eyes. "Not after what happened last time. I'm...just stopping in. To see how you're doing. I'll only stay a minute—I definitely do not want a scene." She glanced at the hibiscus which Steven, or one of the staff, had placed on the windowsill and which now sported three showy, new red blooms. It seemed to like it here.

"I didn't tell anyone, Willoughby. Your secret is safe with me. Don't worry."

Willoughby thought she might faint with the relief she felt. "Thank you, Steven."

"And I won't tell Courtney or Adam what happened either. I'm a vault, my dear."

Willoughby nodded, drew a deep breath, then looked at the floor. "I appreciate that, Steven. If Adam found out, well, he'd probably—"

"If I found out what? What would I probably do?" Adam's voice came from the door.

Willoughby turned, saw her estranged son for the first time in five years, and her heart seized. His dark hair was salted with gray, at thirty-five, and his face was weathered —he was both a runner and a sailor—and his formerly slim frame was now slightly thicker; she wondered if he was drinking more. Willoughby wasn't overly familiar with high-end casual wear, but she recognized that Adam was wearing it: a pair of slip-on leather shoes, sleek jeans, and a soft black T-shirt, maybe made of bamboo. She wanted to rush to him and fold him in her arms, but his bloodshot hazel eyes held such hate that she remained rooted in place, unable to breathe or move, her scalp prickling.

"I'll come back later, Dad." Adam glanced at Willoughby.

"No, don't be silly, Son, you can survive in the same room with your mother for a few minutes," Steven said.

"No, I'm leaving." Adam grabbed the doorknob. "As I said, I'll be back later."

"No, I was just leaving," Willoughby said. This was agonizing. "You came a long way, Adam. You stay." She started to simply reach out and pat his arm as she walked out the door, but he shrank away to prevent her from touching him.

Willoughby walked a long way down the hall before she finally broke down crying. As she sobbed, a memory of Adam as a toddler surfaced, putting his fingers at the edges of her lips and turning them up, saying, *Smile, Mommy, I wuv you.* But she dried her tears quickly and struggled to regain control. She was keeping Clay tonight while Courtney and Scott went to some silent auction fundraiser, and she had to be on her game.

She went to the back courtyard and sat on the bench beside that grizzly old bristlecone pine to hide while she regained her composure. She didn't want to be going past the dining hall or down the hall to her apartment and run into anyone while she was crying. She was at the end of her rope.

Willoughby sat on the bench for a long while.

CHAPTER 15
DESTINY

Well, when Miss Willoughby came hauling freight down the stairs, Destiny waved and had been about to mention something else she'd seen when she looked at that list of banned books on the photo she took, but Miss Willoughby flew by like fire ants were in her pants.

She didn't look all that great. She blasted through the glass door and crossed the courtyard and sat on one of the rocking chairs with her back to the building. Yep, she was crying. Destiny didn't think she'd ever seen Miss Willoughby completely lose it like that before.

Destiny didn't think what she wrote was bad. Why was she freaking out about it? She couldn't tell her that, of course, being that she wasn't supposed to be listening. She sat there for a few minutes, and Destiny started debating about going out to ask if she was all right, except she was not supposed to leave this desk except for an emergency, and she'd already left once without Ms. Robinson's permission today. Just as Destiny decided that hell, yes, this was an emergency, and stood to go check on her, Miss Willoughby stood up, and instead of going to memory care, where she usually went after the meeting, she went over to the health-care wing.

After a minute or two, Destiny opened her photo roll and looked at the list of banned books again. Down at the bottom of the sheet of paper, below the list of books, there was a five-digit number. Maybe it didn't mean anything—maybe Margaret had just jotted down some random number on the closest sheet of paper. But maybe it did mean something.

Destiny went back to sorting the mail. She wasn't listening in on the writers' group as much now that they'd repeatedly invited her to join in. She was thinking about joining it, though she did think that their being so old was kind of weird. It made her think again about how, without the Dancing Divas and Drop the Mic, Destiny didn't really have a friend group. She wondered what it might be like in Durham at nursing school. Probably so much studying there wouldn't even be time for friend groups. Then Destiny looked outside and caught sight of Marcus crossing the courtyard, looking especially ripped, and she waved.

He saw her, took a look around to make sure nobody was watching, and headed over, giving the courtyard one more glance before opening the glass door. He'd been stopping by almost every day since the Elvis concert, just to hang out for a few minutes.

He leaned on the desk, picked up *1984* and stared at the cover, which featured the title, a bright red background, and a ginormous blue eye, watching. He put down the book without one comment. Destiny wanted to stick her finger in that dimple. The sleeve of his uniform barely covered up a tattoo that said "Wakanda Forever."

"So, what are you doing?" he said.

"Leaping tall buildings in a single bound."

"I can see that. Faster than a speeding bullet. More powerful than a locomotive."

"Pretty much. What's happening with you?" Destiny was aware that their bantering sounded stupid just because they were nervous about being together while they were at work.

"Nothing. Sick old people. Old sick people."

"Come on, I've seen you—you're good with them. The way you sweet-talked those old ladies at the Elvis concert; they all love you. 'Marcus, could you come help me with this? Marcus, could you come help me with that.' I mean, maybe I'm too *young* for you, Marcus." Destiny winked at him.

Marcus looked all shy, and his dimple cut deeper. "They remind me of my great-grandma. Don't tell anybody, but I like old people. Even the ones that kind of give you a hard time."

"I know what you mean. They cut through a lot of crap by the time they get to that age."

"There's this one lady in memory care that takes her purse around with her everywhere, keeps it in her lap. There's nothing in it, nothing."

"Yeah, I've seen her."

"One time she collapsed, and we had to take her to health care, and she was losing it, saying, 'Where's my purse?' and one of the CNAs says, 'Forget it, it doesn't matter,' and I said, 'Hey, it does matter. That purse is important to her.' And we took it with us on the stretcher. I mean, show a little respect, you know?"

"That was a nice thing to do." Destiny met his eye, wondering if her school principal mama would like that story. "You're a good person, Marcus."

"I try. What time you get off?"

Her heart did a flip. "Eight."

"Okay." He straightened and slapped his hand on the desk. "Me too. Want to really get together this time? Meet you just outside." He glanced back into the courtyard and backed away, heading for the door.

"No, not here." Destiny was not about to test the employee dating rule again. Her school principal mama would have a hissy fit if she got fired. And her daddy wouldn't be too happy either. "Just text me and I'll meet you."

Marcus gave her a nod, and then he was gone.

Destiny didn't even turn on the intercom for the rest of the writers' meeting. She was floating. Change of clothes in her locker? Check. Lipstick? Check.

She was totally caught by surprise when Miss Jennie and the new lady with spiky silver hair—Miss Alli—came up to the desk on their way out of the meeting.

"Destiny, I would definitely like you to send us copies of that photo of the banned books," Jennie said.

"Oh, right, sure. And I'm reading *1984* right now, for your information." She held up the worn paperback from the library. "I read online that it's been the most banned book of all time, and I wanted to start with number one. So weird to be thinking that 1984 is in the future, right? This stuff about Big Brother watching you isn't that outrageous, honestly."

"Yes!" Miss Alli widened her eyes. "When I read it in college, it seemed like this distant point in time, this impossible set of circumstances. And now...well, it seems even more real and scary."

Destiny scrolled through her phone to find the pic she took of Miss Margaret's scratchy-penned list. "Text it to you?"

"Great." Both ladies gave her their numbers.

"I noticed something else about this photo," she said. "See those numbers scribbled down at the bottom of the page, 83254? Do you think that might mean anything?"

"Hmm. It could just be some kind of passcode," Jennie said.

"Or someone's birthdate," Alli added.

"I mean, it could be the code for a lock," Destiny said.

"I wish we could get into her apartment to take a look around," Alli said.

Before Destiny could stop herself, since she was feeling jazzed about seeing Marcus later, she said, "Well, Miss Jennie, you could pretend you've changed your mind and want to go out with Mr. Roy after all. You could definitely get in then."

Both ladies stared at her.

"How did you know he wants to go out with me?" Miss Jennie said.

Destiny, girl, you've done it now, she thought. *They're going to find out about the intercom.* "Well, I mean, isn't it obvious? Just as obvious as the fact that Dr. Abe wants to go out with you, Miss Alli. So you just need to work it, is all I'm saying. We ladies got to work it."

They both laughed, so hopefully she got away with it. But Destiny decided right then that she was definitely not going to eavesdrop on their meetings anymore.

That night, Marcus texted her to meet him at a spot in downtown Eden Forest called The Black Horse Pub, which she didn't know. But when she got there around eight thirty, she saw a few café tables with umbrellas outside, and big blue and yellow neon letters in the storefront window read: *Karaoke Friday Night.*

She'd done karaoke a few times, with a bunch of girl-friends from Drop the Mic, with spoken word stuff. The parents of one of her friends had a karaoke machine in their basement. But on a first date? A quiet place would have been better, where she and Marcus could get to know each other a little. She'd even dressed up in the famous short red dress. But she went in. When her eyes adjusted to the dark, she spotted Marcus sitting at the booth farthest away from the karaoke setup, in a fitted, blue-collared shirt and black jeans. He was holding a beer and a champagne cocktail, a drink she'd told him she liked.

"Champagne cocktails are half-price on Fridays," he said, handing her the champagne glass, which was the old-fashioned kind, shallow and wide. "Of course, you'd be worth it even if it was full price. You look great."

"Thank you. I'm a lucky girl. Very classy. Looks deli-cious." She almost said, *you look delicious* but fortunately caught herself in time. "You look great too."

"I didn't remember Fridays are karaoke nights," he said. "I thought it would be pretty quiet here. But we can sit outside."

She looked around. Only about a dozen people were scattered around, and no one was singing over at the karaoke corner. "Yeah, outside sounds good."

He stood up and smiled beguilingly, his dimples crin-kling. "I'll get some snacks."

Marcus got a bowl of cheese-filled pretzels and they sat at a café table outside. It was a nice night, and the early May air felt soft on her arms. The bar was in a busy part of town and people strolled by on the sidewalk, and cars buzzed by with their lights on, music playing out their open windows.

"No work talk," Destiny said.

"No work talk," Marcus agreed.

Destiny asked him to tell her about how he decided to become a Big Brother, and he told her about his little brother, Tyrone, who was twelve now, and the plans he tried to make for them each week.

"Sometimes we go to the library. Sometimes we play pickup basketball at the park near my house. I can't afford to take him to lunch every time, but we do that sometimes. We splurged and went to The Gantt Center downtown one day." Marcus shrugged. "My mom signed me up for the program after my dad left, and I'm still in touch with my own Big Brother. It meant a lot to me. So I'm just paying it forward."

Then their conversation meandered around, mostly coming back to family, which made Destiny like Marcus even more. Marcus lived with his mom and grandmom, and his med tech salary took care of a lot of household expenses.

"So I'm graduating with my associate's degree in a few weeks," Destiny worked up the courage to say. "And my parents are having a graduation party for me. I'm going to invite a few folks from work. Daddy's going to work the grill, and whatnot. Mama's making a lot of food. Come if you want."

"Big congratulations! I'd love to come. Sure it's okay with your folks?"

"Yeah, sure." She'd just told Mama and Daddy some friends were coming. No one special. She'd leave it that way. No need to get their antennae up.

"Text me the time and address."

"Okay, great." She ducked her head and smiled.

"Another round?" Marcus stood to take her glass.

"Hey, now that I've had some liquid courage, maybe I'll try karaoke."

"Sure, I bet you're good." Marcus reached for her hand, and Destiny entwined her fingers with his, which felt really nice, and followed him inside. There weren't that many people in the karaoke corner at all. It would be like a personal karaoke session.

After getting another drink for each of them, Marcus went over to the machine. "So since we were talking about Bruno Mars the other night—" He pressed the button, and the song opened with clapping, then a deep bass rhythm, and then the irresistible dance song "Uptown Funk," and Marcus pretended to be Bruno Mars, singing about being "too hot," and it being Saturday night, and daring everyone to just watch. Marcus was a great dancer, which didn't surprise her at all, since he'd talked about being an athlete. And after the champagne, Destiny couldn't help getting up to dance, too, and jumped up and gave Marcus a high five every time Mars sang "hallelujah."

A few other people in the bar got up and started dancing too. Sitting still wasn't easy with that song.

"For a hundred dollars, who wrote that song?" Marcus asked her at the end, when they were breathless, leaning against each other.

She cut a flirty glance at him. "You are definitely a music trivia guy. I guess it was Bruno Mars?"

"Mark Ronson and Bruno Mars, 2014. Half-credit."

"I'll take that. Okay, I'll do one." She went to the machine and right away picked "Girl on Fire," by Alicia Keys. The confidence she felt, knowing that she was graduating and that Marcus was coming to her party, fit the words, yes—on fire, and on top of the world. It was kind of embarrassing to try to sing the great Alicia Keys but, what the hell, they were having fun. She had fun stretching out the word "fire" at the end of that one line, making it "fi-yah!"

At the end, Marcus gave her a standing ovation, and a few of the other folks in the bar clapped, too, which was funny, and she and Marcus hugged.

They agreed to go outside to cool down, and Marcus grabbed a couple of ice waters. They sat down and Destiny pushed her braids back, wiping away the sweat that had popped out on her temples while dancing.

"You never told me what you're majoring in," Marcus said.

"Oh, English. Which is why I have to memorize those Langston Hughes's poems."

"So can you get a job as a teacher?"

"Not unless I go to more school." She took a long sip of the cool water, then plunged in with the truth. "Okay. So. I've applied to nursing school in Durham." Her heart kind of burned when she said this, and she immediately wished she hadn't.

"Durham? You mean you'll move?" Marcus's face dropped. "But we just met."

"I'm not sure I'm going. I haven't even heard whether I've gotten in yet."

"Oh. Will you quit your job at Bristlecone?"

"I haven't decided anything." She swirled the ice in her glass.

"Go to nursing school here in Eden Forest. Then I can still see you."

"You mean you wouldn't keep seeing me if I moved to Durham?" Destiny's throat felt tight. She couldn't believe they were having this conversation on literally their first real date.

"Oh, we could, sure." Marcus ducked his head and took a long drink of water. "My car is pretty old."

"Even if I got in, I wouldn't go until the fall."

"Sure. Hey, you asked if I would listen to your poem—Langston Hughes? Want to do it now?"

"Oh, let's do that next time. I'm not in the mood."

"Okay, sure." He wasn't meeting her eyes now.

Would there even be a next time? Oh, God, why had she even mentioned nursing school?

CHAPTER 16
JENNIE

Jennie opened her computer the day after the writers' meeting to input the changes that the group had suggested for her piece and saw a new email from the publisher she'd queried a few weeks ago. She could read the first few words of the message in the preview:

```
Thank you for giving us a chance to
consider…
```

She would have to open the message to read the rest.

Jennie sat with both hands in her lap, unmoving. She was sure the entirety of the message was: *"Thank you for giving us a chance to consider your work. Unfortunately, your manuscript was not a fit for our list. Best of luck with your writing, etc., etc."* She was so sure, in fact, that she didn't open the email. She didn't feel like a rejection today. She would open it later. Or maybe even delete it.

She went to her manuscript and, with Sir Arthur

purring on her lap, began methodically inputting the changes. The group had been subdued after Willoughby's abrupt exit; the whole situation with her had been odd. Jennie had never known Willoughby to be anything less than completely gracious and poised, including at Margaret's funeral. Yesterday had been a side of her she'd never seen. It seemed as though Willoughby had a panic attack.

Jennie had experienced one of those herself at Michael's funeral. She'd felt so overwhelmed by all the people approaching her, hugging her, expressing condolences, so stunned by the enormity of the hole that Michael's loss had left, the finality of him being gone forever, that she had raced out of the funeral home parlor to a back porch, where she'd tried to get some air.

Elijah followed her to the porch, where she leaned over the railing and took deep breaths of the crisp fall air, ignoring the bare oaks and the blanket of brilliant orange leaves just below the porch.

"Mom, what's wrong?"

Jennie tried to catch her breath, shaking her head. "I just had to get out of there. I broke out in a cold sweat, people were crowding in on me, my heart was beating out of my chest, and I thought I would faint."

Sweet Elijah had put his arm around her, though tears were running down his own cheeks, and stayed with her, his warm body next to hers, until she regained her composure.

The memory made her decide to reach out to Willoughby. She'd never really reached out to her before, mostly because Willoughby always seemed so confident and composed, like such a leader. But maybe now she could help.

Be prepared, came Michael's voice. *She might decline.*

"I know, Michael, but I just have a gut feeling I need to reach out." She didn't want to invite her to the apartment for dinner. Since Michael died a year and a half ago, she'd only entertained in her apartment once—other than lunches and dinners for Elijah and Amanda, which didn't really count—and that was for the Bristlecone book club, which she'd signed up for long before he died.

Several people had offered to host for her, but she'd been determined to see it through, thinking that getting food, flowers, arranging seating, and writing up discussion questions could distract her from her grief. It had in fact been a total disaster. The book club members had been so kind, many writing emails the following day thanking Jennie for the lovely evening, even though she knew it had been a mess. Somehow, the kindness of people made her feel her grief all the more.

Willoughby answered on the second ring.

"Hi, Willoughby, I just wanted to call and see how you're doing. I was a little worried about you yesterday."

Willoughby drew in a breath. "Oh, Jennie, thank you. I'm perfectly fine, please don't worry. You're sweet to call."

"Well, you seemed upset, so I was wondering, would you like to go for a walk or something and then pick up some lunch, either here at Bristlecone or at one of the cute places downtown? I know you've had challenges lately with Gary, and I wanted you to know that I had a panic attack once, at Michael's funeral, really, and so I do understand when things seem to be too much."

"Well, that's really thoughtful, Jennie. I'm really fine, but I'd love to get together. That would be fun. Thank you. Let's see, what time is good?" Willoughby's voice sounded suddenly more vulnerable.

"Ten thirty on Monday?" Jennie hoped Willoughby

would be okay with eating lunch at Bristlecone so her budget wouldn't be stretched.

Two days later, on Monday morning, Willoughby was prompt, appearing right on time beside the bristlecone pine tree in the back courtyard as the sun slanted through its branches. The two women both wore deep-pocketed shorts for their phones, loose yoga tops, and bright walking shoes, and they both carried water bottles.

"Want to walk around Bristlecone and then do the greenway loop through the woods?" Jennie asked. "That's about an hour."

"Perfect."

Willoughby's long legs kept Jennie going at a fast pace. They started out talking about all the health benefits of walking—both physical and mental.

"I walk almost every day," Jennie said.

"Me too! We should do this more often."

As they wound around the Bristlecone campus, they commented on some of the additions provided by the present management, some of which they agreed with, some of which they didn't.

"Look at the tennis courts—they've repainted them for pickleball and there are *so* many pickleball players," Jennie said as they passed. Every court was full, with people swinging and running, their shoes squealing, balls flying over nets and making that perky, hollow, popping noise.

"I play sometimes, do you?"

"No, I have arthritis, and I'm too afraid of a knee injury. Also, the sound of the ball drives me crazy. I'm a yoga girl."

"I've heard other people complain about that." Willoughby laughed. "It doesn't bother me."

"Hey, isn't that Roy, Margaret's husband?" Jennie indicated a man wearing bright red shorts and electric orange shoes with a faded gray NC State T-shirt hugging his round stomach. He zigzagged around the court, serving flamboyantly and volleying with three women, two of whom seemed fit, the third of whom looked nearly ready to drop.

"It is!" Willoughby looked at Jennie with her mouth hanging open, and they watched him practically knock his partner down to reach for a shot. "Well, he doesn't appear to be suffering too much."

"Side-out!" Roy yelled as he won the point.

Jennie looked at Willoughby and laughed. It seemed she'd been laughing at Roy's expense a few times too many lately, first with Alli and now with Willoughby, but honestly, wasn't he bringing it on himself? She shook her head. "I said before, I won't pass judgment. People grieve in different ways."

Fortunately, Roy was far too busy rallying to see them, so they walked past and headed for the oak-lined greenway. Jennie told Willoughby about the time she and Alli were having lunch and both got calls from Roy asking them out.

"Haha, I feel left out!" Willoughby chuckled. "I'm the only woman in the writers' group he hasn't hit on."

"Well, to be honest, Willoughby, he may be aware you already have a husband in the building."

Willoughby laughed, a bit ruefully. "I know, you're right. In fact, I have two."

"Oh, that's right."

Willoughby waved her hand. "More on that later."

"Okay. How is Gary, by the way?" Jennie hoped Michael

approved of the subtle way she'd led up to this topic and hadn't pressed on the "two husbands" issue, though she was definitely curious how it was going.

Willoughby shook her head as they headed off the Bristlecone property into the suburban neighborhood that led to the greenway, with its neat, renovated mid-century modern homes and treed yards. "Not good. He's been throwing things at the staff, throwing things at me, yelling, refusing to eat, losing his temper. He's so angry about what is happening to him. He won't take a shower unless I'm there."

"Oh, Willoughby, that must be really hard." Jennie touched Willoughby's arm briefly as they walked. The writers' group had never addressed this topic. They had talked about many things, but often deep feelings were disguised as the feelings of characters. In a way, writing fiction was therapy, but in another way, it sometimes had an effect of removing the real gut punch of "this has happened to me."

"Oh, when I think about him. Us. How we were. To compare him to who he was before—I can't. It really is devastating."

"I'm so sorry."

They walked along the paved greenway path leading into the woods in silence for a few minutes, saying hello to some harried parents with a double stroller and twin infants swaddled in pink, an energetic goldendoodle, and a determined toddler on one of those tiny bikes, using his feet to push his way along. Then they had the path to themselves, and Jennie enjoyed the dogwoods, the mimosa trees, and the blackberry flowers alongside the trail, as well as the shade from the piney woods.

"I won't complain, because I chose this, I chose Gary. I was absolutely crazy about him. I remember our meeting and I still get goosebumps. And we are married, for better or for worse, in sickness and in health. But dementia is so hard."

"Oh yes, it must be terrible." Jennie nodded and thought about the irony that Willoughby still had her husband alive, yet he was so changed, not able to be a partner, not ever going to get better, and Jennie's was gone forever. Would she trade places with Willoughby?

As if reading her mind, Willoughby went on. "I know you can't ever see your husband again, so I feel absolutely awful when I compare my situation to yours."

"Don't feel bad, Willoughby. Both struggles are equally tough." Jennie settled in to listen.

"Well, I go to see Gary every afternoon. They do tell me he actually behaves better when I'm not around. And my first husband, who's recovering from the Whipple procedure for pancreatic cancer, has just moved to Bristlecone, because my daughter asked me to get him in, and I did. But now I've visited him, too, a few times, to help my daughter, who's pregnant and also has a toddler."

"Oh, my, Willoughby. You're essentially taking care of two husbands."

"Yes, it's definitely crazy." Willoughby shook her head. "But visiting Steven isn't unpleasant. He's another adult, he understands me very well, and I still love him as the father of my children."

"Of course."

"Oh my, Jennie," Willoughby said suddenly, "I am going to have to duck into the woods for a bathroom break, I am so sorry." She seemed distressed but gave a nervous laugh. "Could you watch the path to see if anybody's coming?"

"Sure, it looks clear now!"

Jennie waved her behind a large poplar with a thick

trunk. Jennie saw a flash of white as Willoughby yanked down her shorts, then craned her neck to look both ways down the path. Suddenly, voices sounded just around the corner and five brightly clad bikers in Lycra barreled toward her, talking at the top of their lungs about a guy who'd been convicted of crypto crimes.

"Willoughby—bikers!"

There was absolutely no time; they were coming at breakneck speed and Willoughby wiggled around but could not get her shorts up fast enough. Jennie was pretty sure all five bikers got a prime view of Willoughby's stark, White ass as they whizzed by.

Jennie gasped, then covered her mouth, laughing when she saw that Willoughby was laughing as well.

"Oh my God, I guess I flashed them!"

"You flashed them as they flashed by!"

Jennie and Willoughby stood on the path holding their stomachs, weak with laughter. They couldn't stop.

Sitting at the table together on the patio outside the Bristlecone dining room about an hour later, Jennie ate her usual summer salad and Willoughby had a protein bowl.

"I am sorry about leaving the meeting Friday," Willoughby said. "I think you're right; it was a panic attack. Maybe brought on by the caretaking for both husbands. Tell me what happened during the rest of the meeting."

Jennie gave Willoughby a quick summary of what everyone had shared. Willoughby agreed with Jennie that Alli was a wonderful addition to the group. "Have you had any news about any of your submissions? I've had crickets."

"Well," Jennie said slowly, "I did have a response to my submission to a small publisher. But I didn't open it."

Willoughby sat back, her eyes wide, pushing her bangs from her forehead. "Jennie! You didn't open it? What's the matter with you?"

Jennie laughed. "I didn't want another rejection. To be quite honest, I just wanted it to sit out there in the ether and still be a possible 'yes.'"

Willoughby nodded in deep agreement. "I know what you mean, truly." But now she held a finger up. "But I believe in your writing, and we are going to go on your phone right now and open that email."

Jennie got goosebumps. "Oh, Willoughby, that's okay, I can open it later, I appreciate your support. Besides, I forgot to bring my phone." She patted her pockets to demonstrate.

"No, Jennie." Willoughby slapped her hand on the table and stood. "Then we are going to your apartment, and we are opening that email right now."

Jennie could feel herself flushing—her delight at having Willoughby so in her corner was a bit euphoric—and she stood too. Her support really did feel good.

Willoughby strode out of the dining room, and as they left, Jennie happened to see Roy, sitting alone at a table, still in his pickleball clothes, eating lunch. But he wasn't eating; rather, he was sobbing over his plate, his wrinkled, sodden napkin spread over his face.

Jennie's heart contracted with compassion. Yet, his pain seemed too intense and private to interrupt, so she didn't stop.

She led Willoughby through the side door and down the hall to her apartment. Her hand shook a little as she put the key in the lock. The email was certainly a rejection, and how would that feel, with Willoughby standing by? Even more deflating than usual. Willoughby would be supportive, but it wouldn't erase the defeat.

This was such a bad idea. And she certainly didn't want to hear what Michael might have said.

Jennie led Willoughby into her apartment, and of course Sir Arthur, right at the door, wanted to investigate and wove around both women's legs, meowing, as they came in.

"That's Sir Arthur."

"Not a fan of cats, I'm afraid. I'm allergic."

"Sorry, that means he will bother you even more."

Jennie led Willoughby into her office, shutting Sir Arthur out.

She found the email. "Ready?"

"Go for it."

Her hand shaking, Jennie clicked.

Dear Ms. Jennie Rossi,

Thank you for allowing us to consider *Renegade Priestess: A Story of Enheduanna.* Our publisher, Kathryn Arroyo, would like to call you next Monday at 3:00 p.m. Eastern time. Please let us know if you are available.

Best...

"Oh my God!" Willoughby screamed. "The publisher is going to call you!"

Jennie, her entire body flooding with disbelief and joy, stood up and Willoughby enveloped her in an impulsive hug. They jumped around the room screaming like teenagers.

"What does that mean?" Jennie, breathless, finally said to Willoughby. "That's next week, right? Not today?"

They both peered at the email again. "Yes, next week. Well, she's not calling you to talk about the weather! She must be interested in your manuscript. Tell her yes, Jennie. Right now."

"Okay. You're a true friend, Willoughby." Jennie sat down because she felt dizzy. The surreal nature of the moment settled onto her and sank through her bones.

CHAPTER 17
ABE

Abe thought this was the place. It was a small storefront displaying a logo with the theatrical masks of comedy and tragedy, and the name of the troupe, EF Players, lettered with artistic flamboyance. A potted pink geranium in a decorative cement planter bloomed by the door.

It was Tuesday evening, four days after writers' group, and Abe couldn't believe he'd let the women talk him into doing something he'd had no intention of doing. Especially Alli. Snippets of that guilt-inducing interaction they'd had a few days ago near the bristlecone pine about the breakup kept flashing through his head. He'd even given Solomon a bath, so he'd be looking his best for the audition. Abe decided now that even if Solomon got the part, he would decline it. Like Groucho Marx, who didn't want to be a member of any club that would accept him.

Solomon, eager for anything, wriggled so hard to get to the ground after being let out of his carrier that Abe had difficulty attaching the leash. Abe allowed Solomon to pull him around to the side of the building, where he saw about a dozen people standing in the alley holding small dogs in their arms. There were two pugs, about five or six chihuahuas, a Norwich terrier, a Yorkie, and maybe a Maltese—Abe didn't know dog breeds that well. A dark-haired, seemingly no-nonsense young woman with a clipboard appeared to be in charge, instructing people where to stand and wait, and taking notes of the dogs' and owners' names and contact information.

Solomon raced to join the people and other dogs with unbridled joy, jumping on the woman with the clipboard. Well, obviously stage fright wasn't going to be an issue for Solomon.

"Hi, I'm Mary, the stage manager. So, what's your name, little guy?"

"This is Solomon."

"And Solomon is trying out for Bruiser?"

"I suppose. There's a role for a chihuahua, I heard." Abe felt ridiculous.

"Yes, that's Bruiser." She smiled at Abe, a little patronizingly, he thought, maybe because he wasn't familiar with the play.

Several attractive, high-energy actors came out into the alley, one of whom was a petite young woman with a beautiful smile, freckles, and blonde hair. She bent over to pet Solomon, who jumped all over her as though they were long lost friends.

"You must be trying out for Bruiser!" said the young woman.

"That's right," said Abe.

"I'm playing Elle Woods," she said. "Bruiser's my little poopsie woopsie!" She let her voice go to a high register, which Solomon seemed to adore.

"Oh!" Abe made a mental note to look up the novel, or

maybe the movie, so he wouldn't seem so ignorant. He'd been rather snobbish about the play itself, since he thought it was partly a send-up of academia, but could see now that he needed to educate himself better. Otherwise, he would really seem like an outsider. Not to mention the fact that this delightful young woman, young enough to be Abe's granddaughter, was quite friendly toward Solomon.

Solomon was now running from one person to another, jumping on everyone, pulling on the leash. The other dogs were relaxing in their owners' arms, much better behaved, while Solomon greeted every person present.

"He's like a politician," Mary joked, smiling at Abe. Then she turned to the group. "Let's get a video of each of the dogs." Mary tapped the record feature on her phone. "When I focus on you, just introduce your dog and tell us or show us what tricks your dog knows."

Tricks? Solomon didn't know any tricks. He didn't even know any commands. He didn't even know "sit." He barely knew his name. Abe watched with a sinking heart as the owner of the two pugs demonstrated their ability to do back flips.

Why did he suddenly care whether Solomon got this role or not? The whole thing was silly.

When Solomon's turn came, Abe let the actor playing Elle hold him. "This is Solomon," he said. "His only trick is sticking out his tongue, which, as you can see, he's doing now." The cast members seemed to think the tongue trick was adorable and required every bit as much talent as back flips.

"So does he bark?" Mary asked.

"Almost never," Abe assumed that would be a positive thing, since they wouldn't want Bruiser backstage yapping throughout the production. Plus, it was true. Solomon had probably barked six times in Abe's memory.

"Oh," Mary said. "Bruiser has to bark twice in the play."

"Oh, well, I don't know how I'd make that happen." Abe was so nonplussed about this barking failure he completely forgot to employ Alli's suggested line about Solomon being a Gemini vegetarian.

"Okay, thanks, everyone." Mary said. "We'll be in touch."

"When?" Abe was used to firm deadlines.

"Soon."

Was that it? The entire audition?

"Time for rehearsal," Mary said. And with that, the charming actors went back inside to resume rehearsals and Solomon's audition was over.

Solomon, ecstatic about all his new friends, tried to follow them, pulling on the leash, then looked yearningly at the closed door where all the fun, high-energy actors had disappeared. Abe shuffled back to his car, along with the other dog owners, eventually having to pick up Solomon, who had clearly loved the attention and was reluctant to leave. Abe wished he was as extroverted as his dog.

"Come on, Solomon, let's go home." The whole thing had been ridiculous. Driving home with Solomon resting his head disconsolately on his lap, Abe became furious at himself for letting Alli talk him into it. Especially since she appeared to be angry with him. Once home, Solomon seemed to know that he had failed and curled up in his bed, his back to Abe. Over the next two days, Abe checked his email several times, chiding himself for even caring. The stage manager hadn't even given a firm date for her decision. She'd said only "soon." How unprofessional was that?

On the third evening after the auditions, Abe sat in his

den with his glass of cabernet, reading about previous productions of the play. Many of the reviews characterized the movie as a campy and masterful sendup of stereotypes, and Reese Witherspoon's performance as brilliant. Abe finally broke down and watched the movie. While he made it a rule to never watch silly movies, he had to admit that *Legally Blonde* was very clever and purely delightful. It did spoof stuffy know-it-all professors and intellectuals like, well, ahem, like himself.

In today's world, with memories of COVID, the political situation, the wars, and so many people suffering, it seemed almost irresponsible to be focused on something as silly as this play. Yet, Abe had to admit, it was a refreshing and welcome change.

Abe told himself that he didn't really care if Solomon got the role or not. It had been a rather enjoyable experience to audition, and had gotten him out of his comfort zone, but wouldn't it actually be a relief to *not* get it? The barking failure could have clinched that. He didn't want to spend all those evenings at rehearsal, anyway. It would cut into his writing time.

That third evening, Abe had just finished watching *Legally Blonde* when he received an email from Mary, the stage manager.

Thank you for bringing Solomon to audition for *Legally Blonde: The Musical*. We would like to offer the role of Bruiser Woods to Solomon, and we will fill you in on more details, should he accept.

. . .

Solomon had been offered the part! All of Abe's competitive instincts kicked in and his first reaction was triumph. Abe jumped to his feet and impulsively swung Solomon around in a circle, which completely confused the poor dog, who struggled to get back to ground level. His next impulse was to call Alli and tell her. But he remembered how angry she'd been about him writing about their breakup. He didn't know where they stood with each other, actually.

"Solomon, boy, you were offered the part!" Abe knelt and scratched Solomon's head and ears as he sat in his bed. "You won the part. Do you want it?"

Solomon looked up at him, his brown eyes wide and his tongue sticking out. He seemed ready for anything, whatever it might be. But did Abe want to be obligated to drive over to the theater every night for who knows how long? And what if Solomon urinated on the stage?

Abe weighed the pros and cons.

True, Solomon seemed to love being with all those young people. And somehow it might be a way to reconnect with Alli.

But all in all, Abe felt like he was just a lonely old man with a dog. Weighing everything, this whole idea was absurd. Just the idea of doing it seemed so undignified. Abe decided that he'd follow his initial instincts and decline.

On Solomon's behalf, of course.

CHAPTER 18
WILLOUGHBY

Willoughby was already late for Friday writers' group, but she still dragged her feet as she crossed the scrubby Bristlecone courtyard.

As excited as she'd been for Jennie, she was struggling mightily with the green-eyed monster. Willoughby had published a book, yes, but she'd never once been called by a publisher. Try as she might to quell them, waves of jealousy enveloped her whenever she thought about Jennie's upcoming call on Monday. She'd disguised her envy around Jennie, of course, and didn't want a soul to know about it, but the feelings made her stomach roil to the point of nausea.

"You're in your seventies," she told herself. "Be happy for your friend. Get over this juvenile reaction." But self-talk didn't seem to help.

Frankly, she had considered not going to the writers' group at all, due to her embarrassment about racing out last week. But if there was anything that life had taught her, it was to persevere. She'd go back and face the music, whatever it was. Dammit, she was not a quitter. And she'd be a cheerleader for Jennie. She'd encourage her to tell the group about her mysterious upcoming conversation with the publisher. It would give everyone hope, Willoughby included.

She stopped to say hello to Destiny as she headed for the stairs. "How are you today, Destiny?"

"Pretty good." Destiny gave her a broad smile. Willoughby wondered if it had anything to do with spending time with that nice-looking med tech from the health center. She'd seen Marcus and Destiny together once or twice—they did seem to be trying to keep it low-key, but there was definitely electricity, and flirtation along with it. Willoughby prided herself on noticing things like that, such as the energy between Abe and Alli. But Willoughby didn't want Destiny to think she'd been spying on her, so she didn't mention it. Marcus seemed like a very compassionate and caring young man.

"One thing I wanted to say about Miss Margaret's list of books, Miss Willoughby," Destiny offered, opening a photo on her phone. "At the bottom of that sheet of hers is a series of numbers. I've been trying to figure out what those mean. Could they be a code, maybe to one of the buildings or conference rooms at Bristlecone?"

Willoughby looked carefully and did see five numbers. "Well, I know the passcodes to the health-care unit and the memory-care unit, and that's not them. And it's not the conference room upstairs either."

"Well, maybe a different passcode? Just in case you all are still trying to figure this out."

"Oh, we are, and I think we're going to talk about it today. Is there any chance you could join us for a few minutes and we could talk about it?"

Destiny looked at her watch. "I get off today at four. Would you all still be meeting then?"

"That'll work perfectly. Thank you so much for taking an interest."

"Sure. See you in a couple of hours."

Everyone was already gathered around the scarred, sun-faded table when Willoughby arrived. Jennie, bless her, smiled a welcome and empathetic greeting, giving Willoughby the courage to stride in with almost her usual confidence, catching the tail end of the conversation.

"Well, I'm not sure about it," Abe was saying. "I have to let them know by the end of the day today."

"You have to do it!" Alli said. "What do you have to lose?"

"My self-respect?" Abe said, wryly, laughing, but glancing at Alli with a bit of hesitation.

"Do what?" Willoughby asked as she took her seat. "Oh, and I hope someone remembered to grab that egg timer last week."

"I got it." Alli pulled it from her small satchel and gave it to Willoughby. "Though I'll give it back to you as you're our leader. I don't want the responsibility that comes with it." She winked, then smiled at Willoughby.

Well, apparently showing weakness wasn't always catastrophic. Willoughby relaxed a little. She glanced over to see if Abe was equally as forgiving as the women, but his eyes were only on Alli, as Willoughby had noted last week. Did Alli realize?

"So sorry to interrupt, fill me in," she said.

"I took my dog Solomon to audition for the community theater play, *Legally Blonde: The Musical*, and they offered him the part. I have to let them know today if Solomon will do it."

"Your dog is going to be in *Legally Blonde?*" Willoughby couldn't help a chuckle. Pompous Abe with a showbiz dog. What a funny concept! In truth, Willoughby thought it would be a wonderful thing for Abe.

"He's been offered the part of Bruiser Woods. As his agent, I am considering the offer," Abe said, with mock grandiosity. "I might add that I had never heard of *Legally Blonde* until last week. I'd like to thank you, Alli, for encouraging me to do it."

"Bruiser Woods! My daughter, Courtney, watched that movie a hundred times and can quote entire speeches from it," Willoughby said. "Elle Woods is one of her heroes."

"I think it's a complete no-brainer," Jennie said.

"I could not agree more," Alli said, smiling at everyone. "Abe, you can't say no."

Abe shrugged. "It is somewhat of a commitment—two weeks of rehearsals as well as two weeks of performances." He glanced at Alli again. "Maybe I will say yes."

Willoughby sure wished Gary would still look at her the way Abe looked at Alli. But of course, her situation was so different, and Gary couldn't help what was happening to him. He had actually looked at her that way for many years. She shouldn't forget that.

Willoughby set out the timer, then, and they read their pages. As the group had gotten to know each other a little better, maybe since experiencing the trauma of Margaret's death together, their comments for one another were kinder and possibly more knowing, caring, and less formal than in the months before but no less constructive. Willoughby had not written anything, because she'd had a bad week. But Abe and Jennie and Alli had all had productive weeks. Jennie had written two chapters, so she must have been particularly inspired after the boost of the email from the publisher. As the meeting wound down, in fact, Willoughby waited for Jennie to mention her news.

"Does anyone have anything else to share?" Willoughby tried not to look pointedly at Jennie. "Any writing news?"

Jennie locked eyes with Willoughby, with a slight smile, and Willoughby tried to decipher her wordless message. Don't bring it up? Or was she saying, will you share it, rather than me?

"Jennie, do you—" She didn't want to overstep if Jennie wasn't ready to share.

"Yes, I guess I have some news," Jennie said a bit softly.

"What news?" Abe sat up straighter, turning to Jennie.

"Yes, tell us!" Alli leaned forward, her eyes sparking.

Jennie looked down as she turned her pen over and over. "A publisher is calling me on Monday." She ran her hand through her bristly hair and her face flushed. "At three o'clock."

"Brava!" Everyone cheered for Jennie, and Willoughby smiled despite her jealousy.

"Thank you all for cheering me on," Jennie said. "I am completely overwhelmed by this."

"Tell us about the publisher," Alli asked. "Small? Large?"

"They publish about a hundred books a year. I submitted to them because my manuscript seemed to be a good fit with the historical fiction they publish."

A soft knock came on the conference room door, and Destiny peeked in.

"I just got off. Is now good?"

Willoughby waved her in, and she sat in the empty chair beside Jennie. "Hi, Destiny, thanks for coming. Everyone, I asked Destiny to join us because she's got some ideas about that sheet of paper we found in Margaret's briefcase."

"Right, so..." Destiny pulled out her phone again and zoomed in on the five-digit number at the bottom of Margaret's book list, then showed the screen to everyone. "I didn't really pay attention to this number when I first saw the list. I mean, I agree with you all that this is definitely a list of banned books, but what does this number mean? I was wondering if it might be the code to a safe's lock. Miss Willoughby also suggested it could be a passcode, and I agree."

"So how do we find out?" Abe asked.

Just then, a hard knock came on the conference room door, and Roy, wearing his pickleball clothes, barged in, carrying a rumpled sheaf of papers. "Hey, sorry to interrupt, but I know y'all meet on Friday afternoons, and I had to talk to you."

"Hey, Roy," Willoughby said.

Abe sighed.

Roy plopped in the seat at the end of the table and clapped the yellowed papers down in front of him. "I found this story Margaret wrote. 'Course, she wrote for a long time, and I was married to her, but I never read anything of hers. I figured...well, I don't know what I figured. It was her hobby. I went fishing and golfed, she wrote. But her sister, Eunice, said she wanted to come over and get some things, so I started going through the stuff in the spare bedroom, where she used to write. I picked up this book called *Lady Chatterley's Lover*, and these pages fell out of the back of it, and it was a story that said, 'By Margaret Tinker.'"

"Oh my goodness," Willoughby said. "Did you read it?"

"Yeah, I started reading it. And I don't know if anything is good or not, but I'd like to know if y'all think it's worth beans? Do y'all think I could publish it, or enter it into a contest?" He grinned and shrugged. "Maybe I'd win some money. Some of those contests have pretty big prizes."

A silence, like the buzzing silence before the singing of the national anthem at the Super Bowl, ensued. The group looked at each other. Willoughby immediately knew that Jennie, Alli, and Destiny were thinking exactly the same thing: Margaret's list of banned books.

Willoughby took a breath, knowing that the others were waiting for her to speak first. Margaret hadn't really written anything for their group over the past year; she had only told somewhat disjointed stories, but she must have written quite a lot before they started meeting.

"So the story had been folded and placed in the back of *Lady Chatterley's Lover*?" Jennie asked casually. Roy nodded. "And when is Eunice coming to pick up the mementos she wants from Margaret's things?"

"Day after tomorrow—Sunday. Why?"

"Just curious."

"We're just about finished today, Roy," Willoughby started to say, but then Jennie, of all people, gave her a very direct look, and interrupted her.

"I may be speaking out of order here—but I'd like to welcome Roy to the group and, because it's late, I'd suggest that we stop over at your apartment, Roy, tomorrow morning, around ten, to take a look at the story and welcome you properly."

"With coffee and bagels. Or doughnuts. Or Danish. Or whatever you prefer," Alli added.

Roy grinned. "All of the above."

"Are we sure—" Abe started.

"Absolutely," Alli said, nodding vigorously in agreement with Jennie.

"We'll see you tomorrow morning, Roy!" Willoughby said cheerfully, glancing from Jennie to Alli and back.

"That's great!" Roy shuffled out of the room trailing a distinct scent of sweaty workout shoes.

As soon as the door closed behind him, Willoughby looked at Jennie and Destiny expectantly. "Well?"

"I think I know now what that list of banned books was all about. Margaret hid her stories in the back of the books on that list in her briefcase," Jennie said.

"Yes!" Willoughby saw it all now. "That's why she said, 'Everything is in here.'"

"But why would Margaret hide her stories?" Abe asked.

"I think it has something to do with her sister, Eunice," Willoughby said. "She made a point of telling Jennie and me at her memorial service that nothing Margaret wrote was true."

"Yes, I got the distinct impression that she didn't want people reading Margaret's work."

"Really?" Alli sat forward. "So maybe Margaret reveals something in her writing that Eunice doesn't want anyone to know?"

"Exactly," Willoughby said. "So tomorrow, some of us need to distract him while the rest of us find those banned books." She smiled at Jennie and Alli. "You two might need to pretend you want to date him."

"Anything for the cause," said Jennie.

Alli raised her fist.

"I have a thing, so I have to go," Destiny said, getting up and pocketing her phone. "Do you all want me to come tomorrow? I'm not working until the afternoon. I'd love to snoop around and see if they have a safe and if that code written on the sheet of paper works on the lock."

"We'd love it!" Alli said.

Destiny nodded and said, "See you then!" as she headed out.

Willoughby picked up the timer and put it into her briefcase. She glanced at Abe. "You've always said you wanted the company of another man in the group, Abe. Now you have one."

Abe grimaced.

After everyone left, Willoughby punched in the code to lock the conference room. She leaned against the door, looking at her watch. Time to visit Gary. It occurred to her that Gary, like Roy, had never read anything she'd written either. Her heart truly went out to Margaret for the very first time. The woman had spent her entire life writing, trying to communicate her truth to the world, and no one had noticed. In fact, some people, like her sister, Eunice, were actively trying to prevent Margaret's writing from ever seeing the light of day, for whatever reason. Margaret was essentially a person who had been silenced. Like a book ban.

Willoughby remembered the time during her career as a librarian, to her eternal shame, when she was in the throes of her first few weeks with Gary and not even thinking straight, that she'd knuckled under to a book banning committee and taken a book off a shelf at her municipal library and put it behind the desk, so it would have to be requested. She'd told herself she wasn't really banning the book, since it was officially still in the library. But in fact, she had essentially allowed that book to be banned by making a reader have to request it. The book was *Speak*. Thinking about that later, she'd been so ashamed she'd sworn to herself that she'd never knuckle under to a book banning committee again.

Steven had actually read most of Willoughby's early stuff. He claimed to love it, and declared how talented she was, but she'd never attached much value to his opinion, since he'd usually been stoned. Now she needed to reevaluate that. And in her marriage to Gary, the focus had unquestionably been on Gary at all times. That fact now shone like a beacon that she'd somehow never seen.

She headed over to memory care and input the code for the heavy door. Gary's door was open and Willoughby knocked lightly as she went in wondering, as always, which Gary she might find.

Gary wasn't in the chair, bed, or bathroom. Where was he? Maybe he had stayed at dinner longer than usual. She went out into the hall and looked up and down. Voices sounded from Mrs. Burns's room across the way. Was that Gary's voice?

Mrs. Burns's door stood slightly ajar. Knocking quietly, Willoughby pushed the door a few inches wider and peeked in.

Mrs. Burns's wheelchair sat empty beside the bed. On Mrs. Burns's narrow mattress, she and Gary lay together, holding hands and talking. Gary's silver head lay nestled next to Mrs. Burns's iron-gray pixie cut. What they were saying to each other made no sense to Willoughby.

"So, what do you think about the things that were on the tree?"

"I didn't stop. They were yelling at me."

They seemed to be talking at cross-purposes, about two separate topics, almost a word-salad, but they were chuckling, and the level of trust and caring brought Willoughby close to tears. Pain stabbed her heart so hard she had to grab the doorknob to keep her knees from buckling.

She froze.

Heart pounding, Willoughby made a lightning-quick decision. She pulled the door closed, very quietly, and raced down the hall, not at all sure where she was going. Sweat had broken out on her skin, almost as though she'd had a hot flash. Once outside, with the sun low in the sky, she walked with long strides across the courtyard and around the parking lot, her thoughts angry and jumbled, feeling faint. At one point, she stopped and leaned over to catch her breath.

People strolled over to the main building for dinner. Willoughby could not imagine having a conversation with a single soul right now, so she strode onto the wooded path that she'd taken earlier that week with Jennie, just to hide.

Walking along the path, her thoughts calmed and aligned themselves. Again, she ended up in the private courtyard where the stubby, dwarf-like bristlecone pine with the plaque stood. People in the retirement center liked to make fun of this pine; it was very old and very ugly. People joked that if this was what happened after one got old, maybe they didn't want to live so long. Willoughby sat on a bench across from the maligned tree.

Gary didn't know what he was doing. Willoughby sat and breathed. Mrs. Burns didn't know what she was doing either. Willoughby focused on continuing to breathe. They were like children, finding comfort in one another.

This disease was a horrible one.

Willoughby wiped the moisture from her cheeks. She had offered to stay with Clay tonight for Courtney, in about ninety minutes, and had to be on her toes. She glanced at her watch. This wasn't something she could talk about with Courtney. This honestly wasn't something she could imagine talking about with anyone. She sat on the bench across from the ancient bristlecone, breathed deeply, and tried to regain a measure of composure. Courtney had suggested a therapist. Maybe she should do that.

Through the trees, Willoughby noticed movement in the parking lot and glimpsed Destiny and the med tech Marcus getting into the back seat of a black Toyota. She looked away—she'd glimpsed them once before getting into a car together and certainly didn't want to be watching if they were going to be intimate. But the angle was such that if she got up and left now, they might see her.

She could get on the ground and crawl away, commando-style, but with her arthritis that would be a serious challenge. Her mind raced. Whatever was between Destiny and Marcus was none of her business. She vividly remembered a neighbor of her parents knocking on the car window when she was making out with her high school boyfriend in the driveway and telling her to go inside. She'd never forgotten how judged she felt.

She glanced over at the Toyota again. Destiny and Marcus weren't kissing. Instead, Destiny had pulled out a sheet of paper and was reading him something from it. He listened intently as her expressive hands braided the air. Somehow, this felt even more intimate than a kiss.

Willoughby creakily lowered herself to the ground, ignoring her aching joints. Commando-style it was.

~

"GiGi!" Clay jumped up and down in the front hall, side by side with Keanu, grabbing Willoughby around her thighs with contagious enthusiasm as she bent to greet him. Keanu barked in solidarity. Clay must have graduated from the "no pants" stage because he was wearing a cute pair of baggy shorts over his diaper. And his winsome curls were gone.

"Courtney! You cut his hair!"

Courtney came into the front hall, smelling of perfume, wearing a form-fitting cobalt blue maternity dress. Her freshly styled hair shone. "I did not cut his hair, Mom. Scott took him this time."

"Oh my gosh. He's not a baby anymore."

Courtney made a sad face. "He does look more like a little boy, doesn't he?" She laid her phone on the hall table. "I'll just go to the bathroom one more time."

Scott came into the hall carrying the car keys. "Honey, we're late already."

"I know, I'll be quick."

"I'll be in the car," Scott said. "Thanks, GiGi, as always," he added, giving Willoughby a heartfelt hug, and headed out to the garage.

Willoughby picked Clay up and turned in a whimsical circle as he wrapped his dimpled arms around her neck. "What should we do tonight, Big Guy?"

"*Very Hungry Caterpillar*!"

Courtney's phone rang. On the screen, it read "Dad." Steven calling.

Willoughby picked up. "Hi, Steven, it's Willoughby. Courtney just ran to the bathroom. She'll be right back. They're on their way out to dinner with some friends."

"Oh, hello there. You're babysitting, huh?" Steven seemed delighted to serendipitously speak to her. "How's life with you, Madam Librarian?"

Willoughby started to make a flippant response and

suddenly felt tears running down her cheeks. She drew a sigh and her voice broke. "Oh, fine."

"It doesn't sound fine."

"No, it's not, really." Willoughby could not explain her feelings as Clay, with a wide-eyed and puzzled look on his little face, wiped the tears from her cheeks with his small chubby fingers.

"No cry, GiGi. No cry."

Courtney rushed into the hall, straightening her skirt over her baby bump.

"It's your dad," she told Courtney.

"I'll call you later," she heard him say to her as she handed the phone over.

Courtney, excited to be getting out, exuberantly kissed Willoughby and Clay good-bye, then began to chat with her dad as she headed to the garage. Keanu tried to follow, but Willoughby grabbed his collar in the nick of time.

She and Clay and Keanu had a sweet evening together. She fixed Clay macaroni and cheese, and then they went for a walk around the yard with Keanu, naming plants and looking for chipmunks. And then Willoughby indulged her librarian self by reading Clay lots of her favorite children's books, which had always been her go-to gift for him. He was able to maintain concentration well for age two. They sang songs and Willoughby put him to bed, leaning over the crib railing and running her fingers over his silky cheek for a long time after his breathing became slow and even.

She finally went downstairs, and her phone sang out.

Steven.

Maybe she shouldn't answer. What would it accomplish to tell her first husband about her demented second husband's behavior? How could he sympathize? Did the fact he was calling mean that he still felt something for her?

Did he still love and care for her, after everything? She should just ignore the call. It really wasn't a good idea.

"Hi, Steven," she said.

"Hi, Madam Librarian. What's new at the library?"

"You mean behind the shelves?" This was a line of theirs from when they had been married. Amazing how they could slip so quickly into the old familiarity.

"Yeah."

"Steven, I'm sorry about what happened earlier. Gary isn't doing well. But I shouldn't involve you."

"I'm already involved. Hey, you got me into this facility, and I'm grateful for that. We share children. The least I can do is try to help you if I can."

"I don't think you can help." She started to cry again but wouldn't let him know that Gary had been in Mrs. Burns's room. And honestly, she believed it was a childlike thing, two suffering human beings connecting, lying in bed holding hands. She knew, in her mind, it was nothing more, that she was having an emotional response. She intellectually understood Gary's need for contact, though it didn't make it any easier. "But thanks, Steven, really. You were kind to call. How are you feeling?"

"Pretty good. The docs tell me that I'm graduating from rehab to assisted living in a few weeks. They said I'm a miracle. They never thought I'd make it. I think about that every day."

"That's fantastic, Steven."

"I'm learning all about being present in my life. I've started meditating."

"Really?" After all her years with Steven, this struck Willoughby as hilarious, and she belly laughed.

"Hey, nice to hear you laugh."

She realized she'd been crying when they first started to

talk, and now she wasn't. "You could always make me laugh."

"We had a serious connection, Madam Librarian. I mean, for twenty years, things were pretty good. And maybe..."

"Maybe what?" Her tone came out gruffer than she'd planned.

"Never mind. But anyway, Courtney said she and Scott could come and move me."

Willoughby started to offer to help but bit her tongue. Though she didn't want Courtney doing any heavy lifting, she had too much to do already. She was moved, though, by his unexpected support.

"Stop by sometime," he said after a pause.

"I will."

CHAPTER 19
JENNIE

Jennie did not want to be the first to arrive at Roy's and be alone with him, so she texted Alli and Willoughby and they walked over together, after stopping at the bakery counter in the breakfast room and picking up a pot of coffee and some very sinful-looking pastries to go. Destiny texted that she'd meet them at Roy's.

"How did you guess that Roy was a sucker for pastries?" Jennie asked, chuckling, as they headed across several courtyards toward Roy's building. Visiting families sat on the wooden benches with their loved ones on this warm Saturday morning.

Alli shrugged. "My Spidey senses."

"I mean, it was brilliant, he jumped right on it," Willoughby agreed.

"Is Abe coming?" Jennie asked.

"Abe had a continuing education seminar," Alli said. "He said he hopes we successfully complete the mission."

"Your mission, should you choose to accept it..." Willoughby said. "So, what is our plan? Do we want Roy to know we're looking for more of Margaret's stories? Or is someone going to distract him while the rest of us look?"

"I think we have to play it by ear," Alli said. "Our main goal is to not let Eunice take the stories. I mean, I take it personally. Silencing one of us is like silencing any of us."

"Yes—if she gets them, they'll never see the light of day," Willoughby said. "Talk about book banning." She was determined she would redeem herself from that long-ago mistake, born mainly from fear.

"Exactly."

Just as they arrived at the door of Roy's first-floor apartment, Destiny pulled up in her black Toyota and joined them as they rang the doorbell.

"It's exciting to have a secret mission," she said, her eyes twinkling.

"I know, right?" Willoughby said.

Roy came to the door: face red, hair slicked back, having just showered, presumably after pickleball. "Good morning, ladies!"

When Alli asked where to put the pastries, he led the three of them into his cluttered kitchen. It did not look like a dish had been washed since Margaret died last month. They were stacked sky high in the sink and empty pizza boxes covered the counters and the table.

"Roy, this won't do," Willoughby said in a mother's tone and immediately started gathering up cheese-smeared boxes. "When does your housekeeper come?"

"I don't know," Roy admitted. "Margaret took care of that. The housekeeper knocked on the door a couple times, but I couldn't talk to anyone."

Willoughby handed him the pizza boxes. "That was a mistake. Take these outside to the trash."

Roy obediently took the boxes, stacked nearly to his chin, and went out the back door to the garage.

"Should we lock him out?" Alli suggested.

Willoughby, Destiny, and Jennie burst out laughing.

Willoughby looked under the sink for a pair of rubber gloves. "Are we really going to do this, ladies?"

"I feel like we're in a Charles Dickens novel," Jennie said as she turned on the hot water, squeezed some soap in, and set out the dish drainer. "Where the heroine sacrifices herself to help the hero."

"Any time I do dishes it's self-sacrifice," Willoughby agreed.

Destiny, declaring that dishes were not her thing, nevertheless offered to share a playlist, and everyone danced to "Single Ladies (Put a Ring on It)" by Beyoncé, which Jennie had heard, and "A Bar Song (Tipsy)" by Shaboozey, which she hadn't. But once it started, she couldn't stop bouncing as she scrubbed the dishes. Then Destiny put on "9 to 5" by Dolly Parton, which they all knew, and "Shake It Off," by Taylor Swift, which they knew as well.

Jennie couldn't believe the four of them were dancing around Roy's kitchen having such a good time. Within twenty minutes or so, the sparkling dishes were drying in the drainer, the counter had been wiped clean, and the pastries and coffee were artfully arranged on the freshly polished kitchen table.

"Y'all didn't need to do this!" Roy exclaimed over and over.

"What do you take in your coffee, Roy?" Alli asked sweetly, seating herself. Jennie could've sworn Alli batted her eyelashes. "I'll fix it for you while you get that story of Margaret's."

Roy produced the story, and they huddled around the table, passing the pages around as they drank their coffee, not speaking much except to help each other decipher her spidery handwriting. It was a dream-like story about an old woman from the previous century, her mind winding through memories from when she was young, when girls dressed in white to be presented to society, had their choice of escorts, and were considered to be the belles of the town. Snippets of memories flashed by: the young debutante fell in love with one of her escorts, then spent a predetermined semester abroad, writing him letters nearly every day. But when she returned, her love was engaged to her sister, and for some reason, the young woman was forced to be the maid of honor at their wedding. Then the piece fast-forwarded as the woman later met a young man and married him, though through the decades she never got over her first love. All of them sat in amazed silence after they finished reading.

"What'd y'all think?" Roy said. "I'm no expert, but I thought it was darn good."

"The way Margaret flashed through sixty years of a woman's life in a ten-page story is indeed masterful," Jennie said. "The emotion in the story is powerful. Since Margaret never brought work in to read, I had no idea she could write like that."

"Damn, it was wonderful," Willoughby agreed.

The others, still stunned, agreed that the story was a small jewel, a masterpiece. As each of them praised Margaret's work, Roy became more excited. "So y'all think I could get it printed? Or win a contest?" His eyes went wide and sparked with anticipation.

"You can never predict what will or won't appeal to an

editor," Alli said. "We all think this story is beautifully wrought."

"I also think this is a story that Eunice might not want people to see. Roy, I'd love to see Margaret's workspace, wouldn't you all?" Jennie stood, winking surreptitiously at Alli, Destiny, and Willoughby.

"Sure." Roy led her to the kitchen doorway. "It's a mess —I'd just started putting the books in bags for Eunice but come on in."

"Just curious, why did Eunice want Margaret's books?" Alli asked as Roy led them into the spare bedroom where Margaret kept her spindly oak desk and bookcase.

Roy shrugged. "I don't know, but she asked for Margaret's briefcase, too, so I gave it to her. She said the briefcase and books belonged to their side of the family. I was thinking of turning this room into a workout area, so I didn't care."

The view from the window above Margaret's desk was of the gardens and woods surrounding Bristlecone. A flowering magnolia tree with thick, glossy leaves cast heavy shadows on the window.

Jennie took out her phone and pulled up Destiny's photo of Margaret's list of banned books and, after meeting eyes with Willoughby, Destiny, and Alli, read the first title aloud. "*Are You There God? It's Me, Margaret.*"

Alli ran her finger across the spines of a half dozen children's books, stopped on the Judy Blume book, featuring a preteen girl leaning down to adjust her shoe in a ladylike way, and withdrew it from the shelf. They all watched as, with trembling fingers, Alli opened the back cover.

Ten folded, handwritten pages slid into Alli's hands.

Everyone gasped.

Carefully, Alli opened to the first page. "A Tale of Two Cemeteries," she read. "By Margaret Tinker."

The three of them let out a whoop and Jennie couldn't help herself; she cut loose with an impromptu little dance.

"Is that another one?" Roy asked. "How did you know where to look?"

"Margaret made a list of books," Jennie said, showing him the screen of her phone. "When you found that other story inside one of the books on this list, we guessed there would be stories inside the other books on the list too. Let's do the next one—Orwell's *Animal Farm*."

Willoughby found the book, shelved alphabetically by author. She pulled it off the shelf and flipped to the back, revealing a third story by Margaret Tinker titled "A Southern Girl's Secret."

"This is fantastic!" Roy said. "Give me the next one."

"*Their Eyes Were Watching God*," Jennie said. "It should be shelved under H, for Hurston."

"Oh, one of my favorite books," said Destiny as she opened the closet door in the study and looked high and low, searching, Jennie guessed, for some kind of safe that could explain the five numbers on the sheet with the list of books.

Roy kneeled and searched one of the lower shelves, pulling out an old paperback with a gold cover featuring a wrathful God unleashing a storm on the earth. He gently dislodged a thin story entitled "The Ties of Sisters."

"Hmmm," Willoughby said. "Maybe that's another one Eunice doesn't want the world to see."

One by one, they found Margaret's stories inside the back of *Speak, The Hate U Give, The Catcher in the Rye, To Kill a Mockingbird, Charlotte's Web,, 1984, Animal Farm, The Bluest Eye, The Adventures of Huckleberry Finn, The Color*

Purple, This Book Is Gay, Me and Earl and the Dying Girl, Nineteen Minutes, and *The Absolutely True Diary of a Part-Time Indian.* Inside *Alice's Adventures in Wonderland* was no story but simply a small key on a string, being used as a kind of bookmark.

"Including *Lady Chatterley's Lover,* that's seventeen stories in all," Jennie said, counting them and smoothing her hands over the fragile handwritten pages. She held up the key. "And one unidentified key."

"You had no safes?" Destiny asked Roy.

"No." He shook his head.

"What about safe deposit boxes?"

He shook his head again. "Not that I knew about."

"Hmm," said Destiny.

"Imagine," said Alli. "This represents years of Margaret's work that really went completely unnoticed by anyone in her life."

Roy hung his head.

"I'm sorry, Alli didn't mean to single you out, Roy," Willoughby said. "No one did—we didn't pay enough attention to Margaret's work either."

"But now we can," Jennie said. "Everyone's voice deserves to be heard."

"Roy, if you wanted to submit any of these stories, they'd have to be typed. Can you type?" Alli asked.

"Oh, no. I'm a hunt-and-pecker."

Jennie exchanged glances with Willoughby and Alli and tried not to smile.

"Then, do you mind if we take the stories and get them typed up and saved on a computer?" Jennie said. "We'll be very careful with them, and we'll return them to you with printed copies. Plus, we'll email you the electronic copies for submission."

"Well, I guess that's a good idea. You all will be careful with them. I know I can trust you." Roy scratched his ear. "Eunice didn't put much stock in Margaret's writing anyway. She told me a few times that Margaret's stories were flights of fancy, and she hoped I didn't believe a word of them."

Willoughby headed for the door, obviously in a hurry to get the stories out of Roy's apartment. "Well, we better be going. Welcome to the writing group, Roy. Next week we'll have the stories typed up for you. And be sure, if you find any more, to bring them with you."

"Great to see you, Roy," Alli said, close on Willoughby's heels.

"Bye, Roy," said Destiny.

"Thanks for the pastries. Take care of Margaret's stories, and I'll see you next Friday," Roy called, seeming pleased to be part of the group.

"Bye now." Jennie clutched the stories to her chest and followed Willoughby and Alli. They waited until they had rounded the corner, out of Roy's line of sight, then high-fived each other.

"Yes!" They whooped like college cheerleaders.

"No time to lose," Jennie said. "Who's going to type these up?"

"Two take six, one takes five?" Alli suggested.

"Done," said Willoughby. "Did you find anything that helped with those numbers, Destiny?"

"No, ladies, I hate to say this, but I did not." She shrugged. "Maybe it was nothing. I still want to know what that key unlocks."

"We'll figure it out." Willoughby sounded confident.

"Yes, for sure. And Destiny," Jennie added, "the playlist was fantastic!"

"I'm going to have 'Put a Ring on It' and 'Shake It Off' earworms in my brain for a week," Willoughby said.

"Like that's a bad thing?" Destiny said, chuckling.

"Not in the least."

Jennie settled herself at her desk on Monday a little before three and opened the screen to her manuscript. Maybe Ms. Arroyo would ask her a question about it, and she'd need to quickly look something up. Sir Arthur, sensing her nervousness, paraded repeatedly across her desk, as if to reassure her, waving his tail in her face.

Try some deep breaths. Go to your happy place, came Michael's voice.

"I am in my happy place. With you. Sometimes I wonder though, do I even want success? Or do I really love my existence as a nonentity?"

At that moment, 2:59, Sir Arthur walked across Jennie's keyboard and a quick message flashed on her screen:

Are you sure you want to delete *Enheduanna Priestess* manuscript?

"Ahhh!" Jennie's heart convulsed as she screamed and swept Sir Arthur from the keyboard into her arms. She had another copy somewhere—in some file or another—but it wasn't the absolute latest she'd sent to the publisher. She dumped Sir Arthur to the floor. Blood thundered in her ears, and she broke out in a sweat as, fingers shaking, she tried to click the "No" option.

Another message appeared on the computer screen:

Enheduanna Priestess manuscript successfully deleted.
This file is recoverable for 30 days.

"Sir Arthur!" Jennie screamed again. "What are you doing to me?" Now she was completely in panic mode.

Sir Arthur rubbed up against her ankle, purring.

Then her phone rang. Jennie dropped her head into her hands. With a shaking finger, Jennie tapped to answer.

"Hi, it's Kathryn Arroyo. How are you, Jennie?" Her voice sounded confident and deep, and a bit rushed, as if Ms. Arroyo was short on time.

"I'm fine, thanks, Kathryn." Jennie gripped the phone hard and tried to relax, without much success, taking deep breaths. "Thanks for calling."

"Are you sure you're okay? You sound a little out of breath. Did I call at a bad time?"

"Oh, no, no, please, this time is perfect." Jennie wiped sweat from her temple and tried to read the tiny print instructing her on how to recover the file.

"Thanks for making time to talk with me, Jennie. And for thinking about our press when you sent us your manuscript. We found the subject matter of Enheduanna to be fascinating—very few people realize she was the first writer in history, male or female—and your writing and the storyline flowed beautifully."

"Oh, thank you. I am beyond thrilled that it resonated with you."

"Indeed, it did. You explored some very new ideas about Enheduanna's power, again, as a priestess and as a woman, about her struggle to maintain power, about her poetry, and of course about her sexuality. All subjects that will fascinate today's readers, most of whom don't even know she existed."

Jennie's head buzzed with the praise, yet she was on edge, wishing she could just have twenty seconds to figure out the file recovery procedure, and also listening for Ms. Arroyo to say "*But...*"

"So, what I'd like to tell you today is that...we want to publish your manuscript!"

"My manuscript...?" The manuscript that Sir Arthur had just deleted, *that* manuscript? Okay, wait, she had emailed it to them, it was still in her email. She could recover it there. Relief flooded her. Her shoulders relaxed. She felt she was regaining control of her sanity.

There was a thud as Sir Arthur knocked over Jennie's office trash can and crawled into it.

"Yes, you heard me right. We want to publish your manuscript. Staff members here have fallen in love with your book and insisted to me that, yes, this book needs to be on this year's list of spring releases. That means a very tight timeframe, releasing in March. So nine months."

"Oh my God."

"Sound doable? Are you sure you're all right?"

"Uh...I...I guess so." Jennie was sure other authors were more poised in moments like this. And probably had backup manuscript copies and office trash cans without cats in them. She stood up and began to pace.

"Just two requests. First, we need a bibliography as soon as possible so the fact checker can get to work."

"I could send one in a few days." She hoped she could do that.

"And we need a bio with details about your Iraqi heritage. I assume that you indeed have Iraqi heritage? Otherwise, in today's atmosphere, publishing this would be very tricky."

"Of course. Yes, my mother came as a child from Iraq in

1939, before World War II, and her family settled here in North Carolina. She married an Italian man, though, and then it just became easier for all of us to say we were Italian. And, for many reasons, we never really tried to clarify it." Jennie's thoughts raced. This was practically the first time she'd told that to anyone. Publishing this book meant that she would need to reveal to the writers' group, as well as everyone else she knew, that her mother's family was originally from Iraq. And that would include informing her son Elijah and his fiancée, Amanda.

"Interesting. We'll include that information in your bio —it gives you credibility. Well, you'll be hearing from our contracts person and your editor in the coming week. As soon as we get a contract signed, your editor will start making notes on some of the suggestions she might have for you to strengthen the manuscript even more. In the meantime, congratulations, Jennie, you've written a wonderful book and we're proud to publish it!"

Ms. Arroyo ended the call and Jennie sat down, stunned.

Congratulations, my love, came Michael's voice.

Jennie regretted more than she could say that he wasn't there to share this with her; it was what she'd wanted for so long.

Sir Arthur crawled out of the trash can and meowed at her.

The file! Jennie scooted her chair up to the computer and followed the instructions, and a few minutes later she had a recovered, renamed file. She made a backup file for good measure. She drew a breath of relief but still felt dizzy with all the excitement. Nearly stunned.

This was really happening.

CHAPTER 20
ABE

On Monday, Abe parked in the small front lot at the community players' rehearsal space. He sighed as he climbed out to get Solomon.

He was tired after a disconcerting morning appointment with his cardiologist, in which he was told to schedule a scan for calcium in his heart. He'd spent the afternoon moderating an online panel for the adult learning program in town, on the abysmal state of Middle Eastern relations. The panels were invigorating, making him feel as though he was still in the thick of teaching, but the present political landscape there was so depressing.

Talking about the Middle East roiled his feelings about a number of issues. Abe had not been a proponent of the 2003 Iraq war. Most of his more recent students before he retired hadn't even been alive at the time. It seemed like ancient history to them. Abe's previous loyalty to Israel, which he firmly believed had a right to defend itself, had been tested in recent years, he had to admit. The world was in such a state of chaos.

In the face of all that, had he really committed himself to this silly play?

He took Solomon out of his carrier and attached his leash. As soon as Solomon recognized where he was, he practically dragged Abe along, trying to get into the Eden Forest Community Players' rehearsal space, a glass-walled corner unit in a niche shopping strip. Amazing how a little dog could remember places so well.

There was still light in the evening this time of year. Red chrysanthemums grew in a planter beside the door. Singing and piano could be heard even before Abe followed Solomon inside, where actors rehearsed a campy song and dance number. Were they really singing about whether someone was gay or European? Apparently yes. They were belting it out at top volume. Abe assumed there had been several rehearsals already, since the actors seemed to know their parts. Solomon, he surmised, was like a prop, not needed until the last few rehearsals.

"Hold!"

The singers, dancers, and pianist halted and turned to face a grizzled, white-haired man with headphones, seated behind a table in the back of the room. "Elle, you need to cross to stage left along with the lyric. From the top. Let's try to get a run-through of the whole song."

The actress playing Elle, the cute, freckle-faced blonde who had bonded so immediately with Solomon, raced back to the side of the room that denoted offstage. She wore what appeared to be exercise clothing. Most of the other women rehearsing were somewhat scantily clad as well. Apparently, this wasn't a full-dress rehearsal. The pianist played a few introductory chords, and the scene started again.

No one greeted Abe, so he sat in a metal folding chair

below the table where the director sat. Solomon, on Abe's lap, was entranced. No one who walked by could possibly ignore Sol, who sought every person's eye and leaned in for a pat on the head. Another dog sat with his owner on one of the other metal chairs—the black pug who had done flips during auditions. So there were two dogs in the show?

Solomon seemed eager to make the pug's acquaintance, but the other dog seemed indifferent. Maybe it was a type of social pecking order, only with dogs. The pug was a bit larger and seemed to know more tricks than Solomon (easily accomplished since Solomon, in fact, knew none), but Abe didn't like the idea of Solomon being second best.

"And scene." The scene ended and the director gave more notes about what he called "blocking," which appeared to be where people were moving on the stage. "The tan dog is here now so let's start Act One from the top and try to do a full run-through."

Abe thought the director might possibly have said that the esteemed Dr. Abraham Goodman of the History Department was kind enough to be here with his talented dog, Solomon, but he decided to let it go. The man was clearly very busy.

The director squinted at Abe. "Bruiser has four scenes and a curtain call. The actors will come get him and then deliver him back to you after each scene. That'll give you time to get his costumes changed."

"Costumes?" Abe was afraid he'd inadvertently let his mouth hang open.

"Yes, we don't have anything in the wardrobe department for a dog, so you'll be on your own with that. And we unfortunately have lost our wardrobe mistress—she found a paying gig down in Charlotte."

Abe started to ask where he might obtain such clothing,

but the pianist launched into the energetic and blaring opening number, so Abe went over to the stage.

During the rehearsal, "Elle" came over just before Solomon's scenes and took him from Abe's lap, carried him around the stage while she sang and danced, and then brought him back to sit with Abe until his next scene. Solomon happily went with her, snuggling into her arms and watching all the other actors with his liquid brown eyes. He seemed to be enjoying himself thoroughly.

Abe had to admit, he was beginning to enjoy himself too. The singing, dancing, and clever repartee were mesmerizing.

By nine o'clock, the director called it a wrap. Only Act One had been rehearsed. Abe was beginning to understand why so many rehearsals were required. The stage manager, Mary, who had spoken to Abe during the audition, came over as the rehearsal broke up and the actors gathered their backpacks.

"Do you have any questions?" she asked as she scrolled through her phone.

"Actually, yes. Bruiser requires costumes?"

"Yes. Bruiser's first scene takes place in California, then he has two scenes that take place at Harvard, and a final scene in a courtroom when Elle is acting as a lawyer. Oh, and then he has the curtain call, when all the actors go onstage to take a bow," Mary told Abe. "So that's at least four costumes. Once we move to the rehearsal space, you'll be sitting offstage with Bruiser, and Elle will come get him, just like she did tonight. Any other questions?"

"Where would one obtain a costume for a chihuahua?"

"Mary!" the director called, waving a script. "Notes!"

"Gotta run—text me later." Mary darted away.

The actor playing Elle came to say good-bye to

Solomon, her backpack over her shoulder, blonde ponytail swinging. She petted his head and gave him a peck on the end of his nose. "Bye, Solomon, little man! You crushed it. See you tomorrow night." She flashed Abe a smile and sashayed out the door. Solomon wiggled in Abe's arms as though he wanted to go with her.

"You're too young for her, buddy."

Back at home, Solomon seemed rather tired and curled up in the bed that Abe had placed next to his desk and instantly fell asleep. Abe answered a few follow-up questions from that afternoon's Middle East panel about the two-state solution and scheduled the calcium test for his heart. Then he sat looking at his computer screen. Should he take a chance and write Allison an email asking for her help with costumes for Solomon?

He'd been racking his brain to come up with an excuse to contact her. This was perfect. After all, she was the one who'd encouraged this play nonsense. But would she even talk to him? She'd been slightly friendlier during the writers' group than during that regrettable encounter out in the courtyard. Possibly her feelings toward Abe had warmed after his apology. And obtaining costumes for a chihuahua was innocuous enough, and definitely not his area of expertise.

He looked up her email address from the writers' group email threads and began to compose what he thought could be read as a casual email.

Dear Allison,

I thought you might be entertained to learn that Solomon had his first rehearsal for *Legally Blonde* tonight. He seemed to enjoy himself quite a bit, though what male wouldn't enjoy being carried around in the arms of a beautiful young blonde?

He deleted the last sentence. That was clearly inappropriate. Even he knew that. After four or five more drafts, he finally came up with a message that seemed to carry the right breezy, friendly tone.

Dear Allison,

I thought you might be entertained to learn that Solomon had his first rehearsal for *Legally Blonde* tonight. He seemed to enjoy himself quite a bit. He has bonded not only with the actress who plays Elle, but also with almost the entire cast.

The play is a farcical send-up of academia, as well as a spoof on stereotypes, and I must admit that, at first, I was a bit offended but now am allowing myself to be open to the humor.

I do have an issue with which you might be of assistance: his costumes. I have been told that he needs a costume for each of five scenes: one in California, two at Harvard, one in a courtroom, and one for a curtain call. Do you have knowledge of a place to obtain such costumes? Since you are already familiar with the story, you would be the perfect person to assist Solomon in his efforts to play his part. I, of course, would reimburse you for any purchases or accompany you on any necessary shopping expeditions, though I generally tend to avoid retail establishments. He weighs eight pounds.

Sincerely yours,

Abe

He did not send the email right away, choosing to read it over and contemplate the tone several times. Did it seem too formal? Or perhaps too casual?

The third time he read it over he caught the fact that he'd mistakenly addressed her as "Allison" again. Oof! He must do better to get that through his head. He also realized that he sounded as though he did not want to accompany her to a retail establishment, when, in fact, getting together was the entire point of the email. The present phrasing made it sound as though he was asking her to run an errand for him. It could be a casual first date, could it not? So he deleted the phrase about avoiding retail establishments. Was it presumptuous to mention that Solomon weighed eight pounds, as though he assumed she would accept? He went back and forth on that and finally decided to leave it in.

He realized he was thinking about Alli in terms of how she might react to things quite a lot more than he had in college. Back then he hadn't thought much about her as a person at all. That was illuminating in itself. Age and his life experiences—with women especially—had changed him.

With that, before he could talk himself out of it, he sent the email. She probably would not answer for at least a few hours. She might not even still be awake; it was after ten.

When they'd dated, they used to stay up until two in the morning. He couldn't even remember what they were doing. Well, yes, he could. He went to bed and dreamed of those nights full of passion.

When Abe woke up the next morning, he immediately checked his phone, telling himself not to be too disappointed if she hadn't answered.

But there it was, an email from her.

```
Dear Abe,
    I would be delighted to help with
Solomon's costumes. There is a pet store in
Eden Forest Village called The Bark
Boutique that specializes in costumes for
pets.
    Should we meet there tomorrow afternoon
around 3:30? I know you probably need them
pretty soon. Bring Solomon with you so we
can make sure the costumes fit.
    Sincerely,
    Alli
```

Abe arrived fifteen minutes early at The Bark Boutique. He chided himself for seeming too eager, so he put Solomon on his leash and took a walk down the block to a charming coffee shop, where he could hear "Don't Go Breaking My Heart" by Elton John and Kiki Dee. Then he realized it was the afternoon and past time when he allowed himself coffee, so he walked back to the store again. When he arrived at the boutique, he was only five minutes early and decided that was kosher, so he took Solomon in.

Other dogs in the store caused Solomon to race from one potential friend to another, touching noses (and sniffing butts) with any other canine who would give him the time of day. Abe realized he was smiling and meeting the eyes of people in a way he hadn't done since he and Nicole separated. Strangely, Abe felt a renewed sense of purpose. Several of the bigger dogs acted as though Solomon didn't exist, which irked Abe, though he supposed size was pretty important in the canine world. There was so much merchandise in the store—toys, food, leashes, walls full of various collars—Abe didn't know where to start.

"Abe!"

He turned and saw Alli, and then Solomon saw her and pulled the leash right out of Abe's hand, galloping over to jump on her. Alli wore a simple skirt and top in pastel colors with sandals, and big dangly earrings that, with her spiked hair, accentuated her slim neck and shoulders. She reminded Abe of Nefertiti. She kneeled and petted Sol. "Hello, Mr. Solomon, hello, buddy, so nice to see you again!"

"Thanks for coming to help me with this," Abe said. "Solomon, as you can see, also appreciates it quite a lot."

"Sure. He is the cutest. This place is amazing, isn't it? I get things for my granddaughter's dog here—she loves to spoil her pets. I think the costumes and clothes are in this room over here." Alli pointed to a separate room with dozens of dog outfits in different sizes hanging on the wall, from bright yellow-and-black bumblebees to marine-blue-and-pink mermaids, to red-and-green Santa and reindeer costumes. There were also rows and rows of everyday outfits in a rainbow of bright and pastel colors—shirts, sweatshirts, sweaters, hoodies, dresses, hot pink tutus, and bow ties in all colors and sizes.

"I had no idea places like this existed."

"Oh yes, dressing pets is a big business. I think Solomon is a small—not extra small—those are for Yorkies and teacup poodles. And he needs a California outfit, a Harvard outfit, a courtroom outfit, and a curtain-call outfit?"

"Good memory—yes." Did dogs find it humiliating to be dressed in these ridiculous costumes? On the contrary, Solomon seemed to be reveling in the attention.

Alli took Solomon's leash, and he went obediently with her as she walked around the clothing room. Alli pulled out a tiny pink sweatshirt with "Harvard" written on the front. "Look at this! This is perfect! The tag even has a photo of Bruiser from *Legally Blonde*. Solomon, buddy, do you want to try this on?"

Alli knelt and slid the sweatshirt over Solomon's head. "He is such a good boy," Alli said. "He really has a great temperament." Alli pulled the sleeves of the sweatshirt over Solomon's front legs. "I think this small size fits, don't you?"

"He looks hilarious." Solomon seemed a bit humiliated, with his eyes wide and his ears flattened, but wasn't complaining.

"You can't read 'Harvard' when he is on his feet, since it's written on the chest of the shirt, but when Elle is carrying him, it will be visible." Alli stood, picking Sol up, to demonstrate that the writing on his chest could be seen, and he gave her a lick on the ear.

Alli smiled and snuggled him. Abe wished he could give

Alli a lick on the ear, but obviously that would be inappropriate.

"Okay, the 'Harvard' sweatshirt is a go," Abe said, laughing. "How about a California outfit?" Had he ever imagined he'd actually enjoy himself with something like this?

Searching, Alli found a brightly colored Hawaiian shirt that buttoned up the front and made Sol look like a surfer dog. And then, for the courtroom scenes, Abe and Alli agreed that a large white collar with a huge bow tie would work.

"I imagine it should be really big to be seen from the audience," Alli said.

"Maybe three costumes are enough," Abe said, wondering how much all this would cost.

"Well, how about if he just wears the bow tie for the curtain call?" Alli suggested.

"Good idea." At checkout, Abe was a bit shocked at the cost of the three outfits but didn't want to appear cheap while Alli was around, so said nothing. This was a once-in-a-lifetime thing, anyway.

After Abe paid, they stood outside on the sidewalk in the afternoon sunshine. Abe felt awkward but Alli seemed at ease. He met her eyes and restrained himself from reaching to touch the exact place where Solomon had licked her ear. "Let me buy you a coffee to say thanks for helping me with this. There's a coffee shop about a block away with a patio, so we can take Solomon."

Alli hesitated for an instant, then shrugged, smiling. "Sure, that would be nice."

Abe, hardly able to believe his luck, put the shopping bag with the dog clothes in his Lexus, then he and Alli walked, with Solomon, to the coffee shop. He could hardly believe this was happening.

A memory of walking to restaurants with Nicole and Solomon surfaced. Nicole always wanted to choose restaurants with outdoor seating areas so Solomon could join them. Then an earlier college memory bubbled up, of walking to a deli on a Sunday morning with Alli, slightly hungover after going to a dance. They had both ordered cream sodas and eaten voraciously, Abe a corned beef sandwich and Alli a pimiento cheese. His heart fluttered. He definitely should not be having coffee at this time of day—his pulse would race and he would be up all night—but the sacrifice was worth it.

"Pick a table!" Abe said breezily when they arrived, indicating the patio, with its wrought iron tables and chairs and brightly colored umbrellas. "I'll go in and get the coffees. How do you like yours?"

"Actually," Alli said, looking at her watch. "It's after five. I shouldn't be drinking coffee."

"Me either." Abe held out his hands, showing he agreed. "But I wanted to show my appreciation for your help. For you, I'll drink coffee in the afternoon!" He took a chance saying that, and his heart thumped as he laughed.

She grinned. "Well, I can have wine. And I've been here with my daughter and know they have it. How about prosecco, to celebrate Solomon's fame?"

"Prosecco it is." Abe handed her Solomon's leash and went inside, feeling almost dizzy with success. He stood inside by the bar, waiting for the drinks, watching Alli with Solomon through the window. A song he remembered from his early teaching days, "Somebody's Baby" by Jackson Brown, was playing. Alli leaned down and took Solomon onto her lap and talked to him sweetly, and Solomon curled up. She took out her phone, then, and started texting.

"Cab for you, and prosecco for your wife," said the young man behind the bar, placing the flute and wineglass on the counter and glancing out at Alli.

"Oh, she's not my wife," Abe said quickly.

"Oh, sorry to presume. Just the way you were looking at her."

"We've known each other for fifty years. It's more like a first date...fifty years later." Abe felt a little embarrassed for rambling on, and was embarrassed that the server had noticed his attention toward Alli.

The barista smiled. "Good luck."

Abe blinked and picked up the glasses. "Thank you. You play a lot of good old music here."

"The best music," the barista said with a grin.

Outside, he sat beside Alli and they toasted Solomon's upcoming performance.

"To breaking a paw?" Alli said, with a smile, lifting her glass.

"To breaking a paw," Abe repeated, clinking his glass with hers. "This has been a great help, thank you."

"It was fun to frivolously spend someone else's money," Alli said in a joking voice. Since they were under an umbrella, she slid her sunglasses on top of her head.

"Not so frivolous! Sol will wear those outfits once for each of eight performances as well as a dress rehearsal."

"Yes, cost-efficient. You'll have to become adept at getting him in and out of them. You may not have much time for changes."

"I overheard Elle tell another actress that she has sixteen costume changes. I think by comparison three isn't that challenging. I can handle it." Abe wanted to venture into other topics with her, yet here they were talking about silly dog clothes.

What had her life been like in the fifty years they'd been apart? Had she had a satisfying job, and marriage? How many children did she have, and did they live close by? After the horrible discussion about the breakup though, he didn't dare bring up children. Had she thought of him periodically, as he had thought of her? Their connection seemed to be one that wouldn't ever fade, even if they didn't speak or meet for another fifty years. Yet all such subjects seemed a long leap from the lightness of *Legally Blonde*.

"Do you keep up with many people from college?" she asked, massaging Solomon's ears, as if she'd read Abe's mind.

He shook his head, twirling his wineglass. "Not really. Maybe three or four of my fraternity brothers." He named a few, and she nodded, remembering them. "My wife used to send New Year's cards, before she died, and several people from college were on the list. We used to go to reunions every five years or so. After Ellen died, though, I didn't go anymore. I have to admit, sometimes I looked for you, but you must not have gone back at all."

"No, I didn't." She smiled at him, enigmatically, he thought, but didn't offer any other information. A few seconds of silence ensued.

"We did graduate from different schools, since you transferred," he said, wondering if she'd correct him, since he was pretty sure he'd seen her on the quad that day long ago in her graduation gown.

"We did," she said simply.

He cleared his throat. "How long have you been writing poetry? I'm no expert, but I think your poems are quite good. They speak to me, anyway, possibly because we're of the same generation."

"Well, thank you. I didn't tell the writing group, because I just wanted to be an ordinary person presenting my work, but I've published a few books of poetry."

"You have?" Abe was flabbergasted. "And you didn't tell us?"

She grabbed her sunglasses from the top of her head, put them on, then tore them off again in an agitated manner. "Please don't tell the others. I don't want them to be...I don't know, intimidated, jealous, whatever. I just wanted to be like everyone else."

"Well, Willoughby published a book years ago, so no need to worry about that." Abe tried to understand. If he succeeded on any level with his work, he would announce it proudly. But he had learned, in only the year he'd been in the group, that creative work was different from academic work. Especially memoir. Sometimes people didn't want their work to be noticed. He nodded. "Your secret is safe with me." Then he laughed. "That sounds like a corny movie line." He did like the idea that the secret would tie them together, though.

"Thank you, Abe. I appreciate it. Oh, and I wanted to tell you—Willoughby and Jennie and Destiny and I went over to Roy's apartment last Saturday and found a bunch of Margaret's stories tucked inside the back covers of her books. Seventeen of them! We're typing them up and Roy is coming to our meeting this week to get them."

"That's unbelievable. She'd hidden her stories?"

"Yes. From her sister, we think." She glanced at her watch. "I better get going. I'm helping my daughter plan a wedding and we have to go watch a band tonight."

"Oh, that sounds fun. I remember you used to love to dance."

"Still do!"

They stood and walked with Solomon back to The Bark Boutique and their cars. She drove a silver Prius, which seemed to suit her. He wanted to kiss her; he'd spent hours wondering what it might feel like now, even though both of them had many more wrinkles on their lips than fifty years ago when their lips had first met. But something told him not to try. He just watched her touch noses with Solomon instead.

CHAPTER 21
DESTINY

Destiny was getting ready to go to work that Friday when she heard Mama get home from school after a half-day, and call to her from downstairs.

"Destiny, baby, come down here, quick." Mama's voice was high and excited. "There's an official, snail mail letter for you from NC Central Nursing School."

"Fat or thin?" Destiny, dressed in her navy-and-white work uniform, came to the top of the stairs. Thin ones were rejections and fat ones were acceptances. Everybody knew that. If the snail mail version had come, it was probably on Destiny's online portal too; she just hadn't checked it lately. Reason being, she wasn't sure she wanted to go.

"It's fat. Come on down here and open it. If you don't, I'm going to open it myself. I can't stand waiting." Mama stood at the foot of the stairs in the front hall, waving the business-size envelope at her.

"You're probably going to steam it open anyway. Go ahead and open it."

"That's ridiculous, come on down here. You should open it yourself."

Destiny headed slowly down the stairs, dragging her hand along the oak banister. Now that things had heated up between her and Marcus, why would she want to move to Durham?

Mama handed her the letter and stood with her hands on her hips, waiting. She still had on her school clothes, a black power suit and low heels, and she wore her favorite reading glasses with the rhinestone patterns on the earpieces.

Destiny slowly slid her finger along the flap of the envelope.

"Gracious, baby, do you think you can do that any slower?"

The flap finally came open and Destiny pulled out the letter, unfolded it, and read it aloud to Mama. "'We are delighted to inform you that you have been accepted at North Carolina Central Nursing School for the upcoming fall semester.'"

Mama raised her hands over her head and did a little dance, whirling and whooping. "Congratulations, baby! You did it!" Her voice rose to a happy shriek at the end, and she gathered Destiny in a heartfelt hug. "I knew you could do it!"

Making Mama happy was a powerful thing. There hadn't been too many times in her life so far when what Destiny wanted was different from what Mama wanted. But maybe this was one of them.

Destiny smiled weakly and disengaged from Mama's muscular arms. "Then it lists the supplies I need and gives a website for contacting housing. I have to report for class the week after Labor Day. It says here that most students in the Nursing Program don't have time to hold outside jobs."

"You don't sound that happy, baby. What's wrong?"

Mama took hold of her chin and looked searchingly in her eyes.

"Nothing. 'Course I'm happy. But...maybe I met somebody, Mama. Maybe I don't want to move to Durham."

Mama waved her hand in dismissal. "Destiny, you are too young to even think about settling down."

"You and Daddy got together when you were not much older than me."

"Times were different then. And just because you move to Durham doesn't mean you can't see someone. If the young man cares for you, he'll make the effort to see you, even if you are a few hours away. Nursing school is about you and your future. Who is this, anyway, this person you've met?" Mama cocked her head.

"A guy. Really nice." Destiny didn't want to say "at work" because Mama knew good and well that she wasn't supposed to be dating anyone who worked at Bristlecone.

"And where did you meet him?"

Destiny dodged the question. "And I don't even know if I want to be a nurse. What about my performance poetry?"

"You can still do that. "

"How many hours do you think I'm going to have in a day?" Destiny checked her phone for the time, put the letter on the hall table, and opened the front door. "I've got to go. I'm going to be late."

"It's important for you to have a degree and professional skills, Destiny." Her mother's tone became harder as she stepped away. "You'll thank me later."

"Not sure when I'll be home tonight."

Destiny felt like crying, and once she was on the way to work, she was so busy trying to finish the argument with Mama in her head that she almost missed the turn for Bristlecone.

Later, as she was putting the residents' mail in their mail cubbies, Willoughby stopped at the desk to rearrange the armful of printouts she was carrying. "Hey, Destiny. How's everything with you? You seem kind of down."

"I got into nursing school." Destiny didn't bother to hide her real feelings about it, like she had with Mama.

"Congratulations! I know it's not easy to get in, so good for you, Destiny. And you're a caring, quick-thinking person. You'll be a good nurse."

"Thank you, Miss Willoughby." Destiny tried, without success, to hold back a sigh.

"You seem a little unenthusiastic about it."

Destiny couldn't tell her—or anybody—about Marcus, since according to the Bristlecone rules they were not supposed to be dating. If Destiny lost her job, she wouldn't have enough to live on if she went to nursing school, and she knew Marcus couldn't lose his either. His granny and his mom both counted on him.

"Well, there might be things keeping me here," Destiny said vaguely. She thought about Marcus's kiss in the chair closet after the Elvis concert, dancing at the karaoke bar to "Uptown Funk," the way he listened last week when she recited the Langston Hughes poem, and all the complimentary things he said. He made her feel seen in a new way.

Willoughby put her hand on her hip and tilted her head in a skeptical way. "You mean, like that cute Marcus with the dimples?"

Destiny felt the blush start on her chest and race up her neck to her cheeks. She thought she had seen somebody sitting on the bench beside the old bristlecone pine when she and Marcus were in her car one day. She leaned forward and whispered, "Was that you, on the bench by the bristlecone pine?"

"I apologize—I didn't mean to snoop. I just happened to be there on the bench gathering my thoughts after a tough afternoon."

So it was her. "Miss Willoughby, please don't say anything to anyone about me and Marcus. We would be fired."

She made a gesture of zipping her lips. "I won't, I promise. But I have to ask, is Marcus the reason you are now lukewarm on nursing school?"

"Well, I'd have to move to Durham, and I know that girl Sheba who's the PT in the health-care unit can't keep her hands off him. If I move to Durham, I'll lose him."

Willoughby nodded, started to speak, then waved her hands, as if to discourage Destiny from ever listening to her. "I am absolutely the last person to give anybody advice on their love life. I am literally the poster child for love life mistakes. The best thing I can say is, don't do what I did! I made so many decisions in my life based on men, and I have regretted it."

"Oh, really?" Destiny laughed but wanted to cry. She knew people had been falling in love, no matter who they were, since forever, and Willoughby probably knew something about that, since everybody talked about how she had two husbands at Bristlecone. Probably she knew what she was talking about if she did feel like giving advice. She was seventy-some years old. She had to have learned something in all those years. Hearing the wisdom from residents like Willoughby was one of the reasons Destiny did enjoy this job sometimes.

"Mama says if he cares for me, he won't forget me just because I'm a few hours away. She says if we want to work it out, we can. She says going to nursing school is about me

—about my future. But what about writing? Where does that fit in?"

"I hope you'll listen to your mama. I know you want to write, but everyone needs something to write *about*, and being a nurse is a fantastic place to start. Where else can you see more of life and death?" Willoughby patted Destiny's arm gently. "Your mama sounds smart to advise you to make your decision about your own future, not just your future with Marcus."

Destiny had to laugh. "It's just kind of frustrating—I wish Mama was wrong once in a while, just to keep her humble. My mama's favorite coffee cup says, 'Oh my God, my mother was right about EVERYTHING.'"

Willoughby laughed. "That's so funny—my mother had a dish towel that said the exact same thing. Sounds like we have bossy mothers in common!"

"Oh, that's funny! I admit, I'm stubborn, so I don't always like to listen to her." Destiny then changed the subject, wiping tears, pointing at Miss Willoughby's stack of papers. "Are those Margaret's stories?"

She smiled, showing she accepted that Destiny didn't want to talk about her situation anymore. "Yes, I got my six typed up and saved."

"I just wish I'd figured out what those numbers on the sheet of paper with the book titles meant. If they meant anything."

"Yes, I know. We could never have even gotten this far without you, though, Destiny."

"Do you know why she was hiding them in the first place?"

Miss Willoughby turned and glanced at the front door, just to make sure that no one heard. "After reading six of her stories, I think she's telling family secrets and there are family members still alive—her sister in particular—who don't want those secrets to come out."

"Like what kind of family secrets?"

"Let me just say, they are pretty juicy. And so we are trying to keep Margaret's sister, Eunice, from getting her hands on them. Or we're at least trying to save them for posterity." She gathered the stories, glancing at her sports watch. "Everyone will be here soon, and I need to unlock the conference room. Join us again when you get off, if you like."

"I can't today—I'm on late shift. I wish I could, though."

"Okay. And I hope things work out—whatever that looks like—with nursing school."

"Thanks." Destiny got it about family secrets. Mama had told Destiny that when people in their family started doing 23andMe, it started to look like they were related to everybody in Eden Forest, and maybe all of North Carolina too: Black, White, Brown, Yellow, and every color in the rainbow, through no fault of their own. Everybody made a joke of it, how they were probably related to North Carolina muckety-mucks. But it wasn't all that funny; they were laughing just to keep from crying.

Destiny got back to sorting the mail, thinking about what Willoughby had said. And what her mom had said. She knew they meant well. It just seemed like sensible plans for the future never took *feelings* into consideration. And they counted for a lot.

She came to the last few pieces of mail and filed a notification from a bank reminding a resident that their safe deposit box fee was due to renew for the upcoming year.

What if that number on Margaret's list was a safe deposit box number or the code to one? Maybe Margaret had a secret box that she hadn't told Roy about.

CHAPTER 22
WILLOUGHBY

Willoughby arrived at the conference room a few minutes early, input the code, set her things down, and began rummaging in her briefcase for the egg timer.

She was glad she hadn't opened her big mouth and tried to give Destiny too much advice, that she'd stuck with telling her to listen to her mama. Willoughby was the last person on earth to give love-life advice. Honestly, what did she know?

Today was overcast and it looked like an afternoon thunderstorm was coming in, which kind of matched her mood. She was pissed at herself; she hadn't written a damn thing she could bring to the meeting. After typing up Margaret's stories and seeing how fricking good they were, and especially after Jennie's publishing success, she'd had a fresh attack of impostor syndrome. Also, her whole life was falling apart, so how the hell could she write?

She'd sat down to make herself write for a few hours yesterday but all she could think about were the episodes over the last weeks with Gary, Steven, and Adam. She'd given in, written several achingly honest journal entries, felt somewhat relieved, and promptly put them in the shredder. None of that needed to see the light of day, right? So for two weeks in a row, she had nothing to contribute. That was a new experience for her. She felt sorry for her poor characters, suspended in limbo for the last two weeks as Willoughby tried to navigate her crazy life.

"Hi, Willoughby!" Jennie was in excellent spirits and took her usual seat. "Weren't Margaret's stories fabulous? I am still just blown away by them."

Willoughby nodded. "The ones I typed were good too. I definitely have some ideas about why Eunice doesn't want her to publish them, don't you?"

"I do! I'd love to discuss it, but, of course, not in front of Roy."

"And I want to hear all about that conversation you had with the publisher," Willoughby said, putting her envy aside. "But I will wait with bated breath until everyone else gets here, so you don't have to repeat yourself."

"Well, there's not *that* much to tell," Jennie said, but Willoughby could tell that she wanted to share.

Abe and Alli came in together. They were talking about Alli's poetry. She hadn't thought Abe was into poetry, but obviously he was into anything that Alli was into. Willoughby had to admit that Abe was not quite so pompous now that he was trying to impress Alli, and she found him more likable.

After a few minutes of greetings and catching up with each other, Willoughby placed the timer in the center of the table. "Well, Roy knows what time we start, so let's just go ahead. Before we read today, let's hear about Jennie's talk with the publisher. I know everyone is eager to hear and cheer her on."

"She offered me a book contract!" Jennie blurted out, barely able to contain her excitement.

"Whoo-hoo! I knew it!" Willoughby, determined to overcome the green-eyed monster within, stood up and clapped, and the rest followed. Everyone was yelling, "Congratulations." It was the first time anything celebratory like that had happened in the writers' group.

"We want details," Alli said, squeezing Jennie's arm.

Jennie told them about her seat-of-the-pants conversation with Kathryn Arroyo, her cat Sir Arthur nearly deleting her entire manuscript, which caused them all to practically faint with panic, the book offer, and the promise that she'd receive her contract soon and then hear from her editor. It was a heady few minutes. The air in the conference room felt supercharged.

Willoughby picked up the egg timer. "Well, on that incredible note, shall we start? I arrived first, but shamefully admit to not writing anything this week, so I will pass the baton to Jennie, who arrived second, and I know we're all eager to hear the work of a soon-to-be-published author."

"Well, all right," Jennie said, sorting her papers. "But I hope you write something next week, Willoughby."

The conference room door swung open and Roy burst in, wearing an untucked polo shirt and faded khakis. "Sorry I'm late!" With much loud thumping of chair legs, he plopped into the nearest seat, which happened to be at the head of the table. "Carry on!"

"Hi, Roy. We were just getting started. Jennie will read her work first, then Alli, then Abe, and then we'll talk about Margaret's stories, since you arrived last." Willoughby turned the egg timer over. "Go ahead, Jennie."

"Okay, well, I thought I'd write my author's note,

which is common with historical fiction. Some of the information in my note may come as a surprise to the group." Jennie cleared her throat and began to read with a shaky voice. "My mother, Norah, came as a girl of ten to North Carolina from Iraq in 1939, right before World War II. At age sixteen, she married an Italian man, took his name, and converted from Judaism to Catholicism. To smooth the way, after that she simply told everyone she was Italian, including her children. I didn't know that I had Iraqi or Jewish heritage until my mother told me before she died at the age of ninety-one. I had been taught I was Italian. I was, of course, only half Italian, but I hadn't known the rest." Jennie took a deep breath but didn't look up. "Learning about my own background inspired me to learn and eventually write about Enheduanna, not just the first woman writer, but the first known author of any gender, who lived in the Sumerian city of Ur, in the twenty-third century BC, and was a princess, the daughter of King Sargon, as well as a priestess."

Jennie continued to read her author's note, which outlined the books she'd read and the research she'd managed to do online—much of it during COVID, when she could not get to libraries. She admitted in her author's note that she had never been able to visit Iraq in person. She sat back. "That's it."

"You're part Jewish," Abe said, with a happy grin. "Mazel tov! Welcome to the tribe."

Jennie smiled. "Hey, thanks."

"Alli, comments?" asked Willoughby.

"It must be extremely disconcerting to learn something about yourself that contradicts what you've been taught all your life," Alli said. "The author's note is authentic and honest, and I appreciated the thoroughness of your research."

Other comments were similar—even Abe didn't mention a thing about Iraqi scholars—and Jennie seemed energized to move forward with the edit. "Thank you all so much for understanding my situation. I feel as though I've revealed a lot—this secret that's become so heavy over the years—but yet, it never really needed to be."

"That is awesome that you are being published, and maybe you can give me the name of your publisher so I can send Margaret's stuff," was Roy's comment.

"Yes, Jennie, keep us posted on how things go with this publisher," Willoughby said. "Okay, let's move on to Alli."

Alli read a deeply thoughtful and poignant poem about helping a daughter and granddaughter plan a wedding when your own marriage did not go well. Hope juxtaposed with concerns. Joy juxtaposed with cynicism, hurt, and sadness. Her piece had nearly everyone close to tears.

"Oh, Alli, that was exquisite," Willoughby said with deep sincerity. "I know that poem speaks to many."

Abe, uncharacteristically, said the poem was deeply powerful and he had no suggestions.

"I also have something to share with the group," Alli said. "I confessed to Abe that I'd published several books of poetry in the past, and I feel that the rest of you should know about that as well. When Jennie talked about finding out about her mother's true heritage, and feeling that she had misrepresented herself, it pointed out to me that I have also misrepresented myself to you all."

"Alli, I feel like our group is a place where we are free to be as honest...or as private as we need to be," Willoughby said. "So please, don't worry about it. I'm so glad to hear about your books so I can buy them."

"I'll bring them next week, and I'm happy to talk with anyone about my experiences publishing poetry. Jennie, you inspired me to be more open. And maybe finding Margaret's hidden stories has inspired me too. Thank you." Alli's smile was warm and sincere.

Then, for his turn, Abe read another light blog piece about his dog Solomon participating in the rehearsals for the play *Legally Blonde*. His post was a funny account of Solomon's first rehearsal and the way the cast quickly adopted him as their mascot. Abe received more positive feedback than for his usual pieces, and he was clearly buoyed. Willoughby thought he seemed more relaxed than in the past.

"I hope everyone will come to see the play, which will be showing for two weekends, starting next week," Abe told them. "It's an experience of a lifetime for Solomon and me. I also enlisted Alli to help with Solomon's costumes, so you must come see it for that reason as well."

"Let's all go on the same day," Willoughby suggested. "A field trip for our group! What about the last performance, the Sunday matinee, in three weeks?" Everyone except Roy pulled out their phones and put the date on their calendars. Willoughby felt a frisson of excitement thinking about how fun it would be. Something to look forward to.

"As Solomon's manager, I want to assure you that he's thrilled to have fans." Abe grinned with previously unknown good humor.

"So is it my turn now?" Roy asked, his face flushed with excitement, scooting his chair closer to the table.

"Yes." Willoughby stacked the six stories that she'd typed on the table, and Alli and Jennie did the same. "We've got printed copies for you, Roy. We'll also email you electronic versions of the stories."

Outside the conference room windows, the expected storm arrived, and ominous purple clouds rolled across the horizon, with rain spitting on the window and silent streaks of lightning in the sky. Then, thunder clapped. Willoughby jumped.

"I think seventeen stories is enough for a collection," Alli said. "And Roy, I'd be happy to make some suggestions about how to organize them. And maybe investigate some publishing options. You could publish them yourself, for example, to give to Margaret's family and friends."

"Or maybe I could make big bucks?" Roy said.

"Alli, that's very kind of you to offer to help Roy, don't you agree, everyone?"

Murmurs of agreement went around the room, though no one responded to the big bucks remark.

"I'm kicking myself because I never sat down to actually read her work while she was alive," Roy admitted.

"Well, you can read them now," Jennie said. "I wish I could help, Alli, but I'm facing my own edit."

"I'll help you, Alli, if you'd like me to," Willoughby heard herself say, even though she didn't have time. But she sure could use a distraction.

Alli smiled. "Oh, thanks, Willoughby. It will be a fun project to work on together. I'll text you to set something up."

They separated out the original stories, which they returned to Roy along with his printouts. As they divided up the remaining printouts between the two of them, Destiny's urgent voice suddenly came over the conference room intercom.

"Miss Willoughby, Miss Jennie—heads up that Miss

Margaret's sister is coming up to see you all. I tried to stop her. She's mad as a hornet about something."

"Why would she be coming up here?" Abe asked.

"I might have mentioned something to her," Roy said sheepishly.

Alli gasped. "Hide the stories before she gets here!"

Alli and Willoughby shoved the fresh printouts of the stories into their briefcases just seconds before Eunice burst into the conference room, with a straight back, a patrician air about her, and a look on her face to match the thunderous rumbling and flashing outside. Roy had not brought a briefcase and still had Margaret's original handwritten stories on the table in front of him.

"There they are!" Eunice pointed to Roy's pile of faded pages in a rather imperial way. "I'd know my sister's handwriting anywhere. Roy, I asked you not to bring that drivel to this writing group."

Roy seemed cowed. "Margaret had been coming to this group for a while and sharing her stuff."

"There's nothing worth sharing in those pages, believe me. I told Margaret—and you heard me say this—that she ought to let sleeping dogs lie. No good comes of sharing these stories." She stepped closer to Roy and held out her hand. "If you know what's good for you and our family, you'll give them to me and I'll do what needs to be done with them."

"What are you proposing to do?" Abe asked, rising to his feet in a surprise move. Abe had, until now, not seemed very invested in the fate of Margaret's stories.

"Burn them, of course."

"That's preposterous!" Abe said.

"They're mine," Roy said. "I'm her husband; you can't threaten to burn them." Roy tried to sweep the stories off the table toward his chest, but Eunice grabbed them at the same time and the top page ripped in two. The rest of the pages fell to the floor.

Everyone in the conference room raced to claim the pages closest to them in a wild, chaotic scramble. Eunice grabbed the most pages, but each of the others salvaged a few.

Breathing hard, the writers stood up, facing Eunice.

"It's our view that Margaret wanted these stories to be read," Willoughby said. "She wanted her voice to be heard." She'd promised herself after she allowed that committee to ban *Speak* at her library that she would never fail to speak up about the right to read and to write again in her lifetime. And she planned to stick to that promise.

"I got most of them. The rest of you didn't get enough for anyone to make sense of anything. Margaret had no right to reveal our family history. She had no right to write about Daddy being in prison for embezzlement. It took years for our family to re-establish ourselves here in Eden Forest. "

"She didn't identify anyone," Willoughby pointed out. "Her stories are fictional."

"Well, I see through them. And I'll have you know that my husband never loved Margaret, it was always me! She went to Italy for her semester abroad; she should not have expected him to be waiting for her. Roy, if you try to publish a word of this, I'll sue you." Clutching the fragile pages to her chest, Eunice stormed out of the room.

"I hope she's careful on the stairs," Jennie said, without a touch of irony in her voice, which Willoughby admired.

"Thank God we have the extra copies," Alli whispered.

Then everyone talked at once for the next few minutes

as they calmed down and congratulated each other for their quick actions.

"Can she really sue us?" Jennie asked.

"It's fiction!" Willoughby said. "Of course not." She surprised herself at how outraged she was on Margaret's behalf.

"Are you sure?"

"Well, we should probably be sure to put that disclaimer on the copyright page about any resemblance to real people being a coincidence, but it should be okay," Willoughby said.

The meeting broke up after that, with everyone congratulating Jennie one last time about her book deal. They walked down together and gathered around Destiny at the front desk.

"Destiny, you saved the day! Thank you—your call on the intercom helped us hide Margaret's stories before Eunice got them." Willoughby gave her a thumbs-up and a big smile.

"Really quick thinking on your part," Jennie added. "I didn't even know that intercom was there."

Destiny beamed and shrugged. "Hey, y'all, I'm glad I could help. The intercom is part of the front-desk-job training, for emergencies, I guess. And I had a feeling that was definitely an emergency."

"Thanks, all of you," Roy said humbly. "You've helped me more than I should ever have expected."

"We're glad we're able to help," said Alli. "And now I'm looking forward to arranging these stories into a collection."

"I just realized something," Jennie said. Everyone looked at her.

"What?" Willoughby asked.

"Eunice mentioned a story about their father embezzling from a company and going to jail. Did any of you see a story about that?"

The rest of them looked at each other blankly, and then, one by one, they shook their heads.

Destiny perked up. "Could we be missing a story?"

"The most revealing one of all," Abe said.

"We accounted for all the titles on the sheet of paper, didn't we?" Jennie said.

"Definitely," Willoughby said. "But she might have more reason to hide that one."

"So...maybe those numbers at the bottom of the page have something to do with that last story," Destiny said. "Roy, maybe you could check to make sure that Margaret didn't have a safe deposit box you didn't know about. You have to pay the fee every year, so you should be getting some kind of reminder."

Roy squinted and pursed his lips, thinking. "I have no idea, but I'll take another look."

"Okay, see you all next week, if not before." Willoughby patted her old briefcase, solidly heavy with nine of Margaret's stories, with confidence as she headed to memory care. The flush of success overwhelmed her usual anxiety.

The rain shower, no longer a downpour, dripped big, sloppy droplets, with clouds of summer steam floating off the cars and sidewalks. She'd forgotten an umbrella, but she just let the droplets fall on her scalp, slowly spreading patches of coolness. As Willoughby keyed in the code on the heavy unit door, a rainbow sizzled into the sky like a wavering mirage.

CHAPTER 23
JENNIE

On Saturday, the day after their writers' meeting, Sir Arthur sat on Jennie's lap, purring and kneading his paws on her thighs, as if the near disaster he'd caused last week had never happened. Jennie had bought an external hard drive and also subscribed to a cloud storage service, so she had several backups in case Sir Arthur threatened her manuscript again.

She opened the file with the contract that the publisher had sent. The legalese was nearly indecipherable, but she saw her advance right on the first page. Fifteen thousand dollars! Her heart thumped. She still couldn't believe that her story was going to be shared, let alone that she'd be paid for it!

When she first started out as a social worker, her beginning salary was eighteen thousand a year. Even then it seemed like a tiny amount to be paid for a year's work. Now, she was overjoyed to be getting fifteen thousand for a project she'd been working on for five years. The world of writing sure was a strange one.

You should call Elijah, came Michael's voice in her head.

He was right. She picked up her phone, her heart beating a bit faster than usual. When Elijah answered, she said, "Hey, honey, guess what? I can come to Africa for your wedding after all. I just got my book contract. I'm making fifteen grand."

"Mom, that's great! Congratulations!" After a beat he added, "I have a confession to make."

"What is it?" Her heart sped up even more and sweat popped out on her temples.

"I thought it was cool that you were working on this big project, but did I honestly think you'd actually get it published? I did not. I just thought it was a great way for you to occupy yourself since Dad was gone. Was I wrong! This is so amazingly great."

Jennie laughed with relief. "It's okay to admit you felt that way; I knew it already."

"When I told Amanda you'd had your book accepted she said I needed to apologize to you, for having so little faith in my own mother."

"Apology accepted, no worries." Her temples cooled. "And I'm very pleased to have the support of my daughter-in-law-to-be. I am also thrilled I'm going to be able to be with you two on your special day."

She drew a deep breath, started to tell him about her Iraqi heritage, then completely chickened out. He'd likely wonder why she'd never told him before. So not a good fit during this happy, congratulatory conversation. She'd tell him during another conversation, maybe, later on. "Now that I can do this, honey, I want to pay for the rehearsal dinner, the way the groom's family is supposed to. Your dad would like that. I one hundred percent support your relationship and marriage and am thrilled you've found each other. Since there will only be a half dozen of us, I should be able to handle it."

"Mom, you don't have to."

"I insist."

Elijah gave her the website for the place they planned to have the wedding, and other information, they talked a bit longer, and then she hung up. As soon as she was off the phone, she went to the safari lodge website to try to see what would be involved. The lodge in the Serengeti that they had found looked gorgeous and rustic, with incredible views of the savannah, and amazingly, once you got there, it was relatively affordable. Elijah and Amanda's wedding would be very simple: a ceremony on a hill under an acacia tree near an elephant watering hole, with a champagne toast, a wedding cake, and dinner for six—Elijah and Amanda, her parents, Amanda's younger brother, and Jennie. The official wild animal of Tanzania was the Maasai giraffe, and the photo gallery showed that guests might possibly experience giraffes, with their absolutely enormous heads, interrupting their dinner to lean down for a nibble. Jennie had to admit, it sounded like an experience of a lifetime.

Jennie's rehearsal dinner for six would cost two million Tanzanian shillings. Mind-bogglingly, at the present exchange rate, two thousand Tanzanian shillings equaled one US dollar. She pulled up the calculator on her phone and input the numbers. So her rehearsal dinner would cost one thousand dollars. It would feature traditional Tanzanian bush food, such as the official dish of Tanzania, called ugali, which was a maize porridge, a Tanzanian pulled meat dish resembling barbecue (for the non-vegetarian guests), and tropical fruit. Afterward, Maasai dancers would perform.

During their visit, Elijah and Amanda hoped to go on two safaris into the bush, and a balloon ride, as well as a trip to view Mount Kilimanjaro. They also wanted to visit "Dr. Jane's Dream," the immersive experience dedicated to Dr. Jane Goodall, recently opened in Arusha.

Jennie decided she would go to "Dr. Jane's Dream," but could afford only one of the safaris, and the trip to Mount Kilimanjaro, and she would stay at the lodge and relax at the infinity pool on the day of the second safari.

What about the balloon ride? Michael asked.

Michael, you know I'm afraid of heights. I'm not going.

This is like once in a lifetime.

I'm not going. Now leave me alone. Michael had always teased her about lighthouses, the Golden Gate Bridge, and other famous elevated locations that she refused to climb.

She tried to read the rest of her contract. Was that mid-August as the due date for her edits? A little over two months.

She hoped there wouldn't be massive changes, since she'd spent years doing research, rewriting sentences, correcting every single thing. She waded through more of the fine print outlining paperbacks, audiobooks, and eBooks and how much she'd be paid for each.

She saw a tiny paragraph saying that if she used any copyrighted material, she was responsible for paying any fees incurred.

Go ahead and sign it, came Michael's voice in her head. *Lyrics from artists who worked fifty centuries ago will be hard to come by, so you probably don't need to worry about that.*

Stop giving me so much advice, she thought, then laughed at how ridiculous it was to be having an argument with Michael and laughing at his comments despite the fact he was dead. Yet, she did need to get some real advice. Did she have anyone she could trust? What about Alli? She'd had several poetry books published. And come to think of it, Willoughby also had that book published years ago. She emailed them both. As it turned out, they had planned to meet for lunch the following day to talk about Margaret's stories, and they asked her to join them.

Jennie waited at the end of the long line at Spicy Veggie on Main Street in town, a trendy lunch spot, craning her neck to see if she could see Willoughby or Alli. The crowd was a mix of the dressed-up, Sunday after-church crowd and the more casually dressed folks enjoying their weekend. Willoughby had chosen this new place in town with lots of vegetarian and vegan options. She finally spotted Willoughby, with her long-legged stride, crossing the street, meeting up with petite Alli coming out of the book-store. They headed in her direction, and Jennie waved to them from her spot in line.

A short time later, the three of them were seated at a table near the edge of the patio. Jennie had emailed the contract to both of them, and they pulled folded and marked pages out of their purses. Just as they settled in, her neighbor Bernice approached them with a handful of flyers.

"Hi, Bernice," Jennie said warily.

"Hi, Jennie. Did you know that the new musical, *Legally Blonde*, which is aimed at young people, has *songs* about gay people?" Bernice began without preamble. "Our young people do not need to be exposed to this kind of thing. I have some flyers here about removing books from the Youth Center, which we talked about, and about the play, and I hope you might be willing to pass them around."

Jennie, Willoughby, and Alli were completely silent for a few seconds, frozen in that Southern female moment of determining what would be the polite yet correct response.

Bernice thrust some of the flyers at them. "If you and your friends could just pass them out. We can't have this kind of atmosphere in our wholesome town. I'm also making a presentation at the Town Hall about closing the play down."

"Well, I feel like—" Jennie was starting to say that parents should make the decision about whether their children should go to the play, but Alli touched her arm to quiet her.

"When is your presentation?" Alli asked.

"Tuesday."

"We'll definitely be there," Alli replied, with a smile. Jennie was a little surprised at Alli's ready response.

"Oh, that would be wonderful, thank you," Bernice said, leaving flyers on the table and heading to another table. The moment Bernice turned the corner, Alli stood up and tossed the flyers into the restaurant's outdoor trashcan.

When Alli returned, she said, "We definitely need to be there on Tuesday. To vote down whatever she proposes. Can I tell you one of my favorite book and librarian stories?" She looked at Willoughby in particular. "My daughter fell in love with a book in preschool as a toddler but could only remember that the cover illustration was of a little boy with no clothes on making bread. When we got to the library and asked the librarian about the book with the boy with no clothes on the cover, she smiled and nodded and took us right over to *In the Night Kitchen* by Maurice Sendak. My daughter was over the moon with joy. There is no way that any book should be banned for any reason. So here's to the incredible knowledge and open-mindedness of librarians!"

"Hear, hear! I love having you in our writers' group," Willoughby said, raising her water glass. "To solidarity." After they made plans to go to the meeting, the talk gradually came back to Jennie's contract.

"It's been a long time since my book contract," Willoughby said, "and I had an agent then, but I've tried to mark places I thought you might be able to negotiate some. You can ask for a larger advance, and more author copies. I was able to get them to double the number they sent to me, and that translates into a bit more money." Willoughby leaned forward and sipped her lemon water.

"Me too." Alli raised a fist of triumph. "You did something amazing. You sold a book. I haven't had agents for my poetry books, so I've tried to decipher the contracts myself. I marked on here that maybe you can get yourself some wiggle room in your deadlines. They seem pretty tight, especially if your editor has a lot of changes. I marked the place where you can also try to get them to give you ancillary rights, like audio rights and eBook rights, if they don't use them."

Jennie took notes on their conversation and put her notebook away when the food came. She was so grateful for their support and advice; she never could have navigated this without them. As they ate, the conversation turned to other topics.

"So if Margaret's sister does try to sue once we help Roy publish this book, are we ready for it?" Alli asked, as she speared the pickle beside her chicken salad sandwich.

"I'm a member of the Author's Guild," Willoughby said. "They have lawyers on staff that can help. Maybe I'll shoot them an email."

"Good idea," Alli said.

"You better be careful working on this," Willoughby

joked. "Roy might come on to you again. That was so eerie that Margaret told him to ask you out after she died."

"Oh, it's not that unusual. One of my friends died of cancer in her fifties and she'd actually picked out her husband's next wife," Alli said. "And, in fact, they did get married, and he has been very happy with her choice for him. Best of all, my friend's last months were made more enjoyable as she acted as a matchmaker for her husband."

"You are kidding me!" Jennie cut into the luscious brownie she'd impulsively splurged on, deciding she deserved a treat because of the book contract. "Maybe she loved him so much she wanted him to be happy. Does anybody want a bite of this?"

"No thanks," Alli said. "I'm not worried about Roy. I'm just going to work with the documents."

"Good way to approach it," Willoughby said. "Sure, I'll try a bite." Jennie cut off a piece of brownie for Willoughby. "Mmm, that's yummy!"

"You know," Alli said, "some people just can't be alone. The minute they lose their partner they start looking for someone else, because they like being part of a pair. And I have to say that I liked being part of a pair too—someone to talk to all the time, someone to snuggle with on cold nights —but I'm also mostly okay on my own."

"I miss Michael so much that I'll admit that, in my head, I still talk to him." Jennie didn't think much of what she'd said until she realized that they were staring at her.

"Really? You talk to him?" Alli asked gently.

"Yes, especially when I have to make a decision." Jennie wondered if the others thought she was nuts. "You think that's weird?"

"No, I've heard of people doing that," Willoughby said, after a slight hesitation.

"My marriage wasn't perfect by any means, but in spite of that I did like being part of a couple," Alli said, skirting the topic. "I'll try a bite of that brownie after all."

Jennie cut a square off and slid it onto Alli's plate. Alli was definitely trying to change the subject. The others did think she was weird. Maybe she shouldn't talk so much about Michael. Maybe she did need to move on. Michael had been the love of her life, and the other women hadn't been quite as lucky with their relationships.

"I think Abe is very interested in you, Alli," Willoughby said, raising her eyebrows. "Don't tell me you haven't noticed."

Jennie hadn't noticed, maybe because she'd been too focused on the writing aspect of their meetings, and Alli hadn't mentioned it. How could she have been so oblivious?

Alli, meanwhile, tasted the brownie. "Oh, that's divine." She gazed around at some of the people at other tables in a thoughtful way, and Jennie wondered if she hadn't heard what Willoughby said. Then she said, "I'm not sure how to answer. I sometimes suspect that Abe is interested in the person I used to be many years ago. Not the person that I am now. But he's no longer the person I knew in college either."

"So you *did* have a history back in college?" Willoughby pressed. Jennie had wondered about that but would not have dared to ask the question.

Alli nodded. "Yes, we went out for a little while. And then we went our separate ways. We hadn't been in touch for decades." There was definitely something Alli was holding back. She seemed not to want to talk about it. Which was unusual, because Alli wasn't usually reticent about any topic. "Abe is not a bad man. I mean, he isn't any worse than average." She shrugged.

Willoughby laughed. "Men. Can't live with 'em, can't kill 'em."

Alli and Willoughby exploded in laughter. Jennie smiled, but she didn't think it was all that funny. She missed Michael so much sometimes she thought she was missing a limb. Especially with so many things happening right now, like Elijah's engagement and her publication, that she wished she could share with him, she suddenly felt so lonely for him she started to cry.

"Oh, I'm sorry, Jennie, we didn't mean to say anything to upset you." Willoughby lightly touched Jennie's arm.

"No, no, you didn't," Jennie said. "It wasn't your fault." She used her napkin to blot her tears.

"I hope you know I don't really feel that way about men." Willoughby smiled, lightly squeezing Jennie's arm.

"Sure, I know."

Alli put her hand over Jennie's. "So sorry, Jennie."

Jennie went home and washed her face. Alli and Willoughby were going to meet for another hour or so to talk about arranging Margaret's stories, and Jennie needed time to herself. That lunch had not ended well. But she knew that grief could creep up at unexpected times, and she knew Alli and Willoughby were both sympathetic. Also, they had given her good advice about her contract. Getting together with the two of them had actually been joyous, despite triggering her grief. Friendship could be a transformational thing. She went to her computer and began a letter to her publisher, asking for the changes that Alli and Willoughby had suggested.

Jennie thought about asking Michael what he thought

but changed her mind. This was her dream. She'd remembered Alli and Willoughby's cautious looks when she
admitted talking to Michael all the time. It was time for her
to make this decision on her own. She didn't want the
publisher to think she was some high-maintenance ego-
driven author—she was nothing like that! She signed and,
before Sir Arthur could step on her keyboard and send it
himself, she sent it back.

CHAPTER 24
DESTINY

S weat tickled Destiny's temples under her graduation cap as the morning sun rose higher in the clear blue Carolina sky. Their graduation robes were gray and ankle length, and underneath Destiny wore a short, fitted dress. Mama insisted that she wear white, like a bride or something, which Destiny understood since Mama herself was practically married to her career as a high school principal as much as to Daddy.

On this early Friday morning in June, graduates were seated alphabetically in white folding chairs on the lawn behind the administration building, and Destiny sat in the middle row. Several of Destiny's friends had also earned an associate's degree but hadn't wanted to come to graduation; they said if they made it four years, then maybe they'd go. Of course that wasn't an option for Destiny, being that graduation was a day when Mama got to brag about her baby girl all day long.

"If you think I am going to miss seeing you walk across that stage, Destiny Johnson, you have got another think coming," Mama said last week, leaning over the kitchen counter and shaking her finger, when Destiny brought up the possibility of skipping graduation. "I won't scream and holler when they call your name, as I know that's not proper decorum. But you'll just need to imagine me yelling, 'Go Destiny! Whoo-hoo! You did it!' at the top of my lungs."

Each graduate was allowed only two guests, so only Mama and Daddy were there, and her two younger brothers, Darius and Jayden, had to stay home to make sure their dog, Rosa, didn't eat the food for her party. Mama was hosting family and friends afterward at their house, including what seemed like every cousin in the entire hemisphere. Mama had made enough food for an army. And Destiny had stayed up late last night helping her finish up the deviled eggs and the icing on the cupcakes.

When Destiny arrived on campus that morning, she'd seen the nursing graduates leaving their pinning ceremony. They all wore sparkling white scrubs and shoes and received special pins to show their accomplishment. Starting an IV with long nails would definitely be a challenge. And leaning down to help someone could be complicated with box braids, if they weren't tied back. She touched the tight, ribbed braids on her scalp, which snaked over her shoulder and down to her waist, and rubbed her finger over the elegant and shiny nude-and-white-swirl nail pattern she'd chosen for today. Her hair and nails were so much of her identity. The nursing students kept short nails and fairly short hair. Was that even a way she could see herself?

The speeches had started now. The sun rose higher, and Destiny shaded her eyes with her program. The president spoke for a few minutes, then the dean, who asked everyone to please hold their applause until the end so that everyone's name could be heard. Destiny started thinking back on the people she'd invited to the party. Of course, her friends from the Dancing Divas, and the Drop the Mic spoken word group from high school, had been invited. Then a few days ago she'd sent a casual, off-hand group text to a few of her Bristlecone co-workers about the party, and she'd included Marcus, just to remind him about when they'd talked about it at the karaoke bar. She hadn't even asked Mama and Daddy about it, which had probably been a mistake. But she kept trying to make it not a big deal. Would he come? What would Mama and Daddy think of him?

Destiny spotted her poetry teacher, Ms. Guthrie, sitting up front on the dais, with her shiny hair pulled tightly back, her high cheekbones, her dark skin, and determined yet deep and feeling eyes, and the striking white velvet sash that signified her PhD in Literature. Now Ms. Guthrie stood and approached the dais and said that before she gave out the diplomas for literature, she would present an award for the best student poetry. She'd announced the contest in class and had even asked Destiny if she had a poem she might like to enter.

Destiny had thought about it—she'd even selected one of her poems, about working with the old people at Bristlecone, and read it to Marcus in the back seat of her car in the parking lot. And he'd listened quietly, in spite of her nervousness, and said it was great. Then, they'd kissed, and then she'd had to work, and after that she'd been focusing on Marcus and graduation.

The day to turn in the poem had been during that time when Destiny was stressing over graduation, falling for Marcus, having the misunderstanding with Marcus, and having her disagreement with Mama about nursing school. Also, her brain played crazy tricks on her, like telling her if she didn't enter, then she wouldn't "lose." Like putting herself out there was nothing more than opening herself up to losing. Then the deadline came, and maybe "accidentally on purpose," she forgot.

As Ms. Guthrie called the name of another girl as the winner, a girl that Destiny knew she could outwrite, Destiny wanted to kick herself. How ridiculous was that, to be telling people she wanted to be a spoken word poet but when she had a chance to try, she "forgot"? Dammit, she wasn't going to chicken out like that again.

When Ms. Guthrie called her name to receive her diploma, Destiny remembered Mama telling her to imagine her yelling "Whoo-hoo! You did it!" at the top of her lungs, and she couldn't help but smile a little bit as she crossed the stage in her gray gown, white dress, and pinching white heels.

She took her diploma and shook Ms. Guthrie's hand.

"Congratulations, Destiny," Ms. Guthrie said. "Keep writing."

"I will."

Everyone returned to their seats, and then the president said, "Graduates, please rise." Destiny and her classmates stood. "At this time, you may move your tassel from the right to the left, symbolizing your transition from candidate to graduate."

Destiny grasped the silky tassel and moved it in front of her face, almost like a windshield wiper. Was she different now? And then they all whooped and hollered and threw their caps in the air, and Destiny swore she heard Mama's voice cheering.

The party that night went by in a haze. The table practically groaned with all the food Mama put out, which was a good thing because Jayden and Darius had forgotten to watch their pittie dog, Rosa, during the ceremony and she'd eaten a whole plate of Mama's buttermilk biscuits. Daddy made some special "cap-and-gown mojito" recipe he found online, and Destiny had two of those and was feeling no pain. Darius and Jayden might have snuck some too.

Daddy tapped his spoon on his mojito glass to get everyone's attention and made a speech about Destiny's determination and talents, then he cried a little while telling everyone that he could not wait to see what her future held, whether it was nursing school or not. Then Mama stood up and interrupted him and said, "Excuse me, my dearest husband, her future will indeed include nursing school, so there." Even before that happened, Destiny knew her dad would be happy with whatever she did, but she admitted she felt increasing pressure to live up to Mama's expectations.

Everyone laughed at Mama's comment, though—Destiny too. A few of her friends from the Dancing Divas came, which was really cool, and one girl she'd been close to in high school but kind of lost touch with, Jada, showed up.

"Are you going to nursing school at NC Central in Durham?" Jada asked.

"I got in." Before Destiny could say anything else, Jada screamed and gave her a hug.

"Me too, girl!" Jada did a few dance steps. "We should be roommates."

"Well, I haven't decided, but sure, let's stay in touch." She was thrilled that a few of the folks she worked with came, too, and every time someone came in, she looked for Marcus. It was like all the congratulations and the cards and gifts and plans were in the background of obsessing over whether Marcus was coming, and she knew she shouldn't be doing that, but she just couldn't help herself. Ever since she'd mentioned moving to Durham, did he seem different? It seemed like over the weeks they'd been talking she'd come to a place where she didn't even realize how much she liked him.

And then, after Destiny finally thought it was probably too late for anybody else to show up and was trying not to act depressed at her own graduation party, the doorbell rang and she looked over and there he stood, dressed so nicely in a light blue button-down shirt and khakis and holding a small bouquet of tulips.

"Congratulations. I wasn't sure...do you like tulips?" he said, with such a shy smile his dimples only barely appeared.

"I sure do." A flood of warm emotions and joy washed over her, and just as he handed them to her, he leaned forward and maybe it was the mojitos, but they kissed, right in her front hall. She hoped Mama didn't see, but then, just over Marcus's shoulder, standing in the doorway, was something even worse—Destiny's boss, Ms. Robinson, who Destiny had not invited. But, of course, Mama had to invite her soror! Ms. Robinson definitely could not have mistaken *that* for a friendly peck. Destiny and Marcus pulled apart like they'd had an electric shock, but they weren't fast enough.

"Congratulations, Destiny, everyone at Bristlecone is so proud of you!" Ms. Robinson said with a smile, handing her a graduation card. And giving Destiny no clue whatsoever whether she was going to fire her after seeing her kiss Marcus.

CHAPTER 25
ABE

"So are you taking your Afib meds?"

Abe and his cardiologist, Gerry Goldstein, had wound up their initial collegial greetings that Wednesday morning, discussions of golf games and basketball, and now Dr. Goldstein was getting down to business, rapidly typing Abe's answers into the computer record as he stared at the screen.

"Oh, yes, the amiodarone, absolutely, every day."

"Good." Goldstein, tall and thin, with piercing brown eyes and only salt and pepper in his dark hair, was a member of Abe's golf club and had a much lower handicap.

"Yes. It does make me nervous about falling."

"Of course. I wouldn't be skiing the black slopes these days." Goldstein looked at the screen again. "Your calcium test did show some buildup in your arteries, so I'm going to increase your statin drug. Be sure to take CoQ10 to counteract it. And of course, we have the Factor 5 clotting disorder that we discovered after your heart attack. I would recommend baby aspirin, not just for long plane flights and for any time you might be sitting for a long period of time, but every day. And this is hereditary, so make sure your children are tested as well."

"Yes, I've been keeping the aspirin with me. Both my sons tested, and they were negative."

"Good news. Any questions?"

"Anything to worry about?" Abe was vigilant about his health now.

"Not really. Just pay attention, live healthy."

"Sure, Doc. I tell you, I've really changed my life. I eat healthy, and I've been religious about exercise—well, I'm not really religious about anything—"

"Understood, neither am I." Both of them laughed. "Brisket at Passover—I'm religious about that. But you shouldn't be. The brisket, I mean." Goldstein kept typing.

"I know, I know, I'm eating more fish and vegetables now. Anyway, I've been walking about four miles a few times a week, walking when I play the front nine, and also doing cardio in the workout room in my neighborhood. I'm taking my blood pressure every day and it's been good."

"Yes, I've seen your reports. They look pretty good." Goldstein typed a few more lines, squinted at the monitor, and turned to Abe. "Questions?"

Abe was a bit surprised it was over so quickly. "Anything else I should be doing? Or not doing?"

"You're doing great, Abe. Keep up the good work. Say hello to Nicole."

Abe's gut twisted. He and Nicole used to see Goldstein on the golf course at their club. Goldstein didn't know. "We're separated. Getting divorced, I guess."

Goldstein's eyebrows skyrocketed. "Really? I had no idea. I'm sorry."

"Thanks." Abe didn't want to tell Goldstein that the divorce had actually been triggered by the heart attack. The fear and ominous nearness of death had forced Abe's hand about moving to Bristlecone. He had to have on-site medical care.

"Anyway, it's great to see you doing so well. Live your life. See you in six months." Goldstein clapped him on the shoulder and pivoted out of the exam room, looking at his Apple watch. Abe changed out of his paper gown, feeling down. He felt bad in a vague and unidentified way.

The next night, a Thursday, was the full-dress rehearsal for *Legally Blonde*. On the way into the theater, Abe saw a rather attractive older woman with a coif of silver hair standing outside the stage door with a sign that said, "Not Appropriate for Children!"

"Sir," the woman said as he headed in with Solomon, "would you let your granddaughter or grandson see this play that has songs about gay people?"

"Well, yes, I would," Abe said, puzzled. "It's hilarious. I'm not sure what you mean."

"I'm making a presentation at the Town Hall on Tuesday to close this play down."

Abe took the flyer because he just couldn't refuse it but angled around her into the theater. A crackpot. So far, Abe had thoroughly enjoyed the rehearsals. The exuberant young people and the campy songs like "Omigod You Guys," "Bend and Snap," and "Gay or European" had him belly laughing. In his opinion, it was great for the town to be putting on something so completely entertaining.

Watching Elle sashay across the stage carrying Solomon while singing and dancing never lost its charm for Abe. From the wings, Abe could see that Solomon was as happy as could be, wagging his tail while being handed from one singing actor to another. All the cast members would stick their tongues out at Solomon as they passed or stop to pet him for good luck before going onstage. Abe had to admit, the experience he'd originally thought was so silly and non-academic had made him feel twenty years younger. Maybe Goldstein was right. He should just live his life.

That night, Abe set his chair and Solomon's bag of costumes just offstage left, as before, but noticed that several racks of showy, outrageous, and mostly pink female clothing occupied the spot where he had been sitting with Solomon. Not wanting to cause any trouble—as Abe could see that Mary, the stage manager, had her hands full with a thousand other details—Abe simply moved his chair a bit farther upstage and started sliding Solomon's paws into his surfer dude outfit for his first scene. Pretty soon he noticed that a number of the young ladies in the play were also stripping off their clothes and getting into their costumes right beside the racks of clothing. Being a gentleman, Abe gallantly turned his back.

Within minutes, Mary came up to him with her clipboard. "This isn't going to work," she said. "Elle and some of the other girls have fifteen costume changes and they can't be doing them with you sitting there."

Abe nodded. "I understand. Should I move to the other side of the stage, then?" Abe picked up the costume bag and started to pick up his chair.

"No, since Elle enters and leaves the stage with Bruiser usually from this side, it makes no sense for Bruiser to be on the other side of the stage. It'll be too much of a hassle to get him back and forth. You'll have to give him to one of the female stagehands. You can just sit in the audience tonight for the dress rehearsal. For the performances, you can just drop him off at the backstage door and come get him after the show."

"So I can't sit with Solomon during the performance?

Not even watch him? I should give him to a stranger? I don't like the sound of this at all." He might have been less concerned if Solomon knew any commands, but Solomon went wherever he liked and never bothered to come when he was called if he had anything better to do.

"He seems pretty happy to go to just about anyone. That was one of the reasons we cast him. Emily, the stage-hand who opens and closes the curtain, has a fair amount of free time. I think he'll be all right. We don't have a lot of options at this point." Mary impatiently glanced at her phone.

Abe's mind raced. He was not going to hand off his dog. The idea of Solomon somehow getting loose and running out the backstage door into the street loomed in his thoughts. The backstage help had too many other responsibilities to focus on Solomon. "What if I found someone female that he knows who can sit with him and change his costumes?"

Mary looked at the ceiling, shifted her weight to one hip, and then back, considering his suggestion. "Can she get here in"—she glanced at her watch—"thirty minutes? And can she be here for all the performances this weekend and next weekend?"

"Let me make a call." Abe pulled out his phone. He thought about calling Alli, but he'd already imposed on her once with the costume-shopping. He had no idea if Nicole would be able to do it—she kept a busy social schedule—but he had to try. Solomon knew her better than anyone.

"You lucked out," Nicole said, when he reached her. "I don't have anything going on tonight."

Abe had never been so glad to hear her voice. "Great. Can you be here in about fifteen minutes? It'll just take me a few minutes to run over his costume changes with you."

"Sure, see you in a bit."

Good to her word, Nicole arrived, with wet hair, wearing hot pink yoga pants, a long multicolored T-shirt, and a pair of pink espadrilles. She looked like a *Legally Blonde* cast member herself. And she was gorgeous, as always. Solomon squealed and ran in circles when he saw her, then literally jumped into her arms and licked her cheek in ecstasy.

"You're a lifesaver," Abe told her. "You look wonderful, by the way."

"I'd just gotten out of the shower! You look great, too, Abe. Theater life agrees with you." Nicole's laugh was interrupted by Mary giving the fifteen-minute warning.

"Here, we'll have to hurry, but I'll show you the performance schedule for the next two weeks, and the costume he wears for each song."

After Abe showed Nicole the surfer dude Hawaiian shirt, the Harvard sweatshirt, and the lawyer tie, he showed her the places in the script where Solomon needed to wear each one. He also showed her the performance schedule.

"I can do the Thursdays and Sundays," she said. "But I can't do Friday or Saturday either week. You'll have to find someone else."

Abe nodded. "Okay, I'll work on that. At least we're covered for tonight."

"By the way, these outfits for him are pretty cute. Did you get some help picking these out?" Nicole put her hand on her hip, raising her eyebrows with a flirty smile.

"How did you know?"

"I don't know, Abe. Canine couture has never really struck me as being your forte."

Abe laughed, having really missed her clever teasing, then felt a jolt of embarrassment, remembering that he had, indeed, spent that afternoon with Alli at The Bark Boutique and then drank wine down the street at the little wine bar. That had been a very nice afternoon. Abe had wanted more, yet Alli eluded him.

Abe sat in the third row in the audience during the dress rehearsal, worrying about whether Nicole would get Solomon's costumes right. When it became obvious that she had figured out the progression with no problem, Abe relaxed and let himself enjoy the farcical show from the audience's point of view for the first time. When Solomon was supposed to bark, the audio crew played a tape of a chihuahua bark, and Abe howled with laughter to see Solomon glance around the theater to see what other dog might be barking. A favorite character of Abe's was the UPS driver in the tight brown shorts, who wooed Elle's best friend by announcing with hilarious double entendre that he "had a package." Comic magic.

When the dress rehearsal was over, and the entire cast stood onstage belting out *Legally Blonde*, including Solomon, safe in Elle's arms with his tongue sticking out, Abe stood and applauded heartily, along with the director, assistant director, Mary, and a few others scattered in the audience, then went backstage to retrieve Solomon and his costumes from Nicole.

"Wow," Nicole said. "What amazing local talent we have. I hardly believe these performers all have day jobs. They seem like professionals."

"I know, they're terrific," Abe agreed. "And Solomon is such a natural!"

"He was born for this role. This play is a blast. I'm sorry I can't do it for every performance."

"Don't worry, I'll find someone."

"I would imagine the person who helped you with the costumes could do it," Nicole said, with a wink.

"Oh, yes, that certainly is a possibility, I guess." Abe was surprised by all that Nicole had figured out just from Solomon's costumes. And did Nicole have someone in her life who was preventing her from helping during the weekend? He tried to sound nonchalant as he and Nicole walked together to the parking lot. The tall lights shone on the cars and the asphalt in the darkness, casting shadows and catching an occasional gleam of mica. The earlier heat of the day had dissolved into a soft evening warmth.

"I'm glad you're doing this, Abe. I've been a little worried about you."

"You worried about me? What do you mean? You yourself said you're no caretaker."

"I'm not, but that doesn't mean I can't worry about you at all. I'm not entirely devoid of feelings."

"I know. I was teasing."

"Life should be a joy. If we couldn't make it together, then we each need to find joy with someone else."

"Have you?" Abe's heart beat double-time.

They stood by Nicole's car for a few silent seconds. "Oh, look, a falling star," Nicole said, pointing, not answering Abe's question.

"Where?" Abe glanced where she was pointing and saw the last, fleeting tail of it. "Ah. Very nice. Perhaps an omen... of some sort."

"The old Abe wouldn't have even looked."

"Really? Maybe not."

"You've changed."

"For the better, I hope." Abe did feel he was endeavoring to savor life more.

"I would say so, yes."

At that, Nicole took Solomon's head in her hands and kissed it. "Break a leg tomorrow night, little man."

Solomon clearly thought he was going home with Nicole, which made it awkward for Abe to part ways with her. Abe was finally able to wrestle him from her arms into his carrier in the back seat, but he squealed piteously throughout, clawing at the crate door, craning his neck to see Nicole as she climbed into her sleek white Volvo and drove away.

Abe sighed.

He went home and wrote Alli an email asking if she could help during the weekend performances. He didn't necessarily think Alli would do it for him, but maybe she would do it for Solomon. Then, he went to bed, lifting Solomon up with him, and even letting him curl up on the extra pillow, which he didn't usually do.

He had a restless night. He dreamed about Solomon on opening night, peeing on the stage or running out the backstage door into the parking lot and getting hit by a car. He dreamed that Alli couldn't help and he would have to give Solomon to one of the preoccupied stagehands. He also dreamed that Solomon barked in all the wrong places—the dog version of not knowing his lines or cues, Abe supposed.

He was reminded of his attack of nerves when Jacob played in his first golf tournament at thirteen. He had been more nervous than if he had been playing himself. It felt as if Jacob's putts had only dropped as a result of Abe's sheer will. Maybe he'd spent entirely too much of his life trying to remain in control. He finally fell into a troubled sleep at around four in the morning.

CHAPTER 26
WILLOUGHBY

Willoughby, proud that she had at last eked out a few pages for writers' group, had just put the egg timer on the table on Friday afternoon before the writers' group meeting when her phone rang.

"Mom?" It was Courtney. Willoughby was planning to go over and vacuum, do laundry, and help out with Clay for a few hours after the writers' meeting. Courtney was prematurely dilated and had been put on bed rest for the last few weeks of her pregnancy. Hopefully nothing was wrong.

"Hi, honey? Everything okay?"

"They just called me from Bristlecone. Dad had a heart attack."

"Oh no!" Willoughby's heart pounded.

"I know. He had been doing great. I don't know any details. They're taking him to the hospital. Can you go for me? I really don't think my doc will let me go."

"Of course, sweetie. I'll head right over." Oh no. Poor Steven. After being nearly out of the woods with pancreatic cancer, now this.

Jennie came in as Willoughby got off the phone, followed closely by Roy, carrying his sheaf of papers.

"Hi, Jennie, Roy. I'm going to have to leave, unfortunately. My ex-husband had a heart attack and Courtney's on bedrest, so I need to go do what I can."

"Oh no, Willoughby, I'm so sorry." Jennie's face suffused with sympathy.

"Oh, sorry," Roy said, with a puzzled look on his face.

"Thanks, I'll leave you the egg timer. Tell everyone I'm sorry to miss the meeting."

"All right, I hope your ex-husband recovers."

Willoughby went down the steps where Margaret had fallen not so very long ago, waved to Destiny, and stepped out into the hot summer afternoon. She crossed the courtyard, barely knowing where she was going; her mind raced. She almost walked by her own car. How bad had it been? Would Steven need to be moved to a higher level of care? Courtney was in no position to be able to do that; Willoughby would need to take care of him unless Adam came down. Maybe she should call Adam and tell him he was needed.

She was so preoccupied she nearly had an accident on the way to the hospital when she accidentally turned left into oncoming traffic. The angry horn of the oncoming car jolted her back to her senses. She squealed into the lot and raced through the crowded waiting area to the emergency room desk.

"My husband, Steven Philpott, was just brought in from Bristlecone." She purposely said "husband" rather than "ex-husband"; she didn't want anyone telling her she couldn't see him because she wasn't next-of-kin. Thank God she'd never changed her last name because of the kids. Thankfully, the nurse at the front desk waved her back and into a cubicle where Steven lay on a gurney, attached to an IV, and on a heart monitor. An oxygen mask covered the lower part of his face. He was pale and his eyes looked frightened. Willoughby rushed to his side.

"Steven!" She grabbed his hand, which felt cold and clammy. "Steven, I'm here."

His eyes widened when he saw her. "Madam Librarian."

"Steven, I'm here. Stay with us. You have a grandchild coming. We love you. I love you." And she did. Memories of their times together, vibrant with laughter, music, and color, sped through her mind like a home movie.

His eyes met hers and, very faintly, he squeezed her hand. Then the zigzagging line on the heart monitor went flat, and the machine began to buzz.

Two nurses ran into the room, pulling the curtain. "Ma'am, you need to leave," said one, as she called a code, which sounded throughout the ER. The other one gently pried Willoughby's hand from Steven's and led her out of the cubicle as a doctor rushed in, yelling "Paddles!" Standing outside, dazed and shaking, the horrible gun-like sounds reverberated inside Willoughby's head as the paddles shocked Steven. Willoughby had a sudden memory from one Halloween when the kids were little and Steven, dressed as Gumby, went trick-or-treating for "gummies for Gumby." Willoughby had not been able to stop laughing.

Finally, after what seemed to be an eternity, the nurses and the doctor walked out and closed the curtain behind them. Willoughby could tell from their defeated expressions that something was wrong.

"Is he okay? What's going on?"

"I'm so sorry. We did all we could, ma'am. Your husband didn't make it."

Willoughby's entire brain seemed to go to a blank

screen. One of the nurses took her by the elbow and ushered her into a chair, then stood next to her and held her hand, rubbing and massaging it gently.

The nurse asked if she wanted to see him, and she said yes. The nurse gently removed the oxygen tube, and then Willoughby went in and held his hand, which was already cool. His face looked ashen, yet peaceful, still with his usual whimsical if sardonic expression.

"Steven," she said, hoping he could still hear her somehow. "Your children love you very much and will miss you terribly. I wish you'd been able to meet your new grandchild. That night we spent together getting high was the most fun I've had in years, and I am grateful for it, even if I don't completely remember everything that happened." She kissed the top of his hand and sobbed as uncontrollably as she ever had in her entire life.

Twenty minutes later she still had not called Courtney, as she knew how heartbroken she would be, and any pain that Courtney felt, Willoughby felt also. And then there was the baby. But once it was established at the hospital that she was not, in fact, Steven's next-of-kin, she had to call.

Courtney, as she had predicted, was nearly inconsolable. When she was at last able to talk, she spoke with the nurse, as Steven's health-care power of attorney, about Steven's wishes to be cremated, and all the other arrangements that had been set up.

"What about a memorial service later, after you've had the baby and gotten settled?" Willoughby said after she was back on the line with Courtney. "Now is not a good time to decide anything, or to try to get people together."

"Yeah, that sounds good, Mom." Courtney's voice was low.

"Do you want me to call Adam, or do you want to?"

Courtney sighed. "I know how things are between you and Adam. Do you mind? I just can't talk about it. With all the hormones, I'm freaking out right now."

"Sure, I'll call him." Willoughby briefly wondered if Adam might have blocked her number but tried anyway, still sitting on the plastic bench in the hallway outside the emergency room. Her heart beating erratically, as she stared at a painting on the wall of a stream running over wet rocks with a troubled sky above, she tapped his name on her contacts list.

"Hello, Mom." Adam's voice was, as expected, cold and hostile. Silence stretched out as he waited for her to state the purpose of her call.

"Adam, I am so sorry, I have bad news. "

"What?"

"I hate to have to tell you this. Your father...didn't make it.."

"What?" Adam's voice cracked. "I thought he was getting better. I thought the surgery worked."

"He had a heart attack. About an hour ago. He's gone. I'm so sorry, Son."

More silence, so she went on. "I'm here at the hospital because Courtney is on bedrest. She is in no condition to plan a service. Maybe wait for a little while and have a memorial service later. You two talk about it and work out what you want to do together. I'm happy to help in any way if you need me."

"Okay. I'll get in touch with Courtney."

"Again, I'm sorry to be giving you this bad news. I'm

sorry you couldn't have been with him. I'm sure he would have liked that."

"Are you accusing me of neglecting my father?"

Willoughby drew in her breath. "Oh, Adam, of course not! I was just trying to help soothe your grief. I'm sure you didn't like being so far away from him, that's all I meant. I didn't mean—"

"I suppose *you* were with him?"

"Well, yes."

"Isn't that ironic." Adam's voice started out dripping venom but ended with a crack of absolute despair.

"Adam, we should be kind to each other," Willoughby said in the gentlest tone possible. "I know how hard these years must have been for you. I have always been ready to listen to what you have to say, whenever you were ready to say it."

A few more seconds of silence. "I can't believe that you, the person who hurt him more than anyone, were the one who was with him. You didn't even love him." And Adam began to cry.

"I did love him, Adam." She hadn't heard Adam cry since he'd come home from school in eighth grade and told her he'd gotten cut from the team during basketball tryouts. His letting her listen to him cry now could be a crack in the armor.

"And I love you. I'm so very sorry, my dear," she repeated. She wished she could reach through space and hug him. How distraught she had been when she lost her own father.

He finally pulled himself together and drew a deep breath. "All right. Thanks for calling. It probably wasn't an easy thing for you to do. I'm going to call Courtney now."

After they hung up, Willoughby put on her sunglasses, as she was nearly blinded by tears, and made her way out to the car. She sat in the driver's seat for several minutes, wiping her eyes, thinking about the surprising rekindling and now loss of her relationship with Steven, the anguish of the children, and assessing whether she should try to drive.

It was her usual time to visit Gary. She didn't have it in her. She decided instead to go to Courtney's early to start helping out. There were other family members and friends they needed to call, an obituary to be written. If Courtney or Adam couldn't, maybe, as a writer, the obituary would fall to her. Then there was Steven's room to pack up. So many things to do.

She could go see Gary tomorrow; he wouldn't know the difference.

Willoughby let herself in when she arrived so Courtney would not have to get out of bed. She glanced upstairs and could see that Clay's door was still closed, so he must still be napping.

"Hi, Court, I'm here." Courtney was on the couch in the living room, and Willoughby sat next to her and enveloped her in a long, tight hug. "He almost made it."

"I know. I can't believe it." Courtney's face was swollen and blotchy from crying, and Willoughby noted with a frisson of worry that her ankles looked swollen too. Keanu galloped in and jumped on the couch but, as if he could read human emotions, wasn't rambunctious. Instead, he licked Courtney's cheek and settled quietly next to her.

"How are you feeling, sweetie?"

"Okay. I've had a few Braxton Hicks contractions, but I had them for weeks last time."

Willoughby did laundry, helped Courtney call Steven's relatives, made a shrimp casserole for Courtney and Scott, walked that crazy dog Keanu, and then (separately this time) took Clay down to the playground in the stroller, brought him home, and got him fed, bathed, and ready for bed.

When Scott arrived, he gave her a bear hug. "Thanks, GiGi."

"Oh, I'm so happy I can help." Willoughby got her purse and hugged Courtney again. "I'll clean out Steven's room this weekend. Bristlecone usually gives people a few days, is what I hear."

"Oh, Mom, I hate for you to have to do that."

"I can do it," Scott offered.

"No, that's okay. You stay here and take care of Courtney. He didn't have that much stuff. I'll just bring it here."

Courtney cradled her stomach and reached over the back of the couch to take Scott's hand. "Okay, thanks, you're saving our lives here. Well, Mom, we have a name for the baby. Steven if it's a boy. And Stephanie if it's a girl. We'll call her Stevie for short."

"Your father was a huge Stevie Nicks fan. He would like that," Willoughby said, laughing, but with tears filling her eyes. She had a memory of that last night in Steven's room, floating around and singing "Landslide."

The next day she went to see Gary.

Plodding down the pristine hall toward his room, she almost turned around and went home to crawl into bed and get into the fetal position. But she made herself keep walking.

"Hi, Gary, it's me." She pushed open his door, steeling herself to be prepared for anything—food to be thrown, someone else to be in bed with him, anything.

Gary, sitting in the easy chair next to his bed, was neatly dressed, with his hair freshly washed and combed, looking like a beguiling silver fox. He paged through the photo album that Willoughby had made of the retirement party they'd given him at the station.

"My sweetheart!" he said joyfully. "I thought you'd never get here!" He stood, put the album on the bed, and eagerly enveloped her in a hug, giving her a deeply felt kiss on the cheek. Then he pointed at the photo album. "I have a lot of friends," he said.

"Yes, you do," she agreed.

"But none as wonderful as you." He stroked her hair.

Willoughby melted into his arms.

CHAPTER 27
JENNIE

Jennie rubbed her eyes, stood up from her computer, and stretched; her neck was aching. It was Tuesday evening, and sun rays the color of flames angled through the blinds in her den. She checked the time on her phone; it was after six and she'd been working on edits since mid-morning.

Her editor had a wonderful sense of story; she had made requests for Jennie to move scenes to increase tension, and Jennie found it amazing how much more effective the rearrangements were. She asked for new scenes, too, which Jennie enjoyed crafting. Overall, Jennie felt lucky that she was in the hands of a capable editor who "got" her story and wanted to help her make it stronger.

Jennie's eyes felt blurred, though. She'd lost track of the time. If she didn't go soon, she'd miss the Town Council meeting. She didn't really want to go but had promised Willoughby and Alli so they could all oppose Bernice's motions, and she was supposed to meet them in the lobby at six thirty. Quickly, she ate a bowl of cereal, put on a dash of lipstick, and yanked a brush through her white, corkscrew hair.

Her phone pinged.

It was Willoughby.

Sorry—have to cancel. Courtney has gone into labor!

Jennie had half expected that. So exciting—Willoughby was about to have another grandchild. She was over the moon excited for her. She grabbed her purse and headed down the hall toward the stairs rather than the elevator, hoping to avoid Bernice. She'd managed to steer clear of Bernice lately, except for that one time she had accosted Jennie about the play while she was at lunch with Willoughby and Alli. She hadn't seen her in the hall so maybe Bernice was avoiding her too. Down in the lobby, Jennie noticed that Bernice had put one of her flyers up on the bulletin board, with its verbiage about "maintaining a wholesome community," and fought a desire to rip it off and throw it away. Jennie hated how divided people still seemed to be. Shouldn't they be living in more accepting times by now?

Jennie had been waiting in the lobby for only a minute when her phone pinged again. Alli. Something had come up with her daughter as well. She hated to let Jennie down but urged her to go to the Town Hall and carry the standard for all of them.

Crap! Jennie nearly went back to her apartment. She hadn't planned on doing this alone. Honestly, she wouldn't have done it at all if it hadn't been for Alli and Willoughby. She hadn't really made a stand on her own since she'd met Michael at the march so many years ago. He'd always been with her.

You can do it, came Michael's voice.

Must I?

You must.

After a moment's consideration, she went out and climbed into her Honda, grasped the steering wheel with all the determination she could muster, and headed downtown. Traffic on Main Street was heavy, as usual, with a lot of pedestrians, and the lot near Ben & Jerry's ice cream and the bookstore where she usually parked was full. The Town Hall meeting must be attracting a lot of people. She finally found a spot over a block away, across from the college quadrangle with its small, nineteenth-century brick dorms and had to jog to get there in time.

She climbed the shallow steps to the two-story, marble-trimmed brick Town Hall building and found an impatient crowd outside the meeting room door, waiting to file in. The buzz of conversation rose and fell, and people jockeyed for position. Every time the front door opened, waves of summer heat blew into the air-conditioned interior.

Inside the meeting room, the air-conditioning didn't seem to be working very well at all, and town employees brought dusty, bright orange plastic chairs out from storage and placed them in the aisles to accommodate all the extra people. Townsfolk were wiping off the chairs and fanning themselves with any sheet of paper or other implement they could find.

Jennie snagged a seat in the next-to-last row, close to the door, so she could duck out if things went on too long. Bernice sat in the front row, near the microphone, with her flyer in her lap. Clearly, Bernice was still actually planning to speak. Were all these people here in support of Bernice?

What would Jennie say? Her chest tightened just thinking about it. She should have prepared something about the First Amendment, the evils of book banning, and censorship. But she'd thought Alli and Willoughby would do the talking and she'd only have to be there for moral support. And also, Bernice was her neighbor. She hated confrontation. Cold sweat broke out on her forehead.

As a writer, this is your fight, Michael said. *You need to speak up.*

The Town Council members called the meeting to order and disposed of a few items of town business: The plans for the new Town Hall complex and parking deck were available online. People had been leaving their cars too long on the electric vehicle chargers in front of the building. People were not picking up their dog poop in the park.

Jennie felt a bit embarrassed that she'd never been to a Town Council meeting until now. She really should have done better. She'd been so wrapped up in her own life—in Michael, Elijah, her writing. One of the Town Council members—a slim, high-energy woman with large red glasses and highlighted gray hair—lived at Bristlecone. She'd seen her in the dining hall and on the pickleball court. Jennie had admiration for this dedicated soul.

Finally, the time set aside for citizen input arrived, and the council called on Bernice. Holding herself very erect, Bernice approached the microphone.

"I moved here from the Midwest to be closer to my son, who works for the university in the grounds department," she began. "This is a lovely and wholesome town, and we need to keep it that way. We need to be vigilant against unwholesome influences. Some of the books at the Youth Center, which is a town-supported resource, are about having two fathers or two mothers, or about butts, or about farts, or about poop. One of them has a naked toddler on the front, and it's even by a famous author named Maurice Sendak!" Outrage poured off Bernice.

Jennie sighed. That was the beloved book Alli had talked about at lunch—*In the Night Kitchen.*

"Some of the books are about teen suicide," Bernice went on. "And teen gay love affairs. Our children don't need to see such books. Why should we give them ideas?"

Jennie's heart ached for young people who might have read *The Perks of Being a Wallflower* or *This Book Is Gay* and felt seen.

"I demand that these books be removed from the shelves of this government-supported resource. And now we have this play, *Legally Blonde,* which celebrates sexuality as well as homosexuality, and it generally does not reflect the wholesome nature of our town. I would like to make a motion that the play be closed down or, at the very least, that no one younger than eighteen be allowed to attend."

The council allowed the director of the Youth Center to come to the microphone, and she spoke about the importance of children being able to see themselves celebrated in the books they read and the dangers of book banning. The director of the Eden Forest Community Players also came to the mic, and he spoke eloquently about the play's message of inspiration to young women, and the fact that many of the roles in the production were being played by teenagers younger than eighteen. He pointed out that people could choose whether or not to attend the play, depending upon their preference, but that they should not curtail the rights of others to enjoy it.

Jennie let out a sigh of relief. The two directors were very well-spoken and persuasive. She was proud that they were protecting freedom. There would probably be no need for her to speak.

Then the council opened the mic to comments and a few citizens came down to stand in line behind the mic and express their thoughts. And Jennie was completely amazed by what she heard. Citizen after citizen expressed agreement with Bernice that the books she mentioned should not be available at a government-supported organization and that the play, *Legally Blonde*, was not wholesome entertainment and, at the very least, younger teens should not be allowed to attend.

One middle-aged man in the third row started chanting "Protect our kids!" and shaking his fist in the air, and people joined in until the roar built to the point that it seemed the ceiling would blow off the council room.

Jennie could not believe her ears. Living with Michael, being in a world of mixed culture, and with more liberal leanings, she had never imagined how differently other people might feel or think. During the years she'd been married to Michael, she'd learned over and over again the power of love. Michael's people had endured so much, yet they were among the most loving and open and accepting and fun-loving people she'd ever known. It was humbling to see the way they continually taught her to fight hate with love.

With puzzlement and disbelief, she watched the angry flushes on the faces of the people speaking, their ardor, their conviction, their fury.

With fervor she got up from her seat, amidst the chanting, and went down the aisle to stand in line behind the last person. By the time she came to the microphone, her heart pounded like fireworks on July Fourth.

"Protect our kids!" someone yelled.

The council chair pounded her gavel. "Quiet! If there isn't order, I will clear the room."

"Next." The council chair waved Jennie forward. "State your name and offer your comment."

"Thank you, ma'am." Jennie's hands were suddenly freezing on this hot summer evening, and she clasped them together so others couldn't see them shaking.

"Protect our kids!" someone shouted again.

The chair banged her gavel once more. "This is your last warning. If anyone else is disruptive, you'll be ejected from the room." She waited for ten or fifteen full seconds, for the room to be silent. Then she nodded at Jennie. "Go ahead, ma'am."

"I'm Jennie Rossi and...I am a writer." Jennie realized she'd never publicly acknowledged herself as such but that this was the perfect time to declare it. "I am also Bernice's neighbor." Out of the corner of her eye she saw Bernice glaring at her, her lips pursed, but she grabbed a breath and plowed on. "I have respect for Bernice's point of view. I, too, want a wholesome town. But I also want an inclusive town. I don't believe we achieve that by banning books or shutting down plays." She drew a steadying breath and continued.

"We achieve it with openness, and with freedom of expression, with knowledge and education. By teaching our children to think, and how to make their own decisions. That freedom is what our country is all about. Reading stories is one of the best ways for children to actually learn what the lives of people different from them might be like, and thus reading is one of the greatest sources of empathy. And what our world needs more than anything is empathy and kindness. Parents can decide whether their children should read the books at the Youth Center. And they should decide whether their own children, if they are under eighteen, should attend or participate in *Legally Blonde*. Those artistic expressions should remain available to the people of our town. Thank you." Jennie was totally out of breath by the time she finished and wasn't even sure exactly what she'd said.

She heard the applause of one person, and then several, behind her. A voice she recognized, right behind her, yelled "Go, Jennie!" She turned and saw Destiny standing just behind her, giving her a thumbs-up, the very last person waiting to speak. Jennie smiled with surprise, and they squeezed each other's hands as Destiny stepped up to the mic.

"I just wanted to add to what Jennie said about young readers seeing themselves in books," Destiny said. "My mom told me that her family wasn't even allowed into the library when she was little, because of being Black, and she said that one of the few picture books she could remember that showed a little Black kid was *The Snowy Day* by Ezra Jack Keats. Her mother got it for her and she read it over and over. She told me that later the book was challenged because it hadn't been written by a Black person. But it meant a lot to my mom. And now it's a classic."

The crowd hushed as Destiny spoke—possibly because she was the first really young person to speak. Jennie was impressed with how self-possessed and articulate Destiny was. Michael had told Jennie that he wasn't allowed to go into the library as a child either. Maybe the audience also might have been hushed when reminded of that.

"By the time I was able to go to the library, though," Destiny went on, "there were lots of books that showed Black kids like me. I can't even put into words how important it was to me to have those books. Having those books was like someone saying, 'I see you. I get you.' When I think about kids from all different cultures and countries, or especially kids who think they might be gay, or trans—finding books that tell their stories is a way to be seen, and that's one of the most important things in the world. Please, see us. Let's see each other. Being free means freedom to read. Thank you."

As she left the podium, the applause for Destiny was electric. As there weren't any more people in line behind her, the Town Council said they would then take a vote.

The seven members voted, four to three, to allow the Youth Center to continue to choose books for their patrons and for *Legally Blonde* to move forward with their opening night later in the week. The tie-breaking vote was the woman with the red glasses from Bristlecone. Jennie wanted to hug her.

Someone tapped her shoulder from behind. She turned and saw Abe.

"Great speech," he said, patting her shoulder.

"I didn't know you were here!"

"Your neighbor gave me a flyer at the stage door, and I made up my mind then to come and speak my mind if necessary. But I couldn't have said it any better than you. And Destiny. Very well done."

"Well, thank you, Abe."

As everyone exited the hall, Jennie lost Abe but found Destiny. "Excellent speech, Destiny. You made a great impression." In a burst of affection, she enfolded her in a spontaneous hug.

"Thank you. I didn't know you'd be here." Destiny hugged her back, seeming pleased.

"I didn't know you were coming either! I can't tell you how happy I was to see your friendly face. Alli and

Willoughby were going to come but couldn't make it at the last minute."

"Your neighbor Bernice was giving out flyers and gave me one when I was working the desk," Destiny told her. "I thought, well, I have something to say. And I'm so glad I came!"

"Me too. It was great to have you here. I'm glad the vote went well, but it was a little disconcerting how close it was, right?"

"I know. Something to think about. Definitely a bummer." Destiny spotted her car in the dark parking lot, and they hugged again and parted ways.

Jennie basked in the glow of the vote, in being supported by Destiny and suddenly feeling closer to her, and the applause, but felt chastened by the narrowness of it all. When she opened her car door, she saw a distraught woman a short distance away, kneeling on the asphalt beside her car, riffling through her purse.

"Can I help?" Jennie said, turning on the flashlight on her phone. She shone the light and saw that the person was Bernice.

"I lost my keys. I can't find them anywhere." Bernice stood up, saw Jennie, and hesitated, about to turn away, then added, "I've looked through every pocket."

"Here, I'll shine the flashlight inside," Jennie offered. She shone the light into Bernice's purse, over Bernice's wallet, phone, hairbrush, sunglasses, reading glasses, numerous tissues, and pill bottles, but no keys.

"They must have fallen out," Bernice said. "They must be back inside the Town Hall."

"I'll go help you look," Jennie said.

"No, you don't have to." Bernice's voice sounded dismissive.

"Of course I do." No matter their differences, Jennie still felt compelled to help.

So they walked the block in the dark to the Town Hall and Bernice looked everywhere around her seat, in the aisle, and in the front lobby for her keys. They were nowhere to be found.

"I'll drive you home," Jennie said. "You can get your spare keys, and I'll bring you back tonight, or you can come back in the morning."

"All right," Bernice said in a dull voice, still not meeting her eye.

On the way back to Jennie's car, Bernice told her she never lost anything. "I'm so orderly, so organized. You must believe that this never happens to me. I just...I just had a very difficult conversation with my son before I came tonight and really, I almost didn't come."

"I'm sorry." Jennie automatically slid into her therapist role She had heard pretty much everything during her social work sessions.

"He still won't let me see my grandson."

"Oh, I didn't know that." Jennie's heart fluttered, but she kept her voice even and accepting.

"Yes, when he first met his wife, I was against their marriage. She's from Afghanistan, her religion is different, her customs are different. Well, you can understand my position. I didn't support the wedding. I didn't go."

"Oh," said Jennie. She broke out in a sweat. She had experienced the very same thing with her own wedding. And then she had nearly done that to her own dear Elijah, not because of differences but because of money. How ironic—such a fine and delicate balance in life. And do we ever learn?

"But now I have a grandson who is six months old, and

I'd like to meet him. That's why I moved here—to be close. But my son hasn't forgotten that I didn't come to the wedding, and he won't forgive me, and neither will she, and they won't let me see my own grandson. I haven't even been allowed to see a picture." Bernice was gasping and crying now. "You know, I'm trying. I'm really trying. But I'm struggling."

"Bernice, I'm so very sorry. That must be terribly hard for you." Jennie, abandoning the non-touching adage she'd followed as a therapist, put her arm around Bernice and squeezed for a long moment.

"Thank you," Bernice said gruffly.

"This is my car." Jennie unlocked the car and got in.

Sighing, Bernice climbed into the passenger seat and swung her purse into her lap. She unzipped an outside pocket and pulled out a tissue to wipe her eyes, and a faint jingle sounded. She dug hurriedly into the pocket and produced her car keys. "Oh Lord. They were in this outside pocket all the time!"

"Oh, wonderful, so glad you found them."

"I'm so sorry about all this trouble." Bernice blew her nose.

"Not to worry." Jennie drove Bernice to her car. "Have a good evening, Bernice. You take care. I hope things work out with your son and his wife and the grandbaby."

Bernice's teary eyes gleamed in the darkness as she met Jennie's, opening the passenger door. "Thank you, Jennie."

Jennie, when she arrived home, fed Sir Arthur, then went into the office and sat in Michael's leather chair and called Elijah.

"Yeah, Mom, what's up?"

"I was wondering if you and Amanda could come over tomorrow night after work, or this weekend? I have something I need to tell you."

"Gosh, Mom, is it bad? You sound super serious."

"It's not bad, it's just...it just is. It's something I should have told you a long time ago." Her conversation with Bernice had convinced her that this secret had to be revealed now; it had already been kept too long. She swore she would never be in a situation like Bernice with Elijah.

"Damn, if it's that big a deal, tell me now."

"No, not over the phone."

Elijah and Amanda came over after work on Thursday night, picking up a Mediterranean pizza and a Greek salad on the way. When Jennie opened the door to let them in, Bernice was standing outside her door across the hall, searching for her keys again.

She glanced at Elijah and Amanda, then at Jennie, blushed, and drew herself up. "Hello, I'm Bernice. I assume you're Jennie's son and daughter-in-law?"

"Yes, well, fiancée. We're getting married next spring," Amanda said with a cautious smile.

"It's nice to meet you," Bernice said. "Jennie is a wonderful neighbor. I'm very lucky."

"I'm sure she's lucky too," Elijah said. "It's great to have friends nearby."

"It certainly is. You all have a nice evening. That pizza smells wonderful!" Bernice finally found her keys in the same outside pocket of her purse and went inside her apartment.

"She seems nice," Elijah said as he set the pizza box on Jennie's kitchen counter.

"She does." Jennie decided to say no more. She hoped Bernice and her son could repair their relationship.

They ate around Jennie's table, talking casually about Amanda's upcoming promotion and raise, a half-marathon the kids had signed up to run together, and some of the plans that had been made for the wedding trip to Tanzania. *The Lion King* was coming to Charlotte, and they talked about the possibility of going with Amanda's parents.

Finally, after they'd finished eating and washed the few dishes, Jennie sat down and put both hands on the table. "So I guess you all are wondering what it was that I thought was such a big deal to tell you."

"Yeah." Elijah raised his eyebrows, waiting.

Jennie launched into the story of her heritage, nervous about how Elijah might take the news. She ended by saying, "Even though at that time in the South there was prejudice against Italians, there was more against Iraqis. So many years went by that the true story almost never got told." Jennie took a breath. "I never told you, either, that your grandfather didn't approve of me marrying your father, and I was estranged from my family until he died. After my father died, I had a reconciliation with my mother and your Aunt Sofia. While my mother was dying, she lived with Aunt Sofia, and I went to visit her, and that's when she told me the truth. So you have Iraqi heritage. And Jewish heritage."

"Wow, Mom. You've kept this secret a long time."

"I didn't tell you at first, because it was just easier. I was a little puzzled and angry that Mama never told me the truth, and I decided to do nothing at first. With the war in Iraq, and the way people were feeling in this country, it made my mother keep the secret even longer, and then so did I." Jennie paused. "I realize now that it was wrong. But I've had to mention it in my bio for this book, and I knew you would see it, and I didn't want you to see it there first and be surprised. I mean, this is something you should have known from the time you were a little boy."

"I'm just amazed." Elijah stared at her with a thoughtful look on his face. "So intriguing, Mom. Did you think I'd be mad?"

"I don't know. I need to think about that. I've written it all down in my author bio, if you want to read it." Jennie grabbed the folder that she'd prepared for him and put it on the table. She realized she was waiting breathlessly for his reaction, twisting her fingers around each other.

"Yeah, of course, I'd like to," he said, sliding the folder closer, and then remained quiet for a few minutes. "Mom, I know that was hard for you. I do wish you'd told me before, sure. And our country has a really long way to go as far as equality goes. Our country is torn apart over immigration. But I think our generation—mine and Amanda's—has a different view. Things like this are not as big a deal to us as they are to someone from your generation. And also, you and Dad taught me well."

Jennie felt tears trembling in the corners of her eyes as she reached for Elijah's hand.

"Things like this—someone's background—maybe used to be scandalous but people our age don't judge as much as in the past," Amanda said. She took Jennie's other hand and squeezed it.

Elijah went on. "I mean, I guess my main reaction right now is that I want to find out more about my grandmother and how she got here. First of all, I admire the hell out of her."

"I'm going to research that too." Jennie drew a deep breath of relief and smiled at them.

"And maybe this is something that we can think about for our wedding too. To acknowledge who we are," Amanda added.

Jennie was so very proud of them.

Legally Blonde: The Musical ran for two weeks, every performance a full house, every performance earning a standing ovation. After the final show, on the last Sunday in June, and the exhilarating curtain call, Abe and the others in the writing group went out into the lobby, the applause still ringing in their ears.

Nicole brought Solomon out from backstage to see them. Human actors from the show mingled with the audience too. And Solomon, knowing he was the center of attention, ran excitedly in a circle on the slippery lobby floor from one person to another, wagging his tail and jumping up on their knees. He still wore his lawyer bow tie from the curtain call.

"You are such a superstar!" Jennie said, giggling as she petted his fawn fur.

"I'm not usually a dog fan, but he's adorable," Willoughby said. "And he was perfect for the part. The play was hilarious. Oh, Abe, Destiny said she wanted to come, but she had to go out of town."

"Totally understand. Oh, this is my ex-wife, Nicole, by

the way," Abe said. "She was helping out backstage with Solomon."

"A tough job but someone had to do it." Nicole winked. Everyone gave her a friendly hello.

"I'm Alli, the one who had your job on Fridays and Saturdays, Nicole. And this is my daughter, Maeve," Alli said. "She teaches at the university. And this is her daughter, Sierra."

"What's your PhD in?" Abe asked Maeve. He'd talked with Maeve just briefly before the curtain rose because she had been rather upset and told her mother that she'd forgotten her low-dose aspirin. Alli had asked the entire party if anyone happened to have a baby aspirin, and Abe had gallantly offered one of those he always carried with him.

"Women's studies," Maeve said. "Mom said you used to teach there. What department?"

"Middle Eastern studies."

She nodded. She was taller than Alli and didn't really look much like her. She was also older than Abe expected her to be. Late forties, maybe even fifty. "Well, the play was an amusing send-up of academia, wasn't it?"

Abe thought her comment was a little pompous and humorless but didn't comment.

The granddaughter, Sierra, actually reminded Abe more of college-age Alli than Maeve. Sierra was entranced with Solomon. "He is so cute. I have a Yorkie who's going to be the ring bearer at our wedding. Can I pick him up?"

"Sure." Abe let her hold Solomon, who went to her happily.

"So, Abe, now that the play's over, are you glad you took Solomon for the auditions?" Alli asked.

"I am! I have to say, this is the most fun I've had in a

long time. I might even say this experience has changed my life."

"Oh, really? In what way?" Alli said.

"Yes, I'd be interested in that too," Nicole said, with a smiling glance at Alli.

Abe felt a little pinned down by their question, as the changes he'd experienced seemed difficult to put into words. "Oh, I don't know—I've gotten to know all of you in the writers' group in a more personal way since we've had the play to talk about and share. And the writers' group has come to mean more to me as a consequence. I just...feel more a part of the community. I know we had a lot of discussions about our 'own voices'"—he held his fingers up in quotes—"but writing itself is an amazing exercise in empathy. Trying to write from the point of view of a person different from myself—say, a woman, or say, a person from another country or culture—has been an incredibly illuminating experience." Since Alli and Nicole were both there, and he had tried, in his own clumsy way, to write from their points of view, he didn't go into more detail.

"I totally agree with you, after spending several years writing from Enheduanna's point of view," Jennie said.

"I think I've become less judgmental. I've come to treasure my family relationships more. And widened my circle of friends. I mean, I hope you're my friends," Abe ended self-consciously.

"Of course we are," Jennie said. "And I will always be grateful for having you cheer me on at the Town Council meeting and supporting us in our quest to save Margaret's stories."

"Yes, you helped save *Legally Blonde*! The experience of Margaret's stories has been very profound," Abe said. "It's too bad that Roy didn't make it today. Would anyone like to walk over to the new winery in town for a glass of wine?" Abe added. "They have an outside seating area that allows dogs, so Solomon could join us."

"I wish I could, but I need to go see Gary, and then I promised I'd help out with Courtney's new baby, Stevie," Willoughby said. "I'm trying to take over some of the feedings with bottles so Courtney can get some sleep. Sorry to miss out! I'll see everyone on Friday. I hope to finally have a few pages, after all the time I've missed with these life events. Plus, maybe Alli and I will have the final arrangement ready for Margaret's stories."

"I can't go either," Jennie said. "I've got editing to do."

Alli, her daughter, and granddaughter also demurred; they had dinner plans. Abe was disappointed; he had hoped for a moment or two with Alli, but her daughter and granddaughter's presence obviously made that awkward. Not to mention the presence of Nicole. After a few more minutes of conversation, Abe and Nicole headed out to the parking lot with Solomon.

"I think Alli is a really nice person, but I found her daughter off-putting," Abe said. Abe was always comfortable being honest with Nicole. She really knew him better than almost anyone.

Nicole smiled. "That's very funny, because she reminded me of you, Abe. In fact, she even looked a little like you."

"I can't imagine where you'd get *that*," he said. "Thanks again for helping with Solomon. I don't know what I would have done without you."

"Oh, I have a feeling you would have managed." Nicole gave him a mysterious and somewhat flirty smile.

Abe looked at his watch. It was a little after five. "You

didn't say you had plans. Let me buy you a glass of wine to say thanks."

Nicole gave him an amused glance. "Sure, I'll let you buy me a glass of wine, Dr. Goodman."

Nicole and Abe found a café table on the stone patio at the wine bar and Abe went inside to order. As he waited for the drinks, he watched as Nicole sat with Solomon, running her fingers over his silky ears, talking to him softly. Solomon appeared to be in heaven.

"Cab for you, champagne for your wife," said the pleasant, tattooed bartender she handed over the two drinks.

"Thank you," said Abe. "Though, she's not my wife."

"Oh, sorry," said the bartender, with a widening of her eyes. "I shouldn't have assumed."

"No, please don't apologize," Abe said. "She actually *used* to be my wife."

"Okay, well, I stand corrected. Ex-wife, then."

Abe tossed off a laugh. "I'm sure it's quite confusing."

The bartender shrugged. "No worries. I'll just say, it looks like she means something to you, whatever the name for that is. Would you like a treat for your dog?"

Abe was surprised. "Oh, well, he's watching his weight, better not."

"Come on, let the little fella have a treat." In her multi-ringed fingers, the bartender held out a very tiny dog treat.

Abe nodded and smiled. "All right, he's definitely earned it, you win."

Abe went to the table, gave Solomon the treat, and he eagerly jumped down from Nicole's lap to eat it in peace under the table.

Abe proposed a toast to Nicole. "To my wonderful ex-wife and chihuahua wrangler."

"I'm not actually your ex-wife, Abe, in case you haven't noticed."

Abe's heart flip-flopped. "What do you mean?"

"Did you ever receive signed divorce papers back from me? I don't believe so, since I never signed them." She cocked her head, tossed her strawberry-blonde braid over her shoulder, and smiled at him.

"You didn't? I guess I just assumed…"

"Nope."

"Why didn't you sign them?" Abe felt dizzy. Hadn't she been the one to remind him about the year's separation passing?

Nicole shrugged. "I'm not sure, honestly. Just got lost in the shuffle during business tax season, I guess. Maybe on some level I thought you'd stop being so scared about your health and change your mind about Bristlecone. I can sign them this week, though, if you really want me to."

Abe nodded absently, still stunned by what she had just said. He wasn't divorced. He had no idea what to say next. What did he want? What did Nicole want?

He looked over at Nicole. She was, as she often said, his best friend. Solomon had finished his treat, crawled into her lap, and fallen asleep. When Abe caught her eye, she smiled, smoothing her fingers over Solomon's silky ears. Her strawberry braid snaked its way over her shoulder and her eyes, heavy-lidded after the wine, regarded him with frank desire.

Without thinking, Abe leaned toward Nicole and kissed her.

～

Later, Abe awoke in the depths of the night in his small Bristlecone bedroom, with the mattress that he had to admit hurt his back and the annoying streetlamp that shone in stripes through his blinds.

His mind replayed the *Legally Blonde* production, how everyone had embraced Solomon, the true and loyal friendships he treasured with the other writers, and the rediscovery of Allison—who he realized he had never really known or understood back in college but only imagined as some fulfillment of his own fantasy. And who knows, maybe he was her fantasy as well? He thought most of all about the way he'd kissed Nicole in the candlelight at the wine bar.

He looked over at the streetlamp shining in stripes through his window blinds. Life was so often like that—a light was shining but we still couldn't see.

CHAPTER 29
WILLOUGHBY

Courtney showed Willoughby the beautiful carved wooden cremation urn when she arrived that Saturday afternoon in July for Steven's memorial service, carrying flowers and Steven's favorite chicken enchilada casserole, still hot from the oven, in honor of him.

"Oh, the urn is beautiful. Do you know where you'll scatter the ashes?" Courtney and Adam had decided that they wanted a small memorial, with just the family, at Courtney's house. They each planned to take half the ashes to spread as they saw fit. They had invited Steven's brother and his wife and their children, but the trip from Florida was too long. They had sent flowers and a basket of food.

"I'm just going to put my portion of the ashes near our willow tree by the creek," Courtney said as she took the flowers from Willoughby to put on the kitchen island. The week after Steven died, the island had been covered with cards, food baskets, and flowers sent to her by friends and family. But that had been a month ago, before Stevie had been born.

"That's a good idea; then you can talk to him whenever

you want," Willoughby said, patting Courtney's hand. "And you've got daylilies and gardenias blooming right now too. Their beauty will help." She remembered how bereft and buried in darkness she'd felt when she'd lost her own father and knew that both kids were struggling. It was especially hard for Courtney, having just given birth, with her rampant hormones and loss of sleep.

Willoughby had of course been helping with Stevie whenever Courtney asked but also wanted to give her space. Willoughby doubted Courtney had even had adequate time to grieve, but thought she was doing tremendously well. She'd told Willoughby that she decided the only place she had time to cry was the shower, so that's where she did it.

"Clay, show GiGi how you've been helping to put on Stevie's booties," Courtney said, sitting on the couch and patting the spot next to her for Clay. He climbed onto the couch and proudly slid one bootie at a time over Stevie's pink feet with her tiny corn kernel toes.

"Very good job, Clay," Willoughby said, kissing his round cheek.

People didn't talk about how a person might grieve the death of their ex-spouse. Willoughby had received one card from a longtime friend who had been close when she and Steven had been married, but that was all. She understood; so often divorced couples hated each other and were intensely relieved when the time came that they didn't have to deal with each other anymore. But there must always have been an initial attraction, or fondness, and sometimes that and a deep friendship remained. That had been the case with Willoughby and Steven, due primarily to Steven's generosity of spirit.

Courtney's phone pinged and she glanced at it. "Adam's

flight just landed, and Scott says they'll be here in thirty minutes."

"Great." Willoughby couldn't help but have anticipatory anxiety, even though Adam had, in a turnabout, told Courtney that it was all right with him for Willoughby to be present at Steven's memorial service. The estrangement from Adam had lasted so long that Willoughby, incredibly grateful for the end of it, also hoped she'd know how to act.

It was hard for Willoughby not to smother little Stevie with kisses every minute of the day. The baby was the most adorable and lovable thing she'd ever seen, and she could not get enough of her. Her smell! Her tiny starfish hands!

"Why don't you take a nap before they get here?" Willoughby suggested.

"If you can help me put the kids down, Deborah from Bristlecone will be here in a few minutes."

"Oh! I didn't realize you'd called Deborah. She's wonderful."

"Actually, she called me. She said she knew you, as you'd worked together on your friend Margaret's service, and I thought it was especially nice of her to offer to come. It makes everything so much easier with the kids. We had a Zoom meeting last week with Adam to talk about the service."

Courtney and Willoughby had just finished putting the kids down when Deborah arrived. She didn't wear the clerical robe she usually wore to officiate at Bristlecone. Instead, she wore a colorful shirt, neat white capris, and flip-flops. Her short auburn hair curled attractively behind her ears. Willoughby thought it was a casual way to dress for a memorial service but didn't mention it.

"I admired the way you handled Margaret's service, and

I'm so glad you're here to do Steven's," Willoughby said as they stood by the kitchen island.

Courtney came up beside Deborah, reached down into the cabinet below, and produced a blender. "We're having a very special kind of service, Mom, that I was keeping for a surprise. We're having a Margaritaville memorial service for Dad."

"What?" Willoughby's jaw dropped.

"You heard me."

"That's why I'm wearing a Hawaiian shirt," Deborah said.

"Me, too," said Courtney, unbuttoning her black maternity top to reveal a Hawaiian shirt underneath with a brilliant pattern of luscious fuchsia lotuses and alabaster lilies.

"Lotuses and lilies. As a writer, I'd say that stands for rebirth and new beginnings," said Willoughby, feeling a catch in her throat.

"That's right, Mom."

The front door flew open as Adam and Scott returned from the airport, carrying Adam's bags.

"A Margaritaville memorial service? Did Adam agree?"

"That's right, I'm fully on board, Mom," came Adam's loud voice from the hall.

"Shhhh!" Courtney ran into the hall with her finger to her lips. "Please keep it down so we don't wake the kids."

"Oh, sorry," Adam whispered.

"You're clearly not experienced in the parenting department, bro," Scott stage-whispered to Adam.

Adam gave himself a mock clap on the forehead. "Busted."

Willoughby stood at the end of the hall, wondering whether to hug Adam. He was wearing a pair of tight faded jeans and a Hawaiian shirt with white birds of paradise on a black background.

"Mom, you're not dressed right," Courtney added. "Why don't you go put on a Hawaiian shirt of mine over your black dress. I left one out for you."

"I don't know, Courtney—"

"Mom, this is what Dad wanted. He'd written out his wishes before he had surgery."

"Really?"

"Really." Deborah nodded. "And there's a part for you in the service, too, Willoughby, so go get changed."

"But please be as quiet as a little mouse so you won't wake the kids," Courtney said.

"They'll wake up the minute you turn on that blender anyway, honey." Scott said. "Might as well just get ready for the onslaught."

Willoughby went into Courtney's room and saw that one of Courtney's Hawaiian shirts, with yellow pineapples and blood-red hibiscus blooms on it, hung on the closet door. Clearly this memorial service wasn't going to be anything like what she expected. Or maybe anything she'd ever attended before. As Willoughby buttoned up the shirt over her dress, she remembered that hibiscus plant she'd regifted to Steven after Gary threw it. It had done so well in Steven's room, as though it belonged there.

This, she realized, was indeed exactly what Steven wanted.

Once she'd put on the shirt, she leaned to peek into the bassinet and drank in Stevie's sweet pink sleeping face. She inhaled her intoxicating baby smell. Then she tiptoed out, pulling the door closed behind her.

A few minutes later, Courtney fired up the blender and Scott turned on Jimmy Buffett. Predictably, both children woke up, and the place was bedlam in the most delightful way imaginable. Willoughby gave Clay a snack while Courtney nursed Stevie and Scott took over margarita duty.

Once the kids were fed, everyone went out into the backyard. Courtney and Adam spoke about having such a fun-loving person as a father. Deborah spoke eloquently about the role of joy in life, quoting from philosophers and artists and musicians.

And Willoughby was assigned to read a little-known quote from author Marthe Troly Curtin that essentially said, time you enjoyed wasting wasn't wasted after all.

Courtney and Adam both cried as they sprinkled ashes on the flower bed beneath the willow, between daylilies and the gardenia bush, both of whose blooms, Willoughby reflected, lasted only one day.

Deborah gave a prayer that blessed rock and roll musicians who played too loud, and their fans, who danced too hard. And then she ended on a traditional note with the Lord's Prayer.

Then they gathered the children, went inside, and each adult drank a margarita, while singing Steven's favorite song, "Margaritaville."

They were all crying, of course. Everyone knew the words—even people who don't know Jimmy Buffett know the words to "Margaritaville"—but Willoughby, as she wiped her streaming eyes, figured it wasn't that often that people cried when they sang them. Willoughby's favorite song by Jimmy Buffett had actually been "Come Monday." That was the one that made her think most of Steven and what they'd had together for twenty-five years.

Willoughby served everyone the chicken enchiladas, and after the meal, she made a point of sitting next to Adam on the couch.

"Courtney tells me you bought an apartment in Brooklyn with your partner," she said cautiously. "I'd love to hear about it." She and Adam had spoken twice on the phone since Steven died, and they'd painfully worked through a lot of Adam's feelings. Willoughby was careful to bring up a topic that she knew would be easy for Adam to talk about.

"We adore it," Adam said. "It's the top floor of a 1920s brownstone, with gorgeous refinished floors and those enormous, tall windows that take up the entire wall and let in lots of glorious light. I don't know if Courtney told you, but my partner Diego is an architect, and he's drawn plans to renovate and enlarge the bathrooms and closets."

"That sounds exciting. I'd love to see it. I want to stay around here to help Courtney for the first few months, but maybe I could come up before it gets cold in the fall and see it. And meet Diego." She said this with studied casualness.

Adam hesitated, looking at her for a moment, then drew a breath and nodded. "Sure, that would be fine."

Willoughby nodded calmly, though her heart was pounding with emotion. "Do you have any photos of your house?"

Adam was more than happy to pull out his phone and show her dozens of them. Willoughby could hardly believe that the estrangement between them seemed to have thawed. She was so grateful that she sat very still, barely breathing, as the late evening summer sun shone on the two of them sitting together on the couch. She remembered when he was a boy and she used to massage his neck after a difficult day at school.

Shortly afterward, Deborah left with hugs all around. Soon after, Courtney revealed that Steven had also requested that those attending his service watch *The Big Lebowski*, his favorite cult classic movie.

Before the movie, Willoughby took Clay upstairs and they read *The Very Hungry Caterpillar* and she tucked him in, making him laugh with raspberries on his cheek. After Clay had drifted off, once downstairs, she decided it might be a good time to leave. She had never really liked that movie, she remembered.

"I've got to go," she said, removing the Hawaiian shirt, taking it back into Courtney's room, and leaning to very gently touch the cheek of the sleeping Stevie. How incredibly powerful her love for this little person already was. Once back in the living room, she gave Courtney a hug. "You all can watch the movie without me." She went over to Adam and reached out to take his hand.

But he pulled her close. "Good to see you, Mom."

Willoughby went outside and had to sob and wipe her eyes for a solid five minutes before starting the car. So much reeled through her mind. Her long ago love for Steven, and the new connection they'd been briefly granted. Her absolute love for their children and grandchildren. All the pain and the losses. And oh, God, she was getting so old. Finally, she felt capable of driving. She put on her driving glasses and headed back toward Bristlecone.

She'd planned to skip visiting Gary. As the nurses repeatedly told her, he didn't remember or notice. But she desperately wanted to see him and headed for her usual space in the memory-care parking lot. How many more days did she have with him, after all? It was impossible to know.

CHAPTER 30
DESTINY

In the women's room next to the front desk, Destiny put on the brightest red shiny lipstick she could find. She didn't usually mess with it but today was special. She was going to be channeling Angie Thomas and Amanda Gorman at the same time. And it was going to be awesome.

Destiny picked up her worn, marked-up copy of *The Hate U Give*, and headed to the back courtyard where the old bristlecone pine tree stood, to join the Banned Books from the Big Chair reading. But her boss, Ms. Robinson, came up to her just as she was going outside.

"Destiny, do you have a minute?"

"Yes, Ms. Robinson?" Destiny had just given her notice that morning. She drew a breath. That was quick.

"Destiny, I know you're heading out for the Banned Books event, so I'll be brief. I will be sorry to see you go. I am not saying this just because your mama is my soror. You have done a good job here at Bristlecone, and this front desk job is not as easy as it seems. You really hustled that night that Elvis performed. You've gotten to know the residents, and they trust you. And your efforts at CPR on the day Margaret Tinker fell were stellar. I really think you will be a good nurse. I gave you an outstanding reference. Good luck to you."

"Oh, thank you, Ms. Robinson. I did learn more than I expected from this job." Destiny leaned forward to shake Ms. Robinson's hand, but Ms. Robinson just ended up giving her a hug. She had not said one word to anyone about seeing Destiny kissing Marcus at her graduation party.

"I know you're participating, so run on, we'll finish any formalities another time."

"All right, thanks, Ms. Robinson."

Destiny stepped outside, kind of glowing from Ms. Robinson's compliments, and joined the others gathering for the event. It was the middle of summer and the spring flowers had finished blooming, but the hardy yellow daylilies were like happy spots of hope in the courtyard, and that old bristlecone was still evergreen, kind of like a miracle. They'd lucked out with a glorious day. In the court-yard, the writers' group had set up rows of chairs in a semi-circle facing a really big Adirondack chair. Someone—Destiny thought it was Willoughby—made a sign that said, "Banned Books from the Big Chair."

Marcus said he'd meet her there, and sure enough, he slid onto the seat next to Destiny just as Willoughby was ready to get started. He took her hand. He'd talked Destiny into this. Now that Destiny had given her notice, it didn't matter if everybody knew about them.

Mama had met Marcus at Destiny's graduation party, and even though Destiny tried to make it seem as though he was just another friend, Mama saw through that pretty quick.

"That Marcus seems like a nice young man," Mama said the

next day, eyeing Destiny as she sipped her breakfast coffee. "Did you say he's a med tech?"

"Yes, Mama." Destiny tried to act like butter wouldn't melt in her mouth, but after that she felt relaxed enough to invite Marcus to the house, and their next date was just a walk around a small lake near her family's house with Rosa, their little pittie dog. Then Marcus threw the ball for Rosa at the dog park for nearly an hour.

When they got back to the house, Mama said why didn't he stay for dinner, and he won her over by having two helpings of her cornbread. After that, Marcus played pool in the basement with Papa and Destiny's brothers. And after that, well, here they were, texting each other all day.

Willoughby had encouraged Destiny to participate in this event too—and she also told Destiny she had a librarian friend in Durham who was connected to a slam poetry and spoken word open mic club. Destiny was definitely going to check that out. Marcus had said he'd come listen to her, and he was already checking out concert options in the Durham area for the fall. Plus, she and Jada had already gone to Durham looking at apartments, which was why she hadn't made it to *Legally Blonde*, and they were going to Durham next week again. Destiny had to admit that it was going to be fun.

People started showing up and filling in the remaining seats, carrying their favorite banned books, most of which looked thumbed-through and battered with wear, or maybe that was just love. It kind of made Destiny tear up to see how loved those books were. And they were all putting their names on the sign-up sheet up front. The writers' group had opened the event to the public, so it wasn't just the old people there, but young folks from the staff at Bristlecone and the town of Eden Forest too, of all backgrounds, some college kids, some who were working. There were some parents there, too, with those kids' books that everybody loved.

Pretty soon all the chairs were full, and more people were coming, so Abe and Roy and the other writers brought out more chairs from inside. When everyone got settled, Willoughby called them to attention.

"Welcome to 'Banned Books from the Big Chair.' Hi, my name is Willoughby Philpott. I'm a retired librarian. I am ashamed to say that once I allowed a woman to bully me into placing a book behind the counter at the library, where a person had to ask for it. I told myself, 'I'm not removing this book, so it's not really banned.' The book was *Speak*, by Laurie Halse Anderson, which is about a girl who is sexually assaulted and literally cannot speak afterward. But being behind the counter, the book was effectively banned, because what girl who has experienced that horror has the courage to come to the desk and ask for the book? After I did it, I felt as though I let down readers and vowed never again to let that happen."

As Willoughby took a breath and straightened her notes, Destiny wondered if she might have started feeling emotional just thinking about that experience. It was brave of her to admit that she'd done that. People judged. One thing Destiny had learned from the old people at Bristlecone was that over the course of their long lives, people made mistakes. Almost everybody did. That didn't mean they couldn't correct them later. Or redeem themselves. And that didn't mean they weren't still good people.

Thinking about second chances gave Destiny a feeling of peace about the future, especially when it came to deciding between nursing, spoken word, and Marcus. That was something really valuable she was taking away from this job that she'd thought at first was so useless and boring.

"Later," Willoughby went on, after clearing her throat, "when I went to a conference, they had a wonderful event called 'Banned Books from the Big Chair,' where anybody could sign up and read a portion from one of their favorite banned books. You would be amazed by the number of books that have been banned over the years, and the reasons they've been banned. One, *In the Night Kitchen*, showed a little boy with no clothes on the cover. Another, *Charlotte's Web*, featured talking animals. Another, *Are You There God, It's Me, Margaret*, dealt frankly with a preteen girl getting her period, as well as religious issues. Another, *Huckleberry Finn*, was cited for racist language, when in fact the writer, Mark Twain, could not have been more outspoken against racism. Another, *The Perks of Being a Wallflower*, showed the coming of age of a gay teen."

Willoughby's speech was at times interrupted by people applauding for the books they liked. She smiled and acknowledged the applause each time.

"The freedom to read is one of the most fundamental and important freedoms on earth. From the introduction of people, cultures, and ideas through reading we become empathetic humans and critical thinkers. We'd like to celebrate that today by inviting any of you who'd like to come forward to read a one-minute passage from one of your favorite banned books. And we'd like Roy Tinker, whose wife Margaret was a fervent advocate of the freedom to read, and write, to read first."

Mr. Roy shuffled up to the big Adirondack chair, sat, and read the first page of *Are You There God? It's Me, Margaret*. It was cool to hear a man reading those words that are meant to be coming from a preteen girl.

Roy had finally found the safe deposit box that Margaret had secretly rented at their bank branch, after, as Destiny had suspected, he received a surprise notice to renew the rental. The number on the sheet of paper with Margaret's list of banned books matched the number of the safe. Alli and Destiny had actually gone with Roy to the bank. It was a tense moment when he had slowly slid the little key they'd found inside *Alice in Wonderland* into the lock on the front of the box. Inside was Margaret's eighteenth story, the one that Eunice had most wanted kept secret, which told of their father's embezzling from the company where he was employed, his trial, incarceration, and the family's move to the other end of the state five years after he was released, to make a new start.

In the end, Roy, Alli, and Willoughby decided not to include it in the collection, even though it was very powerful. Not because they were censoring Margaret or themselves, but out of consideration for Eunice's children.

Next, Jennie read from *Huckleberry Finn*, Abe read from *Catch 22*, Alli read from *The Handmaid's Tale*, and then Willoughby read, naturally, from *Speak*.

Destiny was next. She was an honorary member of the Bristlecone Writers' Group, they'd told her, and they'd offered to read and comment on anything she wrote while she was in nursing school. Or ever, really. And they wanted to get her feedback on their work as well.

Marcus squeezed her hand, and she walked up to the front, feeling a little shy, and opened to the first page of *The Hate U Give*. Her voice sounded shaky at first, but as the seconds went by, she gained confidence and power. She loved the rhythm of Thomas's writing as she described Starr's feeling of being out of place at the spring break party and her banter with her friend. You could tell Angie

Thomas was a performance poet as well as an author. She inspired Destiny. And Destiny realized, after she finished reading, that almost every one of the famous books they'd read from had been about belonging. Or the feelings of worthlessness and injustice people had when they felt they didn't belong. And why couldn't there be a world where they could all belong?

Destiny was transported by the wave of applause when she finished, and she floated back to her chair, where Marcus sat, beaming at her.

"Crushed it," he said.

She didn't know if she and Marcus could do the long-distance thing, but they were going to try.

CHAPTER 31
ABE

After the "Banned Books from the Big Chair" event, Abe and Solomon walked Nicole to her car, and they stood and talked in the Bristlecone parking lot while Solomon snuggled in Nicole's arms.

"I'm glad you came today," he told her. "I wasn't sure you'd be interested."

"You know that one of my favorite authors is Jodi Picoult. And her books always seem to be getting banned, maybe for tackling such controversial subjects head-on. I'm all in for freedom to read."

"Oh, that's right, you talked me into reading that book she wrote about the two sisters—*My Sister's Keeper*. Lots of fascinating twists."

"Based on the fact that they shared DNA," Nicole said, nodding. She opened her car door. "See you bright and early tomorrow, Dr. Goodman. Oh, and don't forget to check on Levi's registration for that summer soccer camp on campus."

"Yeah, I'll do that tonight." Abe took her chin in his hand and kissed her deeply. "See you tomorrow."

"And you promised me you wouldn't move anything yourself. That's what the movers are for."

"Yes, dear." Abe waved as she pulled out. Tomorrow he was moving back in with Nicole. And the thought of it made him very happy. He felt indescribably younger at heart just thinking about it.

On the way back to his cottage, which was a mess right now, with all his books packed, he and Solomon wandered past the old bristlecone pine with the plaque. Abe kind of wanted to bid it good-bye. It had been a sort of inspiration to him while he had been here. As old and ugly as it was, it was still alive. For centuries, it had beaten the odds and clung to life. In fact, it had managed to thrive.

Living at Bristlecone had been good for Abe. He'd opened himself up to the possibility of new friends. Of doing silly things sometimes, such as letting his dog star in a spoof of a play. He'd become involved in the continuing education organization in town and begun teaching a few classes a year. He'd come to a new acceptance of the here and now that eased his mind. The Bristlecone Writers' Group even said he could be an honorary member emeritus. He smiled to himself at their facetious use of "emeritus."

For some reason Abe's thoughts wandered back to Nicole mentioning the importance of the sisters sharing DNA in the Jodi Picoult book. And he then remembered that Nicole had also said that Alli's daughter reminded her of him. And then he remembered that odd interaction when he'd given Maeve the baby aspirin at the play.

And suddenly he knew.

That would explain the semester abroad that Alli took so suddenly, and the fact that she had transferred to another school. He'd assumed she'd moved off-campus or found another group of friends. And on graduation day when he'd seen her with her family, those children he saw weren't all her sister's children. One of them was Maeve.

That day so long ago, when Alli asked him if he wanted to get married and start a family, she was pregnant. And after his dismissive response, she must have decided to leave. And not to tell him anything. Could that be true?

Had he truly been so forbidding that she hadn't felt she could talk to him?

And Maeve had inherited his Factor 5 blood clotting disorder. Only about 5 percent of the population had it, and it was completely hereditary.

He tried again to picture Maeve's face after seeing her at the *Legally Blonde* play. Did it look like his? Like him, she seemed to thrive in academic life and the world of learning. But why wouldn't Alli have wanted him to know, for an entire lifetime? Hadn't he had a right to know about her decision? Feelings he couldn't put into words flooded him. Fury. Regret. Puzzlement.

As he traversed the courtyard, he veered crazily between wanting to confront Alli right away and the other extreme—absolutely never being able to come close to addressing the situation. How presumptuous it might be to ask her if Maeve was his daughter. Daughter—he had never in his wildest dreams imagined what it might be like to have one. Yet, how neglectful to do nothing. He didn't see that it was possible to continue to meet with Alli week after week with the Bristlecone Writers' Group without somehow addressing it.

And at that moment, he saw Alli walking alone, talking on her phone. She was concentrating on her conversation and didn't see him. His mind was nearly exploding with the realization he'd just had, and he was so shocked to see her

that he almost took a route to the other side of the courtyard so their paths wouldn't cross.

But of course, Solomon would have nothing of it. The
moment he saw Alli, he started wagging his tail and pulling
on the leash. He pulled so hard Abe finally let go and
Solomon raced across the courtyard at top speed to greet
Alli, the leash dragging on the ground behind him.

"Hi, Sol, buddy, hi little man," Alli said, putting away
her phone and kneeling to pet him. Solomon jumped all
over her until she finally picked him up.

"He hasn't forgotten his caretaker at the play," Abe said.

"Oh, and I haven't forgotten him. He is a sweetheart."

As if in response, Solomon sniffed Alli's cheek and
licked her ear. She giggled and snuggled him. "The Banned
Books event was so great today. I'm so glad I did it.
Willoughby did a wonderful job arranging it."

"I agree. Very inspiring. I was proud to participate."

"So do you think Solomon misses the play?"

Abe shrugged. "Sometimes he goes to the door at
around seven thirty, yes, thinking that it's time to go to
rehearsal. I have to say, he does seem a bit bored just
hanging around with an old man like me."

"Aww, Solomon, do you miss being a star?"

Abe's mind raced. Soon they would run out of conversation about Solomon, and possibly Alli would say she had to
go, and he wouldn't get a chance to ask about Maeve. Even
though he didn't even know if he wanted to know. No, that
wasn't true. Now that he had been knocked over the head
with the realization, he was desperate to know.

"So how are the plans coming along for Maeve's daughter's wedding?" he asked, knowing it sounded awkward.

Alli looked at Abe in surprise. "I didn't realize you'd
noticed we were planning it, Abe."

"Well, yes, I noticed. I enjoyed meeting your daughter and granddaughter at the play. My oldest grandson, Levi, is only nine—it's amazing you have a granddaughter old enough to get married, since we're essentially the same age."

Alli cocked her head at him. "Is it?"

He decided to leap in. "Does Maeve have Factor 5 clotting disorder?"

"Yes. We discovered it when she was pregnant. So do you know about it?"

"It's entirely inherited. And it's not that common. Only about five percent of the population has it."

"Yes, I know," Alli said the words slowly, her eyes searching his face.

"I have Factor 5 clotting disorder. I discovered it after my heart attack." He started to say more but then just left the sentence hanging in the air.

Such a peculiar look crossed Alli's face.

"Plus, Nicole says Maeve looks like me. That she reminds her of me."

Her eyes widened, she looked away, then back, and he saw doubt and fury and then maybe acceptance. She sighed and adjusted Solomon to a more comfortable position in her arms. "I didn't come here because of you, if that's what you think. Maeve wanted to teach here because it was my alma mater. She'd loved Eden Forest and wanted to teach here from the time she was twelve years old. When she received the offer, I just couldn't tell her that I wouldn't be able to come and live near her. It was her dream. I couldn't stand in the way."

"So she is." Abe couldn't even say the rest of the sentence. His brain felt like a white screen. He felt the blood drain from his face. And he wondered if his knees might give way.

Alli didn't speak for a long moment. "My husband was a good father to her. She loved him. That's what she's believed all her life—she was only three when we got married and she didn't remember anything different. My husband and I were not able to have children together and so Maeve is my only child."

"But what I don't understand is why you didn't tell me. I had a right to know. You kept it a secret for fifty years!"

"I did. It was my decision. My body. You made it clear you were not ready for a future with me, so I did what I decided I wanted to do. I don't know that you had a right to know. Thousands of sperm donors worldwide have no knowledge of the children they've created."

Anger flashed through Abe's body. "Oh, that's unfair. I was more than a sperm donor. I was in love with you."

"But Abe, you couldn't foresee a future with me. Or with her. I thought at first that I should do that, too, that I couldn't finish school with a child. But I managed to do it. I transferred to Chapel Hill and, with the help of my parents and friends, I did finish school."

"I know. But you got your degree from Eden Forest. I saw you on graduation day."

"I saw you too." Alli gave him a small smile. "They let me graduate from Eden Forest because I had enough cred-its. I finished my senior year when I transferred, in case you were wondering." She cocked her head in an almost chal-lenging way.

"I wanted to talk to you."

"Why didn't you?"

He tossed his hands in the air with such vigor that

Solomon started. "I don't know. I was young and foolish. I wish things had been different."

"But then you wouldn't have had your marriage to Ellen, or your sons. And you might have resented me. We might have had a horrible marriage. And I wouldn't have had my marriage, which was good for a long time."

Alli's mention of Abe's sons drew him up short. He couldn't imagine life without them, yet he realized that in the turmoil of the last few years, and with their dislike of Nicole, his relationship with them had indeed suffered.

"Well, I don't know what to say," he finally said. "Is there a chance you might be willing to talk about this again? And consider whether you'd agree for me to try to establish a relationship with Maeve?"

Alli hesitated. "I guess I can't stop you. But let me talk to her first. Obviously, it will come as a huge shock."

"Fair enough." Abe reached out for Solomon and, very gently, she handed him over.

"So I hear you're moving back with Nicole tomorrow," she said.

Abe nodded. "But I'm afraid you won't be rid of me. I'll still be coming to writers' group as a member emeritus."

She smiled. "Emeritus indeed. I'm glad. See you there."

He walked slowly back to his apartment with Solomon, his head still whirling from their exchange. Alli was going to have to talk to Maeve. And he, he now realized, would have to talk to his sons and tell them they had a half-sister. None of that would be easy.

Yet, he relished the challenge.

And dawning in him was the realization that not only did he have to establish a relationship with Maeve, but he also had to repair his relationships with Jacob and Noah. And Levi.

Nicole had been right.

EPILOGUE
JENNIE

NINE MONTHS LATER

J ennie looked at herself in the mirror in her sunny new bedroom. Her hair was a wiry white mess. It always was, there was nothing she could do about it. The black skirt and black flats with the colorful and expensive top she'd bought especially for today looked appropriate and writerly, she thought.

Heading into her living room, she opened the door to her new screened porch. "Sir Arthur, come in now. I can't leave you out there while I'm gone." Sir Arthur had, if possible, been even more enthusiastic about the screened porch than Jennie and loved spending time out there, watching birds, bees, and attacking the tails of any lizards hapless enough to accidentally slither under the door. A number of tailless but wiser lizards now lived in Jennie's yard. Reluctantly, Sir Arthur came inside.

After a meeting with her financial adviser, as well as

Elijah and Amanda, Jennie had decided to move out of Bristlecone and into an independent apartment not far from the kids. She didn't need the medical services the way they had when Michael was alive.

She picked up her book and smoothed her fingers over the beautiful cover, which featured a woman's thoughtful and strong profile, supposedly Enheduanna's, with a background of rocks and colorful desert flowers. Authors sometimes complained about their covers, but Jennie adored hers. She opened the front cover to make sure her typed speech—her first—was folded inside.

A knock came on the door and Elijah called "Mom?" He and Amanda had very thoughtfully offered to drive her to the bookstore. She was extremely nervous and could see herself having an accident driving over.

"Hey!" She opened the door and the two of them came in, hugging her, and handing her an enormous bouquet of flowers.

"Oh my gosh, you didn't have to do that!"

Don't tell them that, came Michael's voice. *Just say thank you, that you love them.*

"I mean thank you—I absolutely love them."

Not to be ignored, Sir Arthur wound his way around Elijah's legs. Elijah picked him up and scratched him between his ears. "Here's the culprit. The one who sent in the manuscript. We should be taking you with us, Sir Arthur."

Jennie picked up a framed photo of Sir Arthur. "His photo is going. I am of course going to recognize him as my agent, the one who sent my manuscript to the publisher. He doesn't want to go."

Amanda, who had made herself at home in Jennie's

kitchen from the first day she'd moved, found a vase. "I can arrange these later when we have more time."

"Perfect, yes, we do need to go."

The book launch was scheduled for four o'clock at Main Street Books, the local independent bookstore. On the way over, Jennie sat in the back seat of their Jeep with Sir Arthur's photo next to her and read over her notes one more time. She'd practiced the reading itself at least ten times.

It doesn't have to be perfect, Michael said.

"I guess people expect stumbles," she told the kids. "I just have to make sure I don't read too long. I hate it when people read too long."

"It will be just right," Amanda assured her. "Everyone there is your friend. They all love you and are there to celebrate your success."

"I wish Dad could be here today," Elijah said. "His chest would be all puffed up, and he'd probably cry, he'd be so proud."

"I know, I know. He would."

I am here, came Michael's voice. *Not going to miss this.*

The kids' wedding in Tanzania last February, scheduled to coincide with the wildebeest calving season, had been spectacular. She'd done so much research ahead of the trip and had discovered that the famous saying from *The Lion King*, "Hakuna matata," which meant "No worries," came from Tanzania. There was also a Tanzanian saying about life that she had quoted in her remarks at the wedding, which said, "Every bird flies with its own wings." She'd meant it for herself as well as for Elijah and Amanda.

And, after quite a bit of thought, she'd decided to go on the balloon ride to see Mount Kilimanjaro after all. That and Dr.

Jane's Dream, and the safari—all of it had been an experience she'd never forget. She had been terrified, yes, but she'd recently read a statement from Georgia O'Keeffe, who said something about being terrified to do nearly everything she'd done, but she hadn't let the terror stop her from doing it anyway. And that had convinced Jennie to do it. She didn't know how many years she had left, and she would certainly never get to Africa again. And she had indeed been able to have a breakfast with newly married Elijah and Amanda during which a giraffe, with its long, sloped neck, giant head, black tongue, and enormous, long-lashed eyes, had bent down through the window and gazed at them with gentle fondness.

"Oh, I just noticed how nice you two look," Jennie said, as they parked and climbed out of the car. Elijah had on a dusky rose polo that fit him perfectly, along with off-white khakis, while Amanda wore a striking white top with a swishy black-and-white skirt.

"We're with the VIP, we need to look the part," Amanda said.

"Very sharp, kiddos."

Jennie loved their local bookstore, with its beautiful displays, its intelligent "staff picks" section, fun "date with a book" section, and extensive local author section. Every year they had an event where the entire town read the same book and then attended talks and readings about it. The store was a touchstone for the whole town. The owner, a lovely, whip-smart woman named Dahlia, came from behind the counter when the three of them entered. "Hi, wonderful to see you. So glad to host your event here today."

"Thrilled to be here. I just hope people come," Jennie said, with what she knew was too much brightness.

"Oh, we're counting on it," Dahlia said, and Jennie

knew she wasn't kidding when she saw several rows of chairs—for at least thirty people—arranged across the back of the store.

To Jennie's delight, Dahlia had bought flowers for the store too. Bright sunflowers, which Jennie thought were perfect. She had set them up beside the podium. On one side was a chair and a stack of Jennie's books, and on the other was another chair and a stack of Margaret's short story collection, which Roy had published with Alli's help.

The joint book launch had been Jennie's idea. She wanted to honor Margaret and, quite honestly, she felt less nervous if she was not the only focus of attention. It had been billed as "The Bristlecone Writers' Group Reading." Willoughby was going to introduce Jennie, and Alli had offered to read a page from one of Margaret's stories, with Roy's agreement.

Dahlia had placed cups of water beside the two chairs, as well as pens for signing books. The attention to detail made Jennie feel special.

"We're going to sit in the back, Mom," Elijah said. "To let the fans sit up front. And also, to take photos showing lots of people!"

Jennie got situated in the chair near her stack of books, reviewing her speech notes, but then people started to come in. First Willoughby, with her lovely daughter, Courtney, who was tall and athletic just like Willoughby. Jennie rose to give them both heartfelt hugs.

"You are going to be great. This is so damn fabulous, my dear."

Jennie was so grateful for all of Willoughby's help with this event. Interestingly, since Willoughby's ex-husband had died, she had scrapped the thriller and was now working on a family story that touched Jennie's heart with its honesty and authenticity. Willoughby had recently gone to New York to spend a weekend with her son and returned in euphoric spirits. She now stood up front, getting ready to give introductions, while Courtney found a seat in the second row.

Then Alli and her rather stern daughter, Maeve, came in—Jennie gave Alli a hug of true camaraderie, and she also gave Maeve a hug. Then Dahlia showed Alli the stack of Margaret's books, with the cover showing two sisters playing together with dolls on a Southern veranda.

"I brought a speech. Did you?" Jennie said.

"I usually wing it," Alli said, with a crooked grin. "You'll be great, Jennie. People just want to see the real you."

At that point, the people she used to join for dinner at Bristlecone came in. Tears started in Jennie's eyes—she had never dreamed they even knew about the launch or would want to come. Then more people from Bristlecone, and the community, and several social workers she used to work with before she retired, came in. How on earth did they know about this? Tears of joy spilled onto Jennie's cheeks each time someone she knew came in and claimed a chair. If they only knew how much it meant to her.

Then, believe it or not, Bernice came in, waving her copy of Jennie's book shyly and choosing a seat near the back. Jennie hadn't seen her since she'd moved to her new apartment, but she felt warmer toward her ever since the evening when Bernice lost her keys.

Then Abe and his sexy red-headed wife came—what was her name? Oh yes, Nicole, along with Solomon, of course. Abe had moved out of Bristlecone and back in with Nicole not long after the *Legally Blonde* play, but no one had the heart to kick him out of the writers' group, just as no one wanted to kick Jennie out, either, so they both stayed.

And his writing had become more and more insightful, Jennie thought.

Sometimes he brought Solomon to writers' group, and everyone was glad to see him. Solomon's goal in life was to greet everyone and show them love, which was perfect for the group. And really, for all of life. Solomon was always well behaved, sitting quietly on Abe's lap after the obligatory greetings, and Jennie was sure that would be the case today as well.

"Break a leg!" Abe said to Jennie and Alli, holding up his hand to say hello as he and Nicole found seats in the third row.

Then Destiny came in with her boyfriend, Marcus. Jennie was so moved that Destiny had come all the way from Durham for the event that she really did begin to cry, even though she knew that Destiny had the additional motivation of seeing Marcus. When Destiny had revealed that she'd been listening to their writers' group meetings over the intercom to get writing tips, no one had been mad or offended. They responded by inviting her to attend the group whenever she could, and she had, in fact, come a few times before she left for Durham, and read some of her performance poetry.

Jennie loved her spirited work. Destiny was so clearly a helping soul who would be an excellent nurse, but all of them had emphasized to her that she must always keep writing—just for her own self-actualization and respect. She shouldn't wait as long as they had to reach her writing dreams.

"Is Roy going to even show up for his own late wife's book launch?" Willoughby whispered to Jennie and Alli, glancing at the time on her phone.

"He'll skid in at the last minute, probably," Alli said.

Sure enough, Roy, making a lot of noise as always, and accidentally knocking down an entire stack of romances with ripped bodices on the front, rambled in, his hair disheveled, wearing a wrinkled polo.

Willoughby opened the program with a description of the Bristlecone Writers' Group, adding that if anyone present had an interest, the group always welcomed new members, and actually had spaces open.

Jennie could not remember anything from her part of the program. She had planned to talk about how many years she had researched Enheduanna, how important it was, in the sweep of the history of the world, to have a woman who was the first writer, the first chronicler of human existence, the first to bear witness to the story of humankind. She had planned to thank everyone in the writers' group, everyone at her publisher's office, and of course Elijah and Amanda, and last but not least, Sir Arthur.

She'd planned to read the first two pages of her book, in which Enheduanna experiences her first desire to write a record of the glory of nature, and the incredible power of love for another being, and finds the implements to do so with wet clay and a stylus.

Jennie had no idea if she actually said or did those things during her presentation. Her consciousness shifted into some sort of altered dream state. Somehow, an impression of Alli reading a page from Margaret's story flashed in her mind and then away.

And then it was over, and people were thrusting books at Jennie to sign.

Willoughby came to hug her. "You were fabulous," she said. "Courtney has to feed Stevie, so we've got to go." She kissed Jennie on the cheek.

Jennie glanced at the front of the store and saw Abe and Nicole leaving, carrying Solomon, with Alli and Maeve. Abe had a copy of Jennie's book, which Jennie found so endearing, especially considering how critical he had been at first. He was also trying to put another book in Maeve's hands, but she was refusing. Then, at last, she took it, with a tight and somewhat exasperated smile. Alli had told Jennie about her past with Abe and about a recent lunch that Abe and Maeve had together, peaceably brokered by Solomon.

You did good, came Michael's voice.

I did, she said. *But you don't need to be my cheerleader anymore, love of my life. I am standing on my own two feet. Now, hush.*

All right, then. See you on the other side, my love. Heartbreakingly, silence followed.

"Can you sign this to my daughter?" said a woman, handing Jennie her book, open to the title page. "She wants to be a writer."

Joy bloomed within her.

ACKNOWLEDGMENTS

I realized one day that though writing has been a huge part of my life and identity, I had never written about it in a novel. I had always shied away from it, thinking it might be too "meta." Not to mention, I hardly consider myself a master. Rather, I am someone who has simply been lucky beyond measure to spend my life with stories and to call other writers my friends. I have a YOLO (you only live once) attitude these days, though, so I decided to try writing about writing. Thank you from the bottom of my heart to those who have cheered me on and helped shape this story.

I also wanted to write about older people, whose lives are more complicated than many think. Though the characters in this book are all fictional, the stories—such as a woman having two husbands in the same retirement community, or a wife selecting her husband's next wife for after she dies, two people reconnecting after fifty years, or a couple divorcing over whether to move to a retirement community—are all true stories that have been told to me.

Since this novel is about a writers' group, my fellow writing warriors come first: Betsy Thorpe, Emily Pearce, Michelle Moore, Elizabeth Hatley, Ann Campanella, Tammy Wilson, Richard Dresser, Barbara Johnson, and Desiree Kendrick. These brave souls read and gave feedback on every page, some more than once. They truly midwifed this manuscript.

Lake Norman Writers provided monthly inspiration

and accountability, and I'd like to thank Ann Campanella and Tammy Wilson again, as well as Gilda Syverson, Caroline Kenna, Tootsie O'Hara, Tara Marshall, Connie Fisher, Dede Mitchell, and Sandra Phillips.

Independent editor Karen Alley offered helpful advice about character development, plotting using several points of view, holding back information until the right time, and using backstory. She also gave me a great book anecdote.

I also thank trusted beta readers Mimi Krumholz, Pam Jones, Rosebud Turner, and Sandra Hayes. Thanks to Lucy Thorpe and Sydney Campanella for perspectives from young people.

I learned about Banned Books from the Big Chair when I attended the American Library Association Conference in San Diego in 2024. A huge chair was set up in the lobby, and anyone could sit there, looking swallowed by it like Edith Ann on *Laugh-In* (boy am I dating myself with that one) and read a page from one of their favorite banned books. This simple statement about the importance of freedom to read moved me so deeply that I decided to include it in my book. I am also a member of Authors Against Book Bans (AABB) and have greatly appreciated the tools that organization has offered authors to help fight this dangerous practice.

Thank you to Jenny Hale and the outstanding team at Harpeth Road Press, including Charlotte Fry, Katie Seaman, Lara Simpson, Kamille Parkinson, Kendra Olson, Sarah Hansen, and Emma Sherk, for plucking *The Bristlecone Writers' Group* from the slush pile, dusting it off, giving it a lovely polishing and a timeless cover, putting it out for readers to enjoy, and supporting it. I am so very grateful.

My family is my rock. It means the world to me that my beloved husband, Jeff, reads all my work and gives me his impressions as an avid reader. His faith in me truly is the wind beneath my wings. Our dear daughters, Caitlin and Kelsey, also took the time to read this manuscript and give me their honest feedback, which means the world to me.

Last but not least, pets have always been like family members to us, and I'd always wanted to write about that special bond, so it was a delight to make Joni and Lionman the heroes of this story. Lionman did indeed step on my keyboard and submit one of my manuscripts. And Joni did actually play Bruiser Woods in *Legally Blonde: The Musical.*

A NOTE FROM LISA

Dear reader,

Thank you so much for picking up my novel, *The Bristlecone Writers' Group*. I hope this story touched your heart. I loved writing it. If you'd like to know when my next book is out, you can sign up for new Harpeth Road release alerts for my novels here:

www.harpethroad.com/lisa-williams-kline-newsletter-signup

I won't share your information with anyone else, and I'll only email you a quick message whenever new books come out or go on sale.

If you did enjoy *The Bristlecone Writers' Group*, I'd be so thankful if you'd write a review online. Getting feedback from readers helps to persuade others to pick up my book for the first time. It's one of the biggest gifts you could give me.

Until next time,

Lisa Williams Kline